Thomas Keith Tindale
South Hanover
May, 1968.

THE GIANT DWARFS

Gisela Elsner

THE GIANT DWARFS

A Contribution

Translated by Joel Carmichael

GROVE PRESS, INC.
NEW YORK

CONTENTS

THE GIANT DWARFS

DINNER TIME

My FATHER is a good eater. He doesn't stand on cere-
mony. He sits down at the table and tucks the ends of his
napkin behind his collar. He props the palms of his hands
on the table, to the right and left of his plate, to the
right and left of the knife and fork. He raises his behind
a little from the chair. He leans across the table so that
his napkin hangs down into his empty plate and he can
see what is in the dishes. Then he lowers his behind onto
the seat. Then he pitches in. He serves himself with the
serving fork, with the serving spoon, one forkful after
another, one spoonful after another, until he has a great
heap on his plate. And while my mother is serving me
a heap that could go many times over into my father's
heap, my father is mashing down the vegetables and
potatoes with a fork, my father is cutting up the meat
into big pieces and pouring gravy over everything with
the gravy ladle. And while my mother is mashing down
my smaller heap and cutting up my meat into small
pieces and pouring gravy over everything, my father starts
to eat. His belly touches the edge of the table. There is

1

a gap between his thighs wide enough for a head to fit in. His legs are wrapped around the chair legs. He carries big forkfuls to his mouth and chews them with great care, his eyes fixed on the center part in my mother's hair, who is now serving herself a heap that would go into my heap several times over. Her head lowered, she sits opposite my father. And while my father is still chewing, he holds the next forkful ready at the level of his mouth, the prongs so close to his lips I'm afraid he may hurt himself.

"Lothar," says my mother into her plate, "start eating and don't always keep looking at Father while he's eating, it spoils his appetite."

I am sitting between them, raised up by a sofa cushion, a bib around my neck. The chair opposite is unoccupied. I pick up the spoon and start eating. For a couple of spoonfuls I look straight at this chair across from me. I count the vertical ribs on the back of the chair; I count up to seven, try to count them twice in a row, and get stuck at ten. I can't count any further.

"Father," I ask my father, the high-school teacher, because I know he knows, "what number comes after ten?"

"At meals," says my father at his meal, "we don't talk."

I go on eating, steal a glance to the right, at my father eating, one to the left, at my mother eating; I see how differently my parents eat. My father sits with his back to the window, to the sun. My mother sits with her face to the sun, the door behind her.

"Maybe," I think as I see them eating, "she sits with her head lowered only because of the sun, and when it's not shining she just goes on sitting that way out of habit."

She holds her head so low over her plate that her hair hangs down into the food. She puts down her fork, pushes her hair to the right and the left of the center part behind the right and the left ear, hastily carries a tiny mouthful into her mouth, washes it down unchewed with a gulp of water from her glass, and folds her hands in her lap under the table top. I don't know whether she prays between the mouthfuls. It takes only a few forkfuls for her to start gagging; the intervals, when her hands are resting in her lap, become longer and longer between the mouthfuls that get smaller and smaller. Finally she carries an empty fork to her mouth, pulls it out, carries it to her mouth again—perhaps so as not to annoy my father by sitting around motionless at dinner.

He is in full motion above the tabletop. He doesn't let go of the knife and fork for a second. Chewing, he loads the fork up again, raises it fully loaded to his lips, and while he holds it in readiness in front of his mouth, he uses the knife to push together into one heap all the scraps of food scattered around the plate. When the balls of food in his cheeks get smaller, when they vanish, when my father has finished chewing, his eyes turn away from the center part in my mother's hair. My father glances sideways at the fork being loaded. He stretches his mouth wide open. I can see his gold teeth right and left and above and below, near the corners of his mouth. I start counting them. But by the count of one my father has already moved his mouth onto the fork with a tiny jerk the length of a prong. His teeth snap together over the stem of the fork, and he slowly pulls the prongs out between his teeth, as though he had to gnaw away at them the way meat is gnawed from bones.

Nothing makes his face so animated as eating—the way his mouth opens wide and gets rounder, the way his cheeks rise and fall, and together with the cheeks the balls of food, and together with the balls of food the reading glasses he wears at meals, and under the glasses the narrowing and widening eyes that he keeps fixed on the center part in my mother's hair while he chews. I don't like to look, but I have to look anyhow, and it takes me a long time to finish my smaller heap of food.

After my father has emptied the first plate, he leans back. He takes a deep breath and lets it out with a groan. I see that the seven ribs of his chair are too narrow for the width of his back. My mother looks anxiously into the serving dishes.

"Will there be enough?" she asks with twitching lips, her hands folded in her lap.

My father loads up his plate with another heap, no smaller than the first. At the second half of the second heap his eye wanders away from the center part in my mother's hair. Some scraps fall from his fork onto the plate. When that happens, he kicks his feet against the legs of the chair, and he unloads the whole forkful back on the plate.

"Lothar," he calls to me, the knife and fork sticking up straight in his fists on the tabletop, "don't pick up the spoon with your left hand!" And he calls, "You're slobbering your food, Lothar!" And he calls, "The way you eat, that's the way you are!" And after he has called that, he goes on eating.

My mother pushes her plate away; half of her little heap, her tiny little heap, is still on it. She pushes herself away from the table, toward the door, and waits there submissively, her hands folded in her lap, her head bowed, her hair hanging over her face, for the meal to be over. Only when my father starts belching at his third heap, which is made up of what is left in the serving dishes, my plate and my mother's half-heap, does she suddenly wince. I see that three chair ribs are enough to cover the width of her narrow back.

After the third heap, the last one, my father crosses his knife and fork on the plate. He tears the napkin out of his collar. He takes the reading glasses off his ears. He wipes his whole face. Then he pushes himself and his chair away from the table with his feet.

"That was good," he says.

My mother raises her head. Through the strands of hair she looks at my father.

"I can serve up again," she says.

"I'm no glutton," says my father and gets up.

"May I get down?" I ask, and my mother nods and giggles behind her hair.

Without his glasses my father goes over to the sofa. He lies down with the top of his trousers open. And while he puts on his street glasses, and while he pokes around in and between his teeth with a sharpened matchstick, his mouth wide open and the expression in his eyes that of someone listening intently, and while he peers at what he has picked out of his teeth and swallows it, my mother carries a tray with the empty dishes and plates into the kitchen. I can still hear them in the corridor, clinking against each other, I can hear my mother's giggling.

I stand in front of the window, in front of the three primrose pots on the windowsill. Every year on their wedding anniversary my father gives my mother a pot of primroses. I look over at the schoolyard and see my father's students racing around the chestnut trees, squatting on the wall of the yard with their legs swinging, see them stepping through the iron-barred gate, and behind the opened windows of the brick schoolhouse I see sponges flying up and erasers. The tap is running in the kitchen. My mother is rinsing off the dishes. My father has dozed off with his mouth half open. I can see his teeth. The matchstick has dropped from his fingers. He has laid his hands on his stomach. Underneath, his food is gurgling away. By using the pattern in the carpet, I've memorized the creaking boards: flowers and birds that I may step on, flowers and birds that I may not step on, and in that way I steal out of the dining room.

In the kitchen my mother is already at the pots. Bent giggling over the sink, she is cleaning them with steel wool. And because she is giggling, rattling the pots, rubbing away with steel wool, and because I sneak about on account of my father, she doesn't hear me coming. I tug at her apron string. My mother wheels round with a soft cry.

"Oh!" she says. "It's you!"

She lowers her damp face to me and kisses my hair.

"He's sleeping now," I whisper.

"That's good," my mother whispers.

She leans her head a little to the side, her ear toward the door opening through which I have just slipped. The drops on her face run down diagonally. They are not only the splashes from the dishwater, they are also tears. They run out of the corners of her eyes. Her face is so woeful when she giggles that I don't know whether she is crying while she laughs or laughing while she cries. My mother wipes her face with her apron. She dries the dishes with the towel. While she puts the dishes away there is a creaking from the sofa. My father has waked up. He hurries through the corridor, sticks his red face into the kitchen.

"I've got to go to class," he says, "Luise. Don't upset your mother," he says, "Lothar."

The front door slams shut.

I go into the dining room, stand behind the window, watch my father walking through the iron-barred gate, hear the schoolbell ring. The students run toward the brick schoolhouse, crowd through the entrance in a dense crush. My father strides behind them with long steps, his eyes trained on the doorway and on the backs of the students' necks. Behind the windows of their classroom the students' heads bob up again. Their faces are turned toward my father. The top of his body towers over the students' heads. Behind his desk my father raises his arms to shoulder level, lets them sink, and with them the students' heads sink down below the windowsills of the schoolhouse.

That is how all the midday dinners in the year pass, except those on Sundays and holidays, when my father remains sitting at the cleared table, correcting his students' notebooks, in which my father enriches the blue and white pages with red ink, and except for the dinner once a year, on a holiday.

That is when my mother remains on the threshold of the dining-room door, holding the loaded tray in front of her on her forearms. She looks even more gaunt than usual in her black high-necked, long-sleeved dress which she wears only once a year, on this holiday. She has pierced a new hole in her belt a good distance behind the last hole. The ends of the skirt hang down on both sides almost to her ankles. Her head lifted over the steaming dishes, her hair pulled back, she looks with her white face into my father's red face. He sits at the table as usual, with the serving fork and serving spoon in his hands, ready to pitch in.

"Today's the day again," says my mother.

Only then does she carry the tray slowly and solemnly over to the table and place the serving dishes around my father's plate. My father drops the serving fork and serving spoon. He begins squirming back and forth on his chair.

"Go ahead, help yourself," says my mother.

She sits up straight, hands in her lap, watching my
father attentively. Behind the lenses of his reading glasses
my father blinks like someone who has been roughly
awakened. He pushes away the serving dishes and the
roast, which is brown on the outside and crisp as always,
and rare on the inside. His stomach begins rumbling so
loudly that I think my whole father is rumbling. He clears
his throat, pushes his chair back and forth, scrapes his
feet on the carpet. Finally he starts whistling to himself,
a march. But the rumbling can't be drowned out.

With annoying composure my mother fills my plate
with the best parts, mashes the heap flat, cuts my meat
up into little pieces; my mother fills her own plate, mashes
the heap flat, cuts her meat. And at the same pace we
slowly carry our knives and forks to our mouths, my
mother and I, then to the heaps, then to our mouths, with
my mother's white face always turned toward the now
dark-red face of my father. He pulls his glasses off his
ears, covers his face with the napkin, jumps up from his
chair, and rushes out of the dining room. I hear him
walking up and down in the hall.

When we finish eating, when my mother has put the
still half-full serving dishes on the tray, my father comes
into the dining room. And now it is he who leans over
and kisses my hair, while my mother carries the tray
into the kitchen.

"Today, Lothar," says my father, "we are going to
your father." I can smell that his breath smells badly
when he hasn't eaten.

We put on our Sunday suits, my father and I. My
mother is standing ready at the door, wearing a black hat
whose veil hangs over her eyes. I walk between them,
holding my mother's left hand, my father's right hand,
looking down at the ground as we walk; I see the point

of my father's shoe lagging behind the point of my mother's—my father who generally has such a stalwart stride. We take the streetcar to the edge of the city, to where we used to live—my mother and I and my father who was a teacher. He was a quite ordinary teacher, says my father, the high-school teacher. When we pass our house, my parents look straight ahead. The tenants, those I know, those I don't know, are leaning out the windows next to one another and looking out into the street or at the tenants of the house opposite, who are also leaning out the windows and looking out into the street or over at the tenants of the house opposite. I turn around, see the tenants I know stretching their arms out at us, and hear them calling, "There! There!" calling "Them! Them!" calling "Those! Those!" I see the tenants I don't know and the tenants of the house opposite hanging all the way out the windows with their heads, with their shoulders, and looking after us. My parents pull me along with them.

It is not far to the cemetery. Once there, we walk along the main path. Aside from the cemetery's regulars, a couple of old women who stand around with their heads constantly nodding and their lips moving soundlessly and who now and then, perhaps at the high points of their mute speeches, wave their arms so wildly that their wind-blown figures begin to totter—aside from these old women I see gravediggers chasing after cats with their shovels in their hands. We turn to the left.

I recognize my father's grave. I also recognize the people, some standing at the grave and some hanging around near the grave or circling it like dogs around a scalding feeding bowl. They don't look as though they had planned this visit to the cemetery. They look like casual passers-by, they look as though they had turned up here against their will: a man in hiking boots with a rucksack on his back, a man in tennis shoes with a racket in its cover, a waiter in a white mess jacket, a lady in a sun dress, a couple who have pushed a baby carriage into the shadow of the cemetery wall, a man in a dinner jacket holding a bouquet of flowers—a bouquet wrapped in paper and not intended for my father—and all the other figures: they look past each other or at the ground. I hear their stomachs rumbling.

There is always one among them who hears us coming in time. He nudges the ones standing around. And they all jump apart and away from each other, with their behinds pulled in as though they were afraid someone might try to give them a kick; they squat down behind gravestones and, running crouched over from one gravestone to another, they take to their heels. Only the gentleman in the dinner jacket, a man of great presence, after one precipitate leap away from the grave contains his haste into strides which, even if very long, are still appropriate for a gentleman. He stands there, a few graves to one side of my father's grave, turned toward us; he beckons me over to him with a slightly twisted smile.

I look at my father, who is standing at the grave with his eyes closed, his round hat pressed with both hands against his stomach, which is rumbling, still rumbling; I look at my mother, whose eyes are hidden by the veil; on tiptoe I go over to the gentleman. Just in front of him I turn around to face my parents. They are standing there as before. I don't know whether my mother has opened her eyes behind her veil, I don't know whether my father is looking over at me through a crack between his eyelids. Then the gentleman sticks a big bill damp and crumpled into my right trouser pocket from behind and sticks a bag into my left trouser pocket, and without reaching in to touch it I know it's candy. By the time I turn around he is a few graves further off, the gentleman, so that I can't thank him.

I walk between my parents. They've moved so far away from each other that five children would fit between them.

"Isn't it well tended?" says my father after a while; he sends money every six months to have the grave tended. His eyes are open.

"Why aren't you crying about your father?" says my father after a while.

"We'd better go," says my mother after a while.

I take my mother's left hand, my father's right hand, I start thinking how I can get my left hand loose from my father's right or my right hand from my mother's left, I'd like to get into my left trouser pocket, into the bag. But my parents don't let go.

"I've got an itch," I say, "in my pants."

"When you're home you'll have time enough," says my mother, "to scratch yourself."

And my parents, as if by prearrangement, get a still firmer grip on my left hand and my right hand. My mother pushes her veil away from her face with her free hand. I see that she has fixed her left eye on my right trouser pocket, and I see that my father has fixed his right eye on my mother's left eye.

At home my parents take me to the middle of my room. And while my father leaves, my mother kneels down in front of me, unbuttons my trousers.

"Now," she says," "we'll change your pants. This pair has to be washed, so that it won't itch any more."

She takes off my trousers. I step out of the trouser legs, lift up my right foot, lift up my left, I see her take the bag out of the pocket, put it down on my table, I stand there in my underpants and watch my mother quickly take my trousers out of the room.

Once a year, on this holiday, I have to have dinner in my room. It's still light outside when my mother puts me to bed. I lie on my back, my eyes open, holding the bag in my hand and sucking. At first they are silent, my parents in the dining room, just like every evening, with my mother sitting and darning whatever is torn, and my father lying down and reading the newspaper.

"This time," I think, "they're not going to start in again." And I close the bag, my eyes, and suck.

Then it begins, with my mother's murmur, and my father's clearing of his throat and his shout: "For that I fasted the whole day today!"

I open my eyes, and the bag, I go on sucking and listening. But I can't understand them. Until my father cries, "Will you never leave me in peace about that!" Until my mother throws the darning egg against the wall, cries, "You're going to listen to me! Put your paper away!" pushes back her chair, and jumps up.

The sofa creaks. I hear my mother tearing the newspaper.

"If that isn't the limit!" my father cries. "I have to slave myself sick the whole year with all these muttonheaded kids, just to keep your mouths stuffed!"

"It's not making us any fatter," cries my mother, "because we have to keep on asking ourselves when it will be our turn!"

"What do you mean by that! What do you take me for!" cries my father.

"For a glutton!" cries my mother. "Wasn't I a widow once before, and the child an orphan!"

"And who took his trousers off!" cries my father.

"I'm saving it all up," cries my mother, "for his education!"

Above us and below us I can hear the front doors opening. The tenants go into the stairwell. The tenants creep nearer, up and down the creaking stairs. The tenants listen.

"Can't you see the way he's always watching you when you eat!" cries my mother.

"Because he's greedy!" cries my father.

"No," cries my mother, "because he remembers!"

"He does not remember!" cries my father. "He was only a little squirt then!"

Then the tenants, who can hear everything but can't understand a thing, sneak back and slam their doors. Only then, after Mr. Kecker, who walks on crutches, has raised his crutch, pounded on the floor and yelled, "I ought to hit them with my crutches!"—only then do they begin to fight against my parents' noise with their own noise. They bang canes against the floor, the ceiling, the radiator pipes. They tear open their windows, lean out, yell down and yell up, "The nerve!" "Silence!" "Manners!" "Roughnecks!"

The tenants are yelling for silence.

I stick my head, the bag, under the blanket, I suck.

"Today of all days, a holiday!" I heard my mother crying out in the kitchen.

She ran coughing out of the shorter, narrower, hallway and remained standing on the threshold of our smaller dining room, the one in which there was no room for a sofa.

"Everything's burned," she said.

The thick smoke seeped in from the kitchen through the hall into the dining room. My smaller father and I, we were sitting at the laid table.

"Then we'll just have to eat out," said my father. "Get ready. I'll go ahead with Lothar."

He carried me down the stairs and put me on the sidewalk. Every couple of steps he was ahead of me by the length of a long step.

"What a ridiculous rush!" my mother called out from behind. "Are you running for your life?"

"So they won't be out of their best dishes!" my father called back over his shoulder. "We're late enough as it is!"

Mother caught up with us in front of the hotel entrance.

"Be sure you behave yourself!" she said. "This is a high-class hotel."

We followed my father through the lobby, then through the next room, and through the hotel garden. Only two tables, standing next to each other in the middle of the main room, were still unoccupied. My father and my mother sat down at one of them, opposite each other, so that my father was sitting with his back to the second free table and my mother was sitting facing the second free table. I sat between them.

The tables were covered with white linen. There were white vases with red carnations, glass ash trays, and plates with knives and forks.

"You should have put on your good suit," my mother said to my father.

Three waiters in black trousers and white mess jackets ran back and forth between the tables. Coins jingled in their pockets. They swept off the tablecloths, first here, then there, with their napkins, gave a low bow first to this guest, then to the other who had summoned them to the tables by raising a hand or snapping two fingers; they pulled pencils from behind their ears and jotted down new orders in white notebooks. Then they walked toward the swinging doors and pushed them open with a well-aimed kick. The swinging doors flew wide open and admitted the waiters into the kitchen. For a second I saw the white hats of the chefs, their red faces in the kitchen steam. I heard how the waiters called out their orders to the chefs behind the swinging doors, heard how the chefs repeated the waiters' orders so that there would be no misunderstandings.

"They have good home cooking here," said my mother.

Between the swinging doors and the bar stood the manager, a short man in a black suit, who had to get up on tiptoe to keep an eye on the tables farthest to the rear. His head turned slowly from table to table, from one row of tables to the other, and it was only after he had cast a glance at the last table in the end row that he turned around, stuck his head through the swinging doors into the kitchen, perhaps so that the waiters wouldn't play tricks on the chefs or the chefs on the waiters. He rubbed his hands—or did he wring his hands?—then, interrupting the rubbing wringing of his hands, he signaled a waiter and motioned to our table. The waiter brought the menu and the wine list.

"Wine," said my father, "will run our check up too high."

He pushed the wine list over to the edge of the table. Then my father and my mother read the menu, first looking to the right at the dishes, then to the left at the prices.

"Do you see?" said my father. "The best dishes are crossed off already!"

I got up, went past the bar behind which the girl was rinsing off glasses, drying them, and arranging them on the shelf behind the bar. Sometimes, holding her hands high above the bar, she tapped two empty glasses against each other and indicated a toast to one guest or another, perhaps regulars.

"Lothar," called my mother, "don't bother the other people when they're eating!"

She leaned over, putting her hands on the table, and was about to get up to bring me back when the waiter came over to the table and, hunched over his notebook, started taking my parents' orders.

I looked over at the other tables in the main room.

"But no one is eating here," I thought.

Near our table a well-dressed gentleman clapped his hands together angrily. Two waiters simultaneously leaped over to the right and the left of his chair. The man pulled a watch on a long chain out of his waistcoat pocket, held it away from his body as far as the length of the chain and of his arm let him, and tapped his forefinger on the face of the watch. The waiters tried to calm the man by talking to him softly and raising and lowering their arms over and over.

"The moments take a long time here!" cried the man.

At another table the father of a family divided up the knives and forks among his wife and two grown daughters. They laid them out in front of them, with the knives and forks so far apart that a big plate would have fitted between. With injured expressions the mother and the daughters looked at the tablecloth between their knives and forks.

No one was eating in the smaller room either. I went into the hotel garden. The tables were arranged around a goldfish pool. The guests were staring into the water with greedy looks. Those who had their backs to the pool had also turned their chairs to the goldfish or were sitting backward with their legs wide apart, the backs of the chairs between their legs. Two lovers were sitting with their chairs close together, sucking each other's thumbs. Through the windows I watched the chefs hurrying back and forth. One of them hit his head with empty hands.

"There is no smell of food," I thought, "coming from this kitchen."

The garden was contained by a wall. Over it I saw the balcony of a one-family house. A woman with arms as thick as legs was leaning over the balcony and looking down into the garden of the hotel.

"Grete," she called, turning toward the house, "you can serve up here today!"

The guests glanced up at her for a moment, then stared into the pool again. Some of them turned their heads back and forth as though they were following the movements of the goldfish.

"Hey there, you kid!" a man called out from behind me. "You're obstructing my view of the fish!"

He had a tennis racket lying next to him. He picked it up threateningly. He wasn't joking. I ran back to my parents.

That's where I saw him for the first time. He had taken up the other free table in the middle of the main room. He sat back to back with my smaller father, the backs of their chairs were only a hand's breath away from each other. His stomach was touching the edge of the table. His thighs were spread so far apart that a head could have fitted in between. His legs were wrapped around the chair legs. He was holding his knife and fork straight up and down in his fists on the table top.

"Isn't that the high-school teacher?" whispered my mother.

My father turned around.

"That's him!" he whispered, his face red.

My father had recognized him from behind. He carefully lifted up his chair and moved so close to the edge of the table that he touched it with his chest.

"Is he looking this way?" whispered my father.

"No," whispered my mother.

"Tell me," whispered my father, "when he looks over. Or do you think I should go over to his table?"

"The way you look!" whispered my mother. She shook her head.

At every table hands shot into the air, fingers snapped, fists pounded the table tops. Some guests rose up from their chairs, called out, truthfully, "I'm getting up!" or called out, untruthfully, "I'm going!" because they immediately let themselves sink back again onto their seats. Calling out from table to table, they outdid each other about how long they had been waiting.

"Right now," a man in shorts and hiking boots called out, "I've already missed the third train!" He took a timetable out of a rucksack that hung over the back of the chair, opened it, and handed it to the guests at the next table.

"You wouldn't recommend a place like this to your worst enemy!" they cried.

"This is the first and last time!" they cried.

"This is the last time!" even the regulars cried.

The waiters flitted back and forth, wildly flapping their napkins across the tablecloths, as though they wanted to prove that at least their hearts were in the right place.

"Just be patient another second," they said. "We weren't prepared for such a crowd!"

The ringing of the guests in the rooms could be heard in the lobby. The manager hurried back and forth, from the swinging door to the lobby to the swinging door. The guests in the rooms above our heads began to stamp on the ceiling. The waiters surrounded the manager. They talked at him from behind extended napkins. The manager looked at the ceiling with moist eyes, his fingernails digging into the backs of his hands.

The well-dressed man began clapping his hands again. "This seems to be a resort for professional starvers!" he called to the manager with a nasty laugh.

The manager bowed without a word of protest.

Behind the bar the glasses were clinking together in the trembling fingers of the girl.

I could hear the high-school teacher's stomach rumbling.

The manager went to the lobby, on tiptoe, nodding his head soothingly in all directions. On the way, his knees buckled. He kept on going, crouched over, his hands almost touching the floor. But he did not straighten himself out, though it would have been easier. When he had left the room, the waiters scratched long lines through the menus.

A murmur arose in the garden. I stood up. My mother was paying attention only to the high-school teacher. At all the tables the guests had set out their silver, with the knives and forks so far apart that large dishes would have fitted in between.

"Bring me the special lunches numbers one, two, and three!" called the man in shorts and hiking boots. "As far as I'm concerned, you can mix them all up together, but bring them now!"

Those who had been waiting in the garden had leaped up. They were standing partly on the chairs and tables, so as to have a better view of what was being eaten for lunch on the balcony. The round head and the round shoulders of the woman stuck out above the balcony. I could see only the small head of the man, probably her husband, who was sitting opposite her, either because his

chair was lower than hers or because he was smaller. The
maid stood in the balcony door. She held a tray. At a
nod from the woman she raised the tray over her head
and showed it around. Then she put the tray on the table,
which was invisible behind the parapet, and disappeared
into the house.

"Grace!" cried the woman. The man looked at her in
astonishment. Then he lowered his head. The woman
raised her hands, folded them at the level of her mouth,
and prayed loudly and slowly, like someone leading a
service: "Come, Lord Jesus, be our guest, and bless that
which Thou hast bestowed on us."

And while she was praying, some more guests came
into the garden next to me, and the guests in the rooms
threw open their windows onto the garden. They were
men who hung their bared chests all the way out, drew
the women in underwear to the windows, and pushed them
back into the rooms, calling, "Leave your finger on the
bell!"

The man and the woman began eating, carrying one
forkful after another to their mouths. And with each
forkful the lip-smacking around me grew louder and
louder. The people waiting on the ground, on chairs, on
tables, the ones in the windows opened and closed their
mouths in the rhythm of those eating up there, they
chewed with teeth clicking together with a loud noise.
But the woman wasn't content with these forkfuls becoming visible to her spectators, and those only for a short
time.

"Grete!" she called and rang a bell held high in her
hands. "We need some fat books!"   ·

The maid appeared in the doorway to the balcony,
carrying a heap of books in front of her. The man jumped

up, reached for the highest book, opened it and held it in front of his face. But the woman tore it out of his hand and slammed it shut. As they stood facing each other, I saw that the man was not only a head shorter than she, but that the man was also thin enough to fit into the woman twice over. She went inside and closed the balcony door behind her. And while the man and the maid, carrying out their instructions, disappeared behind the balcony parapet, the table top and part of the table legs came into sight above the parapet.

The woman came back, wearing a shiny dress. They sat down at the table again. They weren't sitting comfortably, they were much too low for the table, and they had difficulty eating. The moment the man emptied his plate, the woman urged him to eat some more. The man spread his hands over the plate and shook his head violently. It even looked as though it were shaking the whole man. But the woman poured the food over his hands. It broke up and dribbled between his spread fingers onto the plate. Whenever the woman wasn't looking, the man flung down whole forkfuls over the balcony into the garden. All around, the guests' stomachs rumbled.

But even that wasn't enough for the woman. Once she pretended, with an empty hand, to throw down something, another time she threw down scraps of food. Some of it fell into the goldfish pool. The water splashed up. The guests kept their eyes fixed on all this and began scraping their feet back and forth. While the greater part of them clung to each other, the smaller part rushed to the pool. "The fish!" they cried. They plunged their hands into the water, they pulled the fish out, they stuffed them into their mouths. Half a fish between their teeth, the other half hanging out and moving back and forth like tongues—

that's how they stood; then they bit into them. The lovers were standing chest to chest. Their lips touched as they bit a goldfish in two.

"That was the appetizer," they said, separating their lips again.

And they went into the room ahead of the other guests.

The high-school teacher sat back to back with my father and rumbled.

"He looked over here!" whispered my mother.

A guest from the hotel came rushing in. His dressing gown had blown open in front revealing his white legs with their black hairs. He looked quickly around at a few tables, then turned on his heel and vanished as swiftly as he had come. "Those in the restaurant," I heard him calling out, "haven't got anything yet either!" Above our heads the hotel guests stamped on the ceiling more violently than before.

"There's no sense," whispered my father, "in going over to his table now. He'll have a right to wonder why I hesitated so long before saying hello to him."

"He looked over here!" whispered my mother.

My father bent his head and sat hunched over the table with his shoulders drawn up high.

"We ordered!" the guests called. "We waited! Now we want to eat!" They all held knives and forks in their hands.

"Is he looking this way?" whispered my father.

My mother shook her head. My mother nodded. The manager stood in front of the swinging door. He had to open his mouth more than once before he could articulate the hoarse words. "Ladies and gentlemen," he said, and he twisted and turned so that he addressed half his sentences at the swinging door, "I beg you to understand. We were not prepared for such a crowd. I did what I could. I asked for extra help in all the restaurants in the city. But there, too, they can barely accommodate the rush, and they are concerned with satisfying their own guests. I beg you, therefore, to leave the restaurant. We are closed." And as though to prove this, a waiter carried a placard saying CLOSED TODAY past the guests to the door and hung it up there.

"This must be a joke!" cried the well-dressed man. He jumped up, he pushed the manager away from the swinging door. The chefs behind it jumped to one side, their hands still touching their ears. The lids of pots fell on the floor, and the well-dressed man laughed nastily. The waiters drew the curtains and let down the rolling shutters. The restaurant was half-dark. They put the unoccupied chairs on the tables.

"He's been looking at you all the time," said my mother.

With his feet the high-school teacher pushed himself and his chair away from the table. The back of his chair touched the back of my father's chair.

The well-dressed man came out of the swinging door. "They are cooking pure tap water in the kitchen," he cried. The guests, holding their knives and forks, moved closer to the manager. He vanished behind the swinging door. I heard that something in the kitchen was pushed up against the swinging door.

"Get hold of something for us!" cried the guests. "No matter what!"

"We'd better go!" whispered my father. "Can't you move a little bit? I can't budge."

The guests behind us had reached the level of our table. The guests in front of us stood in front of the swinging door, as though only waiting for an order to storm the kitchen. My father stood up slowly and carefully. He turned his head to the right, then to the left, with the expression of someone listening, as though he expected someone to tell him how to get out of the restaurant. Behind him the high-school teacher jumped up.

"All right," said my mother, "let's go, then."

"One moment!" the high-school teacher called, standing close behind my shrinking father. "Don't we know each other?" The guests next to our table stopped moving. They looked at my father. The guests in front of the swinging door turned around. My father lowered his eyes. He nodded.

"What do two people who know each other do?" cried the high-school teacher.

"They say hello," whispered my father.

The guests had come so close that my mother was standing among them. My father looked at my mother. But my mother was looking off in another direction.

"I'd like to go now," whispered my father, and he took a hesitating step forward.

"One moment!" cried the high-school teacher. "We're not through yet! Who says hello first?"

"The younger person," whispered my father.

"And which of us two is the younger?" cried the high-school teacher; and then he added, as though he could no longer wait for my father's answer, "You are!" And so that everyone could see whom he meant, he stuck his fork into my father's shoulder.

My father groaned aloud, and as though this, too, were most improper, he put his hand over his mouth.

The high-school teacher seemed astonished himself at how violently he had struck out with the fork. As he pulled it out of my father's jacket, his eyes gleamed a little behind his reading glasses. But the guests nodded to him with radiant eyes.

"Then say hello!" cried the high-school teacher.

"Hello," whispered my father, "sir."

"Well, hello!" cried the high-school teacher. "Aren't you hungry at all? I listened for a long time, but I didn't hear your stomach rumbling. Could you be the one who has eaten up everything here?"

I just managed to jump to one side. Then they all fell upon my father. A great growling tangle of arms, legs, rumps, rolled around on the floor, covered my father. Now and again I saw an arm raise itself high, holding a knife or fork in the hand, and then go whipping back down with great force. My mother was standing a little to one side, upright and motionless. Figures in dressing gowns flitted in through the lobby door and threw themselves on top. Through the growling I heard something crack, break. Then the tangle came apart. First the ones in dressing gowns rolled away from the backs of the others. Then the others crawled under the tables, each one dragging something along. My mother, bumping into the tables, went off toward the stairs that led downstairs to the toilets.

"Grete!" I heard the woman on the balcony call. "We'll have coffee inside!"

As the guests under the tables began to belch, my mother came back up the stairs. "I just," she muttered, "just didn't"; and she winced whenever someone belched. Then she took me by the hand.

We walked between the tables and gathered together the scraps of my father's clothes. Whenever we passed, we startled the gnawing people. They lifted the table-cloths a little, they blinked out at us, like people frightened out of their sleep. They straightened up; they smoothed out their clothes with their hands. They pulled their hats all the way down over their faces. They made off with their heads bent low, with their behinds pulled in, leaving big banknotes on the tables as though settling bills.

When my tongue is sore and the bag is empty, I lift the blanket up high and listen. My parents have gone to bed. I hear my father snoring, I hear my mother clearing her throat.

The morning after, once a year, always at the time my father is teaching, my grandmother comes to visit us.

She arrives with two suitcases and looks like someone at the end of a long trip, though she lives only a few streets away.

"My child!" she cries. "You've gotten even thinner!" She puts her suitcases on the floor and belatedly claps her hands together.

"But it's very nice here," she says, and looks around the dining room. Then she unpacks her suitcases and puts one jar of preserves after another on the table.

"That'll last a while," she says. "How is your husband?" she says.

"Very well," my mother says. "You can see him through the window there."

"No, no!" my grandmother says. "Never mind." She turns away from the window, she even closes her eyes for a second. "Tell me," she whispers behind her hands, "wasn't yesterday the day again?"

My mother nods. "Go and play, Lothar," she says.

I close the door and listen.

"I don't know," my mother says, "whether I was right or not. But I'm not pretty and I don't know how to dress. And he was so attentive to me. Toward the end he came to see me several times a day. He even skipped his classes."

"You're quite right," says my grandmother.

"'You must let me make it all up to you,' he said," my mother says. "And when he came and when he left, the other tenants didn't hide behind the curtains any more. They pulled the windows open. 'There he is again,' they called out. 'The suitor himself!'—'Is the new little widow going to turn him down?' they called out. 'Is he going to stay overnight this time?' 'If you don't let me make it all up to you,' he said, 'I'm going to stay all night.' "

"You're quite right," says my grandmother.

"He doesn't smoke," says my mother. "He doesn't drink. He saves up everything for Lothar. And he eats whatever is put on the table. Come to the kitchen with me. I have to cook the dinner."

"I'll leave you to your cooking in peace and quiet," says my grandmother. "I'd better go now."

My mother goes into the kitchen. I sit down on the stool in the corner and watch my mother cook.

She kneels down in front of the refrigerator, pulls a big lump of raw red meat out of the freezer compartment, carries the meat carefully in both hands over to the sink. The way she goes through the kitchen, lifting her feet very high off the tile floor at every step, with her dress billowing out, her upper arms at an angle to her back, her elbows akimbo, I think the only thing that stops her from flying off is the weight of the lump of meat. She holds the meat with both hands under the tap, washes it, and between her fingers the reddish water runs down the drain. She wraps the meat in a white cloth, dries it, sets it down on a wooden board. She turns around and looks up at the kitchen clock. She bends over the lump of meat, cuts off some scraps of fat with the kitchen knife, rubs it down with salt, with oil, rolls it back and forth in flour. Then she puts it into the simmering grease of the roasting pan, puts the lid on, shoves the pan into the stove, and shuts the door. She turns around and looks up at the kitchen clock.

"Now the water," she says, she sings; lifting her feet high above the tile floor at every step, as though surmounting obstacles, she goes, she rises to the cupboard. Her ankles are as narrow as wrists, the bones stick out to the right and the left through the stockings with a bluish shimmer, bluish like the veins springing out of her calves. My mother fills two large pots with water, puts them on two gas burners. And while she cleans the vegetables, peels the potatoes, the steam rising from the seething pots on the stove lifts up the lids, which fall back with a clatter and are lifted again. And while the vegetables and the potatoes are cooking in the pots, my mother kneels down in front of the oven, my mother puts some pot holders over her hands, my mother pulls the roasting pan out of the oven, uncovers the roast, which is brown now and crisp, looks at it in a worried way, says, "Will there be enough?" Then she scratches the crust of the roast away from the edge of the pan with the knife, pours cream over the roast, pushes it back into the heat of the oven and lets it go on baking. She moves back and forth, going up and down in the kitchen, getting the spices ready, uncovering the pots, stirring spoons around in the pots, and as she moves back and forth and up and down, she says, she sings out, the names of all the ingredients; she turns her face, blotched white and red now, to look up at the kitchen clock, whose black hands on a white background are moving closer to noon, to dinner.

My mother is a good cook.

THE HOST

I AM SITTING on the bed, on the bed, on my bed, between the foot and the head of the bed, in the middle, I am sitting on my quilt folded over twice, on the pillow folded once on the quilt, on top of it, my knees bent over the edge of the bed, my legs hanging down without touching the floor. I put my hands around the edge of the bed, I push my thumbs between the edge and the mattress, I stretch out the other eight fingers, I sit in this way on this mound of bedding and squeeze my behind into it.

I'm no longer all by myself.

In the dining room my parents are busy blaming each other for that. My father defends himself noisily, moving his chair back and forth and scraping his feet on the carpet; he shouts, "I can't eat overcooked meat!" My mother defends herself noisily, banging her knuckles on the table top so that the plates clatter; she shouts, I "can't run miles to the butcher, with the child!" It's after dinner. My mother has not cleared the table. My father hasn't stretched out on the sofa. Between two justifications I hear my father and my mother repeating the main points of their accusations.

"Because you want the meat half-raw!" cries my mother. "As though I would overcook it!"

"Overcooked meat!" cries my father. "No! Because you go to that butcher! You still go! Even though I failed that son of his, that blockhead, who is only good to be made into sausages!"

"I can't run miles!" cries my mother.

"I always said so!" cries my father.

"You never said so!" cries my mother.

"He'll palm a tapeworm off on you!" cries my father.

"Run miles to the butcher!" cries my mother.

"Out of pure revenge!" cries my father.

Between two justifications, between two accusations, I hear my mother complaining.

"The child is thin enough as it is," she cries. "And now he's become a host as well!"

"Host!" cries my father. "What kind of nonsense is that!"

Below us Mr. Kecker, the one on crutches, pounds the floor with his crutch.

"Hit out!" he shouts. "That's what I ought to do, with my crutch!"

"Shh!" says my mother. "Mr. Kecker is taking the day off."

I am sitting on the bed, on this mound of bedding. I squeeze my behind into it. And when it starts sucking inside me, I press back against its sucking. And when it twists and turns, I move my legs against the wood of the bed until the skin is red, until my calves burn and are scraped open.

Then I pull my legs high up on the mound of bedding, I squat there without moving, my legs squeezed up against my chest, my chin caught between my knees, my fingers on the bruises on my calves.

"When," I ask myself, "is he going to let himself be seen?"

"It can't go on this way," said my mother.

I sat the way I am sitting, on this mound of bedding in the morning. And outside, from the bed, I could see my father walking through the school gate made of iron bars, heard the schoolbell ringing through the closed windows. And inside, from the bed, I saw my mother coming toward me through my room, heard her say—and this through the sound of the schoolbell—that things couldn't go on this way. She carried my Sunday trousers, my Sunday shirt in her hand. She put them both down on the bed. She knelt down in front of the bed, for comparison held her emaciated arms against my more emaciated legs.

"Your legs are like arms, like fingers almost," she said. "I'm fed up with letting other mothers look at me that way. Today you're going to have a check-up."

My mother packed some cookies.

"We'll probably have to wait a long time," she said. "Doctor Trautbert has lots of patients."

It is not easy to miss Doctor Trautbert's office. Signs are scattered throughout our whole quarter on the houses, at about the height of a man, picturing a black hand on a white background, with four fingers curled up and one outstretched forefinger pointing horizontally to a second sign. This second sign in turn points to Doctor Trautbert's office. The farther away you get from his office, the greater is the distance between the signs; the nearer you get, the smaller. The word has gone around in our quarter that with every new patient two new signs of this kind turn up. For the patients put in a good word for Doctor Trautbert with house owners and superintendents. If a house owner or a superintendent is especially reluctant, Doctor Trautbert's patients put the signs behind the windows of their own apartments. On Doctor Trautbert's house, all across the front, at the height of a man, hand after hand points to sign upon sign. Doctor Trautbert is the owner of the five-story apartment house.

On the sidewalk in front of the door four piles of dog dung, not yet dried, lay in a row, equidistant, a dog's length from each other. None of these four piles had been stepped on. The people who lived in the house, the people who visited the ones who lived in the house, the patients of Doctor Trautbert, and any others who went in and out of the house, all seemed to be very familiar with this state of affairs.

My mother rang the bell.

In the stairwell, all along the wall, one hand pointed to the other, black on white on black on white, going up the stairs. Doctor Trautbert lets his patients walk up five flights of stairs. His office and his apartment have the same entrance. Above this entrance a vertical forefinger pointed downward, pointed straight at the white cap of Nurse Else, who stood in the doorway, gray-haired, with a whitish-gray face, with gray eyes, a thin-lipped mouth, with a white ribbon all around her whitish-gray throat, in a gray ankle-length skirt. She stood in the doorway as though the door had been fitted to her along with her cap. In width Nurse Else could have fitted in next to herself three times over.

"Have you an appointment?" she said, holding a notebook waist high in her left hand, a pencil in her right.

"Leinlein," said my mother. "It's about Lothar. Lothar Leinlein."

Nurse Else leaned forward a little, looked with the pencil for my name in the notebook, made a check mark against it.

"Please," she said.

And as we stepped into the hall, my mother pushing me in front of her, and as Nurse Else shut the door, her eyes fixed on our four legs, Doctor Trautbert's four dogs began to yap an accompaniment to our passage through the hall, past the coat closet, the consulting room, toward the waiting room, ran yapping into the back of a door with something written on it. The sign clattered at the thud of their four bodies. At the moment of the thud the dogs burst into a frantic yelping.

"What's on that sign?" I asked my mother.

"Dogs' room," my mother read out loud—I don't know whether she lies when she reads aloud to me—"Enter at your own risk."

The seven patients in the waiting room glanced quickly at the door, at us. They first raised their faces to mother, then lowered them to me.

"Hello," said my mother.

The patients, except for one, stared with dull faces ahead of them or at their laps, at the title pages of magazines with pictures of dogs. All seven patients sat with their legs lined up next to each other, touching the floor. They had put little packages between their feet. The wrapping paper showed flecks of blood and had also come apart in places, so that I could see what was inside: bones and meat, little gifts for Doctor Trautbert's dogs. Now and then, when one of them, by mistake and out of habit, crossed his legs, his face contorted for a moment with a seizure of pain, and he cautiously raised one leg off the other and put it down to the floor again as before.

Four of the seven patients sat on the chairs standing

next to each other along the walls, sat in a row in front of the wall with the window. A chair was left unoccupied between each of them. The other three sat on the sofa behind the library table, sat in such a way that between the arm of the sofa and the first patient, between the first and the second patients, between the second and the third, and between the third and the arm at the other end of the sofa there were gaps the width of a patient. Into these gaps they placed their hands as though by arrangement at irregular intervals, as if they wanted to reassure themselves that the one sitting on the other side of the gap had not meanwhile got too close to their bodies.

At first glance I could see only what had brought one of these patients to see the doctor—the one who was sitting between the two others on the sofa. It was in his face. He kept indicating over and over again just where it was by raising his forefinger, by putting the tip of his forefinger into the space between his eyebrows, on a raspberry-red pustule without a pus cap, on the top of which a meager little tuft of hair connecting the eyebrows stood on end. Around it everything was swollen up, worst of all around the eyes. The eyes lay deeply embedded between the rolls of flesh above and below that kept falling over each other when he didn't pay attention, when he didn't raise his forehead and keep it wrinkled. If he wanted to make out anything of consequence beyond his cheeks—our entrance, for instance—he had to bend his head over backward. The pustule had drawn up the skin on the bridge of his nose, and together with the skin the nostrils, and even the upper lip. I could see to the depth of half a finger into the carefully cleaned, hairy interior of his nose. That is how he sat there, this patient, with creased forehead, lips slightly open, tapping with his forefinger between his eyebrows; he did not look dully ahead of him like the others, rather as though he was astonished by his condition and brooding over his condition.

"Don't," hissed my mother into my ear, "stare at that gentleman that way. Do you think it amuses him?" She gave me a cookie.

And while I was eating the cookie, and because I didn't want to look at the man, and because I couldn't tell what was wrong with the other patients anyway, I examined the picture over the sofa.

Picture and sofa were of the same length. So either the picture had been made to order, or the sofa had been made to order, or it was a coincidence. The gold-colored frame enclosed a landscape that someone completely strange to the place would love. You could see it all as far as the horizon. Not a mountain, not a tree, not a bush covered the view of this line of horizon, which was straight as though drawn by a ruler from one side of the frame to the other. The ground in front of the line was a little lighter than sheepskin-colored, and the ground on the other side of the line was grayish. Uninterrupted by sun, moon, or stars, the grayish ground represented a densely clouded sky. On this side of the line sheep stood in a row, sheepskin-colored, their hind parts, except for one, turned toward the observers or art connoisseurs. The bodies of the sheep were scarcely distinguishable from the ground. The sheep on the left, which the painter had plainly painted before those on the right, at a time that plainly preceded his decision to dispense with the grass too for the sake of the view, the sheep on the left kept their heads down at the height of a blade of grass, as though they were grazing. They were painted in such a way that you could make out their heads between their legs. You could look not only between the sheep's legs, but also between the individual sheep's bodies, as though these sheep had willingly moved away from each other so that someone behind them, who no longer fitted into the frame, could have a view of the horizon through the gaps between their bodies. The horizon stretched out a sheepshead higher than the sheep's heads, except for one. The sheep in the middle—that is, not exactly in the middle but on either side of the gap in the middle of the painting —and the sheep on the right were looking, since there was nothing more to graze, at the horizon. At the edge, to the right, a little lower than the sheep and with his bent back pressed against the frame, as though he were afraid of towering over the horizon if he stood up straight, stood the shepherd with a hat on his head. Hat and horizon touched. The shepherd was not watching the sheep. He had turned his face to one side, and not only that: he covered his turned-away face with both hands, as though he were so ashamed of his sheep that he could not endure looking even in the direction away from the sheep. But he seemed to be particularly ashamed of this one sheep that stood closest to him, the farthest to the right in the row. The hind legs of this sheep stood on the same line as the hind legs of the other sheep. But the neck of this sheep had become so long that the head lay on the horizon, even towered above it. In spite of this it was not difficult to imagine the course of the straight horizon behind the sheep's head. One-eyed and with a malevolent squint, this sheep looked past the shepherd at someone who might be standing behind the shepherd and who no longer fitted into the frame. The horizon ran straight into the sheep's muzzle, which this sheep had opened up wide as though it wanted to bite it in two.

The four dogs began yapping, yapped until the front door slammed shut behind a patient who was finished. The sign clattered at the thud of their bodies. The patients, except for the one with the pustule, pulled their shoulders in, they moved closer to each other, so that the gaps grew smaller on one side, and on the other bigger, they looked at the door.

"Next, please!" said Nurse Else.

The next one, the one on the right next to the one with the pustule, raised his little gift high with both hands, carried it in front of him, carried it limping, thrusting out his right leg and putting it down carelessly, dragging his stiff left leg behind and putting it down carefully—in this way he carried his gift out of the waiting room.

"It's for Tobias," I heard him say hoarsely behind the door.

"Tobias," the patients repeated in the waiting room. "What do you know," said the patients, and they looked at each other like people in the know, except for the one with the pustule, for whom it was difficult to see beyond himself. At the same time the gaps between them were again the same as they had been before the yapping.

"Me too," said one of them, the one at the far left in the row of chairs in front of the wall with the window. "Me," he repeated, raised his trouser leg a little in the air, but not so high that I, who was the only one watching, could notice anything worth looking at on the bare part of his leg, and when he saw that the others—aside from me, who probably didn't seem enough of a spectator for him to display a bigger part of his leg with something worth seeing on it—that the others, then, were dully looking ahead of them or staring at pictures of dogs, he let the trouser leg slip down over the sock. Then with an injured air he looked at the floor at the little gift between his feet.

I munched the cookie.

The yapping came on again, sign rattling. The patients

moved away from each other on one side, toward each other on the other. In the hall I heard Doctor Trautbert say, "Nothing will be left, nothing, you can be sure of that, but a scar, consider it a keepsake from Tobias." The one on the left next to the one with the pustule quickly began checking his clothes. He passed his right hand over the knot in his tie, the buttons of his coat, his fly.

"So that's the next next one," I thought.

"Can I," I asked my mother, "have another cookie?"

He tightened his shoelaces with both hands and lifted his little gift up from between his shoes; he moved over to the left edge of the sofa.

"Wait a little bit," said my mother.

He limped when he went out, dragging his right leg along.

"For Susie," I heard him say.

The only one on the sofa, the one with the pustule, plainly a man with a sense of symmetry, reassured himself with side glances to the right and the left that he was still sitting in the middle of the sofa. And the way he was sitting, he was also sitting in the middle with his head exactly under the gap between the two sheep's bodies in the middle of the picture.

"It's taking a long time," said the one who had first said "me too" then "me"; he was trying for the second time to start a conversation, after having started the first time so wrong you couldn't be more wrong, since you can't begin a conversation between patients as you do a conversation between a doctor and a patient: by starting right in to talk about yourself.

"You can say that again," said the other patients, except for the one with the pustule. He mumbled something to himself that sounded like, "I'm not saying anything."

"It always takes," said my mother, "longer than you think. Always."

"He can't go any faster than he's able," said the one next to the one who had said "Me-too-me" and then that it was taking a long time. The one with the pustule mumbled something to himself that sounded like "I'm not so sure about that."

"He could, though, of course," said the one who had said he couldn't do it any faster than he was able, contradicting himself. "All he would have to do would be not to talk about his dogs all the time. But that's just what he can't help doing. That's it."

"He loves them, that's all," said the one on the far right in the row of chairs. "That's the way he is."

"You could bleed to death," said the one who hadn't said anything before. "He doesn't stop until he's finished with the characteristics of all four dogs. But that takes as long as it takes. That's the way he is."

"Mama," I said, and I saw they were all looking at me.

"Child," said my mother, "you drive me."

"Leave him alone," said one of the two who had said that was the way he was and before that something else. "Children will be children."

"We were all children once," said the one who had said nothing before and then had said something after all.

Then my mother gave me a cookie.

"What's your name?" said the one who had said "Me-too-me" and then a few more things.

My mother looked at me sideways. I knew I had to tell him.

I waited for the yapping of the dogs outside to stop, the yapping that accompanied the voice of Doctor Trautbert, who said, "We must be patient. A bite like that doesn't heal overnight. That's the way it is."

"Lothar," I said. Then I chewed on the cookie.

"Next, please," said Nurse Else.

"Now that's a nice name," said the one who had said "Me-too-me," picked up his little gift, started limping, dragging I don't know which leg behind him—I didn't even look, I saw a fly flying and watched to see when and then on what it was going to settle—and limped out.

After that no one said anything. Only I, because I wanted some cookies, asked my mother whether I could have some cookies, asked her so often that she finally gave me all the cookies.

And while the next one, each time summoned by Nurse Else, left the waiting room to the yapping of the four dogs, limping and dragging behind him one leg or the other and mentioning outside one of the four names: Susie, Annie, Tobias, Gabriel; and while the patients inside moved toward each other and away from each other as long as one of them was sitting on the other side of the gaps, and when nobody was, wrapped their arms around themselves and then sat looking dully ahead again or staring at pictures of dogs; and while one or the other, clearing his throat, tried to attract attention, pulled up one trouser leg or the other, opened his mouth as though beginning to make an announcement while looking from one patient to another; and while the others, especially the ones who had tried the same just before, turned their heads away from him, hardly noticeably but definitely; and while the one who had tried it then gave up again because I, the only one looking, didn't seem to him enough of a spectator, I chewed cookie after cookie, I kept watching when the fly would settle and then on what.

The fly settled on the gap to the left, between the back of the sofa and the one with the pustule.

After the four patients who were finished and before getting to the other three, who, aside from us, were waiting to be finished, right in between, Doctor Trautbert took a break. He fed his four dogs.

I heard them going down the hall, Doctor Trautbert and Nurse Else.

"Did you split it up fairly?" I heard him say. "Show me the bowls."

There was a rattling.

"Good," I heard him say, "none of them is being short-changed." He unlocked the door.

The dogs yapped louder than before. And downstairs, somewhere in the house, perhaps because he couldn't stand it, perhaps because he had to practice anyhow, a pianist began to play. And downstairs, somewhere in the house, because they couldn't stand the piano playing, the yapping, babies began to cry, women began to yell because they couldn't endure the yapping, the piano playing, the yelling: "Stop that banging!" And he, the pianist, yelled, "First stop that yapping!" And inside, in the waiting room, the two patients in the row of chairs with one empty chair between them chattered with their teeth, crouched over, pulled in their shoulders, wrapped their arms around themselves. One of the two, the one who had said nothing and then had said something after all, got up and opened the window, which was five stories too high. Then he sat down, pulled a handkerchief out of his trouser pocket, and twisted it into a sort of rope. The other, the one who had said he couldn't do it any faster than he could and then said the opposite right away, looked from the window to the handkerchief to the window, understood, and nodded in relief, as though the idea of a way out were enough for a way out.

The one with the pustule left his finger on the pustule.
The fly flew toward the picture. It settled in the gap
to the left between two sheep.

The dogs threw themselves against the door.

"My little darlings," Doctor Trautbert called out, "my
little babies! Let your master in! I'm bringing you something special. A bowl for each one of you! Now how
about it, you little sillies! How do you think I'm to get
in if you four great big monsters lean against the door?
Each one to his corner! Everyone pay attention! Susie,
Annie, Tobias, Gabriel—to your places! Give me the tray,
Nurse Else. Now!" The door squeaked as he opened it.
The dogs fell silent.

I imagined that he stood in the middle of the room,
holding the tray in front of him with both hands or lifting
it above his head, more likely that way, so that all four
could see it. I imagined that in each corner one dog sat,
wagging his tail and looking doggishly at his own bowl,
at the bowls of the other three. The dogs began to growl.

"Keep your places!" called Doctor Trautbert. "Back to
your corners! That's the only way each one gets what he
deserves!" But the dogs began yelping, they leaped up
high. The bowls rattled. Then the bones splattered, the
meat smacked, the bowls rattled onto the floor. "But all I
wanted," groaned Doctor Trautbert, "all I wanted was
the best for you!" Then he too fell on the floor. "It's me,"
he groaned, "me, your master, lying on the floor. I warn
you! Don't make a mistake! Or you'll be shot down like
mad dogs!"

"Would you like me to help you up?" said Nurse Else.

I imagined that she looked down on him without a trace
of malicious pleasure or of sympathy in her face, that he
was lying flat on the floor, in the midst of bones, of meat,
of bowls, the dogs around him, silent and with their

muzzles full of food. I imagined that he looked up to her as he said, "Just leave me alone," or that he turned aside from her as he said, "Just leave me alone!" I imagined that he supported himself on the palms of his hands, pulled his legs up to his rump, that he paused a moment in this position, propped up on his knees and the palms of his hands, just as high or not quite so high as his dogs, that he then straightened himself up. "It's all right now," he said, and I heard him walking. "Everything's all right now," he said, and he tried a smile perhaps. "You can't be angry with me, after all. They're the way they are, and if I were that way I'd be just that way too." The door squeaked as he shut it.

The one with the pustule took his finger off the pustule.

"I'm not surprised," said the one who had first said nothing and then said something after all. He unrolled his handkerchief, put it into his trouser pocket. "He gives it to them raw."

"And the wallpaper," said the one who had said a little while before that he couldn't do it any faster than he could do it and then immediately said the opposite, "the wallpaper," he repeated and said the rest with his forefinger on his lips, as though he wanted to show that it was a half-secret, "someone told me is supposed to have a pattern of naked legs, large as life."

The fly, which had crawled along the gap as far as the horizon, on the left between two sheep, flew up a few flies' lengths in front of the horizon and settled on the empty chair between the two patients.

"And do you know, actually," said the one who first had said nothing and then had said something after all, in fact a whole lot. The other, who was looking at him with his forefinger still on his lips, jumped up at Nurse Else's request, jumped up a little too quickly, groaningly

held his leg with both hands, and, bent over, limped out.
When he was finished, and before Nurse Else had called
the next next one, he came in once again, handed a card
to the one who first had said nothing and then had said
something after all: "My address," he said. The other one
pocketed the card, nodded, said, "I will." Then he was
summoned.

The fly flew up, flew around the one with the pustule.

"Thank God," said my mother, "I got dinner ready
already."

The one with the pustule started squirming back and
forth on the sofa, first in the gap to the left, between the
arm of the sofa and himself when he was sitting in the
middle, then in the gap to the right between the arm
of the sofa and himself when he was sitting in the middle.

"I can't wait any longer," he mumbled and jumped up.
"I'm going," he mumbled, and without limping he left
the waiting room without being called, and Doctor Trautbert's office without being finished.

"Now it's our turn," said Nurse Else.

And then we walked behind her, my mother pushing
me in front of her, pushing me past the dogs' room, accompanied meanwhile by the yapping of the four dogs, into
the consulting room.

Doctor Traubert stood in the middle of the consulting
room, broad, short, and pink, and in the presence of
Nurse Else still broader, still shorter, still pinker, just
as she in his presence looked still thinner, still taller, still
grayer than he, than she, than both were anyhow. He
wore a clean white coat. In his outstretched hands he held
a second white, partly blood-flecked coat.

"Get rid," he said to Nurse Else, "please, finally get
rid of this coat. One looks more like a butcher than a
doctor, after feeding those four dogs."

Then he gave us each at the same time, to my mother and me, one of his hands; he looked not at our faces but at our legs.

"Mrs. Leinlein is here for the first time," said Nurse Else. She stepped close to him, and afterward too, during the examination, seizing every opportunity she stood close to him, as though she wanted to indicate that in addition there was the possibility of looking like her.

"It's about Lothar," said my mother.

"Well, well," said Doctor Trautbert. And while my mother sat down, he pulled my lower eyelids down with his thumb, pulled my upper eyelids up with his forefinger, and looked at the red inside.

"Where is the trouble?" he asked.

I snapped my eyes open and shut.

"Ah," he said, raised my chin up with his thumbs.

I straightened my shoulders, bent my head backward, looked into his face.

"Well," he said. "Ah." He bent down to me, let me look into his wide-open mouth, in which, at the back, between the two holes, the raised uvula twitched up and down, in which the back part of the tongue was covered with a thick white coating that became thinner and broken toward the tip of the tongue, which lay pink on his pink lower lip.

"Ah," I said.

"Again," he said.

"Ah," I said.

"Address, please," said Nurse Else. She sat at a table and wrote.

"Thirty-three School Street," said my mother. "He should have a check-up. He's thin enough by nature, and a bad eater as well. But now he's losing weight into the bargain."

We sat facing each other, he and I, with my legs between his legs. He inspected the inside of my ear through
a mirror in front of his eye. This ear mirror was fastened
to a metal hoop, which he wore around his head and
over his forehead. He flipped the mirror back.

"Now the left one," he said. "The left, not the right,"
he said, pulling at my left earlobe.

"He's a little confused," said my mother.

"There's nothing wrong there," he said and took the
hoop with the mirror off his head. "Strip him to the waist."

My mother pulled off my shirt, my undershirt.

"Just one more second," he called.

The dogs yapped.

Doctor Trautbert placed the chilly stethoscope on a
few places on my chest, looking past my head with the
expression of a listener. The dogs were yapping so loudly
that I asked myself whether he could hear anything over
their yapping. He took hold of me with his thick warm
fingers, turned me around between his thighs. He placed
the chilly stethoscope on a few places on my back.

"Take a deep breath," he said. "Breathe out. In," he
said. "Now out. Hold your breath," he said. "All right now.
There's nothing wrong there," he said. He gave me a slap
on the behind.

"He's a little confused," said my mother.

"Lie down there," said Doctor Trautbert. "Look at this
finger!"

I lay down on a leather bed. Doctor Trautbert began
pointing with his forefinger. He pointed in all directions,
now slowly, now quickly. I followed the tip of his forefinger with my eyes, squinted when he held it in front
of my nose.

"There's nothing wrong there," he said.

My mother got up, she put on my undershirt, my shirt.

"Well," she said, "then there's nothing wrong with him."

I stood in the middle of the room. I saw that ·they looked at me not without some disappointment, my mother, Doctor Trautbert, Nurse Else.

"Sometimes," I said, "there's something inside me that moves."

"Now that's interesting!" cried Doctor Trautbert. "Well now, please sit down, my dear lady!"

My mother sat down, she crossed her legs, she put her forefinger against her cheek.

"Now just tell me, where does it move? Here?" said Doctor Trautbert. He pointed to his coat, somewhere near his navel.

I nodded.

"The small intestine, of course, I thought so!" cried Doctor Trautbert. "Now we're getting a little closer."

"Sometimes," I said, "it sucks too."

"Why didn't you tell me?" said my mother.

"Leave him be, my dear lady," cried Doctor Trautbert, "he's probably a host."

"Host?" said mother.

"Host," said Doctor Trautbert. "In the sense of host— someone, that is, who shelters someone else."

My mother trembled.

"You doubtless eat your meat half-raw?" said Doctor Trautbert.

"My husband," said my mother, and she couldn't nod, she was shaking so hard.

"I'm almost sure," said Doctor Trautbert, "though we won't be certain until you bring me a sample of his stool."

Doctor Trautbert walked up and down in the consulting room while he said the following, went from window to door to window, rubbed his hands whenever he did not need them to emphasize his words, kept walking between the door and the window always past the lamp in the middle of the ceiling, between the lamp and the window between us, my mother and me, who were sitting opposite each other, I on the bed, she on the chair, pushed a little to one side and moving off further from me during his speech, until just before the end of the speech she pushed the back of the chair against the wall, he walked accompanied by yapping, by piano playing downstairs somewhere in the house, and he interrupted himself only to open the door and to shout, "Quiet!" into the hall. "In our tracts only two kinds need to be considered. One of them is the narrow, or so-called common, the other is the so-called, and actually incorrectly called, black variety, because it's not black but only a darker white than the common. Now if you ask me which of these two I'd like him to have—and I don't want him to have either—I would say the latter, the black. Of course that, like everything else, also has its disadvantages. For it's very difficult to get rid of it, and its full-grown length, after all, comes to more than eight yards. If you add the width of the hall to the length of this wall, you'll have it, my dear lady."

My mother looked, as though she were actually seeing it in the flesh, along the wall of the room. She trembled. "But doubtless it won't be that long yet," continued Doctor Trautbert, and he pointed to me whenever he meant *it*. "Otherwise, that is, he would look more miserable," and he pointed to me when he meant *me*, "in all probability that long," he added, and he indicated the wall that contained the door. "In spite of all that, you should be glad if it turns out that he has that kind. The other, you know, first kind, and not wrongly called the common variety, lays its capsule——" "Capsule?" said my mother. "——its capsule, I'll explain immediately, often, not always, but often enough in the eye, also in the brain of its own

host——" "Host?" said my mother. "——host in the sense
of host, I've told you that, so then, of its own host. When
that happens——" "I don't know what happens," said my
mother. "Then let's start all over again. The tapeworm's
body consists of a head and a chain of segments, and that's
all. No mouth, no anal region, no breathing organ. He
can afford that. He can make do with that. Because it's a
parasite. It feeds itself, it evacuates through its skin. It's,
after all, why are you trembling? the most natural thing
in the world! Now if you'll just imagine its head. Nothing
could be simpler! No eye, no ear, nothing of the sort!
What for? Because that's what its host has," and he
pointed to me. "Instead, it has four strong sucking discs
on its head, and that makes sense, because that's what
it uses to attach itself to its host. Everything else is then
taken care of by this host. In that way everything is
managed for the best. The hosts of the tapeworm are all
without exception vertebrates. Sheltered in the small intes-
tines of its hosts, tapeworms will reach, not a high, but
a comparatively respectable age of several years, if they
let their hosts do as they like, if the hosts provide proper
nourishment. But if a host refuses, if a host begins to fast,
which of course weakens not only the worm but the host
at the same time, if a host begins absorbing nourishment
that's obnoxious not only to the worm but possibly to him,
to the host itself, like horseradish, carrots, pumpkin seeds,
and so on, then they are numbered, the tapeworm's days.
When the host has made the worm less resistant in this
way, and himself too, that's the way it is, which has the
effect on the worm of making it become more loosely attached to the host than before, which has the effect on
the host of finally producing in him severe colic, stomach
cramps, vomiting, as well as anemia, emaciation, dizziness,
epilepsy, it need not, but it can——" "But that's just," said

my mother, "it." "——so then when the host, and with him
the worm, has finished with this preparatory cure, what
was that you said, then the host begins, if he still has the
strength, if he still has the intention, you'll laugh, many
hosts no longer care, let matters take their course, meaning
that they let the worm get longer and longer, then the
host begins the real cure: the host expels the worm out
of its lair. The host—you'll have to excuse me, but that
happens to be the proper phrase—ejects the worm." "Yes,
yes, all right," whispered my mother. "However, the cure
is successful only when the head is ejected. Many a host,
for instance, thinks in his innocence that it's enough for
him to pull segments yards long out of his rectum and
is content with that. Only a few months later he finds
himself in the same situation as before. I don't know a
single host who wouldn't give up then. The head of the
worm, you understand, even if the host has torn away
all its segments, has new segments budding out of his
lower end. Now you'll surely want to know——" My mother
shook her head. "——how the development of the tapeworm proceeds. Quiet!" We shrank back, my mother, I,
Nurse Else, when he yelled for quiet into the hall. "At
one time," he continued, "the tapeworm was thought to
be an individual animal. Today, however——" "My husband," said my mother. "——it is known, you must know,
that it represents a colony of separate animals, correspond-
ing to the single segments. When they are split off from
the chain, these segments go on living for a little while
longer, and creep about by themselves for a little while.
Just remember, please, that the cattle tapeworm, for
instance, consists of over a thousand segments—that is,
individual animals. That corresponds more or less to a
medium-sized village housed in an intestine like that."
"Just now I really can't," said my mother. "The eggs,

reckoned to be about fifty thousand, who would go to the trouble of counting them, after all——" "Exactly," said my mother. "——the eggs are formed in the segments, fertilized, developed into embryos. Together with the segments, surrounded by the host's excreta——" "What does excreta mean?" I asked. "——your poo-poo, they get outside. There they lie in water, in damp places, and wait for the appropriate intermediary host." "Intermediary host," giggled my mother. "Because it's only in the intestine of the intermediary host, I'll explain at once, that the embryos can develop further. They pierce the intestinal walls of the intermediary host, nature has endowed them with little hooks for the purpose, they get into organs like the liver, the brain, the eye, and so forth, to name only a few, and there they develop into capsules." "Capsules, yes indeed," said my mother. "The capsule is a sort of bubble that contains the complete head of the tapeworm and a parent bubble. The capsule carrier, the so-called intermediary host, as it has been arranged by nature, is one of the chief means of sustenance of the carnivorous tapeworm carrier, the so-called host," and he pointed to me. "The bubble is digested in the stomach of this host. What remains is the head. That attaches itself firmly, as I said, to the small intestine and out of its hind end begins budding one segment after another. Every new segment pushes itself in between the head and the segment previously formed, so that the segments keep becoming older and bigger, the farther they are away from the head of the worm. So much for the worm. Now for example! If he," he said, pointing to me, "and for the sake of clarity we'll keep taking him as an example, if he were a cat, he would obtain his capsule from a mouse. For the cat eats the mouse in whose liver a capsule is waiting, that's how it is, to turn into a worm

in the cat's small intestine. Further! If he," and he pointed
to me again, "if he were a butcher's dog, he would obtain
his capsule from the entrails of a steer. Further! If he
were a hunting dog, you can be sure he would get his
capsule from a rabbit or hare. Finally, if he were a sheep
dog, if you can follow me——" My mother nodded, moved
further away bit by bit, stared at me as though I were
cat, mouse, dog, hare, and worm all at once. "——so, if he
were a sheep dog, he'd catch his capsule from the sheep.
This capsule is embedded in the sheep's brain. I have
seen—and all because of the capsule—flocks of sheep in
meadows that turned in circles as though they were dancing. But since he happens to be a human being," and he
stood still, his forefinger pointed at me, and my mother
looked at me, then moved away so that she came up against
the wall with the back of her chair, as though just this, a
human being, were the worst of all, lowered her head, let
her hair hang down over her face, and in this way listened to the end of his speech, "happens to be a human
being, and an inhabitant of these parts, he got the capsule,
and so the worm, if at all, but I'm almost sure, either from
a pig, then it would be the common tapeworm, or from
a cow, then it would be, as I said, the way we would
like it, the cattle tapeworm."

"Doctor," said Nurse Else, "please don't forget the
dogs."

"My God, my dogs," said Doctor Trautbert. He hastily
unbuttoned his coat. He came toward us with outstretched
arms, handed us, my mother and me, each of his hands
simultaneously.

"And, my dear Mrs. Leinlein, bring me a specimen of
his stool," he said. Then he pushed us, my mother to one
side and me to the other side, out of the consulting room,
out of the hall, out the front door into the stairwell.

Only a few steps later, I heard the bodies of the dogs thud against the doctor's door. We went down floor after floor against the direction of the fingers pointing upward. On each floor the front doors were open, as though the noise of the dogs could be endured, if at all, only at full strength. In the doors, leaning over the bannister, the tenants, men and women, stood. They stood idle and mutually reassured each other, from door to door and from floor to floor, that there was just nothing to be done about all this noise from the landlord's dogs but move out or listen to it idly. A few of them pulled my mother by the sleeve, wanted to know whether we were the last patients. My mother nodded. As she opened the door into the street, a tenant began telling the others what he would do with the landlord if the latter were a tenant and he the landlord.

On the way home, past the signs about Doctor Traut-bert that at first lay very close to each other and then were spaced farther and farther apart, my mother went into the greengrocer's shop.

"If you want to, you can stay outside," she said.

On the sidewalk in front of the shop the grocer had set out case after case of vegetables and fruit. Behind the display window hung bunches of bananas and grapes fastened to hooks by cords, and fastened to hooks by nets were oranges, melons, lemons. Beneath these were cases of turnips, red cabbage, spinach. Behind the cases stood stacks of potatoes, peanuts, onions.

I stopped in front of the cases, counted the cases, counted to ten, counted the fruit piece by piece, the vegetables piece by piece, always up to ten. I can't count any further.

"Mama," I said, "what number comes after ten?"

"Baby," said my mother, "I've got to!"

Two rows of customers stood in front of the counter. They held shopping bags, nets in their hands, half or almost all filled by the baker, the milkman, the butcher. And while the greengrocer moved around in a green apron, rushed back and forth, filled bags, weighed things on the scales with weights, asked whether he should put in more or less, since nature didn't happen to let things grow by the pound, and while the cash register showed with a tinkle the prices of the goods, and while the customers counted out the money and the greengrocer counted it after them and handed over their things, and while one customer left after another, the greengrocer's wife lay on the other side of the counter in a niche hidden by a green curtain with a hole in it. She lay on a cot and peeped out of the hole into the shop. I could see through the fruit the fold in the curtain where she was holding it firmly in her hand, so that she could keep the hole at eye-level all the time. In the other hand she held a piece of fruit or raw vegetable. It crunched when she bit into it. Every once in a while the fold in the curtain disappeared. Then I could hear her groaning that it was a hard lot to lie that way, leaning only on one's stomach, on one's chest the whole day long, with both hands full. If the greengrocer had to go past the hole in the curtain, he stooped down. But if it happened when there was a crowd of customers, that he ran past the hole standing up, the woman threw the fruit, the vegetable on the floor, pulled the curtain open, let herself be seen lying down, and called, "How can I look out for things if you obstruct my view! Get to one side!"

When my mother had worked her way into the front row, I heard some rapid steps behind me. Before I could turn around, step to one side, someone jostled me. It was a man who was looking behind him even while he kept hold of my shoulders. He cursed and pushed me—"What are you hanging around here for!"—into the cases and jumped into the shop.

"The dog keeper!" he called out.

The customers turned around, sneaked to the display window, looked out into the street between the bunches of bananas, the grapes, the oranges, melons, and lemons.

Around the corner that we, my mother and I, had just come came Doctor Trautbert, the dog keeper, a hat on his head and his face reddened by exertion. He pulled his four dogs behind him on four leashes, two in his right, two in his left hand. The dogs took the whole width of the opposite sidewalk.

"Lothar!" said my mother.

I stood in the shop door. The customers were again standing in front of the counter, their backs to the display window, to the street. They held pocket mirrors in their hands high above their shoulders. They squinted into the pocket mirrors out of the corners of their eyes. The green-grocer, perhaps because he did not want to turn his back to the customers, stood with his eyes cast down, lifting and lowering weights in his hands.

Doctor Trautbert, the dog keeper, stood still, turned around, said something to his dogs. Then he began pulling them again, step by step. The dogs gave an impression of sleepiness. And whenever three of them were willing to let themselves be pulled forward, the fourth turned stubborn, took advantage of the opportunity—which was offered far from rarely—of a lamppost or a building entrance to raise a hind leg.

When the dog keeper, Doctor Trautbert, had completed half the distance from the corner to the green-grocer's, a man hurried out of the door across the street from the shop door. He came out with his coat open, holding a scarf in his hand, and began walking toward Doctor Trautbert. And because he was busy throwing the scarf around his neck, and pushing the coat buttons of the coat into the buttonholes, he did not see the dog keeper, Doctor Trautbert, until he was only a few steps away. He recognized him, he shrank back, he stood still, he said, "Aha," and did a half-turn backward, toward the entrance to his house.

"And a very good day to you," Doctor Trautbert said. He pulled the two dogs attached to his right hand close to him, so that the leashes reached to his hat, and raised his hat.

"Hello," said the man. He cleared the sidewalk for the dogs, moved over to the street, and making an arc, walked past Doctor Trautbert, his behind pulled in a little.

That seemed to be the signal for the dogs. They straightened up. They began yelping.

The dog keeper, Doctor Trautbert, made an effort to pull the dogs forward. But they squatted on their hind legs, and a tug of war took place between the dog keeper and his dogs.

"Tobias, Gabriel!" cried Doctor Trautbert. "Let the man pass! The man's in a hurry! Be quiet, Susie! Can't you see what a nice man it is?"

The man, the nice man, began whistling to himself. Yes, he forced himself to a lazy, strolling pace. It was no use. The dog keeper, Doctor Trautbert, lost the tug of war. The dogs took the opposite direction, the one taken by the man. They yanked the dog keeper along after them.

"You curs!" cried Doctor Trautbert. "You'll never do it, never! It's only Susie," he called after the man who was running away. "Don't be afraid, for God's sake! Susie

has an enchanting character." Then his breath failed him,
and with his four dogs he chased panting after the man.

The latter threw a glance over his shoulder to measure
the distance between him and the dogs and the chance
he still had to escape their jaws. The distance between the
man being chased and the dogs chasing after him with
the dog keeper grew smaller.

"They'll have him in a minute," the customers whispered
in the shop. They stood behind the display window again.

The dog keeper, Doctor Trautbert, tried to free himself,
to let loose the dogs, since with his short legs—and for
that matter, with only two legs—he had great difficulty
keeping up with his four-legged companions. But because
the leashes had wrapped themselves around his wrists, he
could not untangle them while running.

"My dear sir," he panted, "wait, wait. We'll make it in
a minute. Down, Annie! Susie, down!" His voice cracked.

The dogs had caught up with the man. One of the four
bit him in the right calf. And as he bit into it, and as
the three other dogs looked sleepily around them as though
now quite unconcerned, as the man, standing motionless,
let himself be bitten, his arms hanging down, the dog
keeper, Doctor Trautbert, bowed behind his back. The
man walked on when the dog let go of his leg.

"Sir," called the concerned dog keeper, Doctor Trautbert, "my dear sir! That won't do at all! You can't walk
in that condition!"

The man stood still. Perhaps because he realized that a
dog keeper, through constant intercourse with dogs, is
more experienced in the field of bites than someone who
has been bitten for the first time.

"I'll be right there!" cried the dog keeper, Doctor Trautbert. The four dogs had settled down on the sidewalk,

two to his right, two to his left. Doctor Trautbert pulled them up with the leashes and dragged them along behind him toward the man. The latter turned around warily.

Doctor Trautbert grabbed him under the armpit. And putting a foot respectively in the gaps between the dogs, in the gaps between the leashes, they stumbled toward the entrance into the house opposite the shop.

The customers stood again in front of the shop counter, turned their backs to the display window, the street, the house entrance, held pocket mirrors in their hands.

"Didn't I tell you right away," babbled the dog keeper, Doctor Trautbert. The other was running through the pockets of his coat, trousers, jacket for the house key. "It was Susie. In time you naturally get to know your little beasts. You can guess what they're going to do. This gentleman, I thought to myself at once, is not going to get away without being bitten. That's how it is. Is it very painful? You simply must understand your animals. A great deal of love and care is part of it. You simply can't imagine what different characters these four dogs have! They don't bite just any passer-by, far from it! And Susie is particularly choosy. Don't think for a moment that she'd bite the first one to cross her path. Is it bleeding a lot?"

The man opened the street door.

"I'll come along," continued Doctor Trautbert. "I'll just bandage you up. You're in luck, I happen to be a doctor."

"The dogs stay outside," said the man.

Doctor Trautbert tied the four dogs to a cellar grill.

"Be good dogs," he said.

He went into the house after the man.

"We'll come again this afternoon," said my mother. "A little quicker, Lothar! Your father came back from teaching long ago, and the table isn't set."

And we walked homeward, my mother pulling me

along, my mother constantly murmuring to herself, "First put on the vegetables, then the meat, grease the pan, bake the potatoes, meanwhile set the table, take the food out of the oven, put it into the serving dishes, serve it. First eat, that'll be better, then talk about it."

"Good appetite!" my father called out to us. He had opened all the doors, was sitting at the table in his chair at the table, his back to the window, his face to the door. "What's wrong?" he said, pointing two outstretched forefingers at the empty table.

THE BUTTON

"The same thing every morning!" my father calls out every morning. And as he hurries through the hallway, he stuffs his shirt into his trousers and buttons his clothes beginning at the bottom, first pushing the buttons on one side of his fly into the buttonholes on the other side as far up as the waistband, then putting its button into its hole, then pushing the shirt buttons into the buttonholes of the shirt from the bottom to the collar. And whenever he buttons, when he gets to the top button, the collar button, and my mother is pouring the coffee through the strainer into his mug, that button refuses to go into its buttonhole, and he cries, "The least a man can ask of a button is that it fit into the buttonhole!" And my mother, holding the coffeepot in her hand, cries, "Better let me do it," and he cries, "So that you can pour the boiling coffee over my shirt," and my mother, putting the coffeepot on the table, cries, "Now my hands are free," but my father, yanking and pulling at this button, cries, "Keep your hands off," and right after that, "Now it's off!"

"I'll sew it on again," my mother murmurs, already in

the hall. She picks up the sewing basket from under the little table under the mirror, carries it by the handle into the dining room. "Just go on eating," she says. "Just leave your shirt on, I can sew it on this way, too."

Now I'll tell how they sit, my father and my mother, how I saw them sitting, at breakfast, until one morning my mother, when the thread tore and I was watching them in the dining room, my mother said, "Lothar, you drive me completely! Get out of here. Otherwise I won't be able to." Until my father cried, "If I catch one more glimpse of you in the morning, I'll!" I'll tell now because I know that they are sitting as I saw them sit, even now.

My father sits in his chair. With his right hand he carries the spoon full of sugar from the sugar bowl to his mug. He dumps the sugar into the coffee. He stirs it around with the spoon in the mug. Then he lifts the spoon out of the mug, licks it. Then he taps the egg with the spoon. He spoons out the egg. And between two spoonfuls of egg he bites into a roll. When he has spooned out the egg, when he has eaten half the roll, when he has buttered the other half of the roll, he pours the whole mug of coffee into himself, with his head bent all the way back. He puts the mug on the saucer, clears his throat, my father, holds the torn-off button high in his left hand, raises and lowers this left hand impatiently, as though the weight of the button were an unthinkable burden. Through all this he talks with his mouth full, he is preparing himself for his teaching.

Meanwhile my mother has moved her chair next to his chair, has moved the sewing basket next to her chair. My mother sits down. She rummages in the sewing basket, her back hunched over. Between many-colored spools of silk thread, darning thread, thin thread, she finds a spool of white sewing thread. And holding the spool of thread between her thumb and forefinger, she takes hold of the thread end of the spool with the thumb and forefinger of her left hand, spins off a length of thread, moving her right hand from her left hand, her left hand from her right hand, until with the spool she comes up against my father on the right, until on the left she can't go any farther along her arm with her hand with her fingers with the end of the thread. Then she lets the end of the thread fall from her left hand and with this empty left hand she tears the thread off the spool in her right hand.

"What's this," says my father. "Am I a federally employed button holder or am I a federally employed high-school teacher!" And meanwhile he raises and lowers his hand holding the button so violently that they are lucky, my father and my mother, when he does not drop the button. Because then they have to crawl around, first my mother, then my father, because she cannot find the button on the patterned rug. Because then the thread gets all tangled up, which my mother, crawling around, pulls along behind her. Because then my mother has to tear off a second thread in the described manner, a third, and so forth. But if fate wills it that my father does not drop the button, my mother says, "Right away, right away!"

She throws the spool back into the sewing basket. She puts the thread lengthwise on her lap so that both ends of the thread hang down on the carpet to the left and right of her lap. Then she rummages about in the sewing basket, her back hunched over, for the pincushion. With a sigh she picks the pincushion stuck with needles out of the sewing basket and puts it on her lap. Needles of all lengths and thicknesses are stuck in it, needles with eyes of every width and narrowness. Holding her ten fingers spread out over the pincushion, my mother looks for the needle that will go through the two holes of my father's shirt button. She pulls it out of the pincushion with her left hand. She holds it ready, tip between thumb and fore-finger, eye coming out beyond her fingers. She passes her right hand over the carpet, looking for the end of the thread. When she finds it she raises it with her thumb, with her forefinger, to her lips, moistens it with saliva, pulls it out of her mouth.

And while she brings the moist end of the thread closer to the eye of the needle, my father says, "I can also go without a button, without a shirt as well, what do you think, I can also go naked, stark naked, to school, or for that matter stay here altogether!"

And while my mother puts her head now so close to the needle that it seems to be, not the thread, but her head that has to go through the needle's eye, she makes the end of the thread go straight past the eye of the needle.

On the right, the thread in my mother's fingers begins to twitch. On the left, the needle in my mother's fingers begins to twitch. After this first attempt to thread the needle, my mother moistens the end of the thread all over again. She pushes her lower lip a little forward.

"I can wait," says my father, "for hours." Then he goes on preparing himself for his classes, goes on eating. My mother raises the end of the thread to the eye of the needle for the second time, moistens it, raises it for the third time, and so forth. With every attempt the needle, the eye, twitching up and down, and the end of the thread, twitching up and down, get farther and farther from each other. With every attempt my mother pushes her lower lip another little bit farther forward, my mother passes her nervous right hand with the thread over her damp face with its red and white blotches. With every attempt my father's head gets a little bit closer to her. He, my father, who interrupts his eating, who does not even swallow what he has in his mouth, he, my father, who does not only want to watch these misses very carefully, but also helps them along by crying, even before my mother has reached the eye of the needle with the end of the thread, "Missed!" By doing this he brings about gaps as big as your finger, as big as your fist, between the end of the thread and the eye of the needle.

"I'm going to visit our neighbor now," says my mother, says it as though she were starting on her last journey. She leaves the front door open, rings the bell next door. "Here I am again," she says, "I know it's the same thing every morning, it's an imposition, but I wouldn't be the least bit offended if you shut the door in my."

"But Mrs. Leinlein," our neighbor cries through the stairwell, "it's such a tiny thing, such a silly thing!"

"Can't even thread a thread!" the tenants above us call downstairs, "but she can demand of others to fly through the house!"

"There," the neighbor cries, "it's through."

"I really don't know how I," says my mother.

"Please," cries the neighbor, "I'll only be annoyed if you don't come back again!"

My mother carries the threaded needle through the hall, holding the eye between her fingers, pointing upward, the twisted thread hanging down, into the dining room. She sits down next to my father. He goes on eating, preparing for his classes, he interrupts himself only to cry that he still has, thank God, half a life left in which to hold this button and to wait for it to be put in the right place.

My mother doubles the thread. "Four thicknesses," she says, "would be better." She knots the ends of the thread. And while she sticks the needle through, pulls it out

again, attaches the knot of the thread on the spot where
the button is supposed to sit on firmly, even if it is only
for a single day, my father goes on eating. And just because he has to move his hand from the plate to his mouth
while eating, and just because she has to move her hand
with the needle into the shirt while sewing on the button,
away from the shirt with the thread, into the shirt with
the needle, my father and my mother get in each other's
way with their arms, with their hands, and with what they
are holding in them. My mother gets in my father's way as
he eats. My father gets in my mother's way as she sews.
So it just happens that my mother, needle in hand, has to
wait until my father's hand is at his plate. And it just
happens that my father, his hand to his mouth, has to
wait until my mother has pulled the thread out of the
shirt. Sometimes, not always but almost always, my father's
roll brushes against my mother's thread. Then the thread
gets greasy at best, but at worst it snaps.

And my mother then has to tear off first a new length
of thread, then try to thread the end of the thread through
the eye of the needle, go over to the neighbor, as though
this were her last, her very last journey, have the thread
threaded by the neighbor—a woman, thank God, who's
tranquil by nature—knot the ends of the thread, and
attach the thread.

It is only when my mother has attached the thread that
she finds out whether she has picked the right needle or
the wrong needle—that is, a needle that is too thick for
the two holes in my father's shirt button.

I look away, I turn aside, I can't watch to see what
happens then—that is, how it all starts in all over again.

When my father has handed my mother the button,
when fate has willed it that she does not drop it, because
then they have to crawl around, my parents, and so on,

when my mother has drawn the threaded needle twice, three times, sometimes more, through the two holes of the shirt button and through the shirt beneath, the neighbor first knocks, then rings right after knocking.

My mother leaves my father with the half-sewn-on button with the thread hanging down with the needle and runs to the door.

"I just wanted to ask," says our neighbor, rubbing her helpful hands, "whether I might not just sew the button on? Or am I in the way?"

"That's really, but thanks, it's already," says my mother, and she tries to shut the door. But the neighbor holds out her helpful hands against it.

"Come in," calls my father. "I beg of you. My wife never comes through in an emergency."

Then my mother lets in our neighbor. She goes on ahead through the halls. The great curves of her rump wobble fore and aft. Her legs are spread wide apart under her skirt. She walks along with a firm step, as though she owned the apartment, while my mother, her head bent, shuffles along, groping along the walls as though she were merely tolerated here, if that.

"Come right in!" my father calls. He is finished with his breakfast now.

"But Mrs. Leinlein," says our neighbor, standing next to my father. "You really can't let your husband go out this way! If he were just an ordinary teacher, all right! But as a high-school teacher one must be even more of a stickler than the principal! This button's been ruined, it won't do at all!" She takes the scissors out of her skirt pocket, takes hold of the button and snips it off. My mother, who has meanwhile been standing with her bent back pressed against the wall near the door, winces with a soft outcry, as though the neighbor were cutting not the thread between the button and the shirt, but into her own skin.

Then our neighbor tears off a length of thread, threads the needle, knots the ends, fastens it in the material, sticks the needle through one hole of the button and into the shirt beneath, sticks it into the shirt a little farther off and into the second hole of the button, pulls the thread through, and so on. She sews my father's button on, our neighbor, humming to herself, our neighbor, and my mother looks at her in amazement, and my father looks at her benevolently, he says, "Splendid, splendid," my father; when the neighbor has convinced herself, my father, my mother, and me too that the button is holding by pulling on the button, he repeats, "Splendid, splendid," my father, when our neighbor snaps off the thread and knots the ends of the thread behind.

She goes out of the dining room, the hall, into the stairwell. The great curves of her rump wobble fore and aft. Her legs are spread wide apart under her skirt, wider apart than when she came in.

And while my mother, her head lowered and her arms outstretched, shuffles behind her through the hall, murmuring, "I don't know how I," she shrugs it off, our neighbor, does not allow her helpful hands to be shaken, she says, "On account of such a tiny thing, such a silly thing," and vanishes behind her door.

My father pushes the button on his collar through the buttonhole. He kicks himself and his chair away from the table with his feet, yanks his jacket off the back of the chair, slips his arms into the sleeves, hurries through the hall, picks up his attaché case from the little table under the mirror.

"High time," he calls to my mother, who is holding open the door for him. "I have to go to class!"

My mother shuts the door.

I hear my mother go into the dining room, hear my mother move the plates on the table, hear my mother shift a chair, hear my mother mutter, "I really don't know why I don't. I feel as though I."

I open the window of my room, I see schoolboys walking on the sidewalk opposite, hurrying with lowered heads. The schoolboys carry schoolbags on their backs. My father crosses the street. He goes through the school gate made of iron bars.

The schoolbell rings.

"It's nothing," I hear my mother mutter in the dining room, "it's nothing at all."

The schoolboys run across the schoolyard toward the brick school building. They crowd through the entrance in a dense crush. My father strides behind them with long steps, his eyes trained on the backs of the students' necks. Behind the windows of their classroom the schoolboys' heads turn up again. Their faces are turned toward my father. My father stands behind his desk. The top of his body towers over the schoolboys' heads. He raises his arms to shoulder level, lets them sink, and together with them the children's heads sink down below the windowsills of the classroom. The students sit down.

Now I'll tell how the benches stand in the classroom, how I saw them stand, how the students sit, how I saw them sit, when I went into the classroom one morning with the attaché case my father had forgotten after the sewing on of the button, I'll tell because I know that the benches are standing as I saw them stand, because they must not be moved, I'll tell because I know that the students are sitting as I saw them sit, because they must not change places.

There are three rows of benches in the classroom. Each

row consists of six benches, one behind the other. Two
students sit on each bench. They sit on the right and the
left ends of the bench, so that between them a space as
wide as two students is left. In the last, the sixth, bench
in each row sits only one student. He sits in the middle
of the bench, so that he can be seen from the desk through
the space as wide as two students that is as long as the
row of benches. Behind the three last, the three sixth,
benches, the jackets, coats, and hats of the pupils hang
on the wall from hooks. Between the first row of benches,
on the left, and the second, in the center, as well as between the second, in the center, and the third, the right
row of benches, lanes are left open the width of two
students, so that not only between the two students
sitting on one bench, but also between the two students
sitting on the two benches of the two rows standing next
to each other, and between the students sitting, for instance, on the right bench ends of the first, the left row,
and the students sitting on the left bench ends of the
second, the middle row, as well as between the students
sitting on the right bench ends of the second, the middle
row, and the students sitting on the left bench ends of
the third, the right row, two spaces the width of a pupil
are left free. In addition, the students sitting behind one
another in a row on the right as well as on the left bench
ends are also separated from each other by the writing
desks that are as wide as two students. The students sitting on one bench are not allowed to move into the
spaces and toward each other. The students sitting in
two rows next to each other are not allowed to bend over
the bench ends into the lanes and toward each other. The
students sitting on the two benches standing behind each
other in a row are not allowed to lean forward or backward over the writing desks and toward someone sitting

before or behind them. They sit up straight, they stand straight, they all bend over their desks when writing, and when bent over, are no further away from each other than when they are sitting and standing. In addition, a lane two students wide is left free between the third, the right row, and the wall with the door to the right of that row, as well as between the first, the left row, and the wall with the three windows and the two narrow pieces of wall that are not even as wide as a thin student and therefore do not cover any standing student.

My father goes along this lane, bench by bench down to the last one, turning his back to the students, opening one window after another, calling out, "I've got ears everywhere!" He mounts the dais up to his desk, my father, he takes off his street glasses, puts on his reading glasses, my father, and holding the list of names in both hands, he calls the roll of the students.

And as my father calls out one name after another, one student after another jumps up, one student's head after another turns up above one of the three windowsills, to the left or the right above one of the six benches of the first, the left, and the second, the middle, and the third, the right row; one student after another calls after his name is called out, "Here!" one student's head after another sinks down below one of the three windowsills, one student after another sits down just as, with the next calling out of a name, the next student is already jumping up. And while my father calls out the students' names, in the classroom below his classroom the lesser teacher walks up and down teaching, the one about whom my father, the high-school teacher, says that he is a perfectly ordinary teacher. And because the three windows of the classroom are shut, what this teacher is teaching can't be understood.

And because his students do not tower above the window-sills even when standing, it can't be determined when one is getting up and when one is sitting down. Only now and then hands with outstretched forefingers shooting up above one of the three windowsills indicate that students are reporting. And while my father calls out the students' names, I hear my mother in the dining room moving dishes, I hear my mother mutter, "You can learn everything, everything. You have to practice, practice. You can practice everything, everything."

"Als, Allseits, Aufgelt," my father calls out, "Druck, Eibisch, Einfach, Feff," my father calls out, "Feff?"

"Feff is absent," all the students cry.

"Feff is absent without an excuse," my father cries. He looks at the list. "For three days Feff has been absent without an excuse," my father cries, he puts a cross against Feff's name on the list. "Does anyone know why Feff is absent?" asks my father. "Does anyone know what is the matter with Feff? Does anyone know, perhaps, that there is nothing the matter with Feff? That Feff may be playing hooky?"

No student's arm shoots up above the windowsills.

"Who knows where Feff lives?" my father calls out.

A number of students' hands with outstretched fore-fingers shoot up above the windowsills, one behind the other.

"Who will volunteer to go to see Feff," my father cries, "and ask him what the matter is and ask why he is absent without an excuse, and tell him, in case nothing is the matter, that he is playing hooky, Feff?"

The students' arms sink below the windowsills.

"Then I will decide who is to go to see Feff," my father cries. "Einfach raised his hand. So Einfach knows where

Feff lives. Einfach will go to see Feff together with Aufgelt!" my father cries. "Grein, Grind, Grübel, Hälfte, Hatschel," my father calls out. "Hatschel. Hatschel?"

"Hatschel is absent," all the students cry. "Hatschel has a cough."

"A cough," my father cries. "So, a cough. Hopfen, Impf, Jaul. Stand up straight, Jaul. Look this way. Kiefer," my father calls out. "Kleinlich, Kusch. Lott, what have you got there on your right hand?"

"I burned my right hand," says Lott.

"Then you will have to write with your left," my father cries. "Mündel, Murmel, Quängel. Who shuffled his feet there? Raff, Rohr," my father calls out. "Who shuffled his feet? I've got ears everywhere!"

No student's arm shoots up above the windowsills. No student answers.

"Answer, Rohr, if you please," my father cries, "when I call you, Rohr. Why did no one tell me that Rohr is absent?" my father cries. "Rohr is absent with an excuse. Scholsch, Schorlach, Schnorchel," my father calls out. "Teilweis, Weiter. Open your mouth, Weiter, when you answer."

"Here," Weiter repeats in a loud voice.

"Zahn," father calls out, "Zander, Zündel, Zweifach. Move to the ends of the benches! More toward the ends. In the middle," my father cries. "More toward the middle, whoever sits alone. Hälfte, Quängel, Zweifach are the ones I mean. Sit up straight! Grübel, Mündel, Zündel! Are you old men? Druck is hiding behind Allseits. I have eyes everywhere!"

My father puts down the list of names, he takes off his reading glasses, puts on his street glasses, he checks the seating order of his students by looking over the benches one by one, along the rows one by one, he begins his teaching by crying, "If you get dressed in the morning, if you button your clothes, if you've got to the last, the uppermost shirt button—that is, the collar button—if this button won't go into the buttonhole, if you pull it, then pull it off, this button, and if the button is torn off, Jaul, what do you do then, Jaul?"

"I will go and stand in front of my mother," says Jaul, "I will hold the button out to my mother. And then my mother will quickly sew it on."

"Jaul will not do that. Well now, Grein, what will Jaul do," my father cries, "when his collar button is torn off?"

"Jaul will take his shirt off again," says Grein. "He will hold the shirt and the button out to his mother. And Jaul will show the place where the button is missing. And Jaul will say to his mother, 'The button is torn off.' And Jaul will ask his mother, 'Would you please sew this button on for me quickly?' And then Jaul's mother will quickly sew on the button."

"Jaul will not take off his shirt. Jaul will not go to his mother. Jaul's mother will not sew on the button. Now then, Teilweis," my father cries, "what will Jaul do?"

"Jaul will keep his hand over his throat," says Teilweis, "so that no one can see the button is torn off."

"Jaul," my father cries, and Jaul jumps up and Jaul's head is visible like the heads of all the students who jump up when their names are called.

"I am not calling your name," my father cries. "I am mentioning your name as an example. Sit down and think over the difference between calling your name and mentioning your name as an example."

Jaul's head sinks below the windowsill like the heads of all the students who have sat down again after their names have been called, after they have answered.

"Jaul," my father cries, "will not keep his hand over

his throat. Jaul will leave his house. Everyone will point to Jaul, everyone will cry, 'Look at Jaul! Running around dilapidated and degenerate! He ought to be ashamed of himself, that Jaul!' So then, Als, what will Jaul have to do, whether he likes it or not?"

"Jaul could, if he could," says Als, "sew on the button himself."

"Jaul will sew on the button himself," my father cries. "That is what Jaul will do. What does Eibisch have to say to that? Eibisch!"

Eibisch's head shoots up. Eibisch says nothing.

"What did Eibisch have to say to that, Einfach?" my father cries.

Einfach's head shoots up next to Eibisch's head. Einfach looks at Eibisch.

"What?" my father cries.

"Eibisch says," says Einfach, "that he does not know how to sew on buttons."

"That is just what Eibisch is going to learn," my father cries. "One moment," my father cries. "Murmel, what did Mündel have to say to that?"

"Mündel says," says Murmel, "that his mother sews on the torn-off buttons."

"That is just what Mündel is going to learn; how to sew on buttons," my father cries. "Eibisch, Mündel! Stand up and hold up your brief cases."

Eibisch stands at the third bench of the first row to the right. Mündel stands at the fifth bench of the second row to the left. Over Eibisch's head Eibisch's upstretched hands hold up Eibisch's brief case. Over Mündel's head Mündel's upstretched arms hold up Mündel's brief case.

"It takes a long time," I hear my mother muttering in the dining room. "It's true it takes a long time, but not so long at all, not so long a time as I always thought."

"Is there someone else among you perhaps," my father cries, "who has something to say about this, something to ask? Don't be so reluctant to speak. Up with your hands. I'm all eyes! I'm all ears!"

No students' arms shoot up, except for Eibisch's and Mündel's four upstretched arms. No student wants to answer. Through the classroom below my father's classroom the lesser teacher runs, teaching. Above the windowsills under the windowsills of my father's classroom students' hands pop up, students' hands vanish.

"Then how will Jaul sew on the button? Jaul!" my father calls out. "You have been called on, Jaul! Stand up!"

"I would use a needle," says Jaul.

"Do not call yourself 'I'!" my father cries. "Call yourself 'Jaul' when you mention yourself as an example."

"Jaul," says Jaul, "will sew on the button with a needle."

"If Jaul does that he will have to go on sewing until he is an old graybeard," my father cries. "And when he stands up, finally, to leave his house once again, before he dies, that old graybeard Jaul, the button will fall off like a chopped-off head! How is Jaul going to sew on the button? Hopfen!"

"In Jaul's place I would," says Hopfen.

"I did not mention you, Hopfen, as an example. Jaul is the example for all of us," my father cries. "Stand up, Jaul! Look at Jaul, everyone! Who is an example for all of us? All together!"

"Jaul," all the students cry.

Jaul stands at the second bench of the second row to the right. Jaul raises an arm.

"What do you want to ask, Jaul?" my father cries.

"Please, I would like to ask if I should hold up my case," says Jaul.

"You are to stand there," my father cries. "You are to

let yourself be looked at! That is all that you are to do."

Jaul stands there, pale and speechless, sways a little.

"Now then, Hopfen," my father cries.

"Jaul will take a threaded needle," says Hopfen. "And then Jaul will sew the button on quickly."

"Not so fast," my father cries. "Hopfen thinks that near Jaul there is, of course a needle, lying on the shirt with the torn-off button. And not only a needle, no, it is threaded as well, of course, right next to Jaul, of course. Hopfen makes the sewing even easier for Jaul than sewing is. Jaul does not have to look for a needle. Jaul does not have to find a thread. Jaul does not have to thread any thread through the eye of the needle. Because everyone in Jaul's house knows when, on what shirt, and where Jaul is going to tear off a button, because everyone in Jaul's house will quickly thread a thread through the eye of the needle, because everyone in Jaul's house will, of course, quickly put the threaded needle right next to Jaul, so that the sewing will be made even easier for Jaul than sewing is. Who is going to know that Jaul has torn off a button? Jaul!"

"My mother, Jaul's mother," says Jaul.

"Jaul will be alone in his room," my father cries. "No one will see that the button is torn off. Jaul will not tell anyone that the button is torn off. And Jaul will tell his mother last of all, because otherwise Jaul's mother will say, 'I'll sew it on again.' And Jaul will sew the button on himself. Jaul will look for a thread, a needle. And Jaul will find a thread, a needle. And Jaul will thread the thread through the eye of the needle. Where will Jaul look for the thread and the needle? Scholsch!"

"Jaul will look for the thread and the needle in the sewing basket of Jaul's mother," says Scholsch.

"Not so fast," my father cries. "Before Jaul looks for

the thread and the needle, he will have to look as best he can for the sewing basket and find it. Now where— we're not through yet, Scholsch, stand up—where will Jaul look for the sewing basket?"

"Please, sir," says Scholsch. "I've never been at Jaul's house. I don't even know where Jaul lives. But if Jaul will tell me where he lives, I'll go to Jaul's. I'll look in Jaul's house, I'll surely find the sewing basket. If you please, sir, I'll start off looking for the house and the sewing basket right away."

"That is exactly what you will not do," my father cries. "You will not sneak off that way," my father cries. "Right away he wants to talk himself out of things! Right away he wants to rush off looking for houses, looking for sewing baskets! He would rather rummage through strange houses than learn something easy here, something very easy! Stand up, that is what he will do, and hold his brief case in the air," my father cries. "That is what he will do right away!"

Scholsch stands at the second bench of the third row to the left. Scholsch's upstretched arms hold Scholsch's brief case over Scholsch's head, just as Eibisch's, just as Mündel's upstretched arms hold Eibisch's, Mündel's brief cases over Eibisch's, over Mündel's head.

"Where will Jaul look for Jaul's mother's sewing basket, Zweifach?" my father cries.

"Jaul will go into the room in which his mother's sewing basket is always kept," says Zweifach.

"And how do you know, Zweifach," my father cries, "that Jaul will know in which room the sewing basket is always kept? And how do you know, furthermore, Zweifach, that the sewing basket is always kept in the same room, and that it is not kept sometimes in one room and sometimes in another, and sometimes here and sometimes there, and wherever and whenever it just happens to occur to Jaul's mother to put it?"

"Unfortunately Jaul will not know that," says Zweifach, "because he himself has never sewed anything for himself. And if Jaul has ever happened to see the sewing basket somewhere, by accident, when Jaul was looking for something else, and if he happens to remember, Jaul, where it was that he once saw it, it is certainly not going to be there still. Because Jaul's mother puts it sometimes in one room and sometimes in another, and wherever and whenever it just happens to occur to her to put it. And maybe she even hides it from Jaul. And unfortunately Jaul will not be able to ask his mother where it is or where she has hidden it. Because then Jaul's mother will ask, 'What do you want with the sewing basket?' And that must not happen. Because then Jaul's mother will ask, 'Is something torn off?' And then Jaul will have to say, 'A button is torn off.' And that must not happen. Because then Jaul's mother will say, 'I'll sew it on again.' And that must not happen. Because Jaul will have to sew the button on himself. And Jaul will have to search the house. And the bigger Jaul's house is, the longer he will have to search. In every room, in every closet of every room, in every chest of drawers of every room, in every little table of every room, in every box and chest of every room, behind all, under all, on top of all the furniture in every room, everywhere."

In the third row to the right next to Scholsch's two upstretched arms that are holding Scholsch's brief case over Scholsch's head, an arm shoots up.

"What have you got to say to that? Schorlach!" my father calls out. Schorlach's arm vanishes, Schorlach's head shoots up.

"Nothing, sir, please," says Schorlach.

"Sit down, Schorlach," my father cries, "if you have nothing to say. Who knocked? Why do you raise your hand, Scholrach, if you have nothing to say? I have ears everywhere! Who knocked there?"

"Outside, sir, please," says Schorlach.

"Why didn't you say so at once! Why don't you stand up right away! Why don't you go to the door!" my father cries.

"Feff's mother, sir, please," says Schorlach, "is asking whether she might please speak to you for a second."

"Murmel will report to me who has been talking!" my father calls out. He leaves the classroom, shuts the door.

I hear my mother move dishes in the dining room, hear dishes falling to the floor, breaking, hear my mother mutter, "How easy it is, how it practically finishes itself, how simple it is, how it keeps getting easier."

It seems that my father's pupils speak softly when they speak. I don't hear any noise coming from his classroom. Beneath my father's classroom the lesser teacher walks along the lane between the windows and the first row. He goes past all the benches one by one until the last one, turning his back to the students and opening all the windows one by one and crying, "The conjugation of 'to be.'" He goes back past all the benches one by one, turning to the students and calling out, "All together, conjugate 'to be'!"

"I am, thou art, he is, we are, you are, they are," all his students cry.

My father comes into the classroom. He goes up to his desk. "Murmel, report who said anything," my father cries.

"Aufgelt, Eibisch, Einfach, sir," says Murmel, "Grind, Jaul, Lott, Scholsch, Mündel, and myself, Murmel."

"What did they say, Murmel?" my father calls out.

"They spoke so softly, sir," says Murmel, "that I couldn't understand a word. I myself said they should not say anything so that I wouldn't have to report them."

"What did you, Aufgelt, say?" my father cries.

"I said to Einfach," says Aufgelt, "that we need not, if Feff's mother brings an excuse for Feff, go to Feff's."

"What did you, Einfach, say?" my father cries.

"I said to Aufgelt," says Einfach, "that we must go to Feff's anyways, although you, sir, know what is the matter with Feff, in case you forget, sir, to tell us that we need not go to Feff's. Because Aufgelt no more than I has the confidence to ask whether we still need to go to Feff's or whether we need not go to Feff's anymore."

"What did you, Eibisch, say?" my father cries.

"I asked Murmel," says Eibisch, "whether he would report me if I lowered my arms as long as you, sir, did not see it."

"And what did Murmel say to that? Eibisch!" my father calls out.

"Murmel said," says Eibisch, "that he was saying nothing so that he would not have to report himself."

"So then, you did not only say, I mean you, Murmel, that they should not say anything so that you would not have to report them; you, Murmel, also said that you were saying nothing so that you would not have to report yourself. Why, Murmel, didn't you tell me that? Enough! I know all! What did you, Grind, say?" my father cries.

"I said to Jaul," says Grind, "that he should have enough confidence to speak up."

"And what should Jaul have enough confidence to speak up about? Grind!" my father calls out.

"Jaul would like to ask, please, that he stop being an example for all of us," says Grind.

"Jaul is going to remain an example for all of us" my father cries. "Being an example is even easier than sewing."

Jaul stands, pale and speechless, stands swaying a little.

"What did you, Lott, say?" my father calls out.

"When Eibisch, Mündel, and Scholsch asked Murmel,"

says Lott, "whether he would report them if they lowered their arms as long as you, sir, did not see it, and when Murmel said that he was saying nothing so that he would not have to report himself, I said to them that they had better go on holding up their arms even as long as you, sir, did not see it, because they didn't know after all whether Murmel would report them or whether Murmel would not report them if they lowered their arms."

"So!" my father cries. "Eibisch, Mündel, Scholsch will go on holding up their brief cases. In addition, the following will stand and hold up their brief cases: Aufgelt, Einfach, Grind, Lott, Murmel, and also Jaul, Jaul the example for us all!"

Aufgelt raises his arms in front of Eibisch at the second bench of the first row to the left. Einfach raises his arms next to Eibisch at the third bench of the first row to the right. Grind raises his arms behind Eibisch at the fifth bench of the first row to the left. Jaul raises his arms at the second bench of the second row to the right next to Scholsch, who raises his arms at the second bench of the third row to the left. Lott raises his arms behind Jaul at the fourth bench of the second row on the right, holds his brief case up with one good left hand and with a right hand bandaged in white. Murmel raises his arms behind Lott and next to Mündel at the fifth bench of the second row on the right.

"Conjugate 'to have,' " cries the lesser teacher. "All together: 'to have'!"

"I have, thou hast, he has, we have, you have, they have," all his students cry.

"It's not worth talking about," I hear my mother mutter in the dining room. "It's a triviality, it's not even a triviality, it's nothing." I hear dishes falling on the floor in the dining room, breaking, hear my mother giggling.

A student's arm shoots up above the windowsills in my father's classroom. A student wants to ask something.

"What have you got to say, Zweifach?" my father cries.

"Unfortunately, sir," says Zweifach, "the search for the sewing basket, the needle, and the thread, the threading, the sewing, no matter how hard it will be for Jaul, because Jaul himself never sewed anything on for himself, is going to be the easiest of all. Jaul's mother is going to be the worst. She will see Jaul walking about, searching from room to room. She will see Jaul rummaging about in all the furniture. She will see Jaul pulling chairs over to tall pieces of furniture. She will see Jaul getting up on those chairs. She will see Jaul standing on pieces of furniture. She will see Jaul bending over. She will look at Jaul looking under all the pieces of furniture. She will say, 'Why don't you say something?' She will say, 'Look at me,' say, 'Why do you turn your back to me? Come over here,' say, 'Why are you running away? Why, Jaul, are you hiding? Tell me at once what you've been up to! It must be bad, what you've been up to!' "

"Because he must not tell her," all the students cry, "what he's looking for, or else she will know that he wants to sew something! And then she will do the sewing! Because she must not see his shirt, and so himself, since he has it on, from the front, or else she will know that he wants to sew on a button! And then she will sew on the button!"

"Then, Zweifach, just go on," my father cries. "What will Jaul have to do?"

"He will have to bend over, turn around, hide himself, Jaul," says Zweifach. "He could, if he could, talk himself out of it, Jaul; he could, if he could, start whistling so that she'd think he was just walking around for fun; he could, if he could, spill something, break something, Jaul could. And if Jaul's mother thrashes him, he'll have to let himself be thrashed. And if Jaul's mother hits him, perhaps she won't hit him so hard, maybe only with her hand, and not with a cane. And if Jaul's mother wipes up what's been spilled, sweeps together what's been broken, Jaul might be able, after he's found the sewing basket, be able to look for, maybe to find, a needle, a thread. Jaul will, please sir, not have to look for and find a pair of scissors. Jaul will, please sir, be allowed to tear off or bite off the thread. Jaul will put the thread and the needle in his trouser pocket, Jaul will lock himself in his room. And while Jaul's mother knocks on the door with her knuckles, hits it with her fist, with both fists, and while Jaul's mother kicks at the door, hits the door with the broom, calls, 'Open up,' shouts, 'What are you doing, Jaul?' threatens him: 'If you don't open up, Jaul, I'll break the door down!'—just during this time, which will be very short, before Jaul's mother breaks down the door, Jaul will quickly sew on the button."

"Not so fast," my father cries. "What will Jaul do first? Impf!"

"Jaul will tear a thread off the spool," says Impf. "Better if it's a long thread, sir, so that Jaul won't have to thread it through twice. Because Jaul has no practice, no time. Because Jaul's mother is threatening and shouting outside the door. And then Jaul will thread the thread through the needle's eye."

"How, Zander, will Jaul thread the thread?" my father cries.

"Jaul," says Zander, "will hold the tip of the needle between the thumb and the forefinger of one hand, Jaul will hold one end of the thread between the thumb and the forefinger of the other hand, Jaul will moisten the end of the thread with saliva, Jaul will move the moist end of the thread next to the eye of the needle."

"Jaul's hands," all the students call out, "won't tremble,

please sir, even if Jaul's mother threatens and shouts and tries to break down the door at once. Jaul won't move the end of the thread, please sir, past the eye of the needle."

"All right, Jaul's hands," my father cries, "will not tremble."

"Thank you, sir," all the pupils cry.

"No twitching," I hear my mother mutter in the dining room, "no trembling," I hear my mother sing in the dining room. "A calm hand, quick and nippy, quicker and quicker every time, all by itself, swift as the wind, a hand, this hand, my hand."

"What kind of thread will it be, Kleinlich," my father cries, "that Jaul, with no practice in sewing and nevertheless very skillful—that Jaul, with no time and therefore of course at the very first attempt, will thread with a calm hand while his mother threatens him and pounds away with the broom?"

"Kiefer thinks a thick one is better," says Kleinlich.

"Before Kiefer thinks anything," my father cries, "he has to report. Stand up and hold up your brief case, Kiefer."

At the third bench of the second row on the left Kiefer stands up. Kiefer's upstretched arms hold up Kiefer's brief case over Kiefer's head.

"A thick one would be better, so that it won't break right away," says Kleinlich.

"Very well, a thick one," my father cries, "just as you please. But if Jaul, in such a hurry, picks a thin needle, will Jaul be able to thread that thick thread through the narrow eye of the needle? Jaul!"

Jaul stands there holding up his brief case, pale and speechless, stands swaying a little.

"No," all the students cry. "No!"

"Then Jaul will have to do the best he can and look for a new needle," my father cries.

"No, please sir, no!" all the students cry. "Because that must not happen! Because Jaul can't leave his room before he has put it, the button, in the right place, before he has attached it, the button, before Jaul has pushed the button through the buttonhole of his shirt, before he, Jaul, can say to his mother, 'it was all because of the button I wanted to sew on myself this time. Look, there it is, the shirt is buttoned.' Jaul will pick a thick needle, if you please sir, in spite of all the hurry. Jaul will be very sure to pick a thin thread, if you please, sir, and in spite of all the hurry, one that please won't snap and that can be threaded through the big wide eye of the thick needle!"

"Very well, a thick needle," my father cries, "a thin thread, just as you like! Let him thread it, Jaul!"

"Isn't that right, sir?" all the students call out.

"Jaul is to do as he pleases," my father cries. "It is he who is going to have to sew on a button, not I. What, Grübel, will Jaul do then?"

"Jaul will make the thread double," says Grübel. "Jaul will knot both ends of the thread. Jaul will stick the needle into the shirt, pull the needle out of the shirt, fasten the thread on the spot the button is supposed to be fixed on. And then Jaul will quickly sew the button on."

"Not so fast," my father cries. "Before Jaul sews on the button, he will have to know whether he likes it or not where it is, the button. Where is the button, Jaul?"

Jaul stands there holding up his brief case, pale and speechless, stands swaying a little, without a word.

"Unfortunately Jaul has mislaid his button!" all the students call out. "Unfortunately Jaul has lost his button in the search for the sewing basket, the thread, and the needle. Unfortunately Jaul will have to go searching through the big house for the small button. Unfortunately —if Jaul could only leave his room, because he won't be able to leave his room before he's sewed on the button he's lost, and he won't unfortunately be able to sew it on because he's lost it!"

"Jaul," my father cries. "What is all the lamentation. for? As far as I'm concerned he's put the button down right near him!"

"Thank you very much, sir," all the students cry.

"Not so fast," my father cries. "Unfortunately I'm afraid that will be of no use to Jaul either. So then, Zündel, what will Jaul do then?"

"Jaul will stick the threaded needle through one hole of the button," says Zündel.

"Just as I thought," my father cries. "Just what that slyboots Zündel would say! Jaul is going to stick that thick needle, says the slyboots Zündel, through the small hole of the small shirt button. Do you think, Quängel, he, Jaul, is going to make it?"

"If Jaul could, but Jaul won't be able to, Jaul will have to look for a new needle after all," says Quängel.

"Jaul better not have to look for any new needle," all the students cry. "Please not, sir."

"I'll wait," my father cries. "I'll give you time. Think it over," my father cries. "Think about what Jaul is going to do now."

My father comes down from the dais, he walks along each lane one by one, each bench one by one, back and forth and past the sitting students and past the students standing with their arms up and swaying a little, he, my father, looks at his wrist watch, on his wrist raised to eye level.

"Past tenses," the lesser teacher cries. "All together, all the past tenses of 'to be.'"

"Was, has been, had been," all his students call out.

In the dining room, against the humming, the singing, the giggling of my mother, I hear dishes falling to the floor, breaking.

"Now then," my father cries, "What is Jaul going to do now? Hälfte!"

"Please sir," says Hälfte, "may I request that Jaul, who has found the needle and the thread after a laborious search, who has hidden from his mother, who has shut himself up in his room, who cannot leave his room before sewing on the button that he does not know how to sew on, may I request, sir, that Jaul, who sits, threatened by his mother, behind a door that cannot hold out much longer against his mother's broom thrusts, that Jaul, who laboriously and without any practice in sewing and with no time for sewing has now finally threaded the thick needle, and now has finally knotted the ends of the thread, and now has finally fastened the thread to the shirt, may I please, sir, request, sir, that Jaul be permitted to find in his room a big button with holes so big that he, Jaul, can effortlessly stick the big needle through?"

"Very well," my father cries, "just as you please! Then Jaul will find a big button in his room."

"Thank you, sir," all the students cry.

"Now then, Weiter," my father cries. "What will Jaul do now?"

"Jaul," says Weiter, "will stick the needle into one hole of the button and into the shirt beneath it, Jaul will stick it through a little bit away from the hole in the shirt and through the second hole of the button, Jaul will pull out the thread."

"And so on," my father cries, "and so on."

"Jaul will sew the button on himself," all the students cry.

"Schorchel," my father cries, "what will Jaul do then?"

"Jaul," says Schorchel, "will tug at the button, Jaul will try the button to see whether it's tight, Jaul, if the button is tight, will tear the thread off and knot both ends of the thread underneath."

" 'It was all because of the button,' Jaul will cry," all
the students cry, " 'which I had to sew on myself this
time!' Jaul will step out of the room and cry, 'Look, it's
in the right place! Look, the shirt is buttoned!' "

"Not so fast," my father cries, "Stop! How will Jaul push
the big button through the small buttonhole of his shirt?"
my father cries. "Who has been gasping? Do you think,"
my father cries, "that Jaul is going to make it? Who has
been whining? I have ears everywhere! Jaul, whether he
likes it or not," my father cries, "who is making faces
there, I have eyes everywhere, will have to tear the button
off again! What," my father cries, "will Jaul do now?
Why," my father cries, "are you weeping, Allseits?"

"Because I know," says Allseits, "that I'm not going to
know what you, sir, are going to ask me."

"Listen to the question! Prick up your ears!" my father
cries. "What, Allseits," my father cries, "listen carefully,
what is your name, Allseits?"

"Jaul," says Allseits.

"Stand up and raise your brief case," my father cries,
"until you know what your name is! What's your name,"
my father cries, "listen carefully, Grein?"

"Jaul," says Grein.

"Stand up and raise your brief case, Grein," my father
cries. "Who has been whining?" my father cries. "What
is your name, Kusch?"

"Jaul," says Kusch.

"Stand up and raise your brief case," my father cries.
"Perhaps you are called Jaul too, Raff?"

"Jaul, yes indeed," says Raff, "sir."

"Stand up everyone, raising your brief cases. Everyone!"
my father cries.

All the students stand and raise their brief cases.

"What are you doing?" my father cries. "Everyone!"

"Sewing," all the students cry.

"Where are you?" my father cries. "Look around you! Eyes open!"

"In Jaul's room," all the students cry.

"And what is your name?" my father cries.

"Jaul," all the students cry.

All the students stand holding up their brief cases, stand swaying, stand speechless.

Dishes fall on the floor in the dining room, break. My mother sings and hums and giggles through it all.

I go to look at my mother.

She sits at the dining table, my mother, at the empty dining table, my mother, the sewing basket between her legs wide apart on the floor, between the pieces of the dishes fallen on the floor, she sits and sings and hums, my mother, giggling all the while; with her right hand, her calm right hand with the needle she pulls the attached thread out of the tablecloth, she holds a button in her left hand, her calm left hand, and sticking the needle into one hole of the button and the tablecloth beneath it, and sticking the needle a little bit further away into the tablecloth and through the second hole of the button, she sews, only a button away from the last sewed-on button of the last row, the width of the tablecloth, of this row of buttons, the length of the tablecloth, only a button apart from each other, that button onto the tablecloth.

THE PROCESSION

Everybody in our quarter knows Mr. Kecker. Everyone knows which is his stump, which is his good leg. And that's something. Everyone knows which direction he usually takes, on two crutches and one leg, his stump dangling, while he pants and sweats with the exertion. Everyone knows after two or three words who it is that is making a speech, surrounded and therefore hidden by passers-by, knows without having to listen to it any further, without having to wait for Mr. Kecker to begin brandishing his crutch, for Mr. Kecker's crutch to tower over the heads of the passers-by and swing up and down. And that's something. No one confuses Mr. Kecker with any other invalid, even if he has his stump on the right like Mr. Kecker and his good leg on the left, even if his stump is not only on the right but is also the same length —that is, halfway up his thigh—like Mr. Kecker's stump.

But it hardly ever happens, except for visits, that an invalid like that would turn up in our quarter. Shortly after Mr. Kecker's emergence into the streets of our quarter, the other invalids withdrew to more remote quarters of the city, to suburbs, even to different cities.

They gave up good jobs, steam-heated apartments, they left large families in the lurch. Only a few blind people, deformed people, simpletons remained, whom no one bothered about, not even Mr. Kecker. There remained a one-armed man who tried to hobnob with Mr. Kecker, waved to him with his good arm, ran along behind him wherever he met him, crying, "My best respects, my dear Mr. Kecker," and offered him his services. But Mr. Kecker was repelled by him and rejected him, he called him pushy. And no one in our quarter can say with certainty where this one-armed man has his stump and where his good arm.

Many claim that the whole city knows Mr. Kecker. And that would be something. They say that even those who have not seen him yet in drugstores, in shops, in movie houses where war movies are shown are familiar with his reputation and with the rumors about him. They say that those who see him for the first time say to themselves or to the people they're with, "That must be Mr. Kecker!"

How Mr. Kecker managed it so that even the people in different cities talk about him, so that wives are supposed to tell their husbands, fathers their sons, teachers their pupils, "Don't act so Keckerlike"—that is what is to be discussed here.

His arrival is recognizable not only by his gait, his crutches, his panting, and when he is resting by his speeches, it is also recognizable by the behavior of the passers-by. They suddenly break off conversations in the middle, they separate with hasty words of farewell, they suddenly come to a standstill halfway toward Mr. Kecker, and if they do not go into shops, into doorways, and if they do not cross the street, they turn around and retrace their steps in a great hurry, they postpone what they were going to do or change their minds altogether.

Others, either because they are daring or because they

are bewildered and incapable of a decision, go on walking toward Mr. Kecker, who step by step comes closer to them.

And while behind Mr. Kecker, farther than just out of earshot, the talking starts up again, and while in front of Mr. Kecker, farther than just out of earshot, the talking breaks off, wherever Mr. Kecker is, in between, there is silence, and this silence is only interrupted by the tapping of Mr. Kecker's crutches on the pavement, by the scraping of Mr. Kecker's shoe on the pavement, by Mr. Kecker's panting. And whether it is a daring person or a bewildered person who goes toward Mr. Kecker, a few crutch steps in front of Mr. Kecker his walk will become a shuffle, his knees will give way, and he will not walk on the soles of his feet but will steal past Mr. Kecker on tiptoe in a wider or narrower arc.

Many a daredevil has tried to calculate how an encounter with Mr. Kecker might turn out, has made bets before walking toward him. It can turn out well, it can turn out badly. That depends on Mr. Kecker's mood, which does not depend only on the weather, but which can also change from one step to the next.

Only one thing is certain: to turn away a few crutch steps in front of Mr. Kecker—that no one can do. Because then Mr. Kecker shouts, "So you think the sight of me is as contagious as leprosy! Come over here!"

Otherwise nothing is certain. If someone, because he says to himself or someone else says to him that it would be safer to make a wide arc around Mr. Kecker when meeting him, goes even across the street so that Mr. Kecker has the whole sidewalk for himself, then it can happen—it need not, but it can happen—that Mr. Kecker will stand still, supported only by his left leg and his right crutch, and pointing his left crutch at him will shout, "He's avoiding me! That means he's thinking something bad about me! Or else he could pass me just like everyone else!"

But if this same person, assuming he dares to, passes close by Mr. Kecker at a second meeting, then it can happen—it need not, but it can happen—that Mr. Kecker will put his crutch in front of or between his legs. Then either both fall to the ground or one of the two—and it's better for the two-legged person if he falls—or both clutch each other and so keep their balance, and then Mr. Kecker shouts, "He touched my body! He jostled me! He knocked away my crutch!"

Furthermore, no one knows whether on meeting with Mr. Kecker he should look at him or look away from him.

If someone looks at him, then it can happen—it need not, but it can happen—that Mr. Kecker will shout, "He's staring at me as though a stump were the eighth wonder of the world!"

If someone looks away from him, then it can happen— it need not, but it can happen—that Mr. Kecker will shout, "He's looking away from me as though a stump were as disgusting as a worm!"

Furthermore, no one—whether it's someone who knows him personally or only by sight or whether it's someone who knows only his reputation, the rumors about him— knows whether he should speak to Mr. Kecker or not.

Those who know him and speak to him in a proper way get off lightly if Mr. Kecker, looking straight ahead, pouring sweat and panting, putting down his crutches first, then his foot, moves past them without a word. But it can also happen—it need not, but it can happen—that Mr. Kecker will stop and shout, "Can't you see that just walking makes me lose my breath and sweat? How dare you challenge me to a greeting!"

Those who know only his reputation and the rumors

about him are even more uncertain of how they should behave.

"Perhaps," say some, "it would be better if we spoke to him after all, because he might confuse us with an acquaintance and shout, 'But we know each other! Why don't you say hello? You probably don't want to recognize me any more!'"

"On the other hand," say others, "it would be better if we didn't speak to him, because he might not confuse us with anyone and would shout, 'We don't know each other! You're only saying hello to make a fool out of me! Why don't you admit it!'"

After he has passed by, after he has removed himself, step by step, first putting down his crutches, then his foot, after he is farther off than just out of earshot, the most daring ones say to their best friends, "His main profession is being an invalid, after all."

In addition, Mr. Kecker is employed in a business near our house.

In the beginning, while he was on probation, he behaved in a reserved way, almost shyly, he sat quietly on his chair, the stump on the seat, his good leg stretched out, he did his work and came and went with the other employees, let himself be passed coming to and going from work, and called out, as though he were joking, after someone who passed him, "If you've got it, you've got it!"

During the lunch hour, when the other employees went out, if they offered to help him down the steps, he would shake his head, he kept sitting on his chair, had the window opened, said that was air enough for an old warrior who had let the wind blow around his ears all his life, declined if anyone offered to fetch him some lemonade or a beer, and pointing to his plate, on which the casserole his wife had fixed him the night before was long since lukewarm, he said that was good enough for an old warrior.

He groaned aloud only now and then, holding his stump with both hands or the kneecap of his good leg. But when the other employees rushed over and asked whether they should fetch a doctor or an ambulance, then he would refuse, his face twisted by pain, he forced himself to put on a doleful smile, said, interrupted by groaning and gasping, that they should not worry, that as long as it was no more than that, it could be endured.

"What self-control," the other employees said to each other then.

After Mr. Kecker was taken on for good, he asked for a second chair; he sat there, Mr. Kecker, panting softly, the stump on the seat he was sitting on, the good leg stretched out, the calf and the foot placed on the seat of the second chair, with the knee over the gap between the two chair seats. He groaned aloud more often than just now and then, he held his stump with both hands, or the kneecap of his good leg. And if anyone asked him whether he had a pain in his good leg too, he would shake his head, his face twisted with pain, omitted his doleful smile and said, "Let's forget it! That doesn't ease my pains any."

"What self-control," the other employees said to each other then.

As long as there was another employee in his workroom, Mr. Kecker groaned relatively softly. But if he was alone in the room with the door shut, he would give free rein to his pains, he would groan so loudly that the other employees could hear it even at the farthest end of the hall.

That was at the time when Mr. Kecker would take a

day off now and then, and, supported on two crutches and a leg, still independent, would go off homeward. And the hours in which he sat there groaning, holding his stump or the kneecap of his good leg, corresponded to the hours in which he actually did something.

"It's senseless to have such self-control," the other employees said to each other then. "We ought to get him an easy chair."

"Don't make any fuss over a cripple like me," said Mr. Kecker.

"But please, dear Mr. Kecker," said the other employees. "It's not the least bit noticeable."

They helped him get out of the hard wooden chair and sit down in the softly upholstered easy chair. Even the manager came to see him in his workroom. "Is it better that way?" he asked.

Mr. Kecker nodded, his face twisted with pain. He omitted his doleful smile.

A week later one of the employees, a Miss Annie, made him a gift of a hand-embroidered sofa pillow. Thereafter he would sit this way, Mr. Kecker: his behind and the stump on the softly upholstered easy chair, the good leg stretched out, the calf and the foot on the sofa cushion on the hard chair. And he would spend more time groaning, holding his stump, holding his kneecap, than he would working.

"A little exercise in the fresh air, dear Mr. Kecker," the other employees would say then, "would do you much more good than sitting around in your room." They sacrificed half their lunch hour to helping Mr. Kecker first downstairs, then upstairs. They rushed through their meal, talked mainly about how Mr. Kecker felt, consulted each other how they could make his life easier.

"We ought to get a stretcher," suggested one of the employees.

When the stretcher had been obtained, paid for out of the purses of the other employees, none of whom refused to give his share, the employees divided themselves into couples. They would relieve each other, couple by couple, from lunch hour to lunch hour. One in back, one in front, they would carry Mr. Kecker on the stretcher downstairs, up and down outside, and upstairs again.

At first he lay there on the stretcher, Mr. Kecker, limp and panting. And behind the curtain of the executives' window the manager shook his head in concern. A few days later Mr. Kecker straightened up on the stretcher. With an outstretched forefinger on his outstretched arm he pointed out to his bearers where he wanted to be taken during the lunch hour. He had them bring him beer and frankfurters, although the restaurant was half a lunch hour away. When he did not happen to be pointing, he would eat, or he would eat and point at the same time and give incomprehensible orders with his mouth full. And behind the curtain of the executives' window the manager shook his head. But when Mr. Kecker began while sitting up and eating to give orders not only about the direction but also about the speed at which he wanted to be carried, so that the bearers whose turn it was ran back and forth during the lunch hour, sweating, their stomachs rumbling, and afterward so exhausted that they were incapable of doing their work or collapsed over their work, the more courageous among the employees grumbled.

"How he exploits being an invalid," they said.

"He certainly understands how to take advantage of his disadvantages," they said.

"He takes it easy," they said, "but he's giving us a hard time."

Two of them went to see the manager.

"We have nothing," they said, "please understand us,

sir, nothing against Mr. Kecker's occupying a special place
in the business, against his having an easy chair like your
own, against his spending most of his working hours
groaning, against his taking a day off more often than only
now and then. That's no concern of ours. We also have
nothing against his letting himself be carried on a stretcher
if he is incapable of walking. On the other hand, it won't
do for him to have himself carried when he might just
as well walk by himself—that is, supported by crutches—
and for him to give orders in addition about the direction
and the speed, even though he has nothing to do either
here or there, although he doesn't have to be either here
or there at one time or another, and for him to be brought
food even though his plate is full to the brim with a
casserole, and he harries the poor bearers back and forth
as though in addition to their own four legs they could
also use his missing leg as a fifth."

The manager asked Mr. Kecker to come to see him.

When Mr. Kecker walked through the hall to the execu-
tive room, the tiles cracked, he banged them so violently
with his crutches.

"I'll squeeze out of my stump," the other employees
heard him shout, "whatever can be squeezed out. I'm
basing all my demands on this stump of mine!"

Then he let fall his crutches. Then he fell to the floor.

Two employees volunteered to carry Mr. Kecker home
on the stretcher. A third walked alongside carrying the
crutches. A little farther behind ran the two who had
made the complaint. They assured Mr. Kecker that they
had not meant it the way it had sounded. Mr. Kecker
said nothing. He lay on the stretcher, his hat over his face.
He moaned into the inside of the hat. It was not until
it occurred to the two employees that they could not
behave as Mr. Kecker did—leave their work and run off

—it was not until the two of them turned back that Mr. Kecker took his hat away from his face. He opened his eyes and, full of horror, looked at the crutch carrier. He held the crutches over his shoulder. Mr. Kecker shut his eyes, opened them. Once again, as though he wanted to make sure that he had seen correctly, he looked at the crutch carrier. Then he straightened up. Then from the stretcher he criticized the crutch carrier.

"Crutches are not supposed to be carried like skis," he shouted.

The crutch carrier lowered the crutches at once. He apologized to Mr. Kecker.

"Is this right?" he asked. Now he carried the crutches horizontally and sideways.

"Now you're carrying them like a ladder," cried Mr. Kecker.

The crutch carrier at once started carrying the crutches vertically and sideways, so that they touched the ground as he walked.

"Now," cried Mr. Kecker, "you're making the crutches pointless. You're using them just like walking canes!"

The crutch carrier at once carried the crutches in front of his chest. And in order not to bang into the ends of the crutches with his legs at every step, he walked along beside the stretcher with his legs wide apart and wobbling.

"The way you're carrying them," cried Mr. Kecker, "the crutches have lost their meaning. They don't help you move forward now, they just get in the way!"

Then the crutch carrier stuck Mr. Kecker's crutches under his arms, mimicked the one-legged man, out of virtue and not out of need, by holding one of his two legs bent up, with the foot off the ground and dispensing with walking. Every few houses, and more frequently on the last half of the way to Mr. Kecker's house, the crutch carrier changed over from one leg to the other. He stretched out the leg that had just been bent up and so had rested, and walked on it. He bent the leg that had just been stretched out and so had been heavily burdened, and dispensed with walking.

"Is this right?" he had asked Mr. Kecker after a few successful steps with the crutches.

But Mr. Kecker lay stretched out again, hat over his face, and spoke into the inside of the hat: "A man with one leg, a war cripple, is treated worse in this country than an ownerless dog!"

For a whole week Mr. Kecker was not to be seen at all. He sent his wife.

"I am to inform you," said Mr. Kecker's wife in a trembling voice, "that it is not certain whether he will ever come again on his crutches."

That week the other tenants in the house were very quiet. They sneaked around if anything had to be brought, they whispered if words had to be exchanged. Mr. Kecker's wife ran upstairs, downstairs, fetched medicines, restoratives, food for Mr. Kecker, whose groaning resounded throughout the house, whose cries made the other tenants shrink into themselves with soft cries.

Mr. Kecker came back on his crutches.

Accompanied by two men who had fetched him at home, he set out on his way to the office. The men wore raincoats and hats, and each one had an attaché case. One walked on Mr. Kecker's right, the other walked on Mr. Kecker's left. With earnest faces, with slow, solemn steps, with deference, they followed Mr. Kecker through the gate of the establishment. And while Mr. Kecker resumed his work, they had themselves announced to the manager.

No one could say for sure what was discussed. One of the employees, an eavesdropper or a braggart or a liar, claimed to have heard words like "Inhumanity," "Treating a one-legged man like a dog," "Poor man," "Nevertheless a member of various organizations," "Bring the case before the public."

After this interview, Mr. Kecker only acted as though he were active. There was no more laughter near him. Because then Mr. Kecker called out, "Who laughed there?" And he called out, "Who's been laughing at me!" And if an employee replied, "It was only a joke, really, that I was laughing at," then Mr. Kecker would call, "Your jokes, do you think I don't notice it, are only excuses for you to smile over me!"

Sometimes he didn't even act as though he were active, he sat there with his behind and his stump on the soft easy chair, Mr. Kecker did, his foot and calf on the hand-embroidered pillow on the chair, and made things hard for the other employees.

If it was hot, a passer-by could hear them calling to each other, "A beer for Mr. Kecker! No, not a beer, better make it a lemonade! No, better make it a beer after all!"

If it was cold, a passer-by could hear them calling out, "A heater for Mr. Kecker! Closer! No, not so close, it's better a little way off!"

More often than only now and then a passer-by might hear them calling out, "Mr. Kecker can't walk any more! This time it's the shrapnel! No, it's the stump again, after all! What, so it's the shrapnel after all!"

Because in addition, Mr. Kecker had a piece of shrapnel.

"It's in the right knee," said Mr. Kecker. "Certain motions give me a twinge."

The manager, whether it was the stump or whether it

was the shrapnel, gave Mr. Kecker the day off. And Mr. Kecker had himself carried home in the way described.

"I wouldn't dream," said my father at breakfast, and he shut the books he had opened by mistake and out of habit, "of preparing the lessons. As it is, only half the students listen to me. The other half goes through the city singing and praying behind the parsons. I'll cross-examine them! That's what I'll do!" He wiped his whole face with the napkin. Then he got up from the breakfast table.

"Are you sure," said my mother, "that the shops are open today?"

"When I work," said my father, "then the others work too."

"Its not a legal holiday," said my mother to our neighbor, who knocked in the morning then rang immediately after knocking, asked whether the shops were open as usual or closing earlier than usual or were closed completely. "It's only a religious holiday. But I'd be happy to do your shopping for you. We have to go as far as the fish market anyhow."

And while our neighbor turned the suggestion over in her mind, back and forth, whether she should have fish for lunch or whether perhaps meat would be better after all, turned it over in her mind aloud: "Fish and meat, both have pros and cons," and pondered aloud the pros and cons: "It's true that fish is cheaper than meat, but meat on the other hand is fresher than fish because it comes from the slaughterhouse straight to the butcher shops, to say nothing of the butcher shops that do their own slaughtering, but the fish has a long way to come, in spite of the improved means of transport, from the coast here," and while our neighbor lost herself in her reflections and cried, "I'd rather eat expensive meat than rotten fish! And I can't do it to my husband, either!" And while our neighbor, after my mother protested that no one was demanding that of her, while our neighbor immediately afterward confessed to my mother, "When I think about it, frankly, I really do have a great longing for fish," and imagined to herself, "Do you know, if I lived near the sea I'd eat fish every day of the week, and at the most, though in all honesty I'm not so sure of this, on the weekend a morsel of meat," and while our neighbor suggested to my mother, "if you're going that way anyhow, dear Mrs. Leinlein, please for heaven's sake bring me some fish too, it's all the same whether it's fresh or not, I can always throw it away, after all it's cheap," and while our neighbor, after turning over in her mind in this way whether to have fish for lunch or on the other hand meat after all, finally decided on fish, not until then did my mother dress me, only then did my mother dress herself to go out to shop.

"Very well, then," said my mother, "I'll bring you some fish." As we went out the street door, when we had taken a few steps along the sidewalk, I heard our neighbor call, "Mrs. Leinlein, Mrs. Leinlein, we have to drop it!"

My mother started. We went back, our faces turned upward, looked up at our neighbor, who was hanging her head, her torso alarmingly far out the window. "Thank God," she called out, "I found some meat in the refrigerator. I can't let my expensive meat go to waste just for the sake of the fish!"

"That's all right," said my mother.

"Right, what do you mean, right?" our neighbor called. "Oh, right."

The fish market is in the main business street of our quarter. We went past the establishment where Mr.

Kecker works, past the movie house where Mr. Kecker goes to see war movies. The farther we went, the closer to each other were the shops. They were small stores selling poultry, wool, sausages, toys. Between these stood many-windowed supermarkets, soda fountains, ice-cream parlors, drugstores. Baby carriages, with children in them or without children, stood in front of the shop windows. Bicycles leaned against shop windows or walls or were stuck into bicycle racks. Standing around the streetcar stops or walking up and down nearby or sitting on benches next to them, people waited for the streetcar.

The shopping men and women ran in and out of the stores, waited in line to be served. The selling men and women hurried back and forth behind the shop counters, weighing the merchandise, packing the merchandise, laying the merchandise out for selection.

In the street, on the streetcar tracks or between the tracks, a disorderly crowd of people ran with long lopes. Ahead of everybody ran a long-legged man in shirt and trousers, he had thrown his jacket over his shoulders. The others ran behind him, passing each other on the run, taking their places a few yards behind him, being passed. And even when they ran a stretch, they nevertheless lagged behind the long-legged man, who was running with great endurance and understood the technique of breathing. Because, although he was ahead of them all, even if only by a few yards, he made a much less harried impression than they did. Every few steps he called out, without turning around to the others, and so loudly that you might think they were already separated by the breadth of a river, "But they need a main street for their procession!" After another step, and without turning around to the others, doubtless in order to make them feel their inferiority as runners, he added, "Can you still understand me?"

When he ran past the streetcar stop he called out to the waiting people, "Rather than relying on the street-car, take my advice, it would be better to rely on your own legs!" He ran on without lessening his speed. And while a part of the waiting people joined the crowd at once and began running along, the others called out, "How is that?" "What's the matter?" "Why doesn't it come?"

The long-legged man, by now a stretch further on, left it to the ones with shorter legs to answer these questions.

"The procession," one called, pointing with his thumb over his shoulder, "is passing through here!"

"The street is blocked off," a second one called.

A third one silently pointed in a zigzag, once to the right, once to the left, up at the façades of the houses. At this, another group of the waiting people turned itself into a second crowd and followed, at a few yards' distance, the last runners of the first crowd.

"We'll wait a little bit," the few people who stood around the streetcar stop said to each other with doubtful looks. Then they looked up at the windows above the shops.

Flowerpots with flowers did not, as usual, stand behind the windows, or vases with cut flowers, flower boxes with flowers did not, as usual, hang fastened to the windowsills. More than half the windows above the shops were decorated. These windows were open, framed in greenery and wreaths of flowers. On the windowsills stood statues, images of saints, candles, crucifixes. Little pennants hung from the windows down the house fronts. Next to the house entrances between two shops some little trees, I think birches, stood fastened with cord or planted into pots or leaning against the walls. Men and women, big-eyed, looked out of the decorated as well as the un-decorated windows through spectacles, through field-glasses. Some held children in their arms. They looked at the street or at the window decorations of their next-door neighbors or of the tenants across the street. Some of them were busy decorating their own windows. They dragged over one object after another. They built up the windows and blocked their own view from the windows and themselves and had difficulty seeing through the decorations or past the decorations onto the street. Out of attic windows men and women living on pensions and students leaned out their heads. Over the balcony railings tenants and relatives, or friends or acquaintances of these tenants bent over, layered shoulder to shoulder.

My mother went into the fish market.

Above the fish market, in the window, a woman leaned with her forearms up to her elbows supported on sofa pillows. Her arms and her torso filled out the window so much that to the right and to the left, between her elbows and the casement, there was just enough space for one narrow saint's image apiece. This was how she leaned out the window, the woman: to the right and the left of her a saint, around her a wreath of flowers. She was smiling complacently, as though she were the main attraction and the decorations were in her honor. An old woman in the house across the street was trying to start up a conversation with her. She hopped back and forth behind a crucifix that filled up the window frame and forced her head over the horizontal bar of the crucifix, then under the horizontal bar of the crucifix, and she did this first to the right, then to the left of the vertical bar on which the Saviour hung. "That's my son," she called out, pointing to a photograph at the feet of the Saviour. "My only son."

At the end of the street, above the only house in the cross street that was visible from here, the sun hung and shone into the street. I had to blink or shade my eyes with my hand to be able to look at it. Tenants leaned out of the windows of this house, too. They looked up the side street, their heads turned to the right. I could hear singing swelling up, breaking off, swelling up, in accordance with the varying volume of the surrounding noises.

"They're coming," some people called out in the street or up toward the windows. Some walked faster than before, others stood still. Buyers and sellers came out of the shops, looked up the street to the left before they went on with their buying and selling. The heads in the windows, above the balcony parapets, all turned to the left.

Behind me I heard someone wailing, "Oh, how you're carrying me! How you're carrying me! It's unbearable! You're lurching around and staggering like drunks! You're carrying me like a sack of potatoes, like a sack of garbage! If you want to cook my goose, if you want to drop me, then drop me here, you assassins, and not in a side street where no one will see it!"

"Make way, ladies and gentlemen," a second voice called out, "for a crippled veteran."

The people on the sidewalk stepped aside, making a narrow lane between them into which stuck only the heads of the especially inquisitive. The people on the opposite sidewalk stood still. Those in the windows and over the balcony parapets trained their eyes, their field glasses on the street. A few pushed apart the decorations to have a better view through the gap.

A parade was coming through the street. First of all came a man with two legs, who carried the crutches. This crutch carrier had found a solution for the crutch carrying that Mr. Kecker—it was he whose crutches were being carried—might have been satisfied with. He wasn't carrying them as he had before, first on his back, then sideways, then in front, he wasn't holding them under his arms as he did before, and imitating the one-legged man.

This man carried the crutches the way a flag is carried—
that is, as a flagstaff. Because on account of Mr. Kecker
he wouldn't have dared fasten a flag on top. He carried
them over his shoulder so that they towered above his
head, carried them with his right hand placed across the
wooden shafts and with his outstretched left hand holding their ends. His gait was stately, like that of a genuine
flagbearer. How slowly he walked, how solemnly, and
looking only ahead, never behind!

He had long since made his way through the street and
was walking along on the sidewalk when the two men who
followed him, carrying the stretcher between them one
after the other, arrived in the middle of the street. The
stretcher was pitching back and forth and up and down.
But it was not the bearers who were shaking and swinging
it. It was Mr. Kecker, who was throwing and rolling himself around on it with such force that even the two bearers, who were not weaklings, started stumbling and,
tugged at by his flopping back and forth, had difficulty
keeping their balance. Nevertheless, they stepped along as
carefully as possible. Indeed, when Mr. Kecker flopped
about a little less violently, they even walked on tiptoe
for a stretch.

Mr. Kecker had rolled up his trouser leg and was baring
his stump and the pink scar on the end of the stump. And
as he held it with both hands and moved it up and down,
he kicked against the stretcher with his good leg.

"Stop," he cried when he saw himself surrounded by
people. "Give me a moment's rest!"

The bearers stood still. They waited patiently, heads
bent, hats pulled all the way down over their faces. The
heads of the people stuck out into the lane, which was
narrow enough as it was. Sympathetically they bent over
Mr. Kecker, who let himself fall backward groaning.

"What's he got there?" asked a child, pointing to Mr. Kecker's stump. The child's mother slapped the child's mouth and pulled him away with her.

The singing slowly came closer.

The tenants of the only house in the cross street that could be seen from here pointed their outstretched hands right up into the side street.

"May we go on now?" asked the second bearer.

"Oh," cried Mr. Kecker, straightening up in the stretcher, "they can't wait! They want to go on playing their tricks on me! While all the ladies and gentlemen stand around doing nothing, looking on! Won't anyone interfere when ruffians like that torture a war veteran who gave his leg for his country? I ought to dig it up again and hit them with it! I ought to kick them all the way to the battlefields, these draft dodgers!"

"We were still children then," whispered the bearers.

The people peered searchingly into the red, lowered faces of the bearers.

"We volunteered to carry the stretcher, we really did," whispered the first bearer.

"We could have given ourselves an easier time of it, we really could," whispered the second bearer.

"That's true," cried Mr. Kecker. He let go of his stump. He shook his fists. "You vie with each other to carry me around because you're not men enough to start in with someone with two legs! Just look at you, you miserable weaklings! With me they have an easy time of it, especially since there are two of them!"

The people who stood closest to him took hold of the sides of the stretcher in a gingerly way. A lady bent over Mr. Kecker. With a lace handkerchief she wiped off Mr. Kecker's chin the saliva that spurted out of his mouth with every word.

The singing had come so close that you could catch words like "Lord God," "Gloria," "Seraphim."

Mr. Kecker leaned over the side of the stretcher. He looked down the street past the first stretcher bearer.

"Where is the crutch carrier?" he cried. "Oh, I understand! He's made off so that he can misuse my crutches for his acrobatic tricks! Or—oh. I understand! He wants to hide them, so that he can look out at me from a hiding place while I crawl around looking for the crutches! After him!" Like a coachman with a whip in his hand he swung his arm against the first bearer. But because he had at hand neither a whip nor anything similar to goad anyone on with, he seized his stump again and struck it violently against the stretcher.

The bearers tried at once to go on again. But with many helpful hands the people held the stretcher firmly by the edges.

"How can we assist you?" they asked.

"Should we take you to the bearers' station?" they asked.

"Should we call a car, a health officer, perhaps a doctor?" they asked.

"You can lie down with pleasure! As long as you want, until you feel better!" the people in the windows called out. "We'll gladly give you a sofa to use, if you want! A bed, whatever you want!"

The bearers were not miserable weaklings. But they lacked the giant strength that would have been necessary to carry Mr. Kecker's stretcher together with the people hanging onto it, as well as the people who were hanging on the backs, on the shoulders, of those people. They started out with a long stride. The first bearer pulled at the handles of the stretcher. The second bearer leaned forward against the handles. Probably the whole stretcher would have torn in two if Mr. Kecker had not begun shouting all over again.

"I've got to get the crutches!" he called out. "Get away from the stretcher! Do you want to crush me, to tear me to pieces? Oh, I understand now, you're after my good leg!"

The people were frightened, they let go of the stretcher, and the ones behind let go the coats, the shoulders, of these people.

"No one, forgive my saying so, can do the right thing for Mr. Kecker," said the second bearer.

"After him!" yelled Mr. Kecker.

And as the first bearer fell into a rapid run, and as the second bearer, halfway carried along, stumbled along behind, turning to the furious people and trying to soothe them and saying, "Mr. Kecker doesn't mean it just the way he says it! Mr. Kecker was in the war, remember. Mr. Kecker thinks everyone is against him," the singing grew louder. The running bearers put behind them half the stretch as far as the corner, the side street. Mr. Kecker sat upright between them. He was enfolding his stump with one arm, with the other he was pointing to the back of the first bearer.

"There, there," he cried. "After him! Catch the deserter!"

The crutch carrier stood at the corner, visible to many, just not to Mr. Kecker. The back of the first bearer blocked his view, and he was also afraid to lean over the edge of the stretcher at such a rapid run because he must have been afraid that it would tip over. The crutch carrier looked to the right up along the side street. He took the crutches down from his shoulder. He supported himself on them by leaning them diagonally away from himself against the ground. Mr. Kecker, protected from the sun, to be sure, by the back of the first bearer, but for that very reason unable to see in front, called out, "Stop!"

The bearers stood still. They stood side by side as Mr.

Kecker ordered them to. In this way they took up, with the stretcher between them, the whole breadth of the sidewalk.

The tip of a procession curved around the corner. Some boys walked ahead of everyone, arranged in a row of six. They wore holiday clothes and held song books open in their hands. They sang as they walked, their sleek heads bowed, sometimes looking into the song books, sometimes at the street, sometimes at the tips of their neighbors' shoes, in a tempo set by the real leaders of the procession, two chaplains in skirts. And because these knew the words and the melody of the song by heart, they held up their heads, their empty hands folded, the fingers stretched out skywards, and they only separated them to pull a boy back or push him forward if he did not keep to the leisurely gait of ceremonial occasions. They sang more loudly than the six boys and so helped them along, not only in their walking, but also in their singing. Because the boys, busy enough already with keeping the direction and the tempo, were only singing along now and again, for the most part they twisted their lips in a mute imitation of singing people, humming only the melody in the difficult passages or speaking only the words. The boys who followed them found it easier to keep step between two rows, masking the wrong notes and the wrong words. Because the spectators' attentiveness slackened more and more from row to row. It was only a few mothers and other relatives who ran along on the edge of the sidewalk or on the curbstone and proudly pointed to their children, their nephews, their grandchildren. A couple of mothers shook their fists, thrust their palms up into the air, cried out, "Postponed doesn't mean canceled!" But those boys who felt themselves indicated, who had plainly utilized the procession to postpone their punishment for one or two hours, squeezed themselves with red faces into the middle of the rows.

The girls were led by two nuns, one to the right, one to the left. They carried baskets of flowers suspended by ribbons from their necks. They reached into the baskets. They scattered flowers on the street.

There was only a small number of men. They had been arranged in rows of four, so that there would seem to be more. Anyone who wanted to think of them as the core of Christian manhood in the parish couldn't do it without feeling concern for the parish. Because apart from two rows of Christian youths, with rumps as thick as two men or as thin as half a man, apart from these youths the Christian manhood consisted of old men and pensioners who shuffled along on canes or were mutually helping each other move ahead. The ones who were half-blind kept bumping into the ones in front of and behind them, they also walked for short stretches at the side of the procession, until they were put back in place by a nun, a monk, a chaplain. The ones who were hard of hearing, if they weren't a stanza ahead or behind, would ask aloud, interrupting the singing of the ones next to them, whether the singing was still going on or whether they were praying again or even whether the sermon was being held. Aside from these, a chaplain had collected some idlers and loafers off the street. They turned over in their minds, some of them muttering to themselves, others consulting in rows, whether it was worth joining the parade for the sake of a spoonful of soup. They were asked to join in the singing by a sister who came running along. But they refused, they said they would never join in the singing just for soup, unless they were offered roast. Every couple of houses one would go off, step out of the procession, trot away.

Behind them, all the louder, with all the more self-assurance, went older ladies with a well-groomed look, those who spend their days without doing much more than praying and trying on clothes for church and graveyard visits, for processions. They wore black hats with colored artificial flowers around the brims, and black, also purple, coats. They must have been carrying the song books only for the sake of carrying them, because they did not look into them while singing, did not look even while turning the leaves, no doubt because, aside from the words and the melody, they knew by heart what was on every page. At the deep notes they closed their eyes, at the medium ones they opened them halfway, but at the high ones they opened them wide and turned them upward so that only the whites were still visible. These notes made their thin, lanky figures sway back and forth.

Mr. Kecker sat up straight in the stretcher as they went by singing, sat between his bearers, who, with bowed heads and curved backs, waited for further orders, who only every now and then threw an apprehensive look at him out of the corners of their eyes. He held his stump, both hands wrapped around it, and balanced himself against the stretcher.

Then the crutch carrier kneeled down at the corner, took off his hat. Then the tenants in the windows of the only house in the side street that was visible from here crossed themselves. Then the sextons, in white shirts, in red skirts, in rows, swung around the corner, and behind the sextons came the chaplains and the curates, in rows, in white shirts, in black skirts, some of them wearing black caps on their heads. And as some people imitated the crutch carrier and kneeled down, and others went away shaking their heads or lined up on the curb with their legs spread wide, grinning, and as some of the ones

in the windows began to sing or sank down singing beneath the windowsills and others looked down into the
street, with glasses, without glasses, some also looking
through field glasses and cameras, four sextons came
around the corner carrying a canopy on four poles. In the
middle, under the reddish-gold decoration of the canopy,
from whose sides golden fringes were suspended, there
strode the municipal clergyman. He threw a quick, prob-
ing look over his head, doubtless to make sure he was
still walking underneath the canopy, which made him
look his best. Before him, in both hands, just where his
gold-colored cape fell open, he carried an object wrapped
in gold cloth.

Even before people kneeling around me had straightened up, while the first chaplains and curates were walking by behind the canopy, Mr. Kecker called out, "Forward!"

The people fell back against the walls of the houses.
Mr. Kecker's bearers shrank back.

"But Mr. Kecker," they wailed, "you really cannot ask
that."

Mr. Kecker let the sextons, who were walking ahead of
the canopy, get as far as a few yards away from him. Then
he raised his stump. Then he hit the stump against the
stretcher.

"Cross the street," he cried.

"Please, Mr. Kecker," the bearers pleaded. "Just let the
canopy go past. Then we'll carry you wherever you want
to go."

"Cross the street!" cried Mr. Kecker.

"As far as the equator," promised the first bearer, perhaps because he was more afraid of the heat than of anything else.

"As far as the North Pole," promised the second bearer,

perhaps because he was more afraid of the cold than of anything else.

"As far as the end of the world," they both promised, their voices trembling.

"You are responsible for my body, for my life," cried Mr. Kecker. He beat his good leg against the stretcher, he reared up, he flung himself back, he rolled back and forth. The bearers, in the meantime completely exhausted from carrying him, lurched against a display window.

"Get on then!" he cried.

"God preserve us," wailed the bearers.

Then they set out to cross the street. Their twitching faces bowed down, their backs curved over, their tottering legs giving at the knees, they crept toward the procession.

The bearers reached the procession one row of sextons ahead of the canopy. The sextons stood still. They turned toward the chaplains, the curates, as though expecting an indication of how to behave.

The bearers carried Mr. Kecker past the first, past the second, past the third sexton, between two rows of sextons, one of which was going on and the other of which was standing still.

"Stop," cried Mr. Kecker. The bearers stood still.

And as the first half of the procession went on ahead, singing, the second with a jerk stood still, row by row, in front of Mr. Kecker. But because the boys, girls, men, and women pushing around the corner, those who had been following the chaplains, the curates behind the canopy, could not be held back in time by the chaplains, monks, and nuns running back, the individual rows collided with each other and bumped into each other. In places the procession widened out as far as the curbs on both sides, even beyond them, so that you couldn't tell in

detail who was taking part in it and who was a spectator.
In the midst of this tangle the chaplains, monks, and nuns,
wildly waving their arms, forced their way back in order
to prevent the members of the procession from being
driven into the butcher shops, ice-cream parlors, and back-
yards. And while the singing beyond the corner still went
on for half a stanza, from the canopy to the corner it was
breaking off jerkily and row by row. Only a couple of
the people who were hard of hearing went on singing,
until someone hit them so violently in the side that they
cried out with pain; in addition, a few others went on
singing solos, sunk down below their windowsills with no
view of the outside world and stupefied by the sound of
their own voices, until their neighbors' long-drawn-out
ringing of the doorbells pulled them out of their crouch
and upward. They leaned their terrified faces out of the
windows. They looked for a place on the windowsills
where they could hold on. They knocked over statues,
vases, crucifixes. The knocked-over decorations fell into the
rooms or out of the windows onto the street. But below,
because there was no room to leap apart, the people
leaped on each other. When they stepped on each other's
toes, they groaned but only in a stifled way. But whenever
they crushed and trampled a kneeling person who hadn't
got his footing again, a moaning and wailing began that
for a moment drew eyes, field glasses, cameras away from
Mr. Kecker.

In the midst of this tumult stood the municipal clergyman. With upstretched arms the four sextons held up
the four poles of the canopy. The chaplains, the curates,
stared ahead with dejected looks. Some people had been
pushed to the edge of the canopy, some were under it by
more than a nose. When the municipal clergyman noticed
that he was no longer alone beneath the canopy, he looked

around disapprovingly, then threw up a look for help, this time doubtless intended for Heaven and not for the canopy he was clinging to.

Meanwhile the first half of the procession was distancing itself more and more from the second, just as slowly, arranged in just as long a chain, and just as solemnly as before. A really big shouter would have been needed to call it back, to bridge the gap between both halves. The street between was empty.

Mr. Kecker ordered his bearers to carry him a little way into this gap. The bearers moved with small, stiff steps. A couple of yards on the other side, away from the first, previously the last, row of sextons, Mr. Kecker ordered them to halt. The bearers were not trembling any more. They stood motionless, heads bowed, backs curved, knees bent.

Mr. Kecker stood in the middle of the street, between the two halves of the procession. He looked around like someone with a message. And anyone with something to say was now presented with an opportunity he could not have wished to improve on. Whether out of curiosity, out of a malicious pleasure, or out of consternation, the people in the procession as well as the spectators fell silent. Mr. Kecker spread his arms out wide. "I," he said, opening his mouth, flinging up his fists, "I never wanted war!"

He did not get any further.

The people standing closest to him winced when the door to the house shut behind the second bearer. Mr. Kecker turned around.

No one, later, could say for sure who had opened this door.

"He couldn't have done it himself, of course," some say. "Because he has his hands full just moving forward."

"Of course he did it himself," others say. "With one hand he held himself up, with the other he moved himself forward." And then they show how he, in their opinion and in spite of everything, opened the door for himself. He, who was forced to use his hands if he wanted to move ahead, and this chair with wheels instead of legs. He, who rolled along the sidewalk, rump-high and only a hand's breadth off the pavement. He wore black gloves on the hands he turned the back wheels with. He put them on the tires, put them on, left them there, took them off, in quick succession and always a little way above the pavement, so that he would not run over his own fingers. He was dressed correctly, like a gentleman, with a black hat and coat, with a white handkerchief and white shirt. But at the end of the coat, where other people's legs begin, there he stopped.

When his front wheels had rolled close to the curb, Mr. Kecker turned around toward him for the second time, with a dark-red face now, and with bulging eyes he watched him, Mr. Kecker did, the way he supported himself on the street with his hands, gave the chair a push forward by a violent thrust from his rump so that it slipped over the curb. Then he took his hat off, put it on the seat in front of him, and rolled across the street, putting his hands down and taking them off in rapid succession. In the middle of the street he looked up for a second at Mr. Kecker. Mr. Kecker turned away quickly, but then looked back again, Mr. Kecker did, when the one in the wheel chair, looking straight ahead and completely concentrated on his forward motion, rolled over to the curb on the other side, thudded against it with the forward corner of the seat, supported himself with his hands on the street, gave the chair a push forward by a violent thrust from his rump so that its front wheels were pushed up over the curb onto the sidewalk and the back wheels were pulled along together with his rump between his hands, which were now pressing against the sidewalk.

Mr. Kecker opened his mouth. He wanted to shout something at him. But all he could get out was a rattle. He pressed his lips together and, with a violent blow of his stump against the stretcher, he ordered his bearers to move on. The one in the wheel chair rolled along rump-high and only a hand's breadth off the pavement toward the door behind the first bearer. Nor could anyone, later, tell with certainty how he got in either. Because the bearers ran off into the crowd. The people leaped away from each other and at each other. All they were watching out for now was to leave a lane free between themselves and the stretcher, swaying dangerously back and forth, to whose sides Mr. Kecker was firmly holding.

"What are you still waiting for," a chaplain called to the sextons. "Move ahead!"

The sextons ran off after the first half of the procession, whose singing swelled up and broke off according to the volume of the outcries, the surrounding talk. Without singing the chaplains, the curates hurried off after the sextons. Without paying any attention to whether he was still walking along beneath the canopy, and he wasn't for a whole stretch, the municipal clergyman followed. He was followed by chaplains and curates, followed by boys, girls, men and women, with no show of devoutness and in more or less extreme confusion, in mixed rows of unequal size.

"Pharisees! Stinking inquisitors!" I heard Mr. Kecker shout. "They want to pump me! Me! Not a single dying word will they get from me! No one's going to make me talk! It's not so easy! And they won't do it with such methods, either! I'll bite my tongue off first! I'll tear my tongue out first!" Then the bearers ran around the corner.

THE SHEEP

I HAVE SELDOM seen feet as ugly as mine. But the sight of them upsets me as little as it makes me happy. I look at them when I have a bath, when I cut my nails, when I run barefoot on hot days, I look at them now and then in bed, and more thoroughly than usual when they hurt after long walks, when they swell up, when the veins bulge on my instep, when blisters have formed, corns, new calluses, when the nail of one of my toes, terribly squeezed into my shoes, pierces into the flesh of a neighboring toe.

Their color is white only over the instep. But this strip of white is crisscrossed by the pale blue threads of the veins, which bulge sometimes more, sometimes less, but always enough for me to be able to trace their course with my finger. Toward the toes, toward the rims of the feet, toward the heels the white shades off first into pink, then into crimson. On the balls of the feet, on the ankles, on the heels, indeed just where the angles are sharpest, this crimson shades into purple. My nails are yellowish and brittle, almost half covered with cuticles. A callus of considerable thickness that covers my soles, not altogether, but almost, is of a deeper yellow than my yellow nails. And pink-colored strips can be found only in the grooves between the calluses. And a pink-colored spot can be found in the middle of the sole of each foot.

I have so-called splayfeet as well as so-called fallen arches. And when I stand, I touch the ground with the whole of my sole. And when I put one foot next to the other, only these round, these purple half-circles of my ankles and these round, these purple half-circles of the balls of my feet touch each other. At the same time my big toes reach away from each other almost at right angles and squeeze diagonally against the second-biggest toes, press these second-biggest toes out of the row of toes and upward, so that my shoes swell out not only around the soles of my feet but in addition over the second-biggest toes.

But even with feet like these you could still walk, no matter how bad they are, if there weren't still another problem. Because if I place one sole against the other, with the heels directly against each other, then the big toe of the left foot extends farther than the big toe of the right. It's not enough for my feet to be strikingly ugly in their shape, in their color, but on top of that they're of different sizes. And if I go with my mother to buy shoes, there is always a lot of talk back and forth and pro and con between me and my mother and the saleswoman and me whether I should choose a pair of shoes that will fit the left foot and therefore won't fit the right foot or a pair of shoes that won't fit the left foot and therefore will fit the right foot. The saleswoman as well as my mother leave the final decision up to me. "So that you don't say I'm responsible," says my mother. "So that you won't say I'm responsible," says the saleswoman. And depending on what is decided that day, the outcome of which will decide my walk for the next half-year, I either limp with a pigeon-toed left foot, always swollen and squeezed, or I shuffle along, always turning my ankle, with my right foot first, sliding back and forth, with nothing to constrain it in the roominess of the right shoe and with a polished heel that keeps slipping out of the shoe at every step. And if anyone asked me which type of forward movement I preferred, I would answer, "The other!" And so, every half-year, when the time for buying shoes comes again, I alternate, once deciding in favor of the left, once in favor of the right foot. And from one time to the next, though only until I've come to a decision, only until I've taken the first few steps with the new pair of shoes, I think the kind of movement that is further in the past is the less painful.

That's how it happens that I'm afraid of longer walks, that I try to avoid anything that goes beyond the daily shopping expedition.

And as I sit on a Sunday night, or on a Monday morning, or around midnight, as I sit there and pick up sometimes the right and sometimes the left foot, move it over to the night table lamp, turn the lamp shade around, as I put first the one, then the other foot by turns into the proper light, as I look at these seven blisters, these six white water blisters of different sizes as well as this one dark-red blood blister, the last one of which is longer than all the other six put together, as I sit there so snugly, my father and mother having gone to sleep, I think, "You should have tried to get out of it today, too, or even yesterday."

I hear my father snoring without a break, I hear my mother clearing her throat with a break now and then and at irregular intervals, I hear my mother turning from side to side to the soft creaking of the bedsprings, I hear a clink whenever my mother, groping in the dark over the glass top with the glass tube of tablets bumps into the tumbler into the night table lamp into her wrist watch. Then I hear the springs of their big bed creak still more loudly as she sits up, as she puts the first, the second, the third and if I haven't miscounted the fourth pill into her mouth, gulps some water from the glass, I hear it creaking still more loudly then, as my mother props her-self up between two pills, gets out of the bed, gropes her way through the bedroom in the dark, then shuffles along through the corridor to the bathroom, and fills the glass with water from the tap.

I turn out the light, I sit there as I said, one foot or the other in my hand, but in the dark like that, I wait that way until she puts the water tumbler on the glass top of the night table, picks up and puts down her wrist watch, until she's stretched out again, my mother, to the creaking of the bedsprings, and gives a sigh, but with-out waking my father.

Then I turn on the light, then I look at my seven blis-ters.

There are four blisters, among them a blood blister, on my left foot. There are three—that is, really two and a former blister that has broken now—on my right foot. On the heel of the right foot, on the heel of the left foot, not exactly in the same place but almost, bulges a white water blister as big as a penny. On the ball of each foot a water blister as big as a shirt button bulges, one of them —the one on the ball of the left foot—a little smaller than the other one, the one on the ball of the right foot. It's not noticeable, or barely, and then only when I put them both next to each other and compare them. Another water blister that is more oval shaped than round is squeezed in between the third largest, or, if you like, the third smallest and the fourth largest, or if you like, the second

smallest toe of my left foot. To look at them I have to
spread both toes apart with my fingers. The already men-
tioned former blister, now burst, lies between the fourth
largest, or for all I care the second smallest, and the fifth
largest, or for all I care the smallest of the toes on my
right foot. It's torn open at the edge and through the tear
in the white skin of the blister shines a piece of pink-
colored, moist raw flesh. It also burns worse than the other
blisters when I poke it with my finger. It burned before
in the course of that afternoon, today or even yesterday,
when it burst open in the middle of the woods, and
drained, when my sock grew damp and stuck to it. The
last, the seventh, the blood blister, stretches along the
groove between the big toe and the end of the sole of the
left foot. Its dark-red coloring makes it stand out from
the yellow calluses of the big toe as well as those of the
sole. In its elongated form it's different from the five
round ones, including the former round blister that has
now burst, as well as the blister that is more oval shaped
than round.

And as I sit that way, as I keep busy with my blisters,
as I keep fingering my seven blisters—more carefully, to
be sure, the one that burst than the other six—as I press
down their tops and feel along their edges, as I turn out
the night table lamp in between, turn it on, turn it out,
three or four times—how can I tell how many pills my
mother has swallowed, how many glasses of water she
has gotten for herself—I look over, one foot or the other in
my hand, at the nail scissors, at the cuticle scissors on
my night table. First I pick up the nail scissors, cut the
five toenails of the one foot, the five toenails of the second
foot, toe by toe, snip around among the calluses, cut out
thick pieces of callus from the heels, from the toes, cutting
in as deeply as I can. Then I pick up the cuticle scissors,

cut away the cuticles that grow over the half-moons of my toenails, lay them open, the half-moons, I venture—I admit it—too deeply into every other toenail, I cut into my own flesh, and the half-moons take on a reddish color.

I'll wait for the scabs to form. Probably, I mean without a doubt, I won't be able to wait for the scabs to fall off. I'll lift up the edges of the scabs and, after pulling back and forth a little, I'll scrape off the scabs—I know myself —even before the wounds have closed. No more will I be able to wait—I don't want to deceive myself—until these six blisters burst like the one that did, or until they dry out. I open and shut the cuticle scissors a few times. I bring the cuticle scissors close to the water blister as big as a penny on the heel of my left foot. I stick it in, cut a tear into it, press down with two fingers on the skin of the blister on both sides of the tear, and dry off the drop that oozes out on my sheet.

That was the first, the oldest of my six blisters I had raised in the course of today or yesterday.

Clapping his hands, ready to leave, my father stood on the threshold of my room in the morning, his hat on his head, in a brown sports coat and brown knickerbockers, the handle of his walking stick hanging from his wrist.

"Up, up," he cried. "Today we're off on a hike!" He kicked his boot against the threshold, made an about-face when he saw me getting out of bed, and hurried off to the kitchen with a heavy tread.

"I can't manage any quicker than I can, either," said my mother. She rustled sandwich-wrapping paper.

I pulled up the blinds. The sky, as far as I could see it over the roofs of the houses lying opposite, was pale blue and covered with a number of clouds, comparatively few. Most blinds were still down.

While I dressed, my father walked up and down in the hall, reading the map, looking at his wrist watch, and calling, "I shall be very much surprised if we get out of here before dark!" And whenever he called that, my mother let the knife fall from her hand onto the floor in the kitchen, picked it up with a groan, and complained, "The death of me! Without a doubt, the death of me!"

She stood in front of the kitchen table, in her spinach-green Sunday dress, her hat on her head, in her shoes with medium-high heels, in her thin transparent stockings, through which the bluish veins on her calves glimmered, in places curling all over her thin legs, she stood that way, my mother, and buttered all the pieces of bread one by one, put salami between all of them, slapped two slices together, wrapped them in sandwich paper, and put them into the rucksack on the table between two thermos bottles.

"A rucksack, what a sight," she said. "What a sight," she repeated; she closed the rucksack, her lips pressed together, and shook her head and the hat on her head. My father snapped the rucksack on his back. He took the walking stick in his left hand, took my left hand with his right hand. He led me to the stairwell. My mother ran behind us, turning first the ankle of one foot over the medium-high heel every few steps, then the ankle of the other. We went down the stairs. A corner of the folded map, green with black lines on it, stuck out of the breast pocket of my father's coat. On the sidewalk my mother took my right hand in her left hand.

I'm not exaggerating when I say that we rushed to the streetcar stop. My father walked with long strides, lifting his walking stick together with his left foot and putting them on the ground, sometimes with the tip of the stick half a foot ahead of the tip of his boot, sometimes with the tip of the boot ahead of the tip of the stick. My mother stumbled along, constantly turning her ankle or getting her heels stuck in the cracks between the cobbles, behind my father by the width of two men. I ran between them, a left arm stretched out in front, a right arm stretched out behind.

Around the stop sign, or nearby, as well as around the stop sign on the opposite sidewalk, people stood, family by family. They stood in straight rows or in rows curved into half-moons. Individual members of these large families held on to each other's hands. And only the father on one end of a row, and only the mother on the other end of a row, would ever have a free hand to hold something with or point to something with. For the most part without a word, and interrupting themselves only with terse comments and jerky head movements over toward the mothers, the fathers on this sidewalk looked off to the left down the street, the fathers on the opposite sidewalk looked off to the right down the street along the streetcar tracks. The children stood with bowed heads, arranged in the row according to size, according to age. Some of them carried provisions, blankets, deflated air mattresses on their backs. Now and then they shuffled their feet on the cobbles or kicked a pebble, a butt, over the curb into the street.

"There it is!" cried the fathers. "At last!" With red faces, and with one arm, the free one, stretched out pointing to the oncoming streetcar, with the other they pulled along the members of their family hanging onto it behind them on the street.

The seats were taken by mothers with at least two children on their laps and with one standing gripped between their thighs. The rest of a family like this grouped itself around the seat, holding onto a hand of the father or a strap or clutching hard at a corner of parents' clothing. Only one seat was taken by a young man. He sat there, constantly sliding his behind back and forth on the seat, his face lowered, and staring, with blinking eyes and an upper lip twitching up and down, first at his trousers, then at the fronts of the houses, while shielding his face with his hand against the standing people. These were mothers with angry faces who looked over the heads of the infants in their arms down at him, who were besieging him, who were crowding him with luggage and folding chairs, who kept hissing, "Why doesn't he look around, that one," and, "He'll be sorry when he's an old man and has to depend on the respect of young men!"

More pushed than pushing, we moved up as far as the middle of the car. There the counterthrust of those who were moving toward us, more pushed than pushing, was so great that we came to a standstill. I saw a family of seven hurrying toward the streetcar. There were five children of different sizes who were trying to get to the step between their parents. Four of these five were running on their own legs. The fifth was being carried in the middle of the row, in a sling between them, by the two biggest ones of the four who were running on their own legs. But because these two carriers were also of different sizes, the sling hung down crookedly between them, so that the fifth one, the one being carried, kept slipping down and the smaller of the two biggest ones of those running on their own legs had to carry most of the weight of the fifth one. The bigger of the two carriers—that is, the biggest of all five—held by his other hand, over the handle of a shopping bag, the third biggest, or if you like, the third smallest. The second biggest, or, if you want to put it that way, the fourth smallest, held with his other hand, over the handle of a second shopping bag, the fourth biggest, the second smallest. The latter in his turn held the hand of his mother at the end of the row, while the third biggest or smallest, I mean the one who was hanging on to the hand of the biggest on one side, held his father's hand at the beginning of the row on the other side. Aside from a rucksack, just like the mother, the father was carrying a folding chair in his free hand, just like the mother, in the hand that he, just like the mother, had no child to hold onto with. And pushing the legs of the chair against the passengers on the platform, the father stepped onto the running board of the streetcar. He yanked along the third biggest or smallest, who yanked the biggest of all along behind him into the car.

At that moment, as the one in the sling was hanging over the step, between the outstretched arms of his two biggest, but unevenly big, brothers, the conductor pulled the bell cord. The one in the sling, the infant, dense and mindless, in a position that was still lower than before because of the difference in height between the streetcar and the platform, in the middle of a family half of which was riding away and the other half of which was running alongside, yelling all in a row with the mother on one end and without letting go of each other, this infant bobbed happily up and down, crowing, patted itself on the face with its hands, and fell down backward into the street.

The conductor pulled the bell cord. The streetcar stopped. "It's all right, all right," the mother called out to the father, drowning out the cries of the infant. "Nothing but scratches. Scratches and a few bruises! It always looks worse than it is! Always! We can go on!"

"They've all got a guardian angel," murmured the mothers. "All." And I saw them pass their hands gently over the heads of their children. Then my head was squeezed between the stomachs of my father and my mother by the crowding in of the family of seven. And I stood in the dark for the whole trip, with my face in my mother's stomach and the back of my head in my father's stomach. And I heard the uninterrupted crying of the infant, the occasional crying of other infants, heard the conductor calling out the names of the stops before the streetcar stopped, asking while the streetcar was running, "Who hasn't got a ticket?" ringing before the streetcar started up again. And I heard my father say, "To the end of the line," heard right next to me the conductor groaning whenever he squeezed past the passengers, jingling his change and handing out tickets, all accompanied by the sound of cloth tearing, buttons snapping off, and passengers calling out protests. And at each of the stops I heard a voice cry out, more and more plaintively from the direction of the seat that the young man had occupied, "I want to get off, right away! I'm farther away from where I was going now than when I started." And I heard him banging his fist against the window, more and more feebly. At the last stop, as it grew lighter around me, as the stomachs of my parents moved away from each other, as we got closer step by step to the exit, the young man still sat, now motionless and looking ahead of him with a grief-stricken expression.

We joined the families that had arranged themselves in rows once again. As they walked on, the fathers and the mothers on the edges turned their red faces and tousled heads toward the three conductors of the three streetcars, and with curses stuck their fingers into the rips in their disheveled clothes. The three conductors sat down on a bench next to the sign of the last stop. They took their caps off their heads. Each of them put down his cap between himself and the fellow conductor sitting next to him, they sat bareheaded in the sun and munched their sandwiches.

We walked along between the fences of a settlement of allotment gardens. The tempo was established by the first row of hikers. "If it goes on this way," cried my father, "we'll never get to the woods!"

But it was impossible to catch up with even a single row. Because these big families, together with the luggage they were dragging along, took up, even when they walked shoulder to shoulder, the whole width of the path. The distance between the fathers and the mothers at the ends of the rows and the fences on both sides was so small that at the slightest deviation to the right or the left they got caught on the slats, had to stop, free themselves, and so blocked the advance of the whole procession behind them. A number of them, comparatively few, started a breathless song, which doubtless less because of its melody than because of its volume drew the attention of the gardeners away from their sowing and over to the path. Between the slats of the fences and the ornamental shrubbery I could see them kneeling in front of their flower beds. Smeared with sweat and earth, with bare torsos, they rooted about in their flower beds, throwing stones and weeds into their neighbor's garden, or they stood up, put bottles to their lips, and drank with their heads bent all the way back.

At the edge of the forest, at a distance of only three trees including the gaps between them, families encamped. The fathers lay on air mattresses, their torsos naked and white or peeling. They had pulled off their socks and rolled their trousers up high. Their heads were shielded by white handkerchiefs knotted at the corners, looking like bandages. They had turned their faces to the sun. They moved only in order to scratch themselves all over or to pull off the pieces of skin from their torsos with two fingers or to wipe with the backs of their hands the sweat out of their armpits under their upraised arms. The women sat straddled on folding chairs, their stockings rolled down to the ankles, their blouses unbuttoned. Some wore slips. If they didn't happen to be distributing sandwiches among the children, they were stretching their faces up to the sun. The ones among them who were wearing glasses covered the bridges of their noses with leaves whose stems they pushed in between the frame of the glasses and the base of their noses. Meanwhile the children, naked or wearing underclothes, flinging their limbs up and down, some of them grotesquely twisting and turning their behinds, rolled over the blankets onto the floor of the woods.

Between these families, and with only one tree and the spaces to the right and the left of its trunk between them, other families were settling down. And while the women were spreading out blankets, opening up folding chairs, unpacking provisions, and then, while reassuring themselves with sideglances that the other women were also sitting that way, unbuttoned or pulled out their blouses, the fathers kneeled. They stuck the valves of the air mattresses between their lips, they blew them up, now with cheeks swelling, now with cheeks fallen in, their lungs fully expanded then sinking in again. They they closed the valves, squeezing the valves with two fingers to the sound of the air that came hissing out anyhow.

"Is it still a long way off?" I asked my father.

"Did you hear that?" my father asked my mother, "the question he asked me, the little idler?" He stood still, poked a deep hole in the earth with his stick as though he wanted to mark the place where I had asked whether it was still a long way off, and cried, "Here, here already!"

"Don't you feel well?" my mother asked me.

"If you keep on asking him about it," cried my father,

"he'll think himself even more important, with his worm! He's got to learn what it means to work for his dinner!"

And so I learned what it means to work for my dinner.

We walked along a forest path into which the roots of the trees on both sides were growing. Scattered on the roots along the path, sometimes squarely across the path, torn-off branches lay in the way. And while my father stepped on the branches or over the branches, pushing them aside with the tip of his boot, and the stick too, at every single branch my mother let go of my hand, pulled her skirt up to her knees and walked this way: her head bent, her shoulders drawn up, the elbows standing out akimbo from her rump, and raising her feet off the ground twice as high as necessary, she stepped over them. It was only when a branch stuck so far up that she would have had to raise her skirt as far as her garters that she stood irresolute for a moment, one leg straight, the other bent at right angles and stretched forward, raised her foot until the skirt stretched out between her legs, then pulled it back and, supporting herself with the palm of her hand against the trunks of trees, she lurched around the branch in an arc between the trees. My father stood there, eyes straight ahead, audibly breathing the air in through his nose, letting it out again just as audibly from his wide-open mouth, and poked in the ground with his stick. Whenever we waited this way for my mother, my father and I, I put my left foot forward and let my right foot carry most of the weight of my body. The heel of the left one hurt. I favored it as much as I could, I also bent over and caught the ends of my shoelaces with both hands, but before I could loosen them, but before I could free my left heel from the pressure of the left shoe, even if only for a moment, my mother was there again, stretched out her hand to me with an unsuccessful smile, and I had to move forward again.

There were markings on the bark of the trees alongside the path, white circles with red, blue, yellow crosses and circles inside them. From here the end of the forest —not of our hike, but of this first forest—could be seen in all directions, it was so light, so scantily grown over, so easily seen through. It was a pine forest, or a fir forest, or some other kind of evergreen forest, I think. Definitely not a spruce forest. The spaces between the trees took up far more room than the trees, whose thickest trunk was only as wide as a thin man. Two grown men could lie stretched out in these spaces. The crowns of the trees did not touch each other. The shadows of the long thin trunks, now distinctly, now barely recognizable, now vanishing altogether, set up relations between the trees, which stood in straight, almost dead-straight lines, as though planned. The shadows of the small crowns moved back and forth above the forest floor covered with branches, needles, grass. The hikers, who framed the forest on all sides, all sat facing the sun which was on our backs. The ones we had left behind turned their backs to the forest. The ones to the right and the left looked sideways past the forest. But the ones we were walking toward sat away from the edge of the forest by the length of the shadows of the farthest trees or between the shadows of two trunks without touching them. Where a family was so numerous that the space between the shadows of two trunks was not big enough, they sunned themselves body pressed to body as though they were freezing, shoulders drawn in along the edges of the family row as though they were afraid of bumping into the shadows. They looked into the woods.

Aside from the shadows, aside from the numerous cutdown trees that lay about topless and every which way, there was still another connection between two trees. These were the hikers who were shy of the light, the men without families, who hung in hammocks between the trees wherever the distance between two trunks, wherever the height of the first branches or the beginnings of branches was suitable for what they wanted. They had slung the ropes at the head and foot of these hammocks around the trunks and fastened them to the branches or the beginnings of branches, the length of an arm, wherever possible, above the forest floor. Perhaps so that they wouldn't fall too far in case the ropes broke, in case the branches snapped. While their heads were at just the height of their feet, their rumps hung in the shape of an arc, their behinds deeply squeezed together. And because the narrow bands of the shadows of the trunks did not cover their faces, they hung there, their heads, their torsos above the shadows of the crowns, and snoozed away. It was only when the wind moved the crowns of the trees, when the shadows of the crowns shifted, when the sun shone on them, that they covered their faces with newspapers or sat up in their hammocks, now swaying a little. The skin of their backs was patterned in red stripes, pressed into them by the ropes.

"Do you think the weather will stay nice?" they called out to each other and among each other through the forest, first putting their hands around their lips like a funnel so that the question could be better understood and then pointing skyward with one hand so that the question could be still better understood, while the other hand, so that the answer of the others could be heard more easily, cupped their ears.

"Who can tell, who can tell?" they answered each other back and forth through the forest, their hands placed around the lips again so that the answer could be understood just as well as the question.

Others strode purposefully between the trees with their

hammocks rolled up, made a halt between two trees, unrolled the hammocks, stretched them out in the gap between without calculating whether the distance, whether the height of the branches was right, and then fastened the ropes.

Signs had been carved into the bark of the trees, two identical signs on each of two trees standing opposite each other, which were different from the two identical signs of other trees standing opposite each other. Some hammocks, on those trees where the first branches or beginnings of branches started too high, were fastened to hooks that had been driven in. Clothes hung next to these hooks on clothes hooks. On other trunks, above the heads of the hanging people, little wooden shelves stuck out. Refreshments were placed on them, snacks, and flashlights, plainly so that in case it occurred to them to hang there until darkness fell, they could find the spaces between the tree trunks.

Now and then one would get out of his hammock and with rapid strides, one hand on his fly or unbuttoning his fly, walk toward the only bush of this forest in the middle of the forest. This bush was surrounded by crumpled-up filthy scraps of newspaper, swarming with flies. As soon as someone came close, the flies rose. But the one who was attending to his needs placed himself in front of or behind or next to the bush, depending on the place he was being looked at from, and let a jet patter down on the paper, or he hung his behind over his lowered trousers over the rim of a hole, tore the newspaper into small strips, and with the strip over his fingers, using each strip only once, pass it along the groove between the cheeks of his behind.

"What are you looking over there for!" said my father. He had turned his head toward the hole.

And as we kept on walking, my father sturdily striding on, my mother and I struggling to keep up, my mother
looking at her shoes as though in that way she could
avoid turning her ankle on her medium-high heels, at
the most half a finger high, and myself limping, because
I put my left foot down more carefully than my right,
the hanging people straightened up again.

"He's late," they cried.

"Do you think he's standing us up today?" they cried.

"Do you think he's still coming or do you think something has prevented him?" they cried, first holding their
hands around their mouths, then putting one hand around
their ears while pointing with the other in the direction
of the last streetcar stop.

"Who can tell, who can tell, what's what," they answered
each other.

"That's what I like!" someone called out behind us.

My father turned around. "What do you mean by that!"
he said.

A man came toward us along the forest path, with long
strides and a furious face. He held a rolled-up hammock
clutched beneath his arm, and while executing a sweeping
motion over the forest path with the other as though he
could frighten us in that way out of his field of vision, he
cried, "It's not you I'm after! See to it that you get out of
here!" He turned into the woods and went over to a hammock that was hanging only a couple of trees away from
the edge of the path. In contrast to the other hammocks,
its cords were white and unpatched. A man, his eyes
closed, was lying in it. He had been listening inatten-
tively to the general conversation to the left and the
right without taking part in it.

The other threw his hammock down on the ground,
then with both hands gave the outstretched hammock a
shove so that it swung back and forth.

"I suppose you think," he cried, "when you close your eyes, that no one is going to see you hanging between someone else's trees! I've been hanging here a little while longer than you, my dear sir, every single Sunday, and this isn't my first summer, either!"

"Then you'll just have to change your trees today," said the one in the hammock. He tried to straighten up.

But the other one was pushing his hands firmly against his chest.

"Did you hear that?" he cried. He waited until the last guffaw of the laughter into which all the people in the surrounding hammocks had broken had died down, then he gave a whistle. A well-built young man got up from a tree stump near the hole. Slowly, with legs spread wide, to the noise of breaking branches, he walked over to the man in the hammock.

The one in the hammock was well aware that, lying down and on top of that hanging in the air, he was inferior to an opponent standing with both legs on solid ground with his hands pressed against him. "That's really not right," he complained, "for people to make a fuss about this little place of mine here! There are enough trees in this forest! Just take a look around you!" And in an appeal for help he looked through the cords of the hammock at the people who had hung their hammocks near him. He even began nodding, as though that would get the others to agree with him. The others were getting out of their hammocks, one leg already on the ground. A number of them picked up branches and whipped them through the air. "This forest is taken!" they cried and came close enough so that there was no tree to block the sight of the unpatched white hammock. And leaning against the trunks of the trees, they called back and forth to each other, "We can't let that newcomer bother us! He spoils the whole mood! Cut him down!"

"I want to get out," complained the one in the hammock. But the young fellow was already standing behind his head. He was holding pruning shears in his hands. He separated the two blades, called out, "One," put the cord between the blades, called out, "Two," and as he cut through the cord, calling out, "Three," the other one lifted the hammock at the foot end as high as he could, so that the one in the hammock tumbled headfirst down to the ground. He got to his feet, picked up his clothes, left his hammock to the others, and ran off without dressing. The young fellow cut down the hammock at the foot end too. And as he dragged it off to the hole behind him, the other one began fastening the cords of his hammock.

The people standing around got back into their hammocks, they swung to and fro, they called out back and forth to each other through the woods; "You've got to know how to protect yourself! You've got to know how to protect yourself! Who knows what they'll be trying to do next, these johnny-come-latelys! Putting up hammocks on other people's trees! And the forest getting lighter every week. Because if we deserve a Sunday like this for all our weekdays, then the woodchoppers come in and start clearing everything, without thinking that trees by themselves, without the right distances between them, are no use to us at all! For us to be able to hang our hammocks here at all we have to lengthen the cords every week. Soon we'll have to be looking for shadow with a magnifying glass, soon we'll have to sit on stumps and be exposed to the sun. And it'll be umbrellas protecting us. And it'll be storm clouds we'll be hoping for. That's how it will be! And who can tell, who can tell, when! What nerve, to dare try to put up his hammock there! A lot of us will soon have to take turns standing guard so that everyone will have a chance to put up his hammock! Yes, yes," they kept interrupting each other.

With a tropical helmet on top, barefooted below, with naked, hairy legs, a small bearded man walked along the forest path. He was waving, flinging his outstretched arms in all directions. He was carrying a megaphone around his neck, over a khaki shirt. He stood still in the middle of the path, lowered his arms, put his hands to his body. And as he stood up straight that way, his finger-tips touched his knees. And when he bent over, his finger-tips almost touched the ground without his having bent his back more than is usual. That's how unusually long his arms were. He put the megaphone to his mouth and, while turning around, called in a booming voice through the woods, "Please get ready, ladies and gentlemen! Cover your eyes! I'm beginning immediately!"

And while the ones in the hammocks put black blindfolds over their eyes and lay back, the little man very nimbly climbed a tree in the center. He settled himself in a forked branch and let his legs swing. He sat that way, his hands free, all the way up and in the middle of the forest, and with both hands put the megaphone to his mouth.

"This is the end," he began in a booming voice. "We've lost our bearings completely! No one can count the days, the weeks, the months, we have spent dragging ourselves through this underbrush looking for a way out! Finished! It's all finished! Here we lie! What madness it is to talk ourselves into thinking there's any hope! Let's not fool ourselves! This swamp around us, this underbrush, are impassable! No one can keep track of our companions who have sunk into the quagmire, without a word, without a peep, with hardly an audible gurgle. And we do not have to build ourselves any tombs either, that's certain. Because these swamps are more insatiable than the beasts of prey lying in wait around us. And our bodies won't satisfy them any more than a scrap of bread will a starving man. And the only good thing is that the uproar of the howler apes drowns out the babbling and groaning of our dying people. They're wasting away, our friends, weakened by fever and incapable of shooing away the stinging flies crawling over their faces. And the only good thing is that their fingers are too worn out to take hold of a bush knife. Because who can tell, who can tell, whether they will pounce on our leader? He's sitting crouched over there, his face turned aside, and excuses himself because of the endlessness of this primordial forest. Sooner or later he is going to keel over too and lie there stretched out like all of us here. And the only good thing is that even though everyone is so weak, a feeling of communion in a number of people is more important. Again and again these pull themselves together on all fours, crawl over to a companion, and if they don't collapse on the way over, they whisper a word of comfort to him. That an expedition could end this way, my dear friends, we all know! Yet that this expedition would end this way, which of us would ever have thought it!"

He spoke this last sentence in a trembling voice, then whined into the megaphone, and he interrupted himself only to start imitating wild animals, grunting, croaking, screeching, spitting.

The people in the hammocks began babbling and groaning. Trembling and racked by shivers, they flung themselves back and forth.

"Am I alone," they called out plaintively through the woods, "with the dead bodies of my friends?"

"Is there no one left," they cried, "to hold my hand? No one to give me his ear to hear my last words?"

"Wait a bit, just wait!" others called out. With blind-folded eyes they got out of their hammocks and started out at a crawl.

Hurrying and constantly winding about, we reached the edge of the forest. The people in the hammocks be-gan babbling their last wishes, incomprehensible because of their sobs. Only a few were sitting upright and un-moved.

"As though this couldn't be endured," they grumbled. In order to show how little such afflictions could shatter them, they even whistled to themselves. "Get it over with finally," they cried.

"No, no," whimpered the others. "Not that same hor-rible end again! In that case we'd prefer to be saved!"

"Who can still think it funny? Who is giggling and whimpering here, back and forth? Who doesn't know what he wants any longer? Is there someone here so confused that he can think his own end and the end of us all funny?" the little man whined into his megaphone. And while those who had lain grumbling in the hammocks now began to fling themselves out of the hammocks onto the ground, giggling, whimpering, and waving their limbs as though someone were tickling them, the little man went on whining, "What is it that drives away the stinging flies, the rats, even the beasts of prey? What is it that silences the howler apes? I see the clothes of my com-panions falling off scrap by scrap! I see my companions hitting away at each other's bared torsos! And over their bodies, toward their twisted faces, their feelers out in front, there they advance, giant red columns of ants! They squirt their acid into the eyes of my companions! They blind their victims before plunging their jaws into them, before hooking themselves solidly inside, eating their way in, digging paths and vanishing. Loggy and swollen up with the blood they've sucked into themselves, they turn up in other parts of the body, often a long way off from the points of entry. They pull pieces of flesh from the paths into the open, carry them off, held between their mandibles, piece by piece, my companions, and take themselves off as soundlessly as they came."

He began giggling. I saw no one remain in his hammock. Yelling and laughing, they rolled themselves through the woods, bumping into tree trunks, and they did this until they remained lying unconscious and speechless.

My mother shook herself and scratched herself. We walked along a narrow path, through meadows with yellow flowers alternating with fields, perhaps wheat fields.

"There," said my father, pointing his stick horizontally away from himself at a second forest that looked like the first, which I had taken for a fir or a pine forest or an evergreen forest of some other kind, "there we can rest."

I saw peasants standing in Sunday clothes at the backs of their fields. Their legs, their stomachs, were covered by the grain. They were giving worried looks, now up to heaven, now down at their fields.

"There's a storm coming up," they called out to each other.

Our shadows kept getting less and less visible on the path. I looked down, to make sure I didn't bump into a stone. Meanwhile the heel of my right foot was hurting just as badly as the heel of my left. And whenever my mother stumbled, turned her ankle, stood still with her lips squeezed tight, it was hard for me to decide which foot I should put forward, which I should burden with the main weight of my body.

"Isn't it beautiful here," said my father.

"All right, all right," murmured my mother.

"Stand up straight! Breathe deeply!" said my father to me. "Don't hobble around like an old woman!"

At the edge of the second forest my mother sat down in her green suit on the green meadow, her back to the forest, her face to the sun. And while she pulled off her shoes I sat down next to her, and while I pulled off my shoes my father took the rucksack off his back and then sat down next to me.

We sat that way, in a row, our backs to the forest, our faces to the sun as it came through the gray clouds, and we ate and we drank what we had brought with us.

When my father wasn't looking, I cautiously felt my heels, I tried to pull off my socks. "It's incomprehensible," my father cried then. "There he is with his hands at his feet again! Don't act that way!" After a few unsuccessful tries I pulled my shoes back on. My feet were so swollen that it was hard for me to squeeze them in. "I've got to go," I said, and I limped off into the woods with loose shoelaces with twisted toes.

Except for two bicycles at the edge of the forest, a woman's bicycle and a man's, which were leaning against each other so as not to fall over, I saw nothing at first that doesn't belong in a forest. I went over to one of the few bushes so that I could examine my feet in peace. As I walked, I kept turning around toward my parents. They were sitting motionless, their backs turned to me. In their green and brown clothes they hardly stood out from the woods. I heard a rustle behind the bush. Between the leaves I saw something gray rising and falling and rising, in regular succession. I crept around the bush. Behind it a man and a woman lay on top of each other, as though there weren't room enough in this forest for two. They lay stomach to stomach, the man on top, the woman underneath. The man, in a gray coat and gray trousers, was completely visible from behind. And because he was taller than she, and because he was broader than she, he covered the body of the woman. The woman stretched out her naked arms and legs as far away from herself as she could. Motionless and without even making an effort to shake him off, and only now and again moving her legs, covered with mosquitoes and mosquito bites, or her arms, covered with mosquitoes and mosquito bites, and doing that over his back, moving them toward each other in order to scratch herself, she held up the weight of the man. Her head laid on the side, her face turned away, she was looking between the trees into the distance, without the slightest trace of anger or irritation, not even with any surprise, but as though the whole thing were none of her concern, as though it were customary to lie on top of each other in a forest that a whole village could have fitted into. It's true that the burden was not so heavy seen from the side as it was from behind. Because on his underside the man lay with his legs on the ground between the legs of the woman. Because on top, to the right and the left, next to the shoulders of the woman, the man pushed his outstretched arms against the ground. In that way only their two stomachs were touching. From the stomachs upward, the nearer it came to the heads, the distance between them grew greater and greater. The only thing connecting their torsos was a necktie hanging down out of the man's coat. Their heads were separated from each other by the width of two heads.

The man raised and lowered and raised his behind without let-up. With a red face and red-streaked eyes he goggled past the woman's head toward the forest floor. He was panting so hard that someone who wasn't looking at him might have thought he was the one who had to bear the burden.

"There's someone there again," said the woman.

"That ruins the whole thing!" said the man breathlessly.

He looked at me over his shoulder with a funny expression, his behind pulled in and not moving. "Get out of here, you brat!" he cried. "I'm not going to start in all over again just because of you!"

He had hardly called this out when I heard hurried footsteps behind me. "You ought to be ashamed of yourself, looking over there!" cried my father and with both hands seized hold of my neck and turned it around so that I was looking in the opposite direction with a twisted neck. My mother stood spinach-green between the trees, looking into her handbag with her face lowered and turned away. My father, without giving me time to turn around, his hands on my neck, yanked me toward her. And as I was walking backward, my eyes looking forward, my father was walking forward, his eyes looking backward.

"Why don't you lie down right on the path!" he called out. "Then people can see you a long way off!"

"Anyone who looks," the man called out, quite out of breath, "has only himself to blame! When you get down to it, you have a choice between four points of the compass, and you can always look at the sky if the view everywhere else gets on your nerves!"

"You ought to be ashamed of yourself!" my father called out.

"Get off," said the woman. "I've had enough now."

"You don't have to tell me that twice!" cried the man. I heard a rustle.

"They're not the least bit ashamed of showing their piggishness in broad daylight!" cried my father.

"Don't think about it don't," said my mother. She walked on slowly.

"I suppose you never unbuttoned your pants, either," cried the man. "You manufactured that brat of yours by hand, I suppose!"

"It'll be a long time," cried the woman to the clatter of a bicycle driving off, "before you get on top of me again!"

The man gave a nasty laugh.

"You're not going to get anyone on top of you so quick," he cried. "Leave that to me. Do you think it's any fun when a girl doesn't even resist, when a girl just lies down without the least objection, lies there motionless like a paralytic, doesn't budge the least bit, doesn't make the slightest noise!"

As we caught up with my mother, the man was riding off on his bicycle. My father let go of my neck. The rucksack hung limply down his back. My mother turned her red face toward the path.

"What," I said and was going to ask what the man and the woman had been doing.

"Shut up!" said my father.

"They were doing something," said my mother, "that is not done!" Then my parents walked on even faster than before.

Beyond this second forest there were more meadows with yellow flowers and grain fields, maybe wheat fields. The path ran on toward a third forest, a fir or pine forest, like the first and the second forests, in case these were fir or pine forests.

The pain in my heels had spread evenly over my feet. They ached and burned and hung so hot, so heavy, that it was hard for me to lift them up, so that I often kicked stones.

"Take a look around you!" said my father. "The landscape is full of change."

And I looked around on all sides, though one side would have been enough. Because all around the same thing was repeated with tiny variations. These yellowish-green meadows were followed by these greenish-yellow fields followed by these brownish-green, these more or less light woods always so easily seen through that I could make out the meadows and fields and meadows on the other side.

"There," said my father pointing to the left, holding his stick out flat, "there you can see Field Mountain in clear weather."

My mother and I, we looked off to the left at once. But between the meadows, fields, woods, and the gray clouds that were now covering the sky without a break I saw only the red-tiled roofs of a village and between the roofs the big round crowns of green trees, maybe oaks or ashes or beeches. I didn't know. I didn't want to know, either.

"And behind Field Mountain," said my father, still holding his stick out flat, "you can see Pine Mountain in especially clear weather."

My mother and I, we looked off to the left at once. But the view was unchanged.

"Will you put a pleasant look on your face!" cried my father. He knocked his stick against the ground.

And with a pleasant expression I looked past my father in front, past my father in back, into my father's sports coat, toward the direction in which in especially clear weather you could make out two mountains in a row, looked pleasantly at the clouds, at the roofs, at the peasants, black figures, dwarfed more and more the further away they were, moving toward the village. The smaller they became, the nearer they got to the village, the more loudly the farm dogs yelped. It was a mixture of the high-pitched yapping of the little curs, which would bark hoarsely, pant, soon break off and then only now and then start up yowling again, and the tireless, deep howling, interrupted only by growls, of the great watchdogs. The yelping was drowned out by the bell strokes of the church clock, it was probably afternoon. It kept getting darker. This side of the village the peasants walked over a bridge. They passed one hand along the railing, with the other they held on to their hats. The wind blew the grass, the grain, the treetops to the left.

We reached the edge of the third forest. In the middle of the forest I noticed that a blister on my right foot had burst, that the sock had gotten damp and was sticking.

"Mama," I said, "I feel dizzy."

"Can he lie down for a moment?" said my mother.

"He's got no spunk, the weakling!" said my father. "Lie down wherever you feel like it!"

Between the trees, on the yellowish-green meadow behind this third forest, I saw sheep, the color of sheep-skin.

"Can I lie down over there?" I said, and I pointed at the sheep.

"Stretch out over there!" cried my parents without looking. "I want to have a word in any case with your mother privately, in any case with your father privately. Really?" they interrupted each other at the same time and then added excitedly at the same time, "You too? Well, it's wonderful that at least in this respect we're of the same mind!"

And while my parents moved away quarreling, I slipped over as far as the last row of trees on the edge of the forest, took off my shoes, lay down on my stomach in the grass with my face toward the sheep.

Through the gap between two trees I could see the bodies of the sheep from the side. They were not grazing, the sheep. They stood motionless, one sheep next to the other. Their hindquarters turned toward the right, their sheeps' heads straight ahead and toward the left, they looked past the forest beyond the shepherd. He was walking, leaning against the wind, diagonally across the meadow toward a farmyard. With one hand he was pressing the crown of his hat against his head. With the other hand he was holding his cape wrapped around his body. The moment he loosened this hand, raised it to wave toward the farmyard, the wind blew the cape backward away from his body. The farm dog accompanied his arrival with its yelping. It was not until the shepherd disappeared in the farmyard, in order to get something or to take shelter from the weather or to chat a little—how should I know why he left his sheep—that the dog fell silent. A light came on in the farm house. It kept getting darker. The sheep were not guarded by a sheep dog. And whether it was because it was only from that direction that help could be expected, or whether it was because they had just happened to turn their sheeps' heads in that direction, the sheep kept looking toward the farmyard. There were more sheep than I could count. They stood in an uneven line, so that the trunk of the tree to the left of the gap cut across and covered the heads of the sheep that had moved out further, so that the trunk of the tree to the right of the gap cut across and covered the hindquarters and the hind legs of the sheep that had stayed further back. But it was not only the two tree trunks to the right and the left of this gap as long as two sheep's bodies that cut across and covered the fore- and hindquarters of the sheep in this way, but the sheep's bodies also did that to each other. The hindquarters of the sheep that had moved out further were covered by the heads of the ones standing in the middle, and the hindquarters of the ones standing in the middle were cut across by the heads of the ones that had stayed further back. Besides this, the ones that had moved out further by the same distance and the ones that had stayed further back by the same distance covered each other, as well as some of the ones standing in the middle. And the hindquarters of the sheep that had moved out further touched the heads of the ones that had stayed further back.

I could get a picture, even though it was only approximately clear, of where one sheep stopped and where another began by looking through under their bellies. There between the fore- and the hind legs I could see other fore- or hind legs standing or stamping on the meadow. There I saw every now and again sheeps' heads lowered between fore- and hind legs onto the meadow, and slowly and ungreedily nipping off tufts of grass with their sheeps' muzzles, then being lifted up, with stalks hanging out of the muzzles and disappearing behind the bellies.

Behind the hindquarters of this flock of sheep, to the right along the meadow, and for that matter between the meadow and the adjoining field, there ran a highway. An old car was driving along this highway. When it had passed by half the flock, it came to a stop at the edge of the meadow, blowing its horn. Only a few sheep turned their heads, then, like the others, undisturbed by the noise of the opening, the shutting of the car door, by the noise of the approaching steps, they looked toward the farmyard again.

A broad, short-legged man ran across the meadow, toward the sheep. In his white linen suit, in his pale-yellow straw hat, he was the only living thing that stood out from this brown-green landscape. I looked around in vain for my father and mother. Maybe they were quarreling very softly and nearby, and it was just that I couldn't make them out in their brown-green clothing behind the brown-green bushes and trees of this forest that was getting darker and darker. Maybe, deep in their quarreling, they had moved off farther and farther without noticing it.

"Hey, hey, hey!" cried the man, coming up to the sheep from behind. "But you're all alone, without a sheep dog and without a shepherd! Don't be afraid! I'm not going to hurt you! I'll just watch out for you a little until the shepherd comes back! Because something could easily happen to such sweet-natured peaceful animals as you!"

I did not recognize him, alone and dogless, until he had come up to within a few sheeps' lengths of the sheep. He stood still, Doctor Trautbert, and smiled at the hindquarters of the sheep. The sheep turned their sheeps' heads toward Doctor Trautbert without changing their position. Only one sheep, one of the ones that had moved farther out, kept looking toward the farmyard undisturbed, it even moved a half-sheep's length farther forward and away from Doctor Trautbert.

"Dear, dear," Doctor Trautbert sighed, "what a shepherd!" The sheep that had moved farthest forward bleated in the direction of the farmyard, turned around and slowly walked between the other sheep toward Doctor Trautbert. Then the other sheep turned round and followed it.

"How trusting they are," Doctor Trautbert sighed. "At least sheep are!" He smiled at them.

And though there was meadow all around, and heaven knows the sheep had enough to graze on, he leaned over and began plucking grass with both hands. As he stood bent over in this way, the sheep bleated a second time. It had moved farthest off again, only in the opposite direction. The other sheep bleated back. Doctor Trautbert looked up toward the sheep, astonished and with his face red from bending over. The sheep, the one that had moved the farthest forward, made a little charge at Doctor Trautbert. He fell down, half pushed by the sheep, half slipping backward into the grass. His hat lay a little distance away from his head on the meadow. And before he could straighten up, the sheep had placed itself on top of him with all fours, standing in this way: two legs on Doctor Trautbert's chest, two legs on Doctor Trautbert's stomach, sometimes motionless, sometimes shifting from one foot to the other.

It started drizzling.

Doctor Trautbert lay rigid in the wet, his face trodden, his fingers digging into the tufts of grass. After grasping the position he was in, he tried to shake off the sheep by flinging himself back and forth. But the sheep kept its balance. It was a full-grown sheep. And when he had given up, and when he lay motionless again, it bent down over his head and rooted about in his hair. I think it felt a desire to eat him up. But even this sheep could do nothing against the nature that had destined it to be herbivorous. It let the hair fall from its muzzle and looked hostilely at Doctor Trautbert.

It started raining.

"What can it be about me," moaned Doctor Trautbert, and he covered his face with both hands, then looked over at the other sheep between his outspread fingers, turning his head cautiously from one side to the other. They stood around him, one sheep next to the other, sometimes looking at him, sometimes at the sheep that was burdening him.

The rain came down more heavily. A light was burning in the farm building. The shepherd was probably chatting. I didn't dare look around for my father and mother. The sheep on top of Doctor Trautbert bleated for the third time. A second sheep stepped out of the circle of sheeps' bodies. It settled across Doctor Trautbert's legs.

"I really wouldn't say anything," he moaned, "if you were predatory animals by nature. Not a word out of me, even if I were dying." Then he broke off and started gasping. The burden he was carrying must have been very heavy.

A third sheep stepped out of the circle of sheeps' bodies. It placed itself with its forelegs to the right of Doctor Trautbert's head, its hind legs to the left of his head, its belly over his face. He raised his arms and pushed them against the sheep's belly so that it could not lie down.

"How long," I thought, "is the shepherd going to go on chatting? If he starts talking about the sheep one by one, he won't be able to get back before midnight. Before then they'll have smothered him three times over."

Doctor Trautbert's elbow bent. The sheep's belly came down lower over his head. The circle of sheep closed tighter around him. They stood, one sheep pressed up against the other. Between their legs I saw their sheeps' heads look away searchingly past Doctor Trautbert's body, on which there would have been room for a fourth, if not even for a fifth sheep.

"I can't stand it any more," Doctor Trautbert begged. "Please get off!"

"Just wait until I fetch my dogs!" Doctor Trautbert threatened. Then he began barking, imitating his dogs, in order to drive some fear into them. But the sheep did not move.

And whether it was because he was barking, or because the shepherd now appeared in the light of the farm-yard gate that now opened up, the dog began yelping. When the shepherd stepped out, a second figure, probably the owner of the farm, came into view. He pointed to the sky, perhaps in order to draw the shepherd's attention to the rain. The sky was gray and thickly overcast, and not pierced by either sun, moon, or stars. The farm gate was closed. The light in the farm building went out.

The shepherd approached, this time without holding his hat or cape. The wind had let up. He stood still behind the sheep, looked dumbfounded over the sheeps' backs at whatever it was that was groaning in the middle of the circle and whimperingly imitating more a threatened than a threatening dog. He gave two sheep a clap on the hindquarters, then shoved them apart and stood between them.

"You're a little too free and easy," he cried, stroking the sheep on his right as well as the sheep on his left. "Kindly keep your hands off my sheep!"

He pushed the three sheep away from Doctor Trautbert. They immediately took their places in the sheeps' circle. Bit by bit Doctor Trautbert straightened up until he towered over the backs of the sheep with his head, with his torso. He looked around, probably looking for a gap between the bodies of the sheep that he could squeeze himself through. The shepherd, first placing his hands on top of each other in the posture of someone praying, then holding them apart by the width of a man, ordered the sheep to separate. They opened the circle.

And as the sheep ranged themselves next to each other in an even row again, their heads turned left toward the farmyard, whose outlines were scarcely visible between the sky that was now gray-black, and the gray-black landscape, with their hindquarters turned to the right, Doctor Trautbert walked across the meadow toward his car. And as he walked across the meadow, he kept turning around and calling out, "You ought to be ashamed of your sheep!" The shepherd, his back bent, leaned against the trunk of a tree. He did not look at the sheep. He had turned his face toward Doctor Trautbert and with both hands was covering his face, which was turned away from the sheep. And if you had not heard him giggling you might have thought he was ashamed of his sheep.

When Doctor Trautbert slammed shut the car door and started the motor, only one sheep turned its sheep's head around. It was the farthest forward outside the row. With one eye and with a nasty sideglance it was looking past the shepherd after the departing car, without changing its position. Then it began grazing, greedily and lowering its head jerkily down to the blades of grass and raising it above the blades of grass and lowering it to the blades of grass. The shepherd took his hands from his face, and running behind the sheep clapping his hands, he drove them across the meadow toward the farmyard.

After lying in the wet for I don't know how long thinking over what I should do, I heard, some way off and long-drawn-out, my father calling "Lo" and "thar" and "Lo" and "thar," I heard, some way off and long-drawn-out, my mother calling, "Where" and "are" and "you" and "lost."

"Here!" I called out. "Here!" I stood up.

"Where," called my father, "is," called my father, "here," called my father.

"To the right," called my mother, "or" called my mother, "where," called my mother.

"To the left," called my father. "Answer!"

"Here!" I called. "Here!"

And while my father and mother were calling out "Here" and "there" and every now and then "answer," and while I was calling out "here, here," and every now and then "near the trees" and every now and then "near the meadow" my father and mother were coming closer.

"That's enough for today," said my father.

"What I have to put up with," said my mother. "Really put up with!"

My father lifted me to his shoulders. This is the way I sat: my right leg over his right shoulder, my left leg over his left shoulder, my hands around his throat, while he held my shins over his chest with his arms. He carried me across the meadow, along the highway. And while he was carrying me I fell asleep. And I woke up in my bed. And I heard my father snoring without let-up, heard my mother clearing her throat with let-ups and at irregular intervals. And I didn't know whether it was still Sunday or already Monday morning.

.

THE ROWERS

Not a sound comes from the kitchen: no footsteps, no murmuring, no clattering. No lid rattles, no plates clink, no silver falls to the floor.

"Do you see her coming?" cries my father.

"No," I say, "not yet."

I see women approaching the house, from the right, from the left, I see women moving away from the house, toward the left, toward the right. None of them stands still in front of the entrance. None of them looks up as she walks past toward this window, this dining-room window at which I stand, from which I look at the street.

"Repeat," cries my father, "what she said!"

"She muttered something," I repeat, without knowing any longer how often I've repeated this.

My father sits at the unset dining-room table. He props his elbows on the table top. He looks at the wrist watch on his wrist. From time to time he calls out the correct time, and right after that the length of time he's been sitting there waiting for his dinner, and right after that he asks whether I see her coming.

"What did it sound like?" cries my father.

"I couldn't understand it," I say, without knowing any longer how often I've said this.

"I might be late, something like that?" cries my father.

"No," I say.

"I'll be right back, something like that?" cries my father.

"No," I say.

My father jumps up from his chair. He pulls me away from the window. We stand very close, facing each other.

"You'll have a long time to wait, something like that?" cries my father. "You'll have to look a long time, something like that?" cries my father.

"No," I say. "Certainly not."

"Give me a complete account!" cries my father.

"Perhaps," I say. "Perhaps something like that," I say. I nod.

"So she said: 'You'll have to wait a long time, look a long time,'" cries my father. "Couldn't you have told me that right away!"

"In a way," I say.

"What do you mean, in a way!" cries my father. He pushes me out of the dining room, out of the hall, into the stairwell. "Answer yes or no!"

"Yes," I say.

My father slams the street door.

"We'll look for her!" cries my father. "We'll find her!"

We go off in the direction of the main business street of our quarter. Some of the passers-by turn around to look at us. But though they're walking quickly, my father goes out into the street and at a run catches up with the people walking on the sidewalk. My father goes back to the sidewalk only when the driver of a car blows his horn. Now and again, on this sidewalk or on the one opposite, I hear people speaking to my father with a "How do you do, sir!"

"How do, how do," says my father, without raising his hat, without turning toward the people addressing him.

"Look around you," he calls, "so that we don't miss her!" And as we walk, we turn our heads to the right and to the left.

"What is she wearing?" cries my father.

"What she always wears," I say.

"What does she always wear?" cries my father.

"A sort of skirt," I say, "and a sort of blouse."

"What do you mean by sort of!" cries my father.

"A white blouse, I think," I say, and before I can add that I think she always wears a dark skirt, my father cries, "I don't want to know what you think! I want to know what everyone knows who's not blind or an idiot: what she wears, every day!"

"A white, a slightly yellowish blouse," I say, "and a black, a slightly brownish skirt."

"Are you sure?" cries my father, and he looks at me searchingly.

I nod. I'm not sure.

"Are you sure?" cries my father.

I shake my head.

"Look, look, he doesn't know!" cries my father. "He can't even tell what he sees every single day!"

And as we walk, we turn our heads to the right and to the left. And every now and then, whenever I see a woman with lowered head in a light blouse, in a dark skirt, coming toward us a few houses away, I think I recognize her, I raise my hand to point to her, I open my mouth to cry, "There she is!" and above a similar blouse I recognize just in time a different face whose eyes look past me. And every now and then I see my father stare at a woman coming toward us a few houses away with lowered head, in a light blouse, in a dark skirt, I see his hand clench, I see his mouth open, I see him turn aside suddenly and just in time from another face above a similar blouse, whose eyes look past him.

"I'd like to know," cries my father, and then he breaks off before he has said what it is that he would like to know from me, and then he raises his hat, bows, and then he says, "How do you do, sir," as a car with four open windows, blowing its horn, drives past another car. Behind the bent back of the chauffeur the school principal, hat on head, sits upright. In his right hand he holds a leather glove and hits the chauffeur's back with it. Without being distracted by my father's greeting, he points his outstretched left arm over the chauffeur's shoulders in the direction in which they are traveling and calls, "The same thing every day. Step on the gas!"

"I'd like to know," cries my father.

"There, there she is!" I cry, and I point to her through the people. She is wearing a pale blouse, a dark skirt. She is walking half an arm's length away from a man who is smaller than my father.

"One moment" cries my father. The people in front of us turn around. They step apart. My father passes between them with long strides until he stands close behind the man who is smaller than he is, who winces, says, "How do you do, sir."

"How do," cries my father. "How splendid that we've met! But who is this lady with whom you stroll so publicly and, for that matter, at high noon?"

"My wife, sir," says the man, the teacher. "If I may present my wife, sir," and pointing downward, he adds, "Our son."

Between them I see a small boy.

"Shake hands nicely with the high-school teacher," says the woman.

The boy stretches his hand up high. My father takes the boy's hand and begins blinking like someone who has been roughly awakened.

"We're going to eat out today," says the teacher. "My wife burned the dinner."

"You're doing the right thing," cries my father. He raises his hat to say good-bye, and pulling me along behind him, he runs precipitately down the main street.

The butcher's sign sticks out into the street. It is a pig-colored sign shaped like a life-size pig. Around the shop, around the shop door, the display window, around the windows of the butcher's apartment next door to the shop, people stand in a dense crowd, smacking their lips and now and then yelling "Hurray!" with upraised arms. They take up the whole width of the sidewalk. The nearer we get, the more frequently I see bitten or trampled white sausages or white sausage skins lying on the sidewalk, in the gutter, the more frequently I see dogs snapping at each other over the sausages, over the sausage skins. The cobblestones are wet with puddles of a greasy broth. People, sleepy and belching, squatting on the curb in a row, at irregular distances from each other. They have unbuttoned their coats and waistbands. Some of them hold white sausages in their hands, some of them have dropped sausages without having tasted them, some of them are dropping them.

"Now we ought to be able to get up," they sigh.

"Now we ought to be able to move on," they sigh.

"Even if you could just move forward slowly, just with short steps," they sigh, "then at least there'd be the prospect of being able to stretch out sooner or later and having a little snooze." And supporting themselves with their hands on the curb, they lift up their behinds a little, move forward by the width of a behind at the most, to the right or to the left, according to where they would have wanted to go, then leave it be and lower their behinds onto the curbs again.

"Now we'll have to charter a bus to get us home," they sigh. "It was too much of a good thing."

"What's the matter here?" asks my father.

"The butcher," one of them answers. "The butcher is celebrating his twenty-fifth anniversary today." Sitting on the curb, he speaks down into the street, too exhausted to turn his head up toward my father.

"The butcher," answers a second one, trying in vain to point to the shop with his arm. "The butcher is treating his customers today for free."

"You can eat as much as you want to," answers a third, "if you're a customer. But I advise you." His mouth snaps shut.

"He advises you," a fourth continues the advice of the third, "to eat more moderately than we did."

"Luise!" cries my father. "Luise!"

A few people on the edge of the crowd turn their heads toward us. Sausage ends stick out of their mouths.

"Let us pass!" cries my father.

The people crowd together more closely. In front of us a narrow lane is formed. We squeeze through. Behind us it closes up again at once

Behind the window next to the display window of his shop sits the butcher. He sits visible as far as his belt, above the windowsill on a raised easy chair between two big steaming troughs to the right and left of the arms of the easy chair. A string of white sausages hangs around his neck, over his white smock, down to his belt. He has turned his red face toward the people. His mouth, with its prominent canines, wide open, his eyes closed tight into a horizontal furrow a little below the bald moist top of his skull, he smiles at the people, he reaches both hands into the troughs, he lifts out dripping hot sausages, throws them, without opening his eyes, partly among the people, partly beyond the people onto the street, partly in front of the feet of the ones standing closest to the window. And while some of them raise their arms, catch the sausages, open their mouths, yell, "Hurray!" yell, "Long live the butcher!" and then stick the sausages into their mouths or snap up the sausages in the air with their mouths wide open, sausage ends stick out of the mouths of the others. They let the sausages fall right away in one piece or they bite through them so that only the ends fall off or they stuff them with their fingers completely into their mouths, then stand there speechless and with thick lumps in their cheeks on both sides.

"Stay here," says my father.

He steps over the shoulders of the ones sitting on the steps in front of the open shop door. He moves cautiously and in a zigzag line, his eyes looking down, through the shop behind the marble counter. The floor is probably also covered with sitting or lying people. Because every now and then I hear someone whimpering and sighing, "Won't you watch out!" On the counter, visible and at the same time protected by a glass lid, some sausages lie in layers, the sliced parts in front, turned toward the customers. My father passes along the back wall of the shop. On it cut sausages hang on hooks, long straight ones and curved ones, and lumps of raw meat. Underneath, on a counter, there are dishes with chopped meat with white and dark-red insides. My father pushes open the door in the middle of the back wall. In the steam-darkened lamplight of the room behind the shop I see the butcher's apprentice standing. He is wiping his hands on a rubber apron.

In the display window, between a row of hanging sausages, a doll dressed like a chef stands in a white apron and a white cap. The chef is holding a dish with pieces of roast meat in its left hand. And as it moves its head from the right to the left to the right shoulder, it bangs into the sausages on both sides with its cap. They swing back and forth, banging into the sausages hanging next to them, and these in turn bang into the ones hanging next to them, so that all the sausages keep moving ceaselessly. The chef's eyelids open and shut over the glass eyes. When its head reaches the middle between its shoulders, it comes to a jerky stop, and under its open glass eyes staring straight ahead it brings its right hand to its mouth to the dish to its mouth and distributes silent hand kisses to the pieces of meat.

With his right hand the butcher lifts a sausage out of the trough on the right side, holds it up before his face, and looks at it with half-open eyes.

"The butcher is eating again!" the people standing in the crowd call out. "Bless you!"

The butcher opens his mouth and rounds his lips into a circle a little narrower than the width of a sausage. "Ah," he cries, flicks out his tongue, and licks off the sausage skin. He pushes the sausage into his mouth, slowly and without biting into it, and only deeply enough for the tip to lie between his teeth. Between the sausage skin and the corners of his mouth some saliva trickles out and runs down the butcher's jaws. He pulls the sausage out of his mouth, holds only one end with his fingers, removes the sausage, now standing vertically upward, by an arm's length from his mouth, looks at it, turns it horizontal and toward his mouth, pushes it into the hole of his mouth, so deep inside that his fingertips stick between his teeth. The butcher's eyes brim with tears. He opens his mouth so wide that five sausages would have fitted between his lips. A sound comes out of the butcher's jaws that is not unlike that of vomiting. The butcher draws the sausage out of his mouth. The sausage skin is split open. Between the scraps of skin the stuffing overflows. But before the sausage breaks apart, he pushes it into his mouth, he separates his teeth above the middle of the sausage, lets his teeth snap together, and swallows down the sausage while pushing the second half of the sausage into his mouth with his hand after the first half of the sausage. He knits his eyes again into a horizontal furrow a little below the bald moist top of his skull, he smiles, the butcher, he reaches into the troughs to the right and left of the arms of the easy chair, he throws dripping hot sausages outside.

I force my way through the lip-smacking crowd of people, which keeps replenishing itself even though now and then someone goes off, belching, his hands laid protectingly over his stomach, with small steps. Around it, and keeping only just enough distance so that the people standing on the edges cannot reach them with a kick, dogs pace, sniffing, their tails pulled in.

I see a woman in a light blouse, in a dark skirt, hurrying off toward the center of the city. I run after her, past these shops lying closer and closer together, between all these people running into and out of the shops, these people standing at the streetcar stop signs, these people running toward stopped streetcars and running after streetcars that are just starting up. I run after a woman in a light blouse, in a dark skirt, after a woman in a red blouse, in a green, a blue blouse, in a black-and-white checked skirt, in a red, green, blue skirt.

The streetcars travel across the bridge to the big buildings, department stores, churches, movie houses on the opposite bank of the river.

I go down the steps next to the bridge. The water of the river is brown-green. There is a narrow strip of grass next to the river. Signs are stuck into the grass at regular intervals. I walk along the gravel path between the strip of grass on one side and the empty, backless benches on the other side toward the next bridge. I sit down on a bench. The bridges to the right and left are contained by walls. Aside from the streetcars and the cars driving toward this bank of the river or toward the other I see the heads and the torsos of people, the complete heads or the half-heads of children moving toward this bank of the river or toward the other. From here the streetcars, cars, people on the bridge to the right look as big or as small as the streetcars, cars, people on the bridge to the left. I sit so far away from both bridges that I cannot distinguish the men from the women, the women from the men. I see their light or dark, their more or less colorfully clothed torsos, the light ovals of their faces. They walk bareheaded, they wear hats on their heads. They walk with lowered faces, with torsos bent forward, with curved backs. They walk upright, with faces turned straight ahead. They walk with faces turned upward, their heads bent back, their torsos bent back. They walk behind one another, next to one another, they overtake each other, they pass each other. Next to them I see half-heads or whole ones. I assume these are children's heads. Because why should I assume that some men or women slide across the bridge on their knees and do it without the other people walking across the bridge in the usual way turning around after them or stopping to stare at them.

Of course sometimes a man or a woman turns around, of course a man or a woman sometimes stops, a man or a woman leans over with his head or her head hanging down as far as the height of the wall or sinking beneath

the wall. I see a section of a sagging back or not even a
section of a back. Immediately afterward I see a head
and torso appear at the same place on the wall or I see
a head and a torso not appear again or, at another place
on the wall a little way before it, a little way behind it,
I see a head and a torso turn up. And I think it's another
head and another torso. And I assume that sight is de-
ceptive, especially at such a distance, and I assume that
at the moment when a man or a woman straightened up
I was looking over at the other bridge or at a different
part of the wall on the same bridge, and I assume that
at the moment when another man or woman leaned over
another part of the wall and disappeared I was looking
over at the other bridge or at another part of the wall on
the same bridge. Because why should I assume that men
or women suddenly disappear on bridges, suddenly turn
up on bridges, change their appearances on bridges and
in seconds, especially since I constantly turn my head and
look from one bridge to the other and between times look
at the water, at those brown rowboats, with those rowers
sitting with their backs toward the direction in which
they are rowing, some of whom, oars pulled up, let
themselves be carried by the current toward the bridge
on the left, the others of whom row against the current toward the bridge on the right, their arms swinging the oars over the water in an arc behind them,
dipping the oars into the water, pulling the oars past
them and the boat, swinging the oars over the water
and in an arc toward themselves and the boat, dipping
them. Now and then they throw hasty glances behind
them in the direction in which they move. On the
opposite shore, on one of the backless benches behind
the gravel path behind the strip of grass with the signs
stuck in the grass at regular intervals, I see someone

sitting whom at first I had taken to be a heap of clothes consisting of the rowers' jackets lying on the bench and hanging off the bench, small and made smaller probably by the distance and hard to recognize, I see him turn his head from bridge to bridge and between times casting glances at the water, at the rowers, at the rowers between us, perhaps at me, perhaps taking me at first to be a heap of clothes consisting of rowers' jackets lying on the bench and hanging off the bench, and then for someone sitting small on a backless bench and made smaller probably by the distance and hard to recognize, turning his head from bridge to bridge and between times casting glances at the water.

Sometimes a man or a woman stops on the bridge to the right, to the left, with a face turned down and back, perhaps speaking to a dog, to a child not yet as tall as the wall. Sometimes, between two people walking behind each other on the bridge, something turns up that is neither a back nor a head nor a hat, turns up again an arm's length away from the one walking ahead as well as from the one walking behind, and moves between the two of them. Perhaps it's the top of a baby carriage that the man or rather the woman walking behind is pushing, that the man or rather the woman walking ahead is pulling. Sometimes a man or a woman stops on the bridge, leans over the wall, looks at the water, sometimes a man or a woman leans over, lifts up high a child that wasn't visible before, lets him look over the wall at the water, sometimes a child lifts up high a light skin-colored object that wasn't visible before, holds it over the wall. These objects must be dolls, sometimes they fall into the water. Because no one jumps in after them, although life preservers hang on the bridge wall, because no one rushes down these steps or the opposite steps, tears his clothes off his body while standing on the shore, swims across the river, dives down. The ones standing at the wall put the children on the ground. The children are no longer visible. What is visible are at most the light spots of their hands clutching at the wall. The people standing at the wall lean all the way over the wall. They lower their heads so far that the light oval spots of their faces are invisible. They look into the water, perhaps until the dolls are carried off by the current, until the dolls, if they are dolls, are soaked through with water, sink.

"What are you throwing in the water?" I call out to a rower who is letting himself be carried along with folded-up oars at about the height of this bench, in about the middle of this river, toward the bridge on the left. I stand up, I see the one on the opposite shore stand up, and so that my question will be more understandable to the rower, I raise and lower my arm and point at the bridge, at the water, I see the one on the opposite shore raise and lower his arm and point at the bridge and at the water, as though like myself he wanted to know what was being thrown into the water, as though like myself he wanted to make his question more understandable to the rower by raising and lowering his arm. He, who is just as far away as I am from both bridges, he who must realize just as much as I—that is, that something is being thrown into the water—he who must realize just as little as I—that is, what it is that is being thrown into the water.

"What? What?" cries the rower. He turns his head to the one opposite, to me, then, his face turned to the bridge on the right, he lets himself be carried toward the bridge on the left, with no answer to my question, to the question of the one opposite, without a second question after my question, after the question of the one op-

posite, in case the one opposite had actually asked anything at all, because I didn't hear anything and the rower
didn't understand anything, he lets himself be carried
along further to the left, the rower, perhaps because he
thinks that the one opposite and I had asked a question
not of him but of each other. Because the one opposite
and myself, we're not looking at the rower, we're looking
at each other, because the one opposite and myself,
we're turning toward the benches. I go back to the bench
I had been sitting on until then. While walking I turn
around toward the one opposite, to see whether while
walking he turns around toward me, I see him turn
around toward me while walking, perhaps to see whether
I turn toward him while walking. And we see each other
turn toward each other while walking. And we quickly
turn our heads toward the benches—that is, I don't turn
around any more and can't tell whether he is turning
around, just as he, in case he is not turning around any
more, can't tell whether I'm turning around, just as he,
in case he turns around, knows that I'm not turning
around any more. I sit down on the bench. I see the one
opposite sitting down on the bench, just as he would have
to see me sitting down on the bench opposite. Who sat
down first? I, or both at the same time, or he? If I had
sat down on the bench first, I would have had to see
him sit down. I didn't see him sit down. If we had sat
down on the benches at the same time, he would not
have been able to see me, nor I him, sit down on the
bench. If he had sat down on the bench first, he would
have had to see me sit down.

"Did you see me sit down?" I call, holding my hands
in front of my mouth like a funnel, across the river.

"What does *he* want?" several rowers cry. They turn
their heads to the one opposite, to me, and the other way

around. The one opposite drops his hands, those light small spots, from his face, that light oval spot. Above the light big oval of his face I see a narrow dark strip. It's either his hair or a cap on his hair, if the one opposite has hair on his head. He sits crouched over on the bench, either because he can't lean back or because his back is bent with age. I would take him again for a heap of clothes, just as he would me perhaps, if I hadn't seen him standing up, walking, pointing up and down, turning around, as he has seen me perhaps. He is small, compared with the rowers, perhaps because he is twice as far away from me as the rowers, or even farther than twice as far. Turning my head from bridge to bridge, I see him meanwhile looking at the water, perhaps at me, I see him a little broader, perhaps because like myself he has pushed his arms against the bench to the left and the right. I don't know whether he is looking over here when I, my head turned to the right, to the left, look at the bridge to the right, to the left, whether he, when I'm looking at bridges, looks at bridges, just as he can't know whether I'm looking over when he, with his head turned to the right, to the left, looks at the bridge to the right, to the left, whether, when he looks at bridges, I am looking at bridges. I prop my elbows on my knees, my chin in my hands. With my head lowered, I look between my legs at the gravel. Should I, just because someone is sitting opposite, of whom I don't know whether he wants anything from me, who probably doesn't want anything from me, because what is there for him to want from me, who probably doesn't know whether I want anything from him, what there is for me to want from him, should I lower my head just because of that and look at the gravel, the dust, the butts in the dust? I slowly raise my head. The one opposite sits on the bench, sunk low and caved in as though he had dozed off while I was looking at gravel, dust, butts. What is visible is the big dark spot of his hair or of a cap on his hair, in case he had hair on his head, and a narrow light strip only of his face. The light strip broadens out to an oval spot, the dark spot narrows down to a narrow strip.

And we look at each other again.

Raising my right arm, I wave toward the bridge at the right from where I am. Raising his right arm, he waves toward the bridge at the right from where he is. Everything to the right from where I am is to the left from where he is, everything to the right from where he is is to the left from where I am. Can I call that, can he call that, can we call that a difference? I don't know whether a man or a woman is waving from the bridges to me, to him. Because we are looking at the bridges while waving to each other. And in case a man or a woman on the bridges sees us waving to each other, he would have to, she would have to assume that we are not waving at him, at her, but at each other. And why shouldn't the one opposite not assume that I'm waving at him, and why shouldn't I assume that the one opposite is waving at me? Who waved first? I or both of us at the same time or he?

"Do you know me?" I call out.

"No," calls a rower.

"Maybe," calls a second rower.

"Quiet," calls a third rower. "We're having a race on Sunday!"

The three rowers turn their heads toward the one opposite, toward me, and the other way around. They row next to each other, passing each other, overtaking each other, toward the bridge on the right. Sometimes their boats are at the same level, sometimes one boat is ahead of the other two, sometimes two boats are ahead of the third by half a length, at most by a length. The one opposite must ask questions like me. To whom does he ask questions? Does he ask the rowers? Does he ask me as I ask him? Does he ask me what I ask him? I hear him asking me nothing as he must hear me asking him nothing. Only the rowers feel they are being spoken to. Because they turn their heads to this and to the opposite shore, because they answer, "No, maybe, quiet, we're having a race on Sunday."

Lots of questions can be asked to which these are possible answers.

"Is the water cold?" I call out to three rowers rowing up behind the three rowers.

"No," calls the first, probably because before getting into his boat he stepped into the water.

"Maybe," calls the second, probably because before getting into his boat he did not step into the water.

"Quiet," calls the third, probably annoyed because he is half a length behind the two other boats. "We're having a race on Sunday!"

And again the rowers turn their heads to the opposite shore, to this shore, and the other way around.

Perhaps the one opposite, to find out the questions to which these are possible answers, also asked the rowers the same question or a similar one, for instance, "Is the water deep?" or, "Are you rowing again tomorrow?" or, "Are you going to win the race?" or, "Have you seen my wife, my son, my grandson?"

Perhaps he asked, not me, as I did him, but the rowers or one of the rowers because he looked familiar to him, "Do you know me?"

He sits opposite, extended. He has stretched his arms above his head. I notice that I am stretching my arms.

Sitting on backless benches is uncomfortable. That may be the reason so few people sit here—that is, fewer than few, only two, the one opposite and I. That may be the reason we look at each other. Because if a number, or at least a few were here, we would look at each other only now and then and mostly at the others. I let my arms fall. With my feet I scrape together the gravel, the dust, the butts. The one opposite is covered by a cloud of dust for a moment. Or is it the cloud of dust in front of me that blocks my view of the one opposite, that must block his view of me? The rowboats are being rowed toward shore. A tugboat is passing under the bridge to the right. It pulls along a scow full of coal. Those walking on the bridge to the right stand bent over the wall. The rowboats rock in the waves that quickly move to the shores. The tugboat passing by blocks my view of the one opposite, blocks the view of me of the one opposite. Behind the end of the tugboat receding to the left I see the one opposite leaning all the way over to the right looking at me, he must see me from where he is, leaning all the way over to the left looking at him behind the end of the tugboat receding for him to the right. Perhaps he assumed, feared, hoped that I had made off in the meantime, just as I assumed— that is, hoped, and by no means feared—that he made off in the meantime. The scow passes by. I could jump up, I could run toward the bridge on the left alongside the scow and concealed by the scow. How fast is the boat going? When would the one opposite see me running along behind the boat? The one opposite wouldn't have to wait for me to become visible behind the boat, he would have to wait only until the end of the scow was past. Then he would know what was up. Then he would know that I was running, running away alongside the boat. He wouldn't have to be a good runner to catch up with me.

But perhaps he is one, the one who's jumped up. But perhaps he is one, the one who's now running alongside the scow and, concealed by the scow, toward the bridge on the left, which for him is on the right. Or perhaps he is simply standing up, has stood up, is simply going away, went away. The scow is soon past. I lie down on the bench on my stomach, my head turned toward the bridge on the right. Behind the end of the scow receding to the left, lying on the bench, I look over the river. I straighten up to see more accurately whether the bench opposite is empty, I see the one opposite straighten up, probably to see more accurately whether this bench here is empty. I sit down on the bench. I stretch out my arm to the one opposite, see the one opposite standing on the bench, stretching out his arm toward me. I mean him, he means me. This time no mistake is possible.

"What do you want?" I call.

This time there is no rowboat between us. This time no rower asks, this time no rower answers, this time no rower turns his head.

Did the one opposite ask anything? Did the one opposite understand my question? Did the one opposite answer my question? Is the one opposite asking himself whether I asked him anything? Is the one opposite asking himself whether I understood his question, whether I answered his question?

I walk up and down in front of the bench, I see the one opposite walking up and down in front of the bench. A long procession of people is walking along the gravel path. It blocks my view of the one opposite, it blocks the one opposite's view of me.

Ahead of them all, the woman who is as young and as stout as an old woman, carries a pillow. The man who is as old and as thin as a young man walks behind, keeping two paces away. He has hunched up his shoulders, he casts down his eyes, he presses the crown of his hat against his fly, he puts his chin sometimes on the right sometimes on the left shoulder, as though he were ashamed. Two old women, perhaps the grandmothers, are following him, in their Sunday clothes. Each one pushes an empty baby carriage with lace pillows, a lace coverlet. At each step they throw furious looks at each other or at the carriage of the other from under their broad hat brims. The two old men behind them, perhaps the grandfathers, talk to them soothingly.

"Some use will surely be found for the carriage," they say.

"Necessity is the mother of invention," they say.

"Now we don't know what to do with the carriages," they say, "and soon we won't know what to do with the children." Women join them, perhaps the older, the younger sisters of the woman—that is, the sisters-in-law of the man—perhaps the younger, the older sisters of the man—that is, the sisters-in-law of the woman—perhaps the wives of the men who are walking along behind. These men may possibly be the older, the younger brothers of the woman—that is the brothers-in-law of the man—possibly the younger, the older brothers of the man—that is, the brothers-in-law of the woman—possibly the husbands of the sisters of the man or of the woman. So they would all have to be the daughters and sons as well as the daughters-in-law and the sons-in-law of both couples of parents of the married couple who are walking behind the married couple. The way it looks, these couples of parents of the married couple as well as of the other married couples joining them are the grandparents of the infants, children, schoolchildren, and adolescents, some of whom are being led, some of whom are walking by

themselves between the rows. Hence these would have
to be brothers and sisters or cousins to each other as well
as grandsons and granddaughters of both couples of
grandparents as well as the children or the nephews and
nieces of those sisters and brothers and men and women
married into the family, who must be related or related
by marriage, if it's not a question of friends or married
couples close to the family. But perhaps these older
women whom I take to be the sisters or sisters-in-law
of the woman or of the man, are their aunts and hence
the sisters and sisters-in-law of one of the two couples
of grandparents, in case they're grandparents, in case
they're couples. But perhaps those older men whom I take
to be the brothers or the brothers-in-law of the woman
or of the man, are their uncles and hence the brothers
and brothers-in-law, but perhaps only neighbors or acquaintances of one of the two couples of grandparents,
in case they're couples. And why not brother and sisters,
and why not old people who know each other who have
gotten into conversation with each other while sitting on
park benches, who perhaps said to each other, "Come
along. It can't do any harm. For that matter it's no further to go there than to the park."

But assuming it's a question of grandparents, and the
baby carriages support that view, and the hostile glances
of both old women support that view, then those older
women and those older men would have to be the great-
aunts and the great-uncles, and not the parents or the
aunts and uncles of those children who then, for their
part, only to some extent, if at all, would have to be their
grandchildren and to some extent, if at all, their nephews
and nieces, and hence only to some extent brothers and
sisters to each other or cousins, to some extent nephews
or nieces and uncles or aunts and all sorts of things to

each other, just as they would have to be, for instance, the brothers and sisters, and, and at that, if there is any blood relationship at all, the sisters-in-law and brothers-in-law of the married couple at the head of the procession, in case it's a married couple and not a father and daughter—and then I would be unable to disentangle the relationships of the individuals to each other—because the difference in age is considerable and I hear the man whispering, "My child," and I can't determine whom he means, because he keeps turning his head in all directions—or, to continue, uncle and niece or a male acquaintance who has turned up accidentally next to the woman who to all appearances has not walked on ahead accidentally, and who may not even be an acquaintance of the woman but is only an acquaintance of a member of the procession.

"Show Baby Victor," cry the women.

The man behind the woman at the head of the procession stretches out his arms holding the hat. The woman puts the pillow on them. She lifts an infant out of the hollow of the pillow. He is so small that he fits into her hands, which she has raised to the level of her breast, palms upturned and the hands separated from each other by only the breadth of a hand. His arms and legs fill only half the arms of his baby jacket, half the legs of his baby pants. The ends hang limply down from his motionless arms and legs, the way it is with an amputee. His head is bluish and bald. His head is almost the size of the rump, including the legs. His eyes are closed. But he is not sleeping. He is whimpering, opening wide his toothless jaws, with a soft high-pitched whimper, and as he whimpers, a white liquid trickles in fits and starts from the corners of his mouth.

"Oh how sweet he is, how sweet!" cry the women. They

leave the men and the children. They rush over. They gather in a circle, ringing their hands and shuffling their feet. "You could eat him, you could eat him!" they cry. They bite their lower lips. They move toward this bench.

It is advisable to walk away. I start walking, I see the one opposite walking. We walk to the bridge on the right. Is he going in my direction? Am I going in his direction? Who went first? I lie down on the strip of grass. I do three somersaults. I stand up.

"Hurray!" the rowers call out to the one opposite to me.

That can't be an old man over there opposite, who is doing somersaults like myself, not a grown man, not a young man, who is doing handstands, headstands over there, turning cartwheels like myself, who takes off his jacket and throws it into the water like myself, takes off his shoes and stockings as I do, jumping barefoot over the signs as I do, whom the rowers call to as they do to me, "That's forbidden!" who jumps up on benches over there, runs along benches, moves toward the bridge on the right jumping from bench to bench as I do, who goes up the stairs as I do, who is no longer visible to me as perhaps I am not to him, who may be moving across the bridge to this shore as I move to the opposite shore across the bridge, who perhaps lowers his head, walking across the bridge, so that he doesn't see me, just as I lower my head, walking across the bridge, so that I don't see him.

"I told you to wait," my father calls behind me. "Why didn't you wait?" my father calls behind me.

I wince. I stand still. I hear my father's stomach rumble.

"Be quiet!" cries my father, a little farther away. "I don't want to listen!" cries my father farther away. "Not a word!" cries my father still farther away.

I walk toward the opposite shore, walk through main

streets past big buildings, department stores, churches, movie houses, walk through side streets past apartment houses. I come to a stop in front of a house, lean against the front.

"Come in to dinner now!" a woman calls to me from a window on the ground floor. "Your father has been at the table for quite a while already."

I step back from the front of the house. I look up at the window.

"Come on then, quickly. It'll all get cold!" calls the woman. She turns back into the room. "Standing outside," she says, "acting as though it were none of his business."

The street door isn't locked. I push it open. The front door to the apartment stands open. I step into a hall.

"Close the door," calls the woman.

I close the front door and step into the dining room. A man and a woman sit opposite each other at a covered dining-room table. The woman sits with her back to the dining-room door, her face toward the window. The man sits with his back to the window. The chair between them is empty. The man has tucked the ends of his napkin behind his collar. He props the palms of his hands on the table, to the right and the left, next to the knife and the fork. He raises his behind a little from the chair. He leans across the table so that his napkin hangs down into his empty plate and he can see what is in the dishes. Then he lowers his behind onto the seat. Then he pitches in. He serves himself with the serving fork, with the serving spoon, one forkful after another, one after another, until he has a great heap on his plate.

And as I sit down between them, and as the woman serves me a heap, the man is mashing down the vegetables and potatoes with a fork, the man is cutting up the meat into big pieces with his knife, and pouring gravy over everything with the gravy ladle.

And while the woman is mashing down my heap and cutting up my meat into small pieces and pouring gravy over everything, the man starts to eat. His belly touches the edge of the table, there is a gap between his thighs wide enough for a head to fit in, his legs are wrapped around the chair legs. He carries big forkfuls to his mouth and chews them with great care, his eyes fixed on the head of the woman, who is now serving herself. Her head lowered, she sits opposite the man. As he chews, the man loads his fork up again, lifts it fully loaded up to his lips, and while holding it ready in front of his lips, he pushes scattered fragments of food together on his plate into a new pile with his knife. When the lumps in his cheeks get smaller, when they disappear, when the man has finished chewing, his eyes move away from the woman's head. The man looks askance at the forkful. He opens his mouth wide.

"Eat now," says the woman into her food, "and don't look at your father while he eats, it spoils his appetite."

I take the spoon in my hand. I lower the spoon to the pile on my plate. I see the woman's fingers holding on to the rim of the plate.

"What's the matter with you?" says the woman.

The man is holding the fully loaded fork ready at the level of his mouth, the prongs so close to his lips that I'm afraid he might hurt himself.

"But who are you?" says the woman. She pulls the plate away. I sit there holding the spoon in my hand.

The man overturns the whole forkful back onto the plate. He pushes himself and his chair back from the table with his feet. He jumps up from the chair. He lowers his face very close to my face.

"Who?" he cries. "Who?"

I see his wide open mouth, his prominent canines. I hear my spoon falling on the carpet.

THE LORD

I AM LYING in the dark, covered up to the throat, my face
turned toward a door. Light comes in, between the
threshold and the door, between the door frame and the
door, through the cracks in the door panel, through the
keyhole. I recognize the outlines of two figures. Motionless and silent, one of them leans against the wall next to
the door. Motionless and silent, the other crouches in
front of the figure standing up leaning against the wall.
I straighten up, not soundlessly. And while one figure
remains standing motionless and silent leaning against
the wall, the other gives a soft cry, leaps up with creaking knees, flings itself at the figure standing motionless
and silent, embraces it around the middle with one arm,
reaches over with the other to the door knob, turns it,
and pushes open the door.

Effortlessly, with one arm, she drags out of the room
a man who is taller and broader than she. In the light of
the hall I recognize him from the back. He is all dressed
up, in a black suit and a top hat. He wears white gloves
on his hands. He has spread out his arms. I hear her locking him into the adjoining room.

"Don't you recognize me?" she sings. She switches on the light. I shade my eyes against the light with my hand. I see her standing on the threshold. She is wearing a long-sleeved, high-necked black dress. The tips of the skirt hang down on both sides almost to her ankles. I do not recognize her.

"I'm your grandmother," she sings.

She comes toward me, at every step lifting her feet very high from the tile floor, putting them down with a thump, walking with her skirt blowing out, her upper arms standing out from her rump. As I see her coming toward me in this way, I think that the only thing that stops her from flying away is the weight of her heavy shoes.

"You've grown even thinner, my baby," she says. She claps her hands. They are long-fingered and thin. The bones stand out on the backs of the hands, and over the bones the bumps on the bones and over the bumps on the bones the pale blue veins. On the third finger of her right hand she wears two rings. These rings are so loose that at every motion of her hand they slip down as far as the joint of the third finger, which is bent, with the finger-tip pressed into the palm of the hand.

"You were here once before," she says. She turns around, moves toward the stove, lifting her feet high off the tile floor at every step as though surmounting obstacles. Her ankles are as thin as wrists, the bones stand out to the right and the left. They gleam bluishly through her stockings, as blue as the veins standing out on her calves. She stands motionless for a moment, her hands stretched out in front of her, nine fingers spread out and the third finger bent, she leans over with creaking knees, and picks a hammer from a box underneath the stove.

"It's midnight," she sings. "You'll have to go back to sleep now." And carrying the hammer in front of her with both hands, she goes out of the kitchen.

I hear her opening the door of the adjoining room. I hear her shoes thumping on the floor. She moves back and forth, my grandmother, she opens a closet door, she shuts it.

"What must be," she sings, "must be!"

Then she starts hitting the wall violently with the hammer. And while she hammers, the kitchen clock strikes. I try to count the strokes of the clock. But with all my grandmother's hammering, with the irregular onset of the strokes of all the other clocks above me and below me, with the strokes of a church-tower clock starting up in the middle and drowning out all the other clocks, but not my grandmother's hammer strokes, I lose count.

"God almighty," I hear a tenant yell, "this constant hammering!"

I lie back again. I hear my grandmother murmuring something incomprehensible. Sometimes she sings more than she murmurs, sometimes she murmurs more than she sings. Between times she falls on the floor with creaking knees, she slides over the squeaking boards, and interrupting her murmuring, her singing, she smacks her lips, between times she jumps up from the floor with creak-knees, walks over the squeaking boards to the sound of her thumping shoes, she moves a piece of furniture in one direction, smacks her lips, moves a piece of furniture in another direction, gives a smacking sound with her lips, and all this without going on with her murmuring during the backward and forward motions.

I wake up every hour, whenever my grandmother jumps up to the strokes of the church-tower clock, gives a cry, like someone roughly awakened, whenever she goes on murmuring more loudly and more incomprehensibly, my grandmother, whenever she sings more than murmurs, whenever she mumbles more than sings.

I hear her slamming the front door in the morning, locking it.

I jump out of bed, run along the hall. I press down the latch of the front door, pull at the latch. I hear my grandmother going up the stairs to the sound of her thumping shoes. I turn around, try the latches of two doors by pressing them down. They're locked. No keys stick out of the keyholes. I walk past the hall mirror, which hangs so high that I can't see my face, past the little table under the mirror.

White paper inscribed with black letters hangs in square gilt picture frames behind glass along the walls of the hall, separated from each other at regular distances by the length or the breadth of a frame. It is inscribed in such a way that between the first letter of every line and the frame, so that between the last letter of every line and the frame, so that between all the letters of the first, the topmost line and the frame as well as between all the letters of the last, the bottommost lines and the frame there are identical blanks as wide as a line. There are gaps the size of a letter between all the letters, so that it is hard, not only for me, but perhaps also for someone who can read to tell where one word ends and the following word begins. But it is not only between the letters of one line, but also between the letters of two lines that there are gaps the size of a letter and the length of a line. The letters of all the lines stand one beneath the other, the gaps between the letters of all the lines lie one beneath the other, so that, aside from the horizontally inscribed lines and the uninscribed lines lying between them, vertically inscribed as well as uninscribed lines are formed. The number of letters in a horizontal line corresponds to the number of lines on a sheet of paper, so that the written part, even though broken by the gaps between two letters, between two lines, is in a square shape, like the frame and the margin between the frame and the written part. The intervening spaces between the letters and the written lines take up more space than the letters.

I take a picture off the hook, look at it, look in vain for a period inside the lines or at the ends of the lines or at the end of the last line of the written part, so that it is hard, perhaps not only for me, but also for someone who can read, especially in case it was difficult for him to begin with, to tell where one word ends and the following word begins, and it is even harder to tell where one sentence stops and the following sentence begins, or whether one has been started and finished on the sheet of paper altogether and not just been carried forward or broken off. Because perhaps the writer had chosen too long a sentence to copy out and broke it off, perhaps in the middle of a word, when the square which he intended to inscribed fully was filled up with letters, and carried it forward to the next picture to the right or the left, to the next one after that, and so forth, or else the writer might have chosen short sentences and dispensed with periods, so that the gaps would at least be evenly empty and there would be no difference between empty gaps and ones insufficiently filled with periods here and there. Because the letters, though they're of the same size, have different shapes. Because many letters of the same shape are repeated, it's true, but some are repeated more often, others more seldom, some of them appear only once, and not only that, the letters that repeat themselves are irregularly distributed inside the square of the written part, sometimes they stand next to each other on this side and the other side of the gap the size of a letter, sometimes in the same line, or under each other on this side

and the other side of the gap the length of a line, sometimes they stand a number of lines away from each other
or at the opposite ends of the square. On the glass that
covers the written part, perhaps so that no one will be
able to cross out even a single letter, I see fingerprints,
partly among the letters, partly in the gaps between two
letters. Perhaps they are the attempts of one reader to
point out an important word to another reader, perhaps
the attempts of a reader to keep two words or two
sentences apart from each other. Perhaps, also, these are
the places where the reader was thinking over what he
had been reading and left his finger on the place so that
after thinking it over he would know what word he had
to start in reading.

I turn the picture around. I see that most of the letters
change their appearance and either mean something
different or nothing at all any more, as, for instance, and
in order to pick out a letter that's easier to describe, this
half-circle open on the right, if it is turned upside down,
it opens on the left and then resembles another letter
whose half-circle opening on the left is blocked by a
vertical stroke, or this letter consisting of two strokes
slanting toward each other and meeting at their lower
ends that when it's put upside down resembles another
letter, whose two strokes slanting toward each other and
meeting at their upper ends are united by a horizontal
stroke in the middle. Other letters, even when turned
upside down, keep their shape, and so their meaning,
as, for instance, and in order to pick out a letter that is
more easily described, this letter that consists of a vertical stroke and nothing else, or this letter that consists
of two vertical strokes of the same length standing next
to each other and bound together at half their length
by a shorter horizontal stroke, which when put on its

side is unreadable or would be readable as some other one that the one who wrote on the sheet of paper, if he exists, did not make use of, or this letter that also consists of two vertical strokes the same length standing next to each other and in contrast to the preceding one are not bound together by a horizontal stroke at half-length but at their ends by a diagonal stroke, where this diagonal stroke ties together the upper end of the vertical stroke standing on the left with the lower end of the vertical stroke standing at the right, or for instance this letter represented by a circle that is more oval than round, which if need be could also be deciphered even if laid on its side. Aside from these examples chosen for the sake of greater ease of description, I see a letter that when turned upside down as well as on both its sides remains unchanged and hence readable. This letter consists of two slanting strokes the same length running toward each other in opposite directions and crossing each other in the middle at right angles.

I pass my forefinger under the topmost line from left to right, the way I have observed people do when they read. The first letter after the marginal strip the length of a line after the frame consists of a half-circle open at the right, from whose lower end a short horizontal strip runs into the middle of the hollow of the half-circle. The second, already described letter after the gap the size of a letter consists of a circle that's more oval than round. The third letter, not yet described, after the gap the size of a letter consists of a vertical stroke that is just as long as the stroke of this letter that consists only of this stroke. At its upper end there is a horizontal stroke, a little shorter, that is cut in two by the vertical stroke so that both halves of the horizontal stroke stick out the same length at both sides of the vertical. As the fourth letter and after the gap as big as a letter this third letter already described is repeated. After another gap as big as a letter there follows as the fifth letter one that consists of two interlocking half-circles half as big as the already described half-circles. In which the upper half-circle opens at the right and the lower half-circle at the left, in which the lower end of the upper half-circle is linked to the upper end of the lower half-circle. This letter is one of those letters that even when turned upside down retain their form, and so their meaning. After another gap as big as a letter there follows as the sixth letter one consisting of a vertical stroke that is just as long as the stroke of the letter that consists only of this stroke and has already been described a number of times. At its upper half and actually at the right of the stroke hangs a half-circle that opens to the left but is closed off by the half-stroke, and that is just as big as the two half-circles of the fifth letter that's just been described. The seventh letter following after the gap as big as a letter consists, like the sixth one just described, of this vertical stroke as well as of this half-circle that hangs to the right of the stroke and opens to the left but is closed off by the half-stroke. In addition a shorter stroke slants down to the right from the place where the lower end of the half-circle intersects the middle of the stroke. This stroke ends on a line with the vertical stroke, moved off by only the diameter of the half-circle. If this seventh letter, not very easily described, were followed after the gap as big as a letter by an eighth letter that was just as hard to describe, I don't know whether I'd go on with the description of this topmost line of the written part. But there follows this letter that in my opinion is the most easily described and, on top of that, has already been described, consisting of one vertical stroke and nothing else. As the ninth letter after the gap in the line, along which I pass my finger from left to right in the manner of someone reading, I find a letter that has also been described already and is, if I think of the description of the other letters, relatively easy to describe. It is the letter represented by a half-circle opening at the right. There follows, and why should I keep mentioning the gap, as the tenth letter this letter that is written in front of a large number of letters, perhaps in front of half the alphabet, that consists of two vertical strokes the same length standing side by side and tied together by a shorter horizontal stroke at half-length, which, when it is turned upside down is still read as the same one. The letter following the tenth, and now it would be helpful to know what number comes after ten, corresponds to the already described third letter as well as to the fourth letter that repeats itself after the third. The letter following the one after the tenth I described ahead of maybe an alphabet of letters. It's this half-circle opening to the left, whose opening is blocked by a vertical stroke. The letter that follows the one after the number that follows ten is joined by this letter that's so easily described, which consists of only one vertical stroke.

Now that I have described and counted from left to right the letters beyond more than half the line, now that my forefinger is in the right half of the picture, it occurs to me that I can count those letters after ten, for whose more accurate determination I lack the names of the numbers, just as easily from right to left. I count from right to left another ten letters added to those ten counted from left to right. It turns out that that letter that's so easily described and was described last from left to right, is the tenth counted from right to left. I lack only the names of the numbers of two letters, that is, to the right and left of the gap the size of a letter in the middle of the line, the name of the number of the letter to the right of the letter that's tenth when counted from left to right as well as the name of the number of the letter left of the letter that's tenth when counted from right to left.

I'm going to continue describing from left to right one after another the letters now counted from right to left. This letter that is tenth when counted from right to left is followed by a ninth letter that consists of one vertical stroke and from whose upper, from whose lower end, from whose center a shorter horizontal stroke each runs to the right. These three horizontal strokes are the same length. The description of the eighth letter counted from right to left is going to give me great difficulty. It consists of four slanting strokes of which, and I'm now counting from left to right, the first and the second run slantingly toward each other in such a way that they meet at their lower ends, of which the second and the third run slantingly toward each other in such a way that they meet at their upper ends, of which the third and the fourth run slantingly toward each other in such a way that they meet at their lower ends. If now I cut, and I'll be careful not to, this letter in two at the place where the second and the third slanting stroke meet at their upper ends, then I would twice have that letter already described whose two strokes running into each other slantingly meet at their lower ends. Counting from right to left there follows as the seventh letter, the one already described whose two strokes running toward each other slantingly and meeting at their upper ends are connected in the middle by a horizontal stroke. The sixth letter counting from right to left corresponds to the tenth

counted from left to right. The fifth letter counted from
right to left corresponds to the seventh counted from left
to right. The fourth letter counted from right to left
corresponds to the sixth counted from right to left, which
for its part corresponds to the tenth counted from left to
right. Thus this letter is repeated three times in the line.
In addition, the third letter counted from right to left,
and accordingly repeated twice, corresponds to the ninth
counted from right to left. In addition, the second letter
counted from right to left corresponds to the tenth counted
from right to left, which for its part corresponds to the
eighth counted from left to right. Thus this letter is repeated in the line three times, like the fourth counted from
right to left or the sixth counted from right to left or the
tenth counted from left to right. Finally my finger comes
to rest under the last letter of the line, counted from left to
right, the first letter of the line counted from right to left,
this letter is repeated in the line four times. It corresponds
to the third and the fourth of the letters counted from
left to right as well as to the letter following the tenth
letter that is also counted from left to right.

And as I pass my forefinger along a line of letters that
may produce a word, several words, perhaps even a
sentence, that says something, perhaps something it would
be useful for me to know, I cannot decipher a single one
of the letters, to say nothing of a word or indeed a
sentence. I turn the picture, standing in the hall. I turn
over in my mind which is up, which down, which right,
and which left. Then I take my bearings with the help
of the hanging hook, and thank God there is only a single
one used for the whole picture, and I hang the picture
on the wall. I go into the kitchen and pull up the blind.
I see a brick church opposite. Through the open church
gates walk old men in black suits and black hats, old

women in black coats and black hats. The men take their hats off their heads, the women keep their hats on their heads. The men and the women stick their right hands into a basin near the entrance, take them out, and hold on to their lowered faces. As the bell strokes die away, music and singing sound from the church.

I sit down on the sofa. Above the sofa, on a wooden shelf, between two pots of primroses, stands a photograph with three white margins in a gilt frame behind glass. A frame half as wide would have been enough for the narrow photograph. It shows a front view of a young gentleman who is just as dressed up as the man I saw only from the back and fleetingly when my grandmother dragged him out. He, too, wears a black suit, a top hat, and a white glove on his left hand. He is stepping out of one half of a tall gate not unlike the church gate opposite. And while in the right half of the picture after the narrow white margin, there can be seen besides the gate posts only a dark space as wide as a man, with a few light spots, which is probably supposed to give a view into the interior of the building, and a tiny section of his left shoulder, the left half of the picture is not enough for the man. Before the end of his right shoulder the picture comes to an end without a margin. His right arm with its hand, which is perhaps just as white-gloved, is missing. A section of his right black trouser leg is covered by white cloth. The man is looking earnestly down over his right, his cut-off, shoulder at something that remains hidden from the observer of the picture. Fingerprints are scattered over the visible parts of the man's body.

"That is your grandfather," says my grandmother. She goes into the kitchen to the sound of the church bells. She wears a black hat whose veil hangs down over her eyes. She holds a prayer book in her hands. She comes toward me, with the forefinger of her right hand she puts a new fingerprint on top of the fingerprints on top of the glass cover over the young gentleman's photograph, lifts her forefinger off the photograph, with her left hand embarrassedly turns the two rings around on the third finger of her right hand and, putting her head on her raised left shoulder and indicating the empty place between the frame and the left lengthwise side without a margin of the photograph next to the right, the cut-off, shoulder of the young gentleman, she says, "Those were the days," she sings, "Those were the days!" Then, giggling, she leaves the kitchen with raised shoulders. She opens the door of the adjoining room, she falls on the floor with creaking knees.

"It's Sunday," she sings. "Your suffering will soon be over!"

She carries a black suit on a clothes hanger into the kitchen, hangs it on the hook on the kitchen door.

"That is your grandfather's suit," she says.

She moves a chair a little bit away from the table, drags over an ironing board, puts one end on the tabletop, the other end on the back of the chair, so that it lies aslant between the back of the chair, which is the higher by a hand's breadth, and the table, she puts an iron on the end of the ironing board which lies lower on the table, walks around the table to the stove, pulling the electric cord behind her with the plug in her hand, kneels down with creaking knees and sticks the plug into the outlet.

The cord stretches from the outlet under the stove to the iron on the table, rises from the outlet at the height of her calf past the height of the knee to the height of the thigh to the iron. My grandmother separates the two trouser legs, puts one trouser leg lengthwise on the iron-

ing board so that only a section of the second trouser
leg lies on the ironing board and the other section of
second trouser leg hangs down over the end of the ironing board which is higher, then steps over the section of
the cord hanging at knee height, and moistens a white
rag under the water tap at the sink. She takes a step
toward the ironing board, sinks down on her knees and
with the rag in her hand crawls under the ironing board.
She gets to her feet with a groan, puts the small white
rag on the black end of the trouser leg that lies closest
to the lower-lying end of the ironing board with the iron.
She lifts the iron high with her right hand, licks the forefinger on her left hand, then puts her forefinger moist
with saliva against the iron, and nods at the hissing sound
of the saliva evaporating on the hot iron. She puts the iron
on the damp rag on the trouser leg on the ironing board,
lifts it high, to the hissing sound of the water evaporating
on the hot iron, puts the iron back onto the lower-lying
end of the ironing board. She lifts the steaming, moist,
but no longer wet rag off the steaming trouser leg, with an
effort she steps over a section of the cord that hangs
higher than knee-high, she wets the rag under the tap
at the sink once again, falls to her knees, crawls under
the ironing board and, getting to her feet with a groan,
she puts the wet rag next to that place on the section of
trouser leg on which it had lain when the iron had first
been put down. She puts down the iron, lifts it with the
steam rising, puts it back onto the lower-lying end of
the ironing board, goes to wet the rag once again, and so
forth. I sit on the sofa without a word, gaping. I watch
her stepping now and again over sections of cord hanging
higher, falling to her knees now and again another little
distance away from the ironing board, crawling over the
tile floor of the kitchen, bending more deeply each time

under the board, getting to her feet each time, still without having finished ironing the first trouser leg, with a still louder groan and with a more flushed face, on the other side of the ironing board.

The farther away from the lower-lying end of the ironing board, from the end of the trouser leg, she has to put the rag, the more often she pulls the plug to which the cord is attached out of the outlet. It is true that, if she doesn't have a longer cord, and she may have reasons for not buying one, she could move the table with the chair with the board a little closer to the outlet. It is true that she could move the unpressed section of the trouser leg closer to the lower-lying end of the ironing board and so to the iron and so to the plug and to the outlet. But perhaps she has reasons—she may have, she knows something about ironing—for not setting it up that way. It is true she could stick the plug into the outlet on her way to the sink so that the iron will get hot while she wets the rag, while she crawls across the tile floor, applies the rag. But perhaps she has reasons, now, with the cord lying limp on the floor, now, when it would be easy to step over it, to take the reverse course, the more difficult one. That is, she crawls under the ironing board, the whole distance to the outlet, without straightening up, sticks in the plug, and crawls the whole distance back without straightening up and without wetting the rag on the way, she crawls the whole way back under the ironing board. Then she steps over the sections of the cord that lie closer and closer to the table and hence hang higher and higher, steps over the cord to wet the rag. In doing this, she knocks the iron off the board, catches it as it falls and not without skill, but with such haste that she pulls the plug out of the outlet, not always but often enough. Then she crawls back again the same way, groaning and with her fingers burned, under the board through the outlet and then back again and straightens up and steps over the cord, if she manages to raise her legs to such heights.

After she has pressed the first trouser leg as far as the crotch, she takes the trousers off the ironing board, holds them in her outstretched arms around the waistband and at the level of the belt, so that the trouser legs touch the floor, and looks at the crease, her shoulders hunched and her head laid to one side. Then she puts the second trouser leg lengthwise on the ironing board, so that only one section of the first trouser leg, the pressed one, is lying on the ironing board, the other section of the trouser leg is hanging down over the end of the ironing board that lies higher, and presses the second trouser leg in the way described. She steps across the section of the cord close to the table at the level of her thigh, and in doing this she almost always, hardly ever not, pulls the iron off the table and, as she catches the iron, the plug out of the outlet, she falls on the floor on her stomach, she drags herself panting under the ironing board over the tile floor of the kitchen as far as the outlet and back again under the ironing board, she moves her lips, sometimes without a sound, sometimes she mutters something incomprehensible.

She would have to have—no, she must have—her reasons for making ironing so hard for herself. Because why, if she is going to crawl under the board anyhow, doesn't she crawl under the cord, or why, if she is going to step over the cord anyhow, doesn't she step over the board? Because why, if the crawling and the high stepping are such a strain for her that she groans aloud, that she pants, doesn't she take a bigger rag to wet, or for all I care a small one like the one she does take and put a basin of water to wet the rag next to herself on the table? Because why doesn't she take the way to the outlet that is shorter, far more comfortable, and can be taken by everyone, the way to the outlet, the way around the chair, since nothing stands in her way there, neither a board nor a cord, not even an easily surmounted obstacle like a box or a stool? Finally, why doesn't she stand directly in front of the side of the ironing board that lies opposite her, nearer the sink and the outlet, and because of the moving of the table, the chair, the board still nearer, actually right alongside?

My grandmother presses the trousers until noon. It is not until the church bells ring out that she puts away the iron, leaves the trousers, the rag lying there, leaves the tap running, lets the plug fall from her hand, and goes over to the kitchen window.

I stand next to her. And we look down into the street, see the churchgoers stepping out of the church entrance, see them, while pressing their left hand against their stomach—the men their left hand with a hat—dip their right hand into the basin, take it out, tap it against their forehead, then lower their right hand, tap the middle of their chest, make an arc across their body from the middle of the chest to the left shoulder, tap it against that, then drop their hands, the men putting on their hats. Outside other churchgoers wait for the church to empty, some of them greeting each other in groups and chatting together, some of them alone without saying anything or nodding to someone standing in a group or to someone else also standing alone and without saying anything. There are children there, too. Raising their hats or nodding to each other, the ones going out greet the ones coming in and the other way around, shaking hands and exchanging a few words, the ones going out greet the ones coming in and the other way around. The ones going out also greet and speak to each other. Some of them leave together from the church, in rows reaching across the sidewalk.

"So she's there, he's there," mutters my grandmother. "That one isn't, nor she, so she's not, so they again."

Only now and then, when one of the churchgoers going in or going out or waiting to go in looks up at the kitchen window, my grandmother ducks down below the window-sill, now and then bumps into me and looks at me with a shriek.

"Oh," she says, "it's you. What are you shrieking about?"

I sit down on the sofa, see her going over to the stove, stand there a moment without moving, and stretching out her hands in front of her, with nine fingers spread out and one third finger bent over. She leans over with creaking knees, she pulls a tongs out of the box underneath the stove. And carrying the suit and tongs in front of her, she goes out of the kitchen.

She shuts herself up in the adjoining room.

"Today's the day again," she sings.

I hear her walking back and forth, thumping her shoes on the floor, I hear her moving a piece of furniture, hear her muttering, her singsong, the creaking of her knees, the creaking of the bedsprings.

She locks up the adjoining room.

"Put on your Sunday suit," she says. "There will be company today."

She fills a kettle with water at the tap at the sink, puts it on the stove, lights the gas under the kettle, and sticks a whistling plug on the spout of the kettle. She carries one cake after another on cake plates, whipped cream in crystal bowls, through the hall into the room next to the adjoining room.

A table extended at both ends stands in the middle of

this room. Six places are laid on it, one at each table end, two each along the sides of the table. There is a chair in front of each setting. Five of the six chairs have no arms. They have wooden seats and wooden backs. The sixth chair, at the end of the table next to the door, has up-holstered arms and an upholstered back. But instead of a seat, which is what gives a chair meaning, in this sixth chair there is a square hole framed by three sections con-necting the chair legs as well as the unusually high back of the chair. Behind this chair, on a wooden shelf the length of a wall, stand some white candles. My grand-mother must stretch her arm up high with the lighted match to be able to reach the white wicks.

Colored pictures in gilt frames hang on the walls. They represent heads of men and women, with faces that are pale, or bloodshot, or twisted in pain.

My grandmother draws the curtains.

There are three long rings at the doorbell and right after the ringing there is a rapping of knuckles. And while a whisper in many voices rises in front of the door to the apartment, my grandmother hurries over to the door of the room. It is true that she hurries in such a way that she takes more time. Because she doesn't hurry like other people, who take longer strides to cover a more horizontal distance, she just throws her pointed knees twice as high in the air as usual. And while her shoes make a clatter on the floor of the hall in spite of the lightness of her body, the kettle in the kitchen starts whistling, the guests whispering outside the door of the apartment keep ring-ing in long loud rings and knocking.

"Who's that?" sings my grandmother.

"It's us, the guests," the guests sing outside the door.

"Are you in a state of grace?" sings my grandmother.

"We've kept the vigil," sing the guests outside the

door. "We have prayed. We haven't eaten a thing. You can be of good cheer and let us in."

My grandmother opens the door.

Led by my grandmother, the guests come into the room following each other in a row, pass me, go past me around the table, and contemplate the arrangement of the table. I stand along the wall next to the door. I see them coming toward me, their arms sticking out from their rumps, elbows akimbo, nine of their ten fingers spread out and the third finger with two rings slipped down to the joint and the fingertip pressed against the ball of the thumb. They are wearing black, long-sleeved high-necked dresses, which make their thin, lanky figures even thinner and lankier. And while my grandmother raises her feet higher than anyone else from the patterned carpet of the room, and while she looks biggest because her back is bent least, the three other guests behind her raise their feet less high, each one less than the next, but still strikingly high off the carpet, so that the guest coming in at the end of the row comes comparatively close to a normal walk, the three guests coming in behind her each look smaller than the next because their backs are bent more, each one more than the next. And while my grandmother holds her head motionless while contemplating the arrangement of the table, perhaps because the sight of it is familiar, the three guests coming in behind her nod their heads vigorously, each one more than the next, so that the first one behind her nods plainly with approval because she mutters something that sounds like "Look, look!" or "Good, good," and the second one behind her nods more vigorously, it's true, but plainly only partly with approval and partly because of the feebleness of age, because she mutters something that sounds like "Well, well, yes, yes," and the third one behind her nods more vigorously than the other two, it's true, but plainly only because of the feebleness of age, because without expressing herself she walks around the table, she even tries—in vain, but still she tries—to go against the nodding of her head and to shake her head.

"What's this?" say my grandmother's three guests. They remain standing in a row in front of me, they point at me, their hands shaking violently, each one more than the next, their heads shaking violently, each one more than the next.

"That's my grandson," says my grandmother.

"What's this?" repeat the three guests, as though it were incredible for a grandson to stay with his grandmother, and one after the other they turn their heads to my grandmother.

"My grandson," repeats my grandmother.

"Oh, your grandson!" the three guests cry to each other. Their teeth clatter together, they look at me with gently nodding heads. Only the whistling of the kettle can be heard in the kitchen.

And as I shake hands with each one in turn, as I feel their bent third fingers with the rings, my grandmother mentions the names of the three guests in turn, her three sisters.

Martha is the name of the first one behind her. She can recognize me from the distance of my outstretched and her outstretched arm. Maria is the name of the second. She draws me toward her to arm's length and can recognize me from the distance of my outstretched arm. Minna is the name of the third. She draws me to her by the length of her and my arm and can recognize me at the distance of her outstretched hand.

They take their places. Aunt Minna sits down at the right, Aunt Maria sits down at the left, next to the chair without a seat. Aunt Martha sits down at the right next to Aunt Minna. I sit down at the left next to Aunt Maria. Only the two ends of the table are still unoccupied.

The kettle isn't whistling in the kitchen any more.

"Are you ready," sings my grandmother. She puts the coffeepot on the table.

"We are!" sing my grandmother's three sisters. And as they sit there as straight as their age allows, and as they fold their hands on their laps underneath the table top, and as they turn their faces, with slightly twisted smiles, toward the door, into the room comes my grandmother, carrying before her, in both hands, effortlessly, the figure of a man who is taller and broader than she is. He is all dressed up in a black suit and a white shirt. He wears white gloves on his hands. And because he cannot go through the opening of the door with his arms spread out, she turns him sideways. And because he is standing and is stiff, she puts him into the square circle of the chair without a seat. And because he cannot stand by himself on the tips of his toes, which are pressed on top of each other, she slings a rope around the middle of his body and ties him to the back of the chair.

"Doesn't he look like a lord?" sings my grandmother. She takes a couple of steps backward and, putting her head on her shoulder, she looks at him not without pride, not without shame.

"He looks like a lord," sing my grandmother's three sisters. They smile downward in a shamefaced way, with hunched shoulders, past their black clothes. The man's figure is in the light of the candles, looks with a lowered, pain-twisted face toward the coffee cup into which my grandmother is pouring coffee and milk, into which she drops lumps of sugar, in which my grandmother stirs the spoon around, looking toward the cake plate on which my grandmother is putting a piece of cake with a cake knife, on which my grandmother is putting some whipped cream with a spoon, looking down at the napkin that my grandmother, not without some effort, has forced between his chest and his chin supported by his chest.

Then my grandmother, the hostess, pours one cup full of coffee after another, then my grandmother, the hostess, puts one piece of cake after another on the cake plates, and she does this while the three sisters, the three guests, and immediately afterward I spread napkins over our laps.

"Please help yourselves," she says. She sits down on the chair at the other end of the table opposite the figure of the man.

And the four sisters stick their cake forks into the pieces of cake, they break off bits of cake, they spear the broken bits of cake on the prongs of the forks, they raise them to their thin-lipped mouths. They open their mouths, they snap their upper and lower teeth together with a clicking sound. The forks with the speared bits of cake twitch up and down in front of their heads nodding up and down.

"May the taste please You, Lord," they sing.

And with their eyes directed at the forks, they wait for the moment when their mouths, when their fork prongs begin to twitch at each other, and then they push the prongs between their teeth. They put the forks back on the cake plates next to the pieces of cake. They chew the bits of cake while keeping their teeth carefully away from each other by at most the length of a tooth. Out of the corners of their eyes they observe the man's figure. Then they dip the spoons into the coffee cups, and to the sound of the spoons clinking against the coffee cups they mix the coffee with the sugar with the milk. They do not hold the cups by the handles but encircle them with both hands. They lower their faces, bring them closer to the cups by more than half the distance between the table-top and themselves, then they sit as upright as their age allows, they raise the cups from the saucers, and putting the rims of the cups to their lips, and to the clicking sound of the cup rims banging against their teeth, of their teeth banging against the cup rims, they strain themselves more or less, all according to the strength of the jerks of their heads, of their hands, and hence of their teeth, of their cups, to take a gulp of coffee. The coffee slops over the cup rims into the saucers, onto the tablecloth. Around their places I see more or less big brown coffee spots on the white tablecloth.

"Is it good, Lord?" says my grandmother with a trembling voice into her cup, which is jerking comparatively gently. And covering her face with the cup and with her two hands enfolding the cup, she looks past the cup rim at the figure of the man.

Her three sisters also observe, out of the corners of their eyes and past the cup rims, the figure of the man, who is looking toward the tabletop with a lowered, pain-twisted face, his lips pressed hard together.

They all hold their breath, then they put the cups back on the saucers with such violence that the coffee slops over. They let out their breath. The three sisters raise their cake forks to shoulder height, they stick them, with their heads jerkily turned toward my stooping grand-mother, into Aunt Martha's piece of cake, into Aunt Maria's cake plate, into the tablecloth next to Aunt Minna's plate.

"Is it, Lord, because the question is foolish," says Aunt Maria in a trembling voice, "that You do not speak?"

"Or is it because that one there is impure, Lord," says

Aunt Minna in a trembling voice, "that You do not speak?"

And with their cake forks in their hands my grandmother's three sisters point to my grandmother.

My grandmother pushes herself and her chair away from the table with her feet. With creaking knees she lets herself fall to the carpet. Only her face and her folded hands raised over her face, with nine fingers outstretched upward and one third finger bent and squeezed between the palms of her hands, stick out over the tabletop.

"You spoke to me, Lord!" she cries.

"You can't fool us, you hypocrite!" the three sisters cry to my grandmother. "Get up!"

And as my grandmother slowly straightens up, and as she slowly stretches out her arm, and as she points her forefinger at the tied-up figure of the man, motionless and silent, the three sisters let their forks fall from their hands, jump high up off their chairs, and press their fingers against their lips.

"The Lord be my witness!" cries my grandmother. "May my sisters drop dead on the spot if He remained silent!"

The three sisters, offered to the man in this way, stand living and quivering and awaiting their death. They hold their breath as long as they can, perhaps out of fear that it might be the last breath they will ever draw. They exhale, they sink back into their chairs, sit there huddled up, they are not looking at the figure of the man, they are looking with desperate expressions down at their laps.

"You don't like the cake," says my grandmother.

The three sisters jump like people who have been roughly awakened, they seize the forks, stick them into the pieces of cake, break off bits of cake, spear them on the fork prongs and raise them to their mouths. They snap shut their jaws, wait for the moment when their fork prongs, twitching up and down more violently than before, and their mouths, twitching up and down more violently than before, are at the same level, and then, if the bit of cake hasn't meanwhile fallen from their forks onto their laps, they push the prongs between their teeth or into their noses, whereupon the bit of cake falls onto the laps onto the carpet or onto the chin, whereupon the bit of cake also falls onto the laps onto the carpet. They leave the cups standing in the saucers, enfold them with both hands, they lower their faces and, with their teeth clinking against the cup rims, they lap up the coffee, if it hasn't slopped over onto the saucers onto the tablecloth. From one forkful to the next, whether it gets into their mouths or falls onto their laps onto the carpet, from one gulp to the next, whether the coffee trickles into their mouths or whether it slops over onto the saucers onto the tablecloth, they twitch less violently, finally, when they have emptied the contents of the plates into their mouths, onto the carpet, when they have poured the contents of the cups into their mouths, onto the tablecloth, they twitch no more violently than they did at the first bite, than they did at the first gulp.

They sit up as straight as their age allows. My grandmother pours coffee again, serves pieces of cake again.

"Why are you so quiet," she says, "now that the Lord is ready, perhaps, to grant you a hearing?"

"Now that I shall not be tarrying much longer on earth," says Aunt Minna after a pause, "I should have liked to question the Lord about the four last things."

"About Death," says Aunt Maria after a pause.

"About the Last Judgment," says Aunt Martha after a pause.

"About Heaven and Hell," says Aunt Minna after a pause. They place their hands around their ears. With listening expressions they turn their faces to the roped figure of the Lord sitting motionless and without a word.

"You ought not to bother the Lord with questions," says my grandmother after a pause, "that your confessors can answer."

"We ought to know," say my grandmother's three sisters, "what we can ask the Lord."

They hastily empty the plates, swallowing big pieces of cake or throwing them on the carpet. They hastily empty the cups, pouring great gulps of coffee into themselves or onto the tablecloth. They nod to my grandmother.

"What must be asked," sings my grandmother, "should be asked."

"Have You forgotten, Lord," sings Aunt Minna, "where You once hung, Lord, and where You would still be hanging today if we had not come by? You were hanging alongside a highway, Lord, naked and with no roof over Your head. You were worse off, Lord, than a tramp, a vagrant, a vagabond, who seeks shelter from the storm in barns, in stalls, under trees. No pilgrims moved past You, to rest, to pray, to call You to mind. Herds of cattle, flocks of sheep moved past You. But those who were driving them past, the farm hands, the maidservants, had eyes only for their cattle, their sheep, and not for Your agony, had hands only to keep their herds together with whips, and not to cross themselves with, and not to pray with. We grieved sorely for You, Lord. We prayed until it grew dark. With these hands we dug You up. On these backs we bore You along the highway into this city. And our way was longer, Lord, than the one You took to Golgotha. And our burden was heavier, Lord, than the one You bore. For it was not only like Yourself, a cross we bore, we bore You as well. And we did not fall only three times, like Yourself, our way was all getting up and stepping out only to fall again, and the pauses for rest where we lay stretched out were longer than yours, Lord, and not only in the dust, Lord, until the pains of falling subsided. Your falls, Lord, have been counted, and any-one who knows how to count knows them by heart, our countless falls remain uncounted. We bore You into my house. And You had a roof over your head. You were passed by heedlessly, by those farm hands and maidserv-ants, but the hole impressed them. And they hurried to the peasants they served.

" 'There's a hole,' they said.

"The peasants harnessed oxen, cows, or horses to their carts. They drove, led by the farm hands and maidserv-ants, to the place, Lord, where You had hung. They got out of their carts, they stood around the hole, and they looked into that hole.

" 'Where there is a hole,' they said to each other, 'some-thing is missing.'

" 'Where something is missing,' they said to each other, 'something has been taken away.'

" 'Where something has been taken away without a trade,' they said to each other, 'something has been stolen.'

" 'But how can we catch the thief if we don't know what it was he stole?' they said to each other. And be-cause no one had an answer, they drove back to their village. They went from farmyard to farmyard, they asked who was missing something, and what it was that was missing. Thereupon all the peasants of the village made up long lists of the things they were missing. But these were things that not only would not have fitted into that hole, not into a farmyard, but would not have fitted even into a cathedral. But these were things of such size, of such weight, or of such number that it would have taken an army of thieves to carry them off. But the longer the peasants thought of things they were missing, the greater grew their outcries, their lamentations, their rage at the thieves. They went before the judges and laid complaints against the thieves. But when they were given a hearing, though they could report with great eloquence what expensive things they were missing, they could not report when and where and from whom they had secured them. Some of them fell stubbornly silent. Others stammered out the names of their relatives and friends, living and dead. They also maintained that they had only partly secured these things, inherited them, or gotten them as gifts. But the judge found that the smaller portion of the people named were not richer and not poorer than the peasants, that the larger portion of the people named were poorer than the peasants, even paupers, and would have needed a gift or an inheritance more than the peasants. Then the peasants went back to their farmyards with empty hands. And they grumbled over their fate, which kept things from them that it granted others.

"During Sunday mass the pastor preached to the congregation a sermon against avarice.

" 'You should not lay yourselves up treasure on earth,' he said, 'says the Lord, where moths and rot will consume it and where thieves will dig it up and steal it. The foxes, says the Lord, have holes, and the birds beneath the sky have nests, but the Son of Man has no place to lay His head.' Then he hit his head. 'But I buried Him with my own hands!' he cried, broke off his sermon, abandoned the congregation, and hurried off to the judge.

"He did not lay a charge against the thief on account of theft. He laid a charge against the robber on account of robbery.

"We asked You, Lord, whether we should stand up. Why are You silent, Lord?"

"Have you forgotten, Lord," sings Aunt Maria, "how Minna, our sister, lost weight day after day, how she cried aloud whenever a mailman rang the bell, a gasman, a salesman, how she opened the door, how she cried out, 'I confess,' how she broke down and had to be carried off to bed by mailmen, by gasmen, by salesmen, how she cried out when the kettle whistled on the stove, how she cried out, finally, whenever she heard the bell ring when no one was ringing, how she heard it whistling when nothing whistled?

"We asked You, Lord, if you are content with my house. But You were silent, Lord. We prayed until it grew dark. We took You down from the cross. We dressed You in the finest clothes of the deceased husband of Minna, our sister, who has suffered for You. And because she was down with a fever, there were only three of us to carry You. One carried Your cross. Two walked beneath Your outspread arms. And we carried You through dark alleys. And we mingled with harlots and thieves. And we chattered sinful nonsense, and we danced blasphemously around the cross. And the harlots and thieves laughed and applauded and let us go by without suspicion and held us for their own. And we carried You into my house. And You had a roof over Your head. And we undressed You. And we hung You on the Cross. And we did atonement for our speech."

"Have you forgotten, Lord," sings Aunt Martha, "how our sister Maria became talked about on Your account? 'You must have visitors?' our neighbor asked the very next morning. And when Maria our sister was silent, our neighbor went and spread rumors about her.

" 'She has a man at her place,' she said. 'I saw him with my own eyes. It can't be her own husband, because he's been dead and buried for years. And she never had any sons.'

"And when our sister Maria went to mass, the people called out after her, 'What did you choose, O bride, the veil or the shroud?'

"And we asked You, Lord, if You are content with my house. We prayed until it grew dark. We dressed You in the finest clothes of the deceased husband of Maria, our sister, who has suffered for You. And because she couldn't let herself be seen, there were only two of us to carry You. One carried Your cross. One walked beneath Your outspread right arm. And we walked through dark alleys. But instead of the harlots, instead of the thieves, we saw policemen standing at every corner. They were after a criminal. Him they let go free. But us they followed as far as Martha's house, where we undressed You and hung You on the cross. And when we finished that, they knocked on the door. They seized us and they led us and You away with them. They fetched our sisters out of their houses. And we came before the judge. And the peasants and the farm hands and the maidservants were all assembled, and the pastor of the congregation, too. The peasants had deepened and widened the hole You had been stuck in, Lord, into a big pit. Leaving aside the big things, they read aloud to the judge the small and expensive items on the lists they had compiled. But to the judge the pit alone was not enough proof. But the pastor said, "You have blasphemed against God!' But we answered, 'We love God more than you do!' But the judge said, 'You are poor in the spirit! Let them go!' But to You, Lord, he gave back the peasants. Meanwhile the peasants shouted, 'Him we don't want! When we see Him, we fall into a rage! When He no longer stood in our way, we noticed how much we were missing.'"

"Have You forgotten, Lord," sings my grandmother, "how they threw Your cross and You too onto my back, how they leaped into their carts, how they beat their oxen, cows, horses, how they drove us before them through half the city? Have You forgotten, Lord, how the maid-servants and the farm hands ran along beside us, how they spat on us, how they tripped us, how we fell? Have You forgotten, Lord, how our friends, our acquaintances, even our very confessors, watched from the sidewalks, how they turned aside and said, 'We don't know these women'?"

And my grandmother jumps up and goes into the kitchen. And my grandmother's three sisters jump up and move toward the tied figure of the Lord, sitting motion-less and without a word.

"She carried You into her house, Lord!" cry my grand-mother's three sisters. "She dressed You in the finest clothes of her deceased husband! She served you food and drink every Sunday! We can bear witness to that! We have been silent a long time, Lord, before putting the first question to You! And it was a question that any-one who knows what's right could answer!"

"Who are You, Lord?" cries my grandmother. "We're going to show You who You are and where You belong!" She stands on the threshold, swinging the hammer in her hand. My grandmother's three sisters tear the clothes off the figure of the Lord. He is naked as far as the navel. The lower part of the body is covered by a cloth knotted beneath the navel. The ends of the cloth stick out to the right and the left of the knot. And while my grandmother passes ahead of them with the hammer in her hand, my grandmother's three sisters drag the figure of the Lord into the adjoining room. They press it against a great wooden cross that hangs on the wall between two beds that have been moved away from each other. Each of the three sis-ters holds a nail in her free hand. And Aunt Martha pushes her nail through the hole in the right hand of the figure of the Lord. And my grandmother drives it with the hammer into one end of the horizontal beam. And Aunt Maria pushes her nail through the hole in the left hand of the figure of the Lord. And my grandmother drives it with the hammer into the other end of the horizontal beam. And Aunt Minna pushes her nail, kneeling down with creaking knees, through the hole in the crossed feet of the figure of the Lord. And my grandmother drives it with the hammer into the vertical beam underneath.

"God almighty," I hear a tenant yell, "this constant hammering!"

"What must be," sing the four sisters, "must be!" They fall on their knees. They fold their hands.

THE INMATES

WHEN THEY FLEW below the airplanes, the birds looked as big as the airplanes. If they flew down and settled on the poles or on the cables between the poles, the birds looked bigger than the airplanes. The birds flew from the poles, from the cables between the poles, over to the little gray-green hills in front of us. The airplanes flew over the hills, over the gray poles, over the black cables over to the little gray-green development houses on the edge of the city behind us. The birds disappeared behind the hills more quickly than the airplanes did behind the houses. It looked as though the birds were flying faster than the airplanes. We were walking along a dead-straight road between the houses and the hills. We were probably much nearer to the hills than to the houses. The poles were sticking up in the meadows to the right and left of the road. The cables between the poles stretched out dead-straight as far as the horizon on both sides. The farther away from the road the poles stuck up to the right and left of the road, the shorter they and the sections of the cables between them looked. And the birds on the sections of cable that were farther away looked like knots. On the meadows, which had more weeds than grass, bigger burned spots than grassy spots, tin cans and bottles lay, and charred and filthied scraps of paper or cloth. On the black burned spots there were white butts of the cigarettes, perhaps, lit by the firemakers standing on the burned spot and staring into the blaze or stoking the blaze. The wind drove the trash over the burned spots and the grassy spots until it remained hanging in the branches of the scattered shrubs. And on the shrubs there were more scraps of paper and cloth and cans than there were leaves. Along the road, from the houses to the hills, from the hills back to the houses, drove garbage trucks with three garbage men and one driver. The garbage men stood on the step on the back end of the garbage truck. Two stood to the right and the left of the covered hole in the back end through which the barrels of garbage were emptied, one stood in front of the hole. They held on to the handles on the back end. They wore long dirty rubber aprons and rubber gloves and rubber boots. Their heads were covered by protective caps. Aside from these garbage trucks, an occasional passenger car drove toward the hills. In these there sat at most three to four people, who with gloomily frowning expressions held on to a person who was happily yelling or flinging his arms and legs about or vomiting. If these passenger cars were driving toward the houses, the person who was happily yelling or flinging his arms and legs about or vomiting was missing. The three to four people nodded to each other and looked with gloomily frowning expressions back toward the hills.

"That used to be an airfield," said my grandmother.

We were standing in front of garbage dumps that from a distance had looked like hills. The dumps were as high as the houses in the development. The houses in the de-

velopment were no longer visible from the dumps, just as
the dumps had not yet been visible from the houses in
the development.

"That used to be the railway track," said my grandmother.

The garbage dumps lay to the right and the left of the
track, at regular distances from each other. It was only
the last rubbish heap behind at the back to the left that
had not yet reached the height of the other dumps. Knee-
high weeds had overgrown these piles of useless things.
Not only tin cans, bottles, boxes, scraps of paper and
cloth lay there, there were also mattresses, strips of carpet, lamp shades, there were also closet doors, backs of
chairs, pieces of crockery, china, pots, food debris, there
were also bicycle bodies, tires, umbrellas, books, pictures,
garbage cans.

"Those used to be the airplane hangars," said my grandmother.

The gray tin airplane hangars lay beyond the dumps to
the left of the track. Some of their entrances were open,
some were shut off by closet doors and overhung with
blankets. The holes in these tin airplane hangars were
covered over with pasteboard and stopped up with pieces
of paper or cloth. Before the entrances rags hung on sections of knotted clotheslines. Now and then an old man
or an old woman would hobble toward the dumps, dragging along an empty sack. Now and then an old man or an
old woman would come out from between the dumps
dragging a full sack toward the hangars. And whenever
an old man like that or an old woman like that emptied
a sack in a hangar, to the noise of all the things that
would come rustling onto the floor, old men and women
came out of all the other hangars. They dragged or pulled
backs of chairs, lamp shades, strips of carpet, mattresses,

broken pieces of mirror, pots, food scraps. They overtook each other at a hobble. They forced themselves through the entrance of the hangar. They began bartering, brawling and quarreling with so much noise that it echoed through the hangars and across the airfield.

"Show me! Show me! What did you find? What do you want to keep? What will you give me for it?" they yelled back and forth. "A carpet, a lamp shade, a tile! I don't want that, don't want that! Hey, look at that, a leg! Swap it for something else! What do you want with one leg! Even if you found the other three for it, and you never will, no matter how many garbage deliveries you live through, and you won't live through them, the seat would still be missing, and the seats are rarer than the legs, and you'd have to live through at least twice as many garbage deliveries as you already have. So one leg is a windfall, a find for someone who got three legs together after a painstaking search, by tricky bartering, and a seat to go along with it. So who finds the leg? Someone, naturally, who still hasn't found any other part of a chair or gotten it by swapping something else he's found!"

"What do you offer for the leg?" one of them asked.

"I'd give this blanket for it," another one answered. "It's true it's got a hole. But I ask you, what is there here that doesn't have a hole?"

"One hole, you say!" screamed the first one. "Do you think I'm blind!"

"That's no blanket," they all screamed at once, "that's a sieve!"

"So what else do you offer for the leg?" asked the first one.

"I'd give this pot for it," answered someone else. "It's true it's got a hole in it. But I ask you, what is there here that doesn't have a hole?"

"A pot with a hole in it," screamed the first one, "that's like a house without a roof! And only a numbskull would lie down in it. He might just as well stretch out along the road. And only a numbskull would pour his stew into a pot with holes. He might just as well give it away! He might just as well pour it out! So what else do you offer for the leg?"

"I'd give this table leg for it," answered someone else. "If you just look a little longer, if you just go on swapping a little more, you'll have a table."

"So what should I do with a table?" screamed the first one. "I still haven't found any table parts or got them by swapping. Even if I found the three missing table legs and the table top for them, and I'll never find them because I'm not going to live to see that many garbage deliveries, even if I found the missing nails to nail the table legs to the table top, and I'll never find them because my eyes are getting weaker every single day, I'd still be missing the hammer to drive the nails in with. But the fellow who has the hammer is a usurer, not a businessman, he'd ask the table for the hammer."

"What are you babbling about, you lousy fink!" yelled someone, plainly the one who owned the hammer. "That's a fair deal, swapping a hammer for a table. What's a table by itself? Assuming you had a table, and you never will, you'd be missing the chair for it. Assuming you had the chair, and you never will, because no one here has ever managed to get together a complete table and a complete chair, or even one complete table or one complete chair alone, we all have only parts, because we never come to terms. Well then, assuming you got that far and you sat down on your chair in front of a bare table, and it'll be your luck never to get that far, and it occurred to you that you were missing a pot without a hole, and no one here has ever found one like that yet, then it would occur to you that for the likes of us a pot without a hole is just as useless as a pot with a hole, because you'd still be without anything to put in it. So, assuming you had a pot with a hole, and you won't ever get that even though they're lying around here by the dozen because you can hardly see any more, because you can't do business, but assuming you were sitting on your chair in front of your table with your pot on the table, you'd be hungrier then than you are today."

"Look at him showing off, the lousy fink," they all cried at the same time, "him and his no-good leg! What use is a leg all by itself if a complete table and a chair and a pot on top of it are no use to the likes of us! How far can you get with that! Whom can you kill with that! Just show him what use your hammer is!"

They banged the chair leg with the hammer and the tin wall of the hangar with their fists. The wall of the hangar was smashed. Little bits of wood flew through the hangar entrance.

"I had the leg of a chair," wailed the first one. "One way or the other, it was still worth a blanket, a pot, a table leg! You've smashed it, you bastards."

"I have three legs already," wailed some of them together. "I would have had a chair, with that broken leg! I would have had five legs, with that broken leg!"

Old men and women were crawling or sliding down the rubbish heaps, one hand groping for a hold, the other clinging to half-filled sacks. They hobbled toward the hangars. The ones in the hangars were hitting each other, screaming and whimpering. Others went on rooting around unwaveringly. Digging deep holes in these piles of unusable things, they were looking for something usable. The heads of old men and women appeared on

the peaks of a few dumps. They were stuck in trash up
to their necks. They bent their heads in the direction of
the hangars, listening, cupping their hands around their
ears.

"Just don't get involved," they called to each other.
And their heads disappeared again in the dumps. On top
of the first garbage dump, the one lying closest to the
road, someone squatted, not digging. He was shading
his eyes with his hands from the right and the left, plainly
so as not to be distracted by anything happening on his
right or left, and looking between his palms toward the
road. Putting two fingers between his lips, he gave a
whistle, then crept down the dump and hobbled toward
the last, the smallest, dump in the back to the left. A
garbage truck drove along the road. And as the men and
women rooting around beneath the peaks of the dumps
slowly worked their way out of their holes, and as their
heads appeared, then their arms; and as they, with their
arms propped up on the trash, finally pulled out their
torsos, their rumps, and as they slid or crept down the
dumps and, dragging half-filled sacks behind them,
hobbled across the track toward the dump in the back to
the left; and as out of the entrances to the other hangars,
some knocking over the doors, some tearing off the
blankets in their haste, other old men and women, after
a glance in the direction of the dump lying closest to the
road, after the exclamations of "It's not a false alarm!"
and "He's left his post!" and "He whistled!"—as these old
men and women, dragging empty sacks behind them,
hobbled across the track toward the dump in the back to
the left: the men and women squabbling in the hangars,
screaming and whimpering, and because they were screaming and whimpering not hearing the whistle, kept hitting
each other. They did not fall silent until the garbage

truck, blowing its horn and at a great rate of speed, drove along the track. They pressed out of the entrance to the hangar, some of them with sacks, some without, and forming a second mass, they hobbled toward the track.

There were two gray-brown masses of old people hobbling along the gray track, the first in front of, the second behind the garbage truck that was driving between them at a great rate of speed. The nearer the people hobbling along in the first mass came to the dump in the back to the left, the more densely they pressed forward and hung on to each other, the more tightly they clung to each other. The ones hobbling in front were yanked back, the ones hobbling behind were pulled forward. And stumbling over each other, and plunging together toward the track, and picking up themselves and the others and being picked up by the others, they made such a crowd in moving forward that they were overtaken halfway along the track by the second mass of people that had started out so much later, in which the individuals were hobbling along independently of each other and because of this more rapidly. This happened shortly after the garbage truck had overtaken them. When they overtook the mass of people, the garbage men tapped their foreheads under their peaked caps with the hands they were not holding on to the handholds with, and the garbage men yelled out at the mass of people, "Ragpickers!" The ones hobbling on ahead in the second mass of people stretched their arms out toward the ones hobbling on behind in the first mass of people. They clung to their ragged clothes. And if they didn't seize their arms together with their clothes, fling themselves around their throats, grab hold of their shoulders, then they would be holding nothing but a scrap of cloth and had to snatch at them again. The thick, gray-brown mass of old people that arose in this way was now moving forward very slowly. You couldn't tell which rumps these limbs, intertwined with and clasping each other, belonged to. They clung to each other so tightly that when they tumbled, they tumbled all together and in the same direction. On the section of the track they had put behind them lay scraps of cloth, shoes, sacks, collected trash. Whatever they left behind them on their way to other finds was picked up by another person. He would have got the short end of it, anyhow, in this hobbling race to the dump, and if not the short end, he would only have been able to pick up something that had rolled down in front of the edge of the dump. He who had to use his hands to move forward if he wanted to go any further and use this chair with the wheels instead of legs. He who was rolling along the track rump-high and only a hand's breadth off the concrete. He was wearing black gloves on the hands with which he turned the back wheels. He put them on the tires, left them there for half a turn, took them off the tires, put them on, left them there, took them off, in quick succession and always a little way off the concrete so that he wouldn't drive over his own fingers. He was dressed correctly, like a gentleman, in a black hat and coat with a white hand-kerchief and white shirt. But at the end of his coat, where with other people the legs begin, he stopped. He came to a halt at every object, looked at it, left it there or picked it up, and put it in front of him on the seat he was sitting on. The garbage truck stopped in front of the dump in the back to the left. The garbage men jumped off the step. The driver drove the garbage truck back-ward as far as the edge of the dump. The garbage men vanished for a moment in the cloud of dust that rose when the trash was unloaded. They jumped back to the step. The driver drove with great speed toward the thick, gray-brown mass of old people who were hobbling toward the dump that was still the smallest one though it was now a little higher.

"Just let's see, let's see," they cried, "if anything usable turns up! Sometimes they throw out something brand-new by mistake or in a rage!" They didn't turn aside, they didn't even cry out when the driver of the garbage truck turned the wheel only just in front of them and drove past them in a sharp curve. "Ragpickers!" called the garbage men and they tapped their foreheads under their peaked caps with the hands they weren't holding on to any handholds with. The one in the wheel chair had rolled as far as the edge of the track. He raised his hat as the garbage truck drove past him.

"That used to be a restaurant," said my grandmother.

Only a piece of wall with three window openings was still left of the restaurant. The garbage truck stopped in front of this piece of wall. Through the openings of the windows and above the strips of stone wall overgrown with knee-high weeds above the window openings a heap of ruins was visible, evidently parts of the former restaurant.

"You used to be able to sit inside," said my grandmother, "outside too, in good weather."

Through the window of the garbage truck the driver of the garbage truck handed the three garbage men three bottles of beer and three little packages wrapped in paper. And as he jumped from the driver's seat into the open, the three garbage men, each one holding in one hand a bottle, in the other a little package, walked toward the three window openings. They sat down, each one in a window opening. They sat with their behinds and feet placed against the windowsills, their knees bent, their backs leaning against the stone walls of the window openings, their backs turned to each other. And while the driver, with a bottle of beer and a little package now in his hand, went toward the part of the wall against which the three garbage men sat with their backs, and while he leaned his back against it, the three garbage men put the beer bottles to their lips, the three garbage men unwrapped the little packages and bit into the sandwiches. All four of them looked off toward the dump in the back to the left.

In front of the dump the gray-brown mass of people fell apart. The old men and women flung themselves on the dump. The dump teemed with old people crawling up and down and sliding and rolling up and down and back and forth. The trash rolled and slid between them or under them or over them or together with them. Sometimes you couldn't tell whether it was a human being who was sliding and rolling or whether it was a larger piece of trash. They were rooting around so wildly that great clouds of dust rose. They coughed motionless, until the dust settled. Then they went on picking things. They threw away or into the air only what at the very first glance proved to be completely unusable.

When they had stuffed their sacks, pockets, coats full, they hobbled across the track toward the hangars. And even though they now hobbled along alone and independently of each other, they moved forward still more slowly than they had on the way there. Because the load they were dragging or pulling along was not a light one. Every few steps they halted, put down the sacks or the larger objects. And while they rested, they rummaged about in the trash they had collected. Their lower lips thrust out, they studied what they had collected. They threw out onto the track what they had thought at first glance and in a hurry was usable but what at second glance had proved to be unusable. They stuck back into the sacks, pockets, coats whatever withstood a second glance as well. Only in the case of a few objects did they shake their heads, push their lower lips a little farther forward, then throw the objects away crossly or stick them back.

"You used to be able to see the airplanes take off and land," said my grandmother.

On top of the low dump at the back to the left, some trash moved. There was a stifled whimpering of someone. An arm rose up, five fingers spread wide. The arm moved back and forth, slipped back into the trash as far as the elbow, as far as the wrist, disappeared. The trash did not move any more. The whimpering died down.

The one in the wheel chair rolled toward the three window openings in the section of the wall. The garbage men jumped to the ground. They and the driver who came over handed the one in the wheel chair the empty beer bottles. The one in the wheel chair hid the beer bottles under his coat, raised his hat, and nodded after the driver and the three garbage men standing on the step until they vanished on the road toward the houses in the development.

"Coffee and cake used to cost a bit more than elsewhere," said my grandmother, "but to make up for that, you could sit with people who had traveled everywhere in the world, or with the relatives and acquaintances of people like that."

On the other side of the airfield a narrower road branched off from the dead-straight road. It led behind and along the dumps to a white building that was surrounded by a wall higher than a man and by treetops behind the wall. Behind the wall hands with short sections of arm waved. It looked as though they were beckoning to us. In front of us, the one in the wheel chair rolled between two rubbish heaps to the road and along the road to the wall.

"I'm coming as quickly as I can!" he called.

The hands waved harder than before.

The one in the wheel chair reached the wall before we overtook him. Two hands behind the wall let a package on a string down the wall. The one in the wheel chair detached the package from the string. He unwrapped it and examined the contents, nodding. Then he pulled out the empty beer bottles hidden under his coat, fastened them to the string. The hands behind the wall pulled the string with the beer bottles up over the wall.

"That used to be a tree nursery," said my grandmother. "They tore up everything to make room for a sanitarium for curing addicts. In the beginning they used to cure smokers and drug addicts as well as alcoholics. Now they restrict themselves to alcoholics." She rang. There was a buzz in the lock of the gate. She pressed down the latch.

"If you've come for your son," said a man in a blue smock to my grandmother, "you'll have to wait a little. He's just being examined." The man in the blue smock shut the gate, went along the path to the entrance, squeezed past a ladder blocking the left half of the entrance, stepped over the threshold, obstructed by a series of paint cans with brown and white paint in them and paint cans with water and brushes in them, and over the rims of the paint cans with the handles of paint brushes sticking out of them and into the clinic. All around the clinic, against the sections of wall between two windows, ladders leaned. Painters stood on them, sometimes a rung or two higher, sometimes a rung or two lower, and in their white smocks hardly standing out from the white front of the building. Paint cans with white paint were tied around the middle of their rumps. They dipped broad, thick brushes into these paint cans and whitewashed the outer walls of the sanitarium. In the rooms of the sanitarium, behind the open windows, there were also ladders leaning against the walls. On these the feet and short sections of the smocks of the painters standing on the top rungs were sometimes visible, sometimes the heads and short sections of the chests of the painters standing on the lowest rungs, sometimes the smocks and the paint cans tied around the middle of their rumps, and now and then a hand that was dipping a broad, thick brush into a paint can, lifting it out of the pot covered with white paint, and vanishing.

A cow spotted white and brown stood on the paved path to the entrance, taking up the whole width of the path. Its hindquarters were turned to the right and its head to the left. Around its neck it wore a rope that was fastened to the trunk of a tree at the left of the entrance. In front of the cow, and in his white-and-brown-spotted smock hardly standing out from the cow, stood an artist. He was patting the cow with his white-brown-spotted fingers, and as he patted, he covered white spots on the cow's coat with his brown fingers and as he patted, he covered the brown spots on the cow's coat with his white fingers. And now and then it happened that he patted the brown places on the cow's coat with his brown fingers, and now and then it happened that he patted the white places on the cow's coat with his white fingers. And now and then it happened that he shooed away or killed a fly on the white-brown-spotted coat of the cow, and now and then it happened that he hit the cow's tail that would flip at the white-brown-spotted coat of the cow and drive away the flies. Then the cow mooed and he, the artist, suddenly lifted his hand, freed the cow's tail, and went on patting the cow, talking soothingly to the cow as he patted, talking sweetly to the cow, asking the cow to stand still, to go on standing as it was standing, with its head pointed to the left and its hindquarters to the right, just as he was painting it above the entrance: the same size as the cow and spotted white and brown and with its hindquarters pointed to the right and its neck to the left, so that he could paint the cow's head hanging on the neck pointed to the right and still missing in his painting. Finally he gave the cow a slap, he turned his back to the cow, bent over for a brush, dipped a fine brush into a paint can with brown paint, and then, holding the brush in his right hand, mounted rung by rung the ladder obstructing the left half of the entrance. He touched the brush to the upper end of the neck of the still headless but otherwise completed picture of the body of the cow. This body of a cow was painted from the side, just as he saw it from the ladder. It consisted of a tail hanging down as far as the middle of the hind legs and between both hind legs over the right end of the entrance, of a left hind leg pushed forward and a right hind leg pushed backward, of a thick udder joined to the hind legs, of a cow's rump, of a left foreleg pushed forward and a right foreleg pushed backward. Both forelegs, like both hind legs, were separated from each other by more than the width of a cow's head, so that it looked as though the cow were galloping at great speed above the entrance.

But though at first glance this picture of a cow's body was very true to nature, at second glance decisive deviations could be made out between the picture of the cow's body and the cow's body. Not in the cow's shape, but in the cow's coat. The brown spots on the cow's coat did not correspond to the brown spots in the picture of the cow's coat, not in their size nor in their shape nor in their arrangement, and the white spots on the cow's coat did not correspond to the white spots in the picture of the cow's coat, not in their size nor in their shape nor in their arrangement. No one can tell, after all, just how the cow's coat looked before the artist began patting the cow, and perhaps the cow, before it was patted, looked the way he had copied it. Now no one can tell, after all, whether he had patted the cow before it had been brought to the sanitarium or after he had begun painting or when he was in the midst of painting it, after he had painted half the cow's body. Now no one can tell, after all, when he, the artist, had patted the cow with clean hands, when he had patted the cow with fingers that had turned white and brown in the course of his painting. In the painting, for instance, the cow's tail did not show any white spot, while the cow's tail showed a big white spot at the end, whether it was there naturally or whether it was because the artist, as he was patting the cow's tail that was hitting the cow's coat and flicking away the flies, had smeared it with his white fingers, after having already painted it one solid brown color as nature intended. For instance, it was remarkable that the hindquarters of the cow did not deviate at all from the hindquarters of the painting of the cow, whether it was because the artist had patted them while his hands were still clean, or whether it was because the artist had not touched them out of repugnance, out of disgust. In order to figure that out, one would have had to be acquainted with the cow before it met up with the artist. In addition, the posture of the cow did not correspond to the posture of the painting of the cow. Because the cow, which was tied up, could not make any big leaps like the cow painted over the entrance. Because the cow sometimes lifted a hoof to strike out at the flies on its cow's stomach, because the cow flicked its tail to the right and the left against its hindparts or whipped it high and at its back, because the cow sometimes put first one fore- or hind leg forward or back, because the cow sometimes put its forelegs or its hind legs so evenly next to each other that one covered the other. Because while the artist was studying the cow from the right, he was painting it over the entrance from the left. And the flies that crawled all over the whole of the cow's body, in especially large numbers over the hindquarters and the head of the cow, these flies were left out by the artist. As he stood that way on the ladder, the artist, as he held the brush to the upper end of the neck of the headless painting of the cow, as he turned his head toward the cow so that he could look at the ears, the horns, and then paint them, the cow moved around the tree, stepping sideways, taking big steps with its hind legs, taking small steps with its forelegs, and then it stood there, the cow, on the meadow, the rope around its neck and fastened to the trunk of the tree at the left of the entrance, its hindquarters pointed to the left and the head to the right, and turned its right half to the artist.

"You cow, you," cried the artist, and when he realized, that for a cow the name cow couldn't be an insult, he added, "You hussy, you tart, you! Turn around at once!"

The cow, after circling the tree trunk with the rope, now, moving its head from right to left to right and then jerkily downward, wound the rope down around the tree so far that it could reach the blades of grass with its head. It ripped out one tuft after another, it shook its head to get rid of the flies that crawled around in its red-rimmed, watering, pale-blue eyes, in its nostrils, in its mouth. The artist stepped down a few rungs, he pressed the bell next to the entrance. A man in a blue smock, not the first one, stepped out of the entrance.

"The men and women in the blue smocks are the attendants," said my grandmother.

"How can I paint the cow," the artist cried to the attendant, "if I keep having to get down, to talk to it, and put it in the right position! Tie it up!"

The attendant came back with a long rope. He yanked the cow by the tail around the tree, so that it stood as it was supposed to stand, the hindquarters pointed to the right and the head to the left, he knotted the cow's tail with one end of the rope, and slowly paying out the rope, he walked across the meadow to the next tree at the right. This tree stood a number of windows from the entrance. The attendant wound the rope around the tree, pulled the cow's tail straight with the rope as high as the cow's back, and knotted the other end of the rope to the trunk.

The artist mounted the rungs of the ladder. He put the brush to the upper end of the cow's neck, he turned his head toward the cow's head. The cow mooed, let un-chewed blades of grass fall from its mouth as it mooed, flicked its tail back and forth, and by swinging its tail, started the rope swinging.

"The men and women in the blue-and-white-striped pajamas who look like convicts are the alcoholics," said my grandmother.

To the ringing of a bell, to the hand-clapping of the male and female caretakers ranged by the side entrances, the alcoholics went out of the sanitarium into the grounds. They walked toward the shrubs and trees behind the wall. There stood four alcoholics, only partly blocked by branches, leaves, and tree trunks. They were looking at the four beer bottles that the one in the wheel chair had handed them over the wall. Now and again one of them lifted the neck of the bottle to his lips, and bending his head back, lapped and gulped as though he were drink-ing, and taking the neck of the bottle out of his mouth with one hand, he wiped his mouth with the other as though he had been drinking. And while some of the al-coholics squatted behind the bushes and began digging and dug out corks and corkscrews and bottles and broken parts of bottles and glasses and broken parts of glasses and looked at them, the other alcoholics stood next to the four alcoholics with the four beer bottles. They crooked their fingers into open half-circles as though encircling big glasses. The four alcoholics with the four beer bottles went from one to another, they turned the bottlenecks downward over the hands curved into half-circles as though pouring drinks. Then they all raised their hands as high as their mouths, they toasted each other, they held their hands to their open lips, bent their heads back slowly and a little bit at a time, so that their hands finally lay on their faces that were turned toward the treetops or toward the sky, as though they were emptying in one draught the big glasses they were pretending to hold. Then they belched, lurched up against each other, not imitating people drinking any more, but drunks, and began squalling, at first softly and incomprehensibly, then more and more loudly with each stanza, some drinking songs.

They fell silent, they hid the bottles under their pajamas, the corks, the corkscrews, the broken pieces of bottles and glasses, as a group of burly attendants, smiling and clapping their hands, strode toward them across the meadow.

"To the concert, ladies and gentlemen!" cried the attendants.

The alcoholics trotted toward a terrace. White garden chairs stood around a platform set among white-and-blue-striped parasols. Four musicians in black suits stood on the platform behind music stands with open books of music. They held instruments in their hands. A fifth sat in front of an open piano.

"They play pretty folk songs," said my grandmother. "It's all right for us to join them."

Female attendants in blue smocks were passing out containers of milk on trays, with straws sticking out of the containers. The alcoholics sucked up little gulps of milk through the straws, put them down, and shook themselves. Before drinking again, they cast furtive glances into their pajamas at what they had hidden underneath them. And whenever they glanced under their pajamas, the male and female attendants nodded toward them with jerky movements of their heads, with brief side-glances, with a name that was pronounced in a rapid hiss. Those among the alcoholics who became aware through these nods of the attendants that they or one of their companions had been discovered, tried to slip objects of their own over to others or to get hold of the objects of those who had already been discovered. They succeeded only rarely, and even then they did not fool the attendants. Generally the objects fell out of their hands and onto the paving of the terrace because of their excitement and their fear of being discovered. Bottles and glasses were smashed, the broken pieces splintered, the corks and corkscrews rolled off. A female attendant stood smiling behind the chairs with dustpans and brooms. She swept up everything and carried it into the sanitarium, not without smiling at the alcoholics who were stretching their arms out to the dustpan with imploring looks. Through the open windows above the terrace came the snoring, the groaning, the babbling of sleeping and drunken persons. From the entrance came the cursing of the artist and the mooing of the cow that drowned out the cursing of the artist. The musicians bowed. They began to play. One plucked at his instrument, one blew into his instrument, one beat on his instrument, one drew his bow over his instrument, and the pianist pressed down the black and the white keys with his fingers. The face of a man leaned out of a

window over the terrace. It was full of red pressure
spots and unshaven. His hair hung over his forehead. He
looked at the terrace perplexed and rubbed his eyes as
though he couldn't believe them.

"But what is all this! What does it all mean!" he cried.
"Am I seeing things? Am I crazy or am I dreaming?"

The arm of a male attendant or of a woman encircled
his throat and pulled him back into the room.

"That was someone in deep sleep," whispered my grandmother. "When they're brought here, they're put to sleep
for two weeks straight. When they wake up afterward,
they don't know whether they're coming or going."

"But where am I?" cried the awakened deep-sleeper.
"Is this supposed to be heaven or hell? Hey there, you
sleepyheads! Where did you hide my bottle? Did you
drink up my whole bottle?" He began throwing objects
around.

The musicians played more loudly. The bigger part of
the attendant personnel went into the sanitarium through
the side entrance. A second face appeared in the window
above the terrace. The snoring and babbling that came
through the windows was interrupted and drowned out
by the yawning of other awakened deep-sleepers.

The musicians played one folk song after another. The
alcoholics on the terrace sucked great gulps of milk out
of the straws. They shook themselves. They looked with
avid eyes into their pajamas. The few male and female
attendants standing behind the chairs who were observing
them nodded to each other. They stepped over to the
chairs and reaching beneath their pajamas with one hand
and with a smile bringing out the hidden objects, they
stroked the alcoholics' heads with their other hand.

"Hands off," hissed the alcoholics. Some of them tried
to bite the hands of the attendants or to twist their wrists.

When the musicians had finished playing, only the attendants behind the garden chairs applauded. The alcoholics poured the milk out of the containers onto the terrace.

A female attendant stepped onto the platform. She tried to read aloud a letter of gratitude from a former alcoholic, now cured. But the noise of the awakened deep-sleepers, the cries for help of the attendant personnel in the wards above the terrace, the mooing of the cow, the cursing of the artist, the muttering of the alcoholics sitting on the terrace, all drowned her out. She nodded at the musicians to go on playing. The musicians played as loudly as their instruments allowed. The four alcoholics with the four beer bottles nodded to each other. With unruly expressions they pulled the beer bottles out from under their pajamas.

"We want beer!" they cried. "What do you want?"

"We want wine!" cried the others. "Whisky, brandy, gin—that's what we want!"

They jumped up from the garden chairs.

"Watch out!" cried the painters. "They're brawling again!"

Carrying the ladders under their arms, they ran off across the meadow toward the wall. Some of them had untied the paint cans and put them down in front of the building. The others, who were running off with the paint cans tied to them, left great white splashes of paint on the meadow behind them. And as they leaned the ladders against the inside of the wall taller than a man, mounted them rung by rung, and standing on top of the wall for a moment, pulled the ladders up high, let them down, leaned them on the outside of the wall, and as they went down them rung by rung and one after another and finally disappeared behind the wall, the painters painting the inside walls put the ladders out through the windows, leaned them against the front, swung themselves up on the windowsills, went down rung by rung, and carrying the ladders under their arms, ran off, some of them leaving behind white splashes of paint, some of them, not all, according to whether they had untied the paint cans in their rush or not, across the meadow toward the stone wall.

The alarm bell rang through the sanitarium. From every entrance lurched awakened deep-sleepers and drunks who had been brought in just before. The male and female attendants ran through the grounds, through the wards of the sanitarium. They seized hold of everyone who ran into their arms or across their path. There were not only alcoholics, drunks, awakened deep-sleepers. There were also musicians and painters, who with furious cries of protest pointed to their black suits, their white smocks. Male and female attendants also seized hold of each other and yanked each other back into the sanitarium.

Later it was said that in the general confusion male and female attendants, as well as a number of doctors, had also dragged the head of the sanitarium into the deep-sleepers' ward and injected a sedative into him.

Meanwhile the alcoholics were searching the sanitarium for alcoholic beverages. When they didn't find anything, they ran off to the main entrance. They knocked over the artist's ladder and some of his paint cans. The artist had loosened the rope tying the cow to the tree trunks to the right and the left of the entrance. And while the longer rope that had been tied to the cow's tail lay across the meadow and the path, and was snapped back and forth by the swinging of the cow's tail, the artist was holding the shorter rope, slung around the cow's neck, in his white-and-brown-spotted hand that was twitching either out of fear or because of the cow's head being jerked back and forth. Hardly distinguishable in his white-and-brown-spotted smock from the cow, he was standing alongside the cow in front of the locked entry gate in the stone wall. The cow drew the attention of the alcoholics by mooing.

"Never again milk!" they cried. "We're not calves, and we're not babies! Let's kill the cow, kill it!"

"Don't kill it," begged the artist. "I've rented it. And the rent of the cow comes to more than the paint to paint it with. And the price of the milk is figured into the rent. Because the farmer claims that after painting it, I milk it in secret. I'd have to paint endless cows in order to get up the price for this cow."

But the alcoholics began beating the cow with their fists, with paint cans, sticking it with the handles of paint brushes. One of them hung around the cow's neck. Another pulled the rope knotted to its tail. The cow would not have gotten away with its life if someone in the sanitarium had not pressed the button that opened the entrance. There was a buzz in the lock. The artist flung open the gate. Two alcoholics galloped out together with the cow before the artist managed to slam the gate again. They ran, all four of them, to the garbage dumps: ahead of all of them, spotted white and brown, was the cow, then the artist came behind by the length of the shorter rope, the one slung around the cow's neck, holding this rope in his hand and spotted white and brown and hardly and only through size and movement distinguishable from the cow, and then the two alcoholics came behind by the length of the longer rope, the one knotted to the cow's tail and holding this rope in their hands and striped white and blue and distinguishable not from each other but, to make up for that, from the artist and the cow, and both of them digging their heels into the ground and holding up the cow and perhaps the artist too in their running and bending over for lumps of earth, for stones, for branches, and throwing the lumps of earth, the stones, the branches at the cow and perhaps at the artist as well.

When the cow was beyond their reach, the alcoholics turned to the painting of the cow above the entrance.

"Away with the cow picture! Paint over it!" they cried. And as one of them lifted up the ladder, leaned it against the section of the stone wall over the entrance, seized a paint can with white paint and a brush, mounted rung by rung and, getting to the top, began painting over the headless, white-and-brown spotted painting of the cow with thick white brush strokes, the others grabbed hold of the paint cans with brown paint. They painted onto the white front man-sized brown bottles and glasses, open bottles with corks nearby and glasses filled to the brim or closed bottles with corkscrews nearby or with corkscrews screwed into the corks and empty glasses nearby. They called out to each other through the windows from inside, through the windows from outside, what kind of alcohol was contained in the bottles, the glasses, they were painting. And as they painted, they sang and yodeled drinking songs, lurched through the sanitarium and around the sanitarium.

On the meadow, in the entrances, on the terrace, deep-sleepers and drunks lay around sleeping and snoring. The male and female attendants were dragging them into the sanitarium. They were gradually regaining their authority. The drinking songs of the alcoholics were drowned out by the cries of protest of the alcoholics who had been seized inside the wards of the sanitarium. The alcoholics who were painting over the front broke off their drinking songs. They listened, they put down their paint cans, they threw the brushes away, they hid their brown fingers. The attendants took up positions in the entrances, smiling and clapping their hands.

"Upstairs now, upstairs for your afternoon rest period!" they cried.

With heads lowered, the alcoholics trotted off toward the entrances. The alarm bell was turned off. Above the main entrance a white spot covered the white-and-brown-spotted painting of the cow.

Between two gray-green garbage heaps the cow and the artist emerged, spotted white and brown, and separated by the length of the longer rope and still behind and striped white-and-blue, the two alcoholics. Immediately afterward a gray-brown mass of old people clustered between these two heaps. They stood tightly pressed together and looking after the cow, the artist, the alcoholic; the alcoholic, who now disappeared behind one heap, now turned up in the gap between two heaps, now disappeared behind the next heap, and so forth.

Across the green-and-white-spotted meadow alcoholics in white-and-blue-striped pajamas with big white-and-brown spots trotted into the white-and-brown-painted sanitarium toward the male and female attendants in blue smocks with great white-and-brown spots. Behind the stone wall appeared sections of ladder followed at once by painters' heads.

"They've calmed down!" cried the painters, and standing on the stone wall for a moment, they lifted the ladders over the wall, leaned them against it, and descended into the garden rung by rung.

"If you've come for your son," said an attendant to my grandmother, "you may come in."

He led us into a room.

Motionless and speechless before the foot of an iron bed stood the figure of a small, slight man. He wore blue-and-white-striped pajamas and looked down at the figure of a stout woman crouching at his feet. She was wearing a blue smock. And as we went in, my grandmother and I, and as the woman, evidently an attendant, jumped up and stood for a moment facing the man, evidently an alcoholic, and in her height, in her width, completely covered the man, and as she turned around, flung herself on my grandmother, crying: "Mama," crying, "At last," and then immediately embraced my grandmother, so violently that she started swaying and tumbled against the wall next to the door, the man who until then had been standing motionless and speechless began trembling and moaning in a smothered way. He raised his head and with moist eyes, with eyes full of tears, he looked at the back of the attendant who, in her height, in her width now completely covered my grandmother and pressed her against the wall in greeting. For he was unable to do more than tremble a little, the man, even if he had wanted to hit and kick out. Because his hands were tied together at the wrists, because his feet were tied together at the ankles, because his tied hands and feet were fastened to the bars of the iron bedstead. For he was unable to do more than moan a little, the man, even if he had wanted to curse and scream. Because his mouth was stopped up by a white cloth. "You can congratulate us!" cried the attendant. "Just look at his left hand!" She stepped to one side, so that my grandmother could see the man's left hand. But because the man's hands, tied to the bars of the bed, were hidden behind his back, the attendant, with a twinkle, as though there were no difference between his hand and her hand, held her left hand, with a ring on the third finger, before my grandmother's face.

"My God!" cried my grandmother. She looked through the attendant's outspread fingers toward the slight little man, trembling a little, moaning a little, who was her son and so my uncle.

"I completely forgot to untie him!" cried the attendant. "I have to keep on tying him up, so that he doesn't start brawling with the others! Just take a look at his fingers!" She unloosed the man's wrists, first from the bed, then from each other. His hands were smeared with brown paint. He was wearing a ring on the third finger of his left hand.

"How do you feel?" said my grandmother. And as she took out of his mouth the chewed cloth, wet with saliva, so that he could answer her, and as he, this man, the son, the uncle and so my mother's brother, with tear-filled eyes and shaken by a fit of retching, almost inaudibly managed to say he was feeling all right, the attendant crouched down in front of him and unloosed his ankles, first from the bed, then from each other. When he was loose, this man, he didn't strike out about him, he didn't kick, he didn't curse or scream. He sat down on the bed, he gave a worried look at his brown fingers and then at the brown rendering of a bottle on the white wall above the bed, neckless and of a brown streak the width of a finger which extended along the wall toward the foot of the bed. With a damp rag the attendant wiped the rendering of the bottle and the streak from the wall and the paint from the fingers of the man. Giving the man her left hand, she pulled him up off the bed with her right hand. Hand in hand they both stood in front of the bed, she, the attendant, in a blue smock and to the right and a head taller and twice as wide as he, the man standing at the left and a head shorter and half as wide.

"Am I guessing right?" cried my grandmother and stepped toward her with outstretched arms.

And as the attendant cried, "Absolutely right! Absolutely right," and as the man, with moist eyes and still shaken by a fit of retching though no longer so violently, almost inaudibly managed to say she had guessed right, a number of alcoholics pushed open the door to the room and called, "Just look at him, what a bridegroom! Just look at her, what a bride! What a couple! What a sucker he is! He thinks he's the first, hand-picked! He thinks he's the only one who was ever shackled here so that he can't brawl with the others any more, so that he can be discharged!"

They were yanked back by male and female attendants. My grandmother let fall her outstretched arms. In an embarrassed way she turned both rings around on the third finger of her right hand. The man, the bridegroom, and the woman, the bride, had freed their hands from each other. They had moved far enough apart from each other so that five children would have fitted in between them. They held their left hands with the rings on their third fingers behind their backs. They stretched out their right, ringless hands to my grandmother's right hand, trembling a little, hesitantly reaching out, with the third finger whose two rings had slipped down to the joint bent and pressed against the ball of the thumb. They were smiling past each other with slightly twisted smiles, my grandmother through the gap between the bridal couple, the bridegroom past my grandmother's left shoulder toward the door, the bride past my grandmother's right shoulder toward the mirror on the wall next to the door. She was blinking like someone roughly awakened.

We walked on the dead-straight road between the houses and the hills. The birds flew from the poles, from the cables between the poles, toward the small gray-green hills behind us. The airplanes flew over the gray poles, over the black cables toward the little gray-green development houses on the edge of the city ahead of us. The birds disappeared behind the hills more quickly than the airplanes did behind the houses. It looked as though the birds were flying faster than the airplanes. We were probably closer to the houses than to the hills. Garbage trucks drove along the road, from the houses to the hills, from the hills back to the houses. Aside from these garbage trucks an occasional passenger car drove toward the hills, with three or four people who, with gloomily frowning expressions, were holding on to a person who was happily yelling away or flinging his arms and legs about or vomiting.

"Do you remember the state you were in when we brought you here?" said my grandmother.

And the bridegroom answered that he couldn't remember.

"Now you can begin all over again," said my grandmother.

And the bridegroom answered that now he could begin all over again.

"You'll have to make up for everything now," said my grandmother.

And the bridegroom answered that he would make up for everything now.

"She's no longer so very young, your bride," said my grandmother, "and she doesn't know how to dress. But she has a bright face. She's set aside everything for her trousseau. She comes from a respectable family. And she's given herself such pains for your sake. You have no idea what you owe her."

And the bridegroom answered that he had no idea what he owed her.

We walked along between the gray-green development houses to the right and left of the dead-straight road. The development houses were as high as the garbage dumps.

The garbage dumps were no longer visible from the development houses, just as the development houses had not yet been visible from the garbage dumps. The development houses had numbers next to the street doors and names above the mailboxes and doorbells next to the names. The streets leading at right angles into the development at the left and the right carried signs with street names on them. The fences of the little gardens in front of the development houses were painted white. In the little gardens were neatly mowed squares of lawn with narrow flower beds framing the squares of lawn. In the middle of the squares stood sprinklers that kept turning without a stop and sprinkling water over the lawn and the flowers, or there were baby carriages, the tops turned down, in which sleeping and yelling infants lay, or there were square playpens in which little children, standing up and holding on to the bars, ran around in one direction or another. Variously colored strips of rugs or white sheets were hanging out of some windows. Behind the windows you could see lamps, closets, housewives running through the rooms. Leaning against the houses there were bicycles, in front of the houses cars were parked. On the sidewalks, in the streets, children were roller-skating, children were riding on two-wheeled, on three-wheeled bicycles. Next to the houses, hidden by bushes, stood garbage cans into which the housewives, stepping out of the street doors, emptied vacuum cleaners, dustpans, garbage cans with the remains of food, broken dishes, boxes, scraps of paper and cloth, cans and bottles.

THE EIGHTH

We are standing in front of the windows, staring down into the street. If someone comes along from the right or the left, we lean all the way out of the windows and look down the street with our heads turned to the right or the left. If two people come along, and one of them comes from the right, the other from the left, then we, turning our heads alternately to the right and the left, look down the street and sometimes at each other. Then my grandmother turns away from me with a soft cry, then my grandmother holds her hands in front of the face she has turned away from me, then my grandmother withdraws into the adjoining room the face turned away from me behind her hands held in front of it. Probably when she's there she turns it, probably with her hands still held in front of it, away from the wall that divides the adjoining room, there, from the kitchen, here. She prays a little while, probably for the Lord to spare her the sight of me, before she ventures back to the window, before she leans out with her face turned to the left and away from me.

We are waiting for Doctor Trautbert.

From the pastor's house next to the church across the street the municipal clergyman steps out in black skirts down to his ankles. He strides upright past the open church gates to the right down the street. My grandmother snaps open her mouth, as though she wanted to call out something to him, perhaps call him over, the pastor, instead of the doctor. Then the pastor stands still and my grandmother puts her hand in front of her mouth. She looks horrified at the pastor, who lifts up his skirts, does an about-face, who, crouched over and casting hurried glances behind him, leaps toward the church gates and slams them behind him.

His behavior is explained immediately by the yelping of dogs to the right, by the heavy thudding, repeating itself in rapid succession, of heels on the pavement, by Doctor Trautbert's calling, "Make sure you get behind the dogs! Those street doors are open," the wailing of a woman, "I don't know how, behind the dogs," and outcries from various tenants, "You'll simply have to make a detour," "We've got our hands on the buzzers," "We've got our hands on the latches!"

On the opposite sidewalk, very close to the house fronts, a woman runs with head lowered, with disheveled hair hanging over her face. She staggers into the house fronts. Her light blouse blows open: her dark skirt, the skin of her white, thin arms. She bangs the bells next to the front doors with her hand, she bangs the house doors with her fist, then she turns her head to the right, looks behind her, and before the tenants can press the buzzers to open the doors, and before I hear the buzz in the locks of the street doors, she has gone on a few windows further. And tenants call out contradictory advice to her from the windows of the houses she has left behind her:

"Just stand still, then they won't do anything! Running away is what excites them!" "Run as hard as you can, otherwise they'll tear you to pieces!" Some tenants throw sausages and meat out of the windows, perhaps in the hope of holding up the dogs that way.

The width of a house away from the woman the four dogs' heads appear at the same level, their muzzles yawning, then the four dogs' bodies, separated from each other by the width of a dog, and the four leashes at most the length of a dog's body that run at a slant toward Doctor Trautbert's fists, pressed tightly against each other. The dog keeper stretches his arms out in front, he digs in his heels, pulling back the dogs with his torso thrown way back, he even, because his hands are not free, puts a leg around a lamppost and stands there, the lamppost between his legs, his arms stretched out toward the dogs, his torso curved over and almost forced down to the height of a dog, and in spite of everything he holds the dogs back long enough for the woman to put behind her a distance of three windows and the sections of wall between the windows. Meanwhile the dogs yank at their leashes, they jump up, their throats rattling with the pressure of the collars encircling them. Doctor Trautbert's legs slip off the lamppost. With the dogs he chases along after the woman, now with his torso leaning all the way forward. He too gives her advice while running: "Think up some trick!" he cries. "Anyone can run away! As it 'is, we caught up with you right away! We've caught up with better runners than you!"

The woman presses against the church gates with both hands. They do not open.

"This is a house of the Lord," I hear the pastor's voice sounding through the church. Perhaps he is standing pushing against the church gates.

"Halt!" cries Doctor Trautbert. "Stand still there!" And while the dogs think only of chasing after the woman and he, the dog keeper, thinks only of keeping pace with the dogs, the woman winces and comes to a standstill in front of the pastor's house.

"Are you out of your mind?" cries Doctor Trautbert. "I didn't mean you, I meant the dogs!"

And while the woman keeps on standing there, her face turned away from the dog keeper and his four dogs, he, the dog keeper, adds, "For heaven's sake keep on running!" And while the woman runs on at a stagger past the pastor's house and to the left down the street, until I can no longer see her from this kitchen window, Doctor Trautbert calls out, "Forget what I said! Listen! I don't want to interfere, or you'll blame me for everything! Do whatever you like!"

"Doctor," calls my grandmother, "here it is!" She stands with her left arm propped up on the windowsill, she waves with her outstretched right arm so violently that the rings on the third finger of her right hand slip off over the joint and off the finger. I don't hear the rings falling. I don't see where the rings roll. My grandmother looks after the rings in dismay, she leans all the way out of the window.

"You have to appeal to their lordships the dogs!" cries Doctor Trautbert, and before disappearing from my field of vision, he turns his head toward our house.

I hear my grandmother slamming the street door, hear her going up the stairs to the noise of her thumping shoes, hear the dogs' yelping coming from the left, the heavy thudding, repeating itself with each step more and more slowly, of heels on the pavement, Doctor Trautbert's panting, the outcries of several tenants: "Ohhh-ohhh," and "Ow-ow-ow!"

Then the thudding of the heels on the pavement, the yelping of the dogs break off, then I hear Doctor Trautbert calling, "That was Tobias! I knew it at once! What a piece of luck for you! Just wait a little there!"

The church gates across the street open a chink. The pastor looks out, astonished, at my grandmother creeping across the sidewalk. He steps out of the church and, casting a hasty glance behind him, strides off to the right down the street.

Out of the house entrances, behind their dogs at distances the length of a leash, the dog keepers among the tenants come out. They greet each other, raising their hats with the hand that is not holding the leash. And partly pulled and partly pulling, they are led off to the left down the street by their dogs, they lead their dogs off to the left down the street. There are poodles, bulldogs, dachshunds, spitzes, or dogs that look like one or the other or like two or three or like none of these breeds of dog or like all these breeds of dog or dogs of breeds I don't know. The dogs look more like their dog keepers than they do like each other. The dogs and the dog keepers move forward not steadily, but jerkily. It is not that the dog keepers bring the dogs closer to each other. It's the dogs that bring the dog keepers closer to each other. They stand next to each other, separated from the lampposts by the length of a leash. They look each other over smiling indulgently at each other's and their own dog lifting its leg and leaving puddles behind or squatting with bent hind legs and raised tail and leaving little piles behind, as though it were appropriate to exercise indulgence, not with the dogs, but with each other. They don't introduce themselves to each other, they introduce to each other each other's dogs. They start up conversations without any introductions, in which they talk at each other and enumerate the qualities and peculiarities that distinguish their dogs. They speak in loud voices, so that nothing is missed, so that nothing has to be repeated. They speak rapidly, so that at least the most important things will be said about their own dog. Because the following morning another dog will bring them together with another dog keeper, with whom they will chat about dogs in loud and rapid voices, standing a leash's distance away from lampposts. Because they don't know when an accident—that is, the dog—will bring them together with someone else again. And breaking off their conversations and without saying any good-byes, they chase after the dogs chasing after each other. I see dog keepers standing separated from each other by two leash's lengths and by two dog's lengths standing on the sidewalk trying to pull apart one dog's hindquarters from another dog's muzzle. I see dog keepers separated from each other by two leash's lengths and one dog's length turning around two dogs turning around each other. And while the dog keepers keep themselves separated from each other by as great a distance as possible—that is, by a half-circle—their two dogs hang with their rumps curved almost in the shape of a half-circle, with the head of one at the hindquarters of the other. And no matter how violently the dog keepers yank at their leashes, they can get away the head of one dog from the hindquarters of the other and the head of the other dog from the hindquarters of the first dog only when the dogs themselves have had their fill of sniffing.

My grandmother straightens up. She sticks the rings on the third finger of her right hand. She runs along behind the dogs and dog keepers going off to the left.

The sidewalk, as far as I can survey it from this kitchen window, is empty. I hear the heavy thump of a cane on the pavement, the whining of a dog. An old, gray-haired woman moves backward from right to left, supported by a stick. Her back is bent. She stands still the moment she is visible from here, hits out with her stick, and, drawing in the leash, yanks a small, white, resisting dog over to her. The dog squats at her feet on the sidewalk. It turns its head to the right. The old woman hits it with the stick. The dog jumps up, whining. The old woman loosens the leash. She pulls the dog farther by two windows and the section of wall between the windows, supporting herself on the stick again and walking backward and turned toward the dog. The dog squats on its hind legs. It turns its little white head toward the big brown head of a dog that little by little grows visible at the right. The big brown dog yanks a little white-haired resisting old man toward itself by the leash. The man moves forward, supported on a stick. His back is bent. He stands still the moment he is completely visible from here and braces himself with the stick against the dog. But the big brown dog pulls the resisting old man further along, toward the little white resisting dog that is being pulled along by the old woman with blows of the stick. But because the big brown dog is pulling the old man forward faster than the old woman is pulling the little white dog, the two dog muzzles touch, in spite of the efforts of the woman to move ahead, in spite of the efforts of the man to stay behind. The old woman raises her stick and lets it fall without striking a blow, probably because she is afraid of hitting her own dog and the stranger's. The dogs push themselves close to each other, each one with its head alongside the other's body, toward the hindquarters. The big dog is twice as long and twice as tall as the little one. And while the dogs are each sniffing each other's hindquarters, the old man and the old woman bend over. They bend their heads as far down as their age allows, and they study searchingly the hindquarters of each other's dog.

And perhaps because they trust their own eyes less than information from a stranger, they put their heads close to each other above the bodies of the dogs. They raise their hands with the leashes hanging from them up to their ears. They put them to their ears. With the sticks twitching back and forth so violently in their trembling hands that it's hard to tell just what they want to show, they point to each other's dog's hindquarters. They ask each other a short question that for me here is incomprehensible. They give each other vigorous and long-drawn-out nods, perhaps because the way each one asks the question sometimes gives evidence of adequate eyesight. They tell each other in answer, "Yes, yes," perhaps because each other's answer to the question sometimes gives evidence of adequate hearing. Perhaps they nod to each other and answer each other in order to make quite sure of mutual understanding, because they don't know each other and they don't know what has suffered from age more, the other's hearing or the other's vision.

The big brown dog and its dog keeper stand still, their heads turned to the left, the hindquarters to the right. The little white dog pulls its old woman around the big brown dog and its old man, until it has its head turned to the left, its hindquarters to the right, behind the brown dog that's twice as long and as tall and stands beneath the leash going from the brown dog to its dog keeper until she, the old woman, with her head turned to the left, her hindquarters to the right, stands behind the dog keeper, who is being rubbed up against at the height of his thigh by the leash reaching from the white dog to the old woman. And while the dogs touch each other with head and hindquarters, the white dog and old man are standing farther apart from each other than the old man and the old woman, who are separated by about the length of the little white dog. The old woman moves her arm with the leash by about half the length of the little white dog toward the back of the old man at the moment when the white dog, supported only by its hind legs, is trying to mount the back of the brown dog with its forelegs. The old man, the dog keeper, with his stick now pointing at both dogs, turns toward the old woman dog keeper, who is also pointing at both dogs with her stick. They ask each other a question that for me here is incomprehensible. In answer they shrug their shoulders. To strengthen their shoulder-shrugging they call, "How should I know!" Shaking their heads, they then contemplate the dogs' behavior.

And because the old man dog keeper blocks the old woman dog keeper's view of the dogs, she steps over next to him. The old woman's leash now hangs loosely and in the shape of an arc beneath the old man's leash. The old woman's back is bent more than the old man's back. They both stand propped on their sticks and stare at the dogs. The big dog stands motionless and expectant, while the little dog jumps up on its hindquarters, looks for a hold on its back with its forelegs, slips off. The big dog, after numerous futile efforts on the part of the little dog, willingly lowers the height of its back, by bending its hind legs so far that its hindquarters are at the same height as the legs of the little dog. The little dog slides with its forelegs along the big dog's back as far as the length of its rump will allow. It doesn't even cover half the length of the big dog's back, and the heads of the dogs are farther apart than the little dog is long. The old man, the dog keeper, turns toward the old woman dog keeper next to him. He hits his forehead with the hand with the stick, hangs the handle of the stick over the wrist of the hand he's holding the leash with. "Hey, you," he cries, and claps the old woman dog keeper on the back with his free hand.

"What?" cries the old woman dog keeper.

The old man puts his head close to the old woman dog keeper's head. And while shielding his mouth and the old woman's ear with his free hand, he whispers something to her.

"Them?" cries the old woman dog keeper, and she points at the dogs with her stick.

"What else!" cries the old man dog keeper.

Then they both burst into shrill laughter. They press their hands with the leashes against their stomachs. They thump the pavement with their sticks. They step close to the dogs. They loosen the leashes. The little dog slips off the big dog's back, stands up on its four legs, turns its head to the right. The big dog gets up.

"Rascal!" cries the old woman dog keeper, and she strokes the little dog's back

"Doll baby!" cries the old man dog keeper, and he scratches the big dog's brown coat. For a second the dog and the dog and the dog keepers bent over the two dogs stand there tightly pressed together. Then the dogs squeeze between the dog keepers' legs. The big dog stands at the left, with its head turned to the left and separated from the dog keepers by the length of the leash. The little dog stands at the right, with its head turned to the right and separated from the dog keepers by the length of the leash.

"Once upon a time," I hear the dog keepers say. Each of them stretches an arm with the hand with the leash toward their dogs pulling in opposite directions. They brace themselves with the sticks against the dogs. The dogs pull them apart, first by the length of the little white dog, then by the length of the big brown dog. And because the big brown dog pulls the old man forward more quickly than the old woman can pull back the little white dog, in spite of the man's efforts to stand still, in spite of the woman's efforts to follow the man, the old man dog keeper and the old woman dog keeper get farther and farther away from each other.

When they are separated from each other by the width of a house, perhaps the limit of their hearing, even if they bellow, they brace themselves with all their strength against the dogs, with their faces turning crimson with the exertion and their bodies trembling. They turn toward each other.

"So what's your name?" they bellow.

"Me?" they bellow, and they give each other violent, long-drawn-out nods.

"What?" I hear the old man and the old woman call out as they keep running away. I see the way both of them raise their hands with the leashes and the sticks to the level of their chests with the expression of people listening, the way they then start running helplessly behind the dogs and the leashes, disappearing from my field of vision.

I turn toward the kitchen. I step into the gaps between the objects lying around or turned over or fallen on the floor. I sit down on the sofa. I'm going to stay this way, waiting, staring at these four gray-green kitchen walls with the spots of whitewash under the chipped-off paint, these two clotheslines hanging between two walls with the damp, white-gray washed underwear of my grandmother and of the Lord, with the Lord's black socks, my grandmother's brown stockings dragging on the floor, my grandmother's flowered nightgowns and aprons, waiting, staring at this white sink with the greasy pot filled to the brim with water, the ragged dishcloth, the garbage can with the open lid underneath the sink, in which lie whitish-gray cooked bones and pea pods, eggshells, crumpled scraps of paper, these red, blue, yellow open cardboard boxes with stuff to wash, rinse, and clean that stand on a shelf above the sink, this row of canning jars next to them, with these green peas that are hardly distinguishable from the walls, this white stove on which the soup boils over, this thick gray-green soup that comes bubbling up between the edges of the pot and its lid, that runs down the outer sides of the pot, that leaves behind it lines that are gray-green on top and brownish toward the bottom of the pot and the gas flame, and that flakes off at the bottom in black-brown burned chips, waiting until my grandmother comes back, opens the kitchen door with the damp gray cleaning rag hanging on the latch, and ventures into the kitchen or sends someone else in.

The foamy water from the overturned cleaning pail runs over the square tiles of the kitchen floor. It runs along the narrow white grooves between the tiles, runs under the table with two white soup bowls on it, an empty soup tureen with a serving spoon, two glass dishes with two heaps of light-yellow pudding and two pools of red juice around the edges of the heaps, it runs under the overturned chairs, it wets the cushions that have slipped off the seats of the chairs, the darning thread, the buttons, needles, zippers, balls of wool out of the overturned darning basket. In these pools of water, and in its white-gray coloring scarcely distinguishable from the gray tiles, the white grooves between the tiles, the white-gray streaks of foam on the water, there lies the worm, or a piece of the worm that is almost as long as the kitchen.

It looks like a soiled string of uneven strength. On one side it ends up as thick as a cord, at the other as thin as a thread. In the thicker sections, as far as the middle of the worm or of the piece of the worm, the notches between the segments, and thus the individual segments, are clearly recognizable. In the thinner sections the notches, and thus the individual segments, are not recognizable. The needle's-eye-sized head, with the four suction cups, would have to be sitting at the thinnest spot. But I can't make it out, because it's too small, or because it's swimming around, perhaps, by itself or covered by or sucking itself into one of these torn-off finger-long sections of worm or streaks of foam, or because it's still inside me and goes on forming one segment after another and replacing the torn-off segments. If there weren't these gray square tiles with the white grooves, these objects scattered over the tiles and the grooves, these streaks of foam on the water, I would think it, or this piece of it, was lying there motionless. But its thick end and its thin end are moving. Now they push toward each other, then they move away from each other. It stretches out to a straight line that sometimes lies parallel to the grooves and that divides the tiles. It pushes along the grooves. It twists itself into a half-circle, cutting across the grooves on one side to the right, on the other side to the left. It twists itself into a knot, cutting across the grooves on both sides from the left or on both sides from the right. It stretches on one side and twists itself on the other side into the shape of a walking stick. It stretches out on both sides in the same direction into the shape of a horseshoe. Now and then one end or the other end or both ends at the same time, when they twist themselves, touch a segment hanging more or less far away in the chain. Then the ends don't creep over this segment, but move away, twisting less and stretching out piece by piece, farther and farther away from the chain, as though it were an obstacle like the table legs, the chairs, the chair cushions, the buttons, needles, zippers. The direction of the worm's ends, or the ends of this piece of the worm, and thus the movements, are determined by the obstacles even when it looks as though it were not moving arbitrarily but toward something. The moment an end comes up against an object, even if it's something so easily moved as a button, or against another segment, it gives way and moves in the opposite direction, only to move right back again the moment it comes up against an object or another segment. It would probably move back and forth between two obstacles constantly if it were not drawn past these objects or pushed between these objects accidentally and by being shortened or lengthened through the bending or the stretching of the segments in the interior of the chain. The segments inside the chain bend and stretch like the ends of the worm when they touch one end of the worm or when they are pushed by one end or the other into one direction or another and graze an object.

In just the same way behave the individual sections of the worm that lie to the right and left of the worm that are at most as long as a finger and then consist of several segments, and at the least are as long as a fingernail and then consist of only a single segment. It's possible that in addition there are some pieces of worm creeping around here that are covered up by objects or are tiny and not recognizable by the naked eye. The pieces of worm as long as a finger twist about in the shape of knots, of walking sticks, or horseshoes, without moving forward like the worm. Only when their ends approach each other, on one side at the right on the other side at the left, they don't stay in the shape of a half-circle, but approach each other until they touch and for a moment close up in a shape that is not, it's true, like a circle but looks like a pretzel, before they separate and lie there in the shape of a half-circle, stretched out, twist themselves into a half-circle opening in the opposite direction and closing into a pretzel. Only the individual segments move over several tiles, until the end of the segment farthest forward touches an object or a section of worm. Then the end of the segment pointing back on the way over several tiles moves forward—that is, on the way back—with deviations that are recognizable only because of the tiles and the grooves between the tiles, until it touches the next object or a piece of worm, creeps backward or forward, which means the same, and goes past accidentally, and once here and then there, some object or piece of worm that has been touched several times before.

I hear a car stop in front of the house, hear someone opening and shutting a car door. I step into the gaps between the objects and pieces of worm that lie around, have been turned over, or have fallen to the floor, lean out of the window. A taxi driver holds open the back door of a taxi. My grandmother steps out of the taxi. She opens the street door. She comes into the house with the taxi driver. I hear them coming up the stairs.

"For a second, here, if you," says my grandmother.

I hear them going into the adjoining room, hear their shoes thumping on the floor, hear them opening and shutting the closet door, hear them dragging some object across the floor, then saying, "Only what's fair," and then right after that, "Has its limits," and repeating right after that, "Only what's fair."

I hear the taxi driver walking up and down the hall, sometimes standing still in between, sometimes for a shorter, sometimes for a longer time, perhaps to look at himself in the hall mirror, perhaps to read the written things hanging up in gilt frames behind glass along the walls of the hall.

"There's the suitcase," says my grandmother. "If you'd just another second, here."

She turns the key in the kitchen-door lock three times.

"Lothar!" she calls.

I open the door only a chink and squeeze through.

"Close the door!" calls my grandmother.

She stands in front of the taxi driver, her back turned toward me. Only the light coming through the open door of the adjoining room lights up the narrow hall. The taxi driver holds a suitcase and a peaked cap in his left hand. He stretches his right hand out to my grandmother, who is rummaging around in her purse, looks over past my grandmother's shoulder at me, raises his right hand and passes his forefinger across the bridge of his nose. My grandmother holds a big bill out to him. The bill quivers a little in her hand

"I suppose this'll be enough," she says. "Take him to his father, Mr. Leinlein, thirty-three School Street."

"The suitcase, okay," says the taxi driver, and then he puts the suitcase on the floor and then he holds the peaked cap in his hands behind his back. "But the child," he says and then he shakes his head, "No! Put your money away. I'll never let myself in for that again. You don't imagine you're the first one who ever had an idea like that. It's pretty common, in fact, for someone to want to get rid of a child that way. So they call a driver. So they make a big show of pulling out their purses. So they're pretty big-hearted with tips. So they pay with big bills that'd be enough for a trip around the city. So they say, 'Take him to his father.' So they tell me a street, so they tell me a name and an address too. You said School Street? Leinlein? Thirty-three? And now you'll swear that that street, that number, that name exists."

"But I swear," says my grandmother.

"You see!" says the taxi-driver. "I won't claim you've invented the address. Leinlein and School Street and thirty-three sounds too improbable for an out-and-out lie. But assuming the address is real, assuming his father isn't sitting here behind one of these doors, who's going to guarantee me that this Mister Leinlein is his father and not an enemy of his father's who'll tell me, 'I can't stand the sight of him any more than I can that of his father! Get him out of here before I lose my temper,' and who's going to guarantee me that this Mister Leinlein, in case he is his father, won't pass himself off as an enemy of his father's and say, 'I'm his father's enemy,' and give me the enemy's address as that of his father. I'll be driving back and forth, from the enemy to the father to the enemy, and each one will pass himself off as the father's enemy, and each one will pass the enemy off as the father. They'll stop opening the doors when I ring, they'll lean out of the window: 'Oh,' the enemy will call. 'Oh,' the father will call, 'Just drop him in the street. He's no better than his father!' The only odd thing is that I always have this tendency of thinking the enemy's the father. The only certain thing is that you won't let me into the house any more than the father and the enemy when I bring the child back here, because the suitcase is too big and heavy, because the child looks too tricky and you yourself too exhausted."

"Only what's fair," says my grandmother in a trembling voice, pointing to the kitchen door.

"I believe you that he did something bad," says the taxi driver, and he shrugs his shoulders. He moves toward the door on his way out. He puts on his peaked cap. He puts his hand on the latch.

"No one," he begins, "understands you as well as I do. But believe me, I'd think myself lucky if I only had one like him. He's thin, that means he doesn't eat much. He's weak, that means you don't have to put out much energy to cope with him. What else do you want. I've got four. But believe me, my brother, for instance, would think himself lucky if he only had four like mine. And today I ask myself, what's the big deal? They cling to me. They stop me from moving forward. They cause tremendous quarrels between me and my wife. They rob us of our sleep at night. They spoil our fun. And we never get a day off from them. But what does all that amount to? My brother, he's got seven children: five boys and two girls. My brother's a hard-working father. He's fed them well. He's served them rich food. He ate only after they'd all had their fill. And they were insatiable. All he got was what was left in the pots. He scraped out the pots, he rinsed them out with water, and he drank that water. They put on weight and he lost weight. He turned them into big, into strong children. He was happy when they came back home victorious from fights with other children.

" 'They'll make their way in life,' he said, full of pride.

"But as time went on, a victory over other children was no longer enough. They attacked passers-by. They won. The parents had to lock them up because they were making the streets of the city unsafe.

"At home the children fought with each other. They divided themselves into two groups: three of them, one of them a girl, fought against four, among them two girls. Of course the fight always turned out in favor of the bigger group. They debated what to do in order to divide up the chances of victory fairly.

"They tried the following solution: One of them would occasionally stay out of a whole fight and watch them fighting. After the fight was over, he would leap into one of the two groups to replace the one who had been most badly weakened by the fight. He in his turn would rest throughout the next fight in order to collect his energies so as to be in the position of leaping in after the fight to replace the one who was now most useless for fighting.

"But this solution was unfair too. Because after only a couple of fights it turned out that it was the group in which the one who had rested fought that always won.

"They debated again. 'We need,' they said, 'one brother more or one brother less. We'd manage to have a fair fight quicker if we killed one brother. The likeliest one is the youngest, he's the weakest and most useless.'

"The youngest started screaming. The mother came in, not because he was screaming. The room was full of screams night and day. She came in every hour, bandaged the children's more dangerous wounds and swept out the smashed objects. 'Mother,' cried the youngest at once, in order to save himself, 'mother's got to get into the fight!'

"'But children!' said the mother.

"But the fight had already begun.

"At the start there were two groups: the smaller one did not touch the mother because she had decided to fight on their side. The bigger one, which fought against it, from the very beginning directed the main attack at the mother. The mother made one mistake: she hit out all around her, hit out at anything in her way, hit out at both groups. Then the children, after trying first to talk to her earnestly, then to protest, closed their ranks and made a joint advance against the mother. They overpowered her. They carried her into the bedroom. They tied her to her bed with a clothesline. They let her lie that way until evening and debated what was to be done now—that is, in what way they could evade being punished by the father.

"In the evening the father came home, exhausted from work, from his overtime. And when he rang and when the door wasn't opened for him, he bent down to the lock, put the key into the lock. But before he could open the door, before he could straighten up, the door was yanked open from inside. The children fell on him. They hung on him. They pulled him down to the floor. And as he lay there, they spread themselves across his full length. They tied him up hand and foot. They carried him—he wasn't heavy—into the bedroom and tied him to his bed.

"So there they lay, the parents, alongside each other, they lay there and were so ashamed of their children that they didn't dare look at each other. Their eyes wide open as though astounded, they stared up at the light-green, the transparent glass bowl of their bedroom lighting fixture in which a pile of dead flies had collected during the course of their marriage.

"All seven were still minors. The eldest son was thirteen years old, and of his brothers one was always a year older than the following one, until they got to the two youngest, the daughters, one of them eight, the other seven.

"With his salary the father was able to support the first, the second, the third son. And the food the parents ate at that time was sufficient and kept up their strength. The fourth one, too, caused no grief. The father took care of him with the pay from his overtime. And what the parents had to eat was enough. For the fifth, the last son, the father moonlighted on Sundays and holidays. And if they couldn't get any sleep at night, the parents, then it was not hunger that kept them awake, it was only the noise of the five sons, of whom every single night one woke up the four others with his screams and egged them on to scream along with him or to make peace. That was no less loud than the screaming, because in order to get a hearing, the peacemakers had to outshout the others. When the mother was brought down with the sixth child, the first, the older, daughter, and the father said he could do no more than he was doing, the mother started doing work at home. She sat bent over, the mother, evening after evening until late into the night, sewing under-clothes, the mother. And what she earned was enough to feed the sixth, the first daughter.

"But when the seventh child, the second daughter, arrived, when the sixth, the first daughter, had not yet outgrown her swaddling clothes and was still crawling and could stand up only with her mother's help, when the fifth, the last son, could walk, but rather badly, was always flopping down and looked beat up and miserable because he had to wear the overlong pants of the fourth, when the fourth was able to run upstairs, downstairs, to press the doorbells of the other tenants and the mother had to run upstairs, downstairs in order to quiet the furious tenants, when the third left the house without knowing which way was right and which left, and the mother had to watch out the window to make sure he didn't cross the street, when the second could, it's true, buy cabbage and go for milk, but meanwhile lost the rest of the money or spent it on candy, and when the first one, finally, the oldest son, was of school age and needed a suit, a school bag, a stack of books, what there was to eat was only enough for the seven children.

"Then there followed seven years of the parents' ab-stinence. Then the mother said to the father, 'We'd better stop doing it, dear. My body, says the doctor, can't stand it again.' Then the father said to the mother, 'You're right, dear, the short sweet pleasure isn't worth the years of toil. A raise, says the manager, is something that can't be done.'

"The children stood around the parents' beds. They looked at the parents as though they weren't quite sure of what was to be done now.

"My brother's daughters put their heads together. They whispered softly to each other. They began giggling. They stepped over to the father's bed. They pulled off his trousers, they said, 'We'll just take a look, at it, that,' they said, 'We'll just touch it, that,' they asked the brothers: 'Does Papa make wee-wee with it, that?'

"The brothers gaped at the sisters at first, then they nudged each other. 'What they can do,' they said, 'we certainly can do too!'

"And the brothers went over to the mother's bed.

"The rest came about by itself. They looked everything over at their leisure, and it wasn't long before they discovered the point.

" 'It's the same as it is with dogs,' they said.

"They loosened the father from his bed. They left his hands and feet tied. They rolled him over onto the mother and tied both of them to each other in such a way that a couple of inches of space was left between them to move about, just the amount of freedom the father needed for the back-and-forth movements the children were demanding of him.

"And while up above the father's spirit manifested itself in ugly oaths and curses, down below the weakness of his flesh manifested itself with growing strength. The mother looked steadfastly up at the light green, transparent glass bowl of her bedroom fixture, she seemed to be seeing through the father's head, which blocked her

vision. She lay there, the mother, and looked off toward
the lamp bowl, and she held her breath, the mother, as
though she were expecting at any moment the resurrec-
tion of the heap of flies, the flying up of the flies, the
flying about of the flies of this bed, as though she expected that a swarm of flies could conceal this scandal
on the white linen sheets. The scratched hands, the seven
right hands of the sons and daughters, were placed on
the father's sleek white behind, they pressed it down the
moment it got to the edge of the space for moving about
in and had reached the height allowed, then they light-
ened the pressure so that it could be raised again, then
they pressed it down. The father's oaths and curses
became more and more breathless. And after a half-curse,
one broken off in the middle, he yielded what he had to
yield.

"'He's finished,' said the eldest. He lifted his hand off
his father's behind.

"When hunger plagued them more than fear of punishment, the children loosened the parents from each other.
They were given a beating, all seven of them. For seven
days the parents beat them, and on Sunday, too, there
was no rest from the beating. First the father, then the
mother, that's how they changed off and thrashed them
to the limit of their strength. It was only because they
were no longer able to that they didn't kill them, all seven
of them. But what does a thrashing amount to? Children
are thrashed for stealing a penny. Children are thrashed
for breaking a plate. Children are thrashed for nothing
at all, in a fit of temper.

"Now she's running around, the mother, my sister-in-
law, with a round belly beneath her big smock, can't see
the tips of her shoes without an effort, the mother, sits a
little bit away from the table when she finally gets to sit

down. And when she cooks for her husband and children, she has to clutch the stove between tossing two potatoes into the simmering salt water, in between beating two eggs into the pan. And when she does the laundry for her husband and children, she has to clutch the washtub between two socks, two undershirts. And when she wipes the footprints from the floor, the dirt that her husband, that her children bring in, she suddenly stays there, lying on the wet floor, between the scouring rag and the bucket, sometimes holding the rag in her hand, the mother lies there, breathing heavily or sometimes not at all.

"The doctor isn't giving her any guarantees that it'll be all right when it gets to the point. And it can't be a long way off now. But the children talk about it in their own way. 'Once he's there,' they say, 'then we'll launch the ninth.'"

THE WEDDING

IT WOULD HAVE been advisable not to enter that hall, at least not now.

"In with you," says someone. "Gently now!"

In that silence no one could have gone in without being noticed. They look this way out of the corners of their eyes, without turning their heads. They smile without smiling at you. Perhaps they've been expecting some newcomer, someone else whom they would have greeted by jumping up, with outstretched arms, crying, "Aha!" and "At last!" or "So there you are!" and "What a surprise!" They train their eyes straight ahead of them again. One of them snorts with annoyance.

A chandelier hangs down from the middle of the ceiling. The hall is brightly lit. The tables have been moved together to make one long banquet table. They sit behind this table, almost as long as the hall, a little bit away from the wall. Some of them at regular distances away from each other stand behind the sitting people. On the table stand full glasses and empty plates untouched. Between the glasses and the plates, set out along the

272

table at regular distances from each other, there are vases with bunches of flowers. The vases are not high enough, the flowers are not long-stemmed enough, to cover the important parts of the bodies of the people sitting down. Between the glasses, plates, vases their hands lie, flattened and with outstretched fingers. The heads of the sitting people are under the picture on the wall behind the table. The heads and the more or less long parts of the upper bodies of the standing people stick up into the picture. But they block only unimportant parts of the picture, like the table legs or the feet standing between the table legs, and, hanging down to the floor, the hems of the dresses and the trouser legs of a wedding party eating and drinking and turned to each other in groups and turned away from each other in groups.

The wall above the table consists of a succession of mirrors and windows. Half of those present and of what is in the hall is visible in the mirrors. The other half of those present and of what is in the hall is visible through the windows for the spectators leaning in the windows of the house across the street. The view through only one window is blocked by a man in a black suit. He stands opposite the bride.

"Go away," he hisses, "you're blocking me!"

It's advisable to make an about-face here, just before the middle of the table, shortly before the bride, advisable to create no sensation now, to slip without a sound along this narrow lane behind the chairs, between the backs of the chairs and the wall with the picture, not to graze any of the people standing behind the backs of the chairs, not to stand there too long, to duck occasionally, not to go on to far, not so far as the middle of the table. The chairs have been moved together into a row without a space. The seats are occupied. The seven vertical bars of the backs of the chairs have their upper ends stuck into one horizontal bar. The two outermost vertical bars of the back of a chair touch the outermost vertical bars of the backs of the chairs on both sides. The horizontal bars of the same height have their ends touching each other so as to make one horizontal line the length of the whole row of chairs. The people's backs are partly above this line, partly at the same height as this line, partly slanting and above the line on one side and below it on the other, and cutting across the horizontal line above one vertical bar or above a gap between two bars. The backs are motionless, they are shorter or longer or more or less stretched out or curved. There are narrower or broader backs. The narrower backs are separated from each other at the most by the width of the two outermost vertical bars of two backs of chairs that touch each other and the gaps between these bars. The broader backs touch, or are pressed against each other with hunched shoulders. The broadest backs are pushed past each other, shoulder to shoulder, with the shoulder pushed back drawn up above the shoulder pushed forward. There are many black and some light-blue, yellow, or pink backs. Only the bride's back is white. In many backs some pieces of skin are visible, in many there are straps that have slipped into the pieces of skin. Between the bars pieces of people's backs are pressed through the bars, those of the upright backs by the length of a bar and those of the bent backs by the length of half a bar at least, and from there on farther and farther away from the backs of the chairs. Behind the sitting people, sometimes three chairs away from the next one standing at the right or the left, one person stands behind the shoulders of two people sitting down not far from each other or touching each other or pushing past each other, his head above the heads and between the heads of the ones sitting down, his hands placed against his back or drumming his fingers on his back or his hands with his arms hanging down on the sides pressed against his thighs or behind the backs of two people sitting and propped up on the horizontal bars of the backs of the chairs. The heads are motionless and turned aside, narrower and broader. They are brown-haired, gray-haired, bald heads with smooth, with curly hair, shorter or longer or pulled up high. The faces are turned front. No head blocks any other. No head turns sideways and toward or up to someone sitting alongside and back and toward or up to someone standing behind and toward someone sitting in front.

"Call me when it starts again!" calls a spectator outside from one window of the house across the street, shakes his head as he looks into the hall through a window between two mirrors, withdraws his torso. His head goes down below the windowsill. Perhaps he lies down on a sofa, sits down on an easy chair next to the window ready to jump up and expecting someone to give him a call.

Sometimes one of the sitting people scrapes his shoe on the parquet floor, kicks his shoe against a table leg, sometimes one of the standing people pushes forward a foot that had been placed backward and backward a foot that had been placed forward, sometimes someone sitting cautiously squeezes his hand between himself and the one sitting alongside, scratches an itching part of his back, sometimes someone sitting leans back a little bit further, and as he does that pinches the hand of someone standing behind him that is supported by the horizontal bar of the back of the chair or is clasped around the bar, instantly and carefully moves his back from the back of the chair while the one standing behind lifts his hand off the bar, puts it at his side or on his back.

That's all that's happening, or almost all.

No words are exchanged. Sometimes someone clears his throat, sometimes someone yawns, sometimes someone coughs a little, murmurs "Dear, dear," or "My, my!" sometimes someone murmurs "It's not so easy," or "It doesn't matter," or "It'll soon be over," or "Let it go." No one looks at him. No one says anything in answer. No one asks what he means.

They look into the mirrors that stretch from the floor to the ceiling, they look through the windows that stretch from the floor to the ceiling at the spectators leaning in the windows of the house across the street or into the brightly lit rooms behind the backs of the spectators, they look into a mirror with one eye and out of the window with the other eye.

Between their turned heads and above and past their shoulders, wherever no one else happens to be standing, their faces and half-faces directed at themselves are visible in the mirrors. They smile at each other, unsure of themselves, perhaps they've been looking at themselves smiling at themselves too long by now. They smile uncertainly, some with the corners of their mouths twitching, some with their upper lips, their lower lips, twitching with a trace of helplessness, as though they were not quite sure of how they were going to maintain their smile over a long period and without any reason. Before it loses itself, before their lips fall together, they open wide their jaws. Their faces are contorted, for a moment they take on a vicious look, as though they wanted to rend something. When they see themselves that way, some of them lower their eyes in confusion, they look around at the different parts of the table, parts of the glasses, the plates, the vases, in the mirror, at parts of their legs and feet under the table-cloth, their legs touching the floor next to each other or next to other legs or next to table legs, their legs placed far apart from each other on the floor between them, with the table legs of two tables moved together, their legs flung over each other and squeezed between the table legs of two tables moved together, they improve the position of their feet by scraping their shoes on the floor whenever they see themselves sitting with the tips of their shoes slanting together and sometimes separated from each other by more than the length of a shoe, by moving their soles together and the tips of their shoes apart.

"Is something else happening again?" calls someone outside who wants to know what is going on even if he can't see it himself. Perhaps because he lives one story below the hall and opposite the hall.

"Nothing," cries a spectator outside, who would surely be visible between the heads and past the shoulders of two people sitting down farther at the right looking out from here and opposite a window between two mirrors.

When they see themselves that way, with jaws wide apart, with twisted, vicious faces, as though they wanted to rend something, the others, in confusion, and as though they were searching for points of support for a gayer expression, look off upward, above their heads, if they're sitting, or behind their heads, if they're standing, at the parts of the picture of the wedding party that are visible in the mirrors.

The members of the party in the picture, some of them sitting, some of them jumping up, some of them having jumped up, turned toward each other in groups and turned away from each other in groups, are sitting behind a long banquet table made up of tables moved together. Jugs of wine stand on the table, goblets of wine, goblets of wine falling over, overturned goblets of wine lie about on dark spots. On the table stand platters with lumps of meat with serving forks and knives stuck in the middle. The jugs of wine cover the faces of the sitting ones as far as their nostrils, the handles of the serving forks and knives, sticking up almost vertically, divide the faces of the sitting ones into two halves. Next to overturned goblets the ones jumping up clap their hands together, while the ones sitting or standing next to them, executing with their hands a throwing-away motion or one calling over a waiter, cover up parts of the faces of those sitting or parts of the bodies of those standing. Some of them hold pieces of meat with both hands in front of their faces, so that only their eyes are visible, looking past the pieces of meat or looking down at the pieces of meat. Some of them hold up goblets before their faces, toasting each other, some of them, too, over their heads with their arms outstretched in front of their faces. Behind the heads two waiters hand around two trays, now blocked by the heads, now visible between the heads, one of them with something to eat on it, the other with something to drink. A few members of the wedding party in the painting stretch out their hands before them defensively, some of them hold their hands in front of their stomachs, with eyes closed, as though it were impossible not only to eat and drink any more but even to look at anything to eat or drink. Others, on the other hand, the backs of whose heads can be seen, grasp avidly and with both hands at the waiters' coats, if they are turning their backs to them, or at the glasses and pieces of meat as though their thirst, their hunger, were so unbearable that they can't wait for the waiters to come and serve them. The bodies of the groups of people facing each other cut across and block each other. The long-haired curly heads of the sitting women lie rumpless across the black-coated backs pushing past them of men jumping up. The rumps of two men leaning toward

each other behind the back of a sitting woman are lying
headless and black-coated to the right and the left of this
woman's red-clad torso. A hand lies between two heads
on the naked shoulder of a woman. You can't tell which
of the three men standing behind her back doubled up
with laughter has put his hand on her shoulder. The
mouths of most of them are wide open, the eyes narrowed
to slits, as though they were squalling and screaming.
They look for support, for the most part with one hand,
on the edge of the table, on the backs of the chairs, at
the one standing or sitting next to them, if they don't
happen just to be gesturing, drinking, eating, starting to
drink, to eat, as though they were afraid, through drunken-
ness, of lurching against the walls, the windows, the
waiters, each other, of falling off the chairs to the floor,
into the broken bits of wine goblets, into the pools of
wine, the scraps of meat between the feet of the others.
And the ones standing up with outstretched arms gesticu-
lating wildly must be talking in loud voices, their faces
are so red, their mouths are so wide open. One or another
on the edge of a group stretches out his arm to someone
sitting in the next group and claps him on the shoulder
with his hand, holding his other hand funneled in front
of his mouth, as though he were shouting something at
him.

A landscape is recognizable behind the windows, above
the heads in the painting or between two groups or above
an arm stretching horizontally from one group to another
and underneath that arm. The heads of people who have
jumped up are lying against the light-blue sky, against
the yellowish strip at the edge of the sky that perhaps is
supposed to indicate a sunset that had just taken place
or a dawn that is about to take place in case the wedding
party in the painting has been celebrating through the

night. The heads of the people in the process of jumping up are set against the blue mountains beneath the sky. The heads of the people sitting down are set against the yellow strip beneath the mountains, which perhaps is supposed to represent a ripe wheat field. The shoulders are set against the green meadow, against the brown and sheepskin-colored spots that break up the green of the meadow. Wherever two different groups that have turned away from and toward each other allow a view down to the windowsill, the outlines of these spots are more distinctly recognizable. They are outlines that look like sheep, sometimes like cows, sometimes like light-colored dogs. But perhaps they are also mounds of earth or sand thrown up by moles, dug up by farmers, by dogs. Perhaps they are also spots of earth or sand that have come about perhaps a short while before, because of flocks of sheep or herds of cows that just before the sunset, or in the dawning light before the sunrise, were being driven on, ravenously hungry, all too eager and in spots cropping the meadow down to the earth.

At the edges of the reflected parts of the picture headless rumps bend all the way over toward someone. The rumpless heads, as well as the one they are bending toward, would have to be recognized by any spectators looking between two mirrors through the windows out of the windows of the house across the street, if the distance, by the width of the hall and the street, is not too great. At the edges of the reflected parts of the picture rumpless heads lean toward something visible that, though partly blocked by objects or by other members of the party, is blocked in the mirror. The headless rumps would have to be recognized by any spectators looking between two mirrors through the windows out of the windows of the house lying across the street.

But the spectators are not looking out of the windows over into these windows to look at the parts of the picture that are visible between two mirrors and not even at the whole picture, for which they would have had the opportunity every single day, perhaps for decades.

"Is something else happening again?" calls the one who wants to know what's going on even if he can't see it himself. Perhaps because he lives a story below the hall and opposite the hall.

"The same thing! Nothing!" calls the spectator outside, who would certainly be visible, between the heads and over the shoulders of two people sitting down now further to the left, looking from here, and opposite a window between two mirrors.

"But there must be something going on?" calls the one who wants to know what's going on even if he can't see it himself, mistrustful, perhaps, because he can't see it himself.

"Still nothing?" call out several people who want to know what's going on, cannot see it themselves, perhaps cannot even understand exactly the reports of the one who can see it, perhaps because they live one story below the hall and opposite the hall, perhaps even below the one who wants to know what's going on, can't see it, and while he understands the reports of the one who can see it and says that nothing is going on, he doesn't believe them because on the one hand he can't see anything himself and on the other hand he can't believe that at a celebration like this nothing could go on for such a long time, and who now calls out, "Probably a whole lot goes on over there!"

"Then come and look for yourself!" calls the spectator outside who had just called out that there was still nothing doing.

"I'd be ashamed of myself," calls the one who perhaps after all doesn't want to know it as exactly as it might have seemed at the beginning and judging by the way he called, who perhaps prefers to believe something that is unbelievable for him rather than to go up a flight and assure himself with his own eyes of what is going on—whether, that is, nothing is happening or whether on the other hand something is in fact happening, who is perhaps afraid that the other has told the truth and he'd be going up in vain, "ashamed of myself to enter the house of such an impudent liar!"

After they have looked down at the floor, after they have looked up at the picture, the members of the party sitting motionless and those standing at regular intervals from each other behind the ones sitting move their eyes back to their faces. They look at themselves, the sitting ones earnestly and meditatively, the standing ones full of concern, with their carefully groomed heads in front of such a devastated background as the floor of the picture, between the feet, pieces of meat, broken crockery, pools of wine, fierce and one-eyed those among the sitting ones, the standing ones, half of whose faces reach into and over the rim of the picture, the other half of whose faces stick out of and over the rim of the picture, the two halves of whose faces push each other in one direction or another by at most the width of the bridge of a nose.

"Idiotic," one of them murmurs, lowering his eye, visible in the mirror and probably also visible through the window next to the mirror, perhaps he means his face when he murmurs, "Idiotic," the face of a spectator outside, perhaps he means this when he says, "Idiotic": the way he sits between the mirror and the window and has to look at two different faces at the same time, his own and someone else's, perhaps he means the banquet at which nothing is happening or almost nothing.

For a moment their faces take on a startled, even flabbergasted look, when they see someone popping up behind them in the mirror.

Then it is advisable to move on farther by a few backs.

"It's started again!" cries a spectator outside.

The man in the black suit raises his arm and lets it fall. He stands opposite the bride behind a window, still bent over, with his head and the black box of the camera covered with a black cloth. He pulls the cloth off his head and the box. He straightens up.

"Thank you," he says. And perhaps he sees the way the members of the wedding party wince at this first loud and understandably pronounced word before he starts unscrewing the camera from the tripod and collapsing the black legs of the tripod. He goes toward the exit of the hall, first trying to say good-bye with one joint nod to all those present, who are still glancing past each other, then trying to say good-bye individually to all those present by nodding step by step within the field of vision of each one, then gives it up when he sees them, disconcerted by the black spot of his coat, which blocks their picture in the mirror for a moment, their view of the window, making a dismissing motion with their hands, and with his head lowered, and rubbing the bridge of his nose with his forefinger, he leaves the hall, quickly enough to look just as though he were walking and not quickly enough to look as though he were running.

"So that's that," says someone. And it is not at all sure what he means when he says, "So that's that": the photographing, this banquet, this wedding, the photographing nowadays at banquets like this wedding nowadays, and it is not at all sure that he means something when he says, "So that's that," and isn't confirming or taking up the opinion of someone else about something that had come up in conversation before the photographing of the wedding party, and it is not at all sure that he means anything at all or is simply confirming or taking up the opinion of someone else about something that had come up in conversation before they had all fallen silent because of the photographing, when he says, "So that's that," and isn't simply saying something so that after such a long silence something is finally said, something that will make the others start talking too, and then this sentence, no matter what it may mean, or just because it doesn't mean anything, would be well chosen because the ones sitting or standing near him turn toward him and say, "God knows, God knows," and it is not at all sure whether they mean that the photographing at banquets like this wedding nowadays for instance is yes indeed that way, or whether they, just like himself if that is what he is doing, are confirming or taking up the opinion of someone else about something that had come up in conversation before they had all fallen silent, or whether they are not simply saying, "God knows," because they don't know what is meant by "So that's that," not so very much by "so" or by " 's," as by "that" and "that," or whether they are saying "God knows" so that after this first sentence, "So that's that," another silence should not occur as it had before this sentence.

"They are saying something!" cries a spectator outside.

"What, what?" cry several spectators.

"A word," cries the spectator who had cried that they had said something, "that sounds like God!"

"God, what's that, God?" cry several spectators. "Don't tell me there's a minister there!"

"There he goes, along there behind the table," cries a spectator. It is not the same one who had cried that they had said something.

The ones standing in the lane between the backs of the

chairs and the wall leave the lane. It is advisable to follow along behind them, because now the sitting ones are pushing themselves and their chairs so far away from the table that the backs of the chairs bang against the wall, because they are already blocking off the passage, advisable to let the ones going out ahead bend over to the sitting ones with the request to move back again to the table for a moment.

And while some of the people stand around in the hall, now looking around as though they were looking for chairs, the ones sitting in a row behind the table move apart from each other. Half of them move to the left and the right and around the table with their chairs. They sit down leaving gaps the width of a chair between themselves and their neighbors to the right and the left, along the second long side of the table, with their backs to the mirrors and windows, opposite the ones also sitting separated from each other by the width of a chair and behind the table and turned toward the mirrors and windows.

"I'm sitting underneath the bride!" cries the bride.

"The bride," cry the spectators outside, "says she's sitting underneath the bride!"

The bride raises her veil. She bends her broad, rounded torso all the way back. She places her red face, which because of the white veil looks redder perhaps than it is, against the back of the chair, looks at the bride, the bride, the little pale bride painted above her, who is smiling down at her folded hands with such a simple-minded, woebegone look that you can't tell whether she's crying when she smiles or whether she's smiling when she cries.

"You too!" cries the bride, and the spectators outside don't call out to the others this time that the bride has called, "You too," perhaps because they think that the bride is going to call something else after "You too!" But now she is laughing, the bride, she bends her torso back again, brings her head around, shuts her eyes to slits, throws up her thick arms, the bride, and with her red hands, which through the white veil, through the white arms of the bridal gown seem to look even redder than they are, with the gold ring on the third finger of her right hand, she raises her veil. The bride's mouth is even redder than her face, the bride's mouth is open all the way. Between the white rows of teeth above and below, next to the corners of her mouth, there is a great black hole, a hole that through the white teeth looks even blacker than perhaps it is.

"And the bridegroom is sitting underneath the bridegroom!" all the members of the wedding party sitting at the table and standing in the hall now cry out, and they turn their heads toward the big, broad-shouldered bridegroom in the painting above the bridegroom, who with a swaggering expression points a long, thick red forefinger at the bride in the painting next to him above the bride. "Long live the happy couple!" And while the ones sitting at the table reach for their glasses, and while five waiters in white jackets and black trousers step into the room and pass five trays with full glasses to the standing ones, and while they all raise their glasses, sitting and standing motionless for a moment as they had been during the photographing, only in a different order, only to the laughter of the bride, the spectators outside call out that it was said that the bridegroom was in fact sitting underneath the bridegroom and that the bride was now laughing about it.

"Is the bridegroom laughing too?" cries someone who wants to know what's going on even if he can't see it himself. It's someone different from the one who wants the same thing—that is, wants to know what's going on without seeing it himself—but who doesn't call out anything now, perhaps because he doesn't want to annoy the spectators by constantly calling out until they won't give him any information at all, perhaps because he can find out what's going on through the calls of the others, without seeing it himself, for that matter without calling out himself.

"Right away! Right away!" cries a spectator, and it's neither the one who had called out that they had said something nor the one who had called out that there he went, along there behind the table, and who by "he" meant the minister. "They're drinking to the health of the happy couple!"

The bridegroom sits small and pale underneath the great, broad-shouldered bridegroom in the painting pointing swaggeringly at the bride in the painting above the bride. He has stretched out his arms, the bridegroom, and at the right has got caught between the back of the chair and the back of the laughing bride, his bride, bending all the way back, and at the left between the back of the chair and the back of my grandmother, sitting upright with her back pressed against the back of the chair, his mother, my mother's mother. His head lowered, he looks toward the plate before him on the table. He raises his head, the bridegroom, he opens his mouth, the bridegroom. With his jaws all the way apart he doesn't look as though he were smiling.

"Heavens! What kind of a face are you making!" says my grandmother. And as she leans over a little to look at him, she frees the bridegroom's left arm.

"No, he's not laughing!" cries the spectator who had just cried "Right away, right away!" and then that they were drinking the health of the happy couple.

"Doesn't he look like a lord?" sing my grandmother's

three sisters. They smile shamefacedly, their shoulders hunched, down at their black clothes.

"He's wearing my deceased husband's suit," says my grandmother.

"Now he does look like something after all!" cries the bride. And as she leans over to look at him, she frees the bridegroom's right arm too. And as the bridegroom folds his hands in his lap, the bride cries, "He always used to look like a criminal in his blue-and-white-striped suit!"

"Criminal! Is there a criminal there too? An escaped convict? Finished his sentence?" cries one of those, and there must be a whole bunch, who want to know what's going on even if they can't see it themselves, because it's neither the one who when nothing had yet happened had called out to find out whether something was going on again nor the one who after something had gone on again had called out to find out whether the bridegroom was laughing too.

"Psst, psst!" hiss the spectators outside, perhaps so that, while repeating what has been said, they don't miss hearing what's being said.

"We'd like to know what's what with that criminal up there!" cry men and women, perhaps married couples, and there must be a great many of them after all, who want to know what's going on even if they can't see it themselves, because their shouting drowns out the cries of the spectators who are now calling for quiet, drown out their promises, their vows that the moment they hear they'll pass it on, yes, even the conversations here in this hall, the cries of the five waiters who are now coming into the hall with five trays covered with meat, salads, gravies, "Should we shut the windows here?" and the answers of the members of the wedding party: "No, we'll die of the heat!" "Yes, yes, it's better to die of the heat than of the noise!"

"We'd like to know what his crime was! Murder, robbery, murder and robbery, breaking and entering?" cry the men and women. "Otherwise we'll call the police! It's always the most interesting thing that you never tell us! Wait, just wait, until there's something going on down below again! We won't tell you a word! Not even what it is that's going on down below: a wedding, a christening, a funeral!"

The waiters have dragged in chairs.

It's advisable, now that no one is standing any more, to sit down at the table, on this last unoccupied chair, advisable to put the palms of your hands to the right and the left of the plate, to wait like everyone else until a waiter steps into the gap on the left between two chairs, and, holding a tray in his left hand, serves with his right hand, with the serving fork, loads up the plate with the serving spoon, meat, gravy, salad, potatoes, until a waiter steps into the gap on the right between two chairs and, holding a bottle in his right hand, pours out wine, to say, "Thank you," but not too loudly, before the heap on the plate is too big to eat and the glass is too full to drink, to say, "Fine," the way the others, when they hear someone eating, say, "The chicken is fine," not even repeating the first part, to say, "And how," like some people and to say, "You have to drink wine with it," like some of them right afterward, when they join in with the exclamation of someone eating that "The sauce and the salad are too highly spiced," while the others are still talking about chicken, to call out, "There's nothing you can do to spoil it," and one of these others plainly wants to demonstrate the opposite because he exclaims, "There's nothing you can't spoil, nothing! Only yesterday for instance I," because he moves his mouth and then goes on talking about what for instance yesterday he, because he moves his mouth but it's incomprehensible to the ones sitting further

off and also from this chair, because he is talking by himself and there are a great many who are saying "And how"
and "You have to drink wine with it" and now "Just don't
start in on the potatoes. There are other things to talk
about besides eating."

"Does it taste good?" says my grandmother to the
bridegroom.

"Eat, just eat!" says the bride. She holds a drumstick in
her hand, she bites into it. "Eat, all of you, eat with your
hands!" says the bride. "It's chicken!"

The members of the wedding party lay down their
knives and forks in such a way that the handles lie on
the tablecloth and the blades of the knives and the prongs
of the forks lean against the edges of the plates. They
go on eating with their fingers.

"Yes, yes, it does," says the bridegroom, and he takes
a little bite between his thumb and forefinger, pushes
it hastily into his mouth, washes it down unchewed with
a gulp from his glass, and before the next bite he folds
his hands on his lap under the table top.

"How is Mrs. Leinlein?" says a woman.

"She's busy," says my grandmother, her voice trembling
a little, her eyes blinking a little.

"I was a witness at her first, that is, I say her first
marriage, not at her other one," says a man next to the
woman, perhaps the husband of the woman who had asked
how Mrs. Leinlein was. "I'm always a witness at weddings.
Here now, too. At every wedding, that is, of course not
at every single one. To be exact, there have been three
and with this one today, four. So I've been a witness at
really very few weddings, if you just think of how many
weddings take place in one year in the world, no, better
not, how many weddings take place only today alone,
and in this city. But in spite of that, I have the feeling

I've been at them all, that is, that I've been, I just don't know. Perhaps you'll all understand what I mean!"

He looks at the others one by one.

"Well, more or less," say some of them.

The others are silent.

"He always has such tremendous ideas," says the woman next to him, the one who had asked how Mrs. Leinlein was. "You feel it right away! You can tell just by looking at him! Isn't it a calamity that he can't express them!"

"Can any of you perhaps tell me what I mean?" says the man, and he looks expectantly at the others one by one.

But they lower their heads. But they stuff great pieces of chicken into their mouths, perhaps so that they can justify their silence by their full mouths and not by their lack of understanding.

"Tell us at least what's happening now," several men and women ask. They probably belong to the ones who wanted to know a little while before what was up with the criminal up above.

"They're at the third course!" cries a spectator. This is the one who had first cried, "Right away, right away," then a lot of other things in between, but last of all, "No, he's not laughing," and who by "he" meant the bridegroom. "In the beginning, when they were eating with knives and forks, they talked a great deal, dirty talk probably. 'You can spoil everything,' someone called. 'There are other things to talk about,' the others then said, probably because there's a child present. And then they went on eating with their fingers, probably because it's chicken they're eating. And then one of them said a great many things, among others that he's been a witness at every wedding. And then the woman sitting next to him said it was a calamity. Then they all lowered their heads. Now they're going on eating. Now they're saying nothing or talking in very low voices, probably secrets. Now the bride is crying."

"But why is the bride crying?" several people call out who want to know what's happening even if they can't see it themselves.

"Probably from happiness," the spectator who had begun by saying they were at the third course goes on with his report. "No, she's not crying. She's wiping her face with the napkin."

"It was very good," says the bride. With her feet she pushes herself and her chair a little away from the table.

"The bride," the spectator who had begun by saying they were at the third course goes on with his report, "says it was very good. Now she is looking at the bridegroom and the bridegroom is saying something!"

"I'm no glutton," says the bride.

The members of the wedding party laugh. It's advisable to laugh along.

"What are they laughing about?" cry several people outside.

"Probably at a joke," the spectator who had begun by saying they were at the third course goes on with his report. "Now the waiters are carrying out the plates, the silver, the piles of bones. Some of them are wiping their mouths with their napkins. The others are licking their lips. The waiters are bringing in bowls, probably with fruit. They stick their fingers into them. No, they're not fruit bowls. They're finger bowls. They're washing their hands. The band, the band is coming! This time it's a five-piece one. There's no singer. There are four musicians, as always. They're carrying the instruments, as always— an accordion, a drum, a bass violin, a saxophone. Instead of the singer the fifth one, the bandleader, is carrying the

microphone. The four musicians take their places in front
of the window. The bandleader leans over, and just as
the singer does, he sticks the plug of the microphone into
the outlet near the entrance of the hall. He holds the
microphone in his hand, pulls the cord after him, stands
in front of the four musicians in front of the microphone
that as usual sticks up as high as his mouth. He bows with
a nod of his head. The four musicians lean all the way
over in a bow, they bend their backs so much that their
heads hang down as far as their thighs. 'Good evening,
ladies and gentlemen,' says the bandleader. He turns his
back to the wedding party. He turns toward the musicians,
rocks up and down on his feet, bends at the knees, twists
his torso back and forth. Why is it that he's so excited?
Now he begins conducting. Now they're playing the
usual thing as usual. Do you hear it? He's turning around,
the bandleader, he's turning toward the microphone, the
table. Now he's beginning to sing as well. He's singing
and conducting at the same time, the bandleader, he's
conducting as a professional and singing as a kindness,
probably, to take the singer's place. And he doesn't sing
badly. Do you hear it? The musicians lose the beat because he turns his back to them, probably. Now he's trying
to sing against them. Do you hear his squalling? To start
singing against four people with four instruments! Not
even a professional singer could manage that. He tries to
conduct while singing, turning toward the wedding party.
Several start singing along. They probably think he's calling on them to sing along. The musicians put down their
instruments. The bandleader goes on singing, he turns
around, he turns toward the musicians while singing. The
people singing at the table fall silent. Now the bandleader
is conducting the musicians while singing. They're probably not used to so much honor. They lay their heads on

the side. They look at the bandleader, they look at each
other, probably mistrustfully. They whisper something
to each other. They shrug their shoulders. They turn
around, looking out of the windows so as to see whether
perhaps there's someone there whom the bandleader is
singing to. He's surely not singing to us, not to us, my
dear musicians! They shake their heads. They listen to
him, to the bandleader, probably moved, because they
wipe their eyes with their hands. The bandleader is waving his arms wildly in the air. He looks more like a boxer
than a singer. Now he's breaking off. Everyone applauds.
The musicians applaud the loudest. The waiters close
the windows. What a mean trick!"

The waiters have closed the windows.

The bandleader beckons to a waiter. The waiter carries
the microphone out of the hall. The musicians pick up
their instruments. The bandleader conducts, he leaves off
singing.

"The happy couple must dance!" cries the wedding
party. "Long live the happy couple!"

And as all raise their glasses, the bride gets hastily to
her feet, holds her hand out to the bridegroom, pulls him
up off his chair. And as the bridal couple, the bride in
front, the bridegroom behind, the bride—separated from
the bridegroom first by two, then by three, finally by four
chairs and the gaps as wide as a chair between the chairs
—walks along the lane between the wall and the backs of
the chairs and the members of the wedding party, who
turn first after the bride then after the bridegroom and
nod at the bride and the bridegroom, the spectators
visible between the mirrors look through the glass panes
of the closed windows after the bride, after the bridegroom. They open their mouths, they shut them, the
spectators, they wave their arms around, they tell those
who want to know what's going on without seeing it,

understanding it themselves, what they see and how they understand what they see without understanding anything.

And from here too, and also without understanding anything, you can see what they are telling the ones who see and understand nothing. They hold their hands separate from each other at the height of their heads, they open their mouths either to call out, "The bride is a head taller than the bridegroom," or to call out, "The bridegroom is a head shorter than the bride!" There is no doubt that it is a question of the difference in size, which now that the couple is walking upright is more striking to the eye than before, when the couple was sitting down, which now that the couple is dancing, head to head, shoulder to shoulder, breast to breast, stomach to stomach, is more striking to the eye than before, when the couple was walking one behind the other and separated from each other by a few chairs. The spectators hold their hands separated from each other by the width of the bride, they bring their hands closer to each other from the width of the bride to the width of the bridegroom. They open their mouths, either to call out, "The bride is twice as broad as the bridegroom," or else to call out, "The bridegroom is half as broad as the bride!"

The couple dance through the hall. Thin and black and because of the black of his suit looking even thinner than he is, the bridegroom is stretched up with his head and torso, his lower body stretched back, lies aslant across the bride, who, broad and white and because of the white of her white bridal gown looking even broader than she is, with head and torso thrown back at a slant, with her lower body stretched out forward, is pulling him along after her. With great strides the bride goes backward. With little steps the bridegroom goes forward. The bride is holding her left hand propped on the bridegroom's right shoulder. On one side the bridegroom holds fast to the bride's dress with his right hand. On the other side the bride holds his left hand clasped with her right hand. The bride's veil is hanging over both these hands and covering the hands.

Step by step she, the bride, pulls him along, the bridegroom, tripping along behind, painfully keeping step, pulls him from one end of the hall to the other, turns him around herself, the bride, him, the tumbling bridegroom, then pulls him along, the bride, from the other end of the hall back to the first end of the hall, and so forth. Now she stops moving her right leg, slanting forward, then she stops moving her left leg, slanting forward, the bride, bending her torso still further back she pulls the bridegroom along one or the other outthrown leg, so that for a moment he squats, the bridegroom, on one or the other of the bride's thighs thrust between his legs, able to touch the floor only with the tips of his feet at the right and left of the bride's leg, he sits there so black, so thin, so light on the bride's thick leg pressing through under the white dress that it looks as though she could flick him up to the ceiling with a flip of her foot and catch him without swaying and merely by putting back on the floor the uplifted tip of her foot.

The members of the wedding party applaud after this first dance of the bridal couple. Men and women sitting next to each other, perhaps married couples, nod to each other, stand up.

The couples dance with each other, some of them pressed against each other, some of them as far apart as the length of their arms, the stoutness of their stomachs, will allow, some of them with their bodies touching each other only fleetingly. The men go forward, the women go backward. Sometimes the men push the women, and then it looks as though the women were falling back. Sometimes the women pull the men, and then it looks as though the men were resisting. The couples push against one of the four walls of the hall, turn around just before the wall, push off, pull back to the next wall. The couples' legs are pushed in between each other, now a man's leg between a woman's two legs, now a woman's leg between a man's legs. The legs of these four-legged couples stand still. And while the band goes on playing, the couples step apart from each other to form a broad lane. Through this lane comes a two-legged couple, accompanied by the music, and not to the beat of the music, to the loud squeaking of the boards, panting and dripping sweat with exertion. They are two men, who had been sitting at the table taciturnly and next to each other, not distinguishable from the other members of the wedding party above the table and under the table sitting leg to leg, perhaps, so that the left leg of the one sitting at the right was placed next to the right leg of the one sitting at the left. And while they had perhaps been sitting leg to leg, now they are walking stump to stump, with the left stump of the one walking at the right hanging next to the right stump of the one walking at the left. The stumps are separated only by two crutches: the crutch to the left of the left stump in the left hand of the one walking at the right, and the crutch to the right of the right stump in the right hand of the one walking at the left. They pause a moment, each one supported on his leg and his two crutches.

"Don't let us disturb you," they say.

"If you like, we'll stop the dancing at once," say the couples, who have separated.

Both the one-legged men shake their heads with a pained smile.

"Don't trouble yourselves on account of us veteran warriors," they say.

They set themselves in motion. Simultaneously they

set themselves a temporary goal with their crutches, the width of one step, they fling out their legs at the same time and for the same distance, they set down their feet between their crutches and fling out their crutches, supporting themselves on their legs. The longer stump of the one walking at the left, almost as long as a thigh, dangles back and forth more slowly than the shorter stump, half as long as a thigh, of the one walking at the right. In front of the entrance to the hall the slightly younger one, the one walking at the left, with the longer and more slowly dangling stump, waits, supported on two crutches and one leg, for the slightly older one, the one walking on the right, with the shorter and more rapidly dangling stump, to go on ahead, and follows him, while the slightly older one waits beyond the entrance to the hall, supported on two crutches and one leg, until the slightly younger one has stepped out of the entrance. Then they go on together, striding forward on their crutches on their legs on their crutches.

The couples are dancing again, some with stomachs touching and with torsos and heads far away from each other, one looking forward, the other looking backward, and with stomachs and legs far apart away from each other, and some with heads, bodies, legs pressed close to each other and moving on one spot without advancing, some with heads, bodies, legs so far apart from each other that they could have taken in two people of medium stoutness.

The bridal couple dances between these couples, past these couples. The bridegroom keeps his face lowered. The bride looks past the bridegroom's head with a red face, still redder from dancing than it had been before. She bends her head to the bridegroom's head, and it looks as though she were kissing his hair. She raises her face, the bride, laughs aloud, the bride, has hair in her mouth, the bride, she's bitten some hair off the bridegroom's head, she spits the hair out on the floor, and as though she were ravenous for hair, she again bends her face over the head of the bridegroom, who now places on his head the hand that she, the bride, is not clasping protectively, and she bites him in the hand, the bride, as though hair or hand were all the same, laughs aloud, above the head of the bridegroom, who now cries aloud, and then she cries, the bride, "Just listen to the way he's laughing!"

The bandleader lets fall his hands, he turns toward the couples on the dance floor, to those sitting at the table. The musicians put down their instruments. And while the couples stand still, applaud the band, and then go off to the table, and while the ones sitting at the table applaud the band or the couples, and while the bandleader bows with a nod of his head, and while the musicians lean all the way over in a bow, the bridegroom says more loudly than you usually say such things, "I'll be right back," and he leaves the hall, swaying a little.

Two waiters come in by the entrance to the hall and pointing upward with their forefingers, look at the bride. The bride nods at them. The waiters disappear.

"He'll be right back," says the bride in a louder voice than you usually use to say such things. Broad and red and breathless from dancing, she sits down, the bride, underneath the thin, pale bride in the painting. The bridegroom's chair underneath the bridegroom in the painting swaggeringly pointing to the bride in the painting is unoccupied.

My grandmother nods to her three sisters. The four sisters fold their hands in their laps underneath the table top. They start murmuring to themselves incomprehensibly. Sometimes they sing rather than murmur, sometimes they murmur rather than sing.

"Who would have thought it," says someone. It's the

one who had said after the lengthy silence that that was that. And this time, too, it is not at all certain what he means when he says, "Who would have thought it."

"God knows, God knows," say the ones sitting near him. These are the ones who after he had said that that was that had already said "God knows, God knows" once, who perhaps are repeating "God knows, God knows" because this time they have no more of an idea of what is meant by "Who would have thought it" than what had been meant by "So that's that."

The band is playing again. No one dances. They are all looking at the door out of the corners of their eyes.

The two waiters come into the entrance to the hall, and pointing downward with their forefingers, they look at the bride. The bride nods at them, and the waiters disappear.

"That's the way inside there," say the waiters outside the hall.

"I got lost in the entrance," says the bridegroom.

The hands of the two waiters, with two outstretched forefingers pointing into the hall, with two white sections of sleeve, appear at the right and left of the entrance. The bridegroom comes into the hall between these two waiters' arms pointing inside.

"So there he is again," says the bride, more loudly than you usually say such things.

"You make mistakes," says the one who said, "So that's that," and then, "Who would have thought it."

"We all make mistakes," they all say, "all of us."

"Well, sit down then!" cries the bride.

"Don't mind if I do," says the bridegroom.

"Now's he's sitting underneath the bridegroom again, the bridegroom!" they all cry. "Long live the happy couple!"

They lift their glasses, they drink to the happy couple. The waiters pour wine.

"Who would have thought it would turn out this way," says the one who had said that everything, everything could be spoiled and that only yesterday for instance he.

"Things turn out the way they turn out," says the one who had said, "So that's that" and "Who would have thought it."

"They always turn out different from what you think," says the woman next to the man, perhaps her husband, who said he'd been a witness at every wedding and right afterward that he'd been a witness at only very few weddings and who then asked for someone to tell him what he had meant by that after all.

"You have to keep that in mind," say several people. These are the ones who said "Fine" and "And how" and "You have to drink wine with it" and said this after someone eating had called out, "The gravy and the salad are too highly spiced," and who now calls out, "That's the way it is! And it's better this way than some other way!"

"It'll all turn out all right," says the woman sitting next to the woman sitting next to the man who said he'd been a witness at every wedding and right afterward the opposite and then had asked the others whether they knew what he had meant and some had then said, "Well, more or less" and the others had been silent. "You have to know how to look after yourself."

"Who knows, who knows, what's going to happen," says one of my grandmother's three sisters, who look so much alike that you can't tell whether it's Martha, Maria, or Minna, who besides, when they said something said something at the same time, who at the same time said the same thing, that is, that he looked like a lord.

"Where would we end up," says someone who has not

yet said anything by himself but only when they had all said something, such as, for instance, "And the bridegroom is sitting underneath the bridegroom," or "We all make mistakes, all of us," or "Now he's sitting underneath the bridegroom again, the bridegroom," or "If we thought of everything."

"When I consider, on the other hand," says the man who had said he'd been a witness at every wedding and right afterward the opposite, and he looks helplessly at the woman next to him who had said he always had such tremendous ideas, who now cries, "Tell me, just tell me," who gives him a push in the side and then he adds, "No, everything finally comes to the same thng, that is, the opposite."

"They've got a house like ours," says the woman sitting next to the woman who said he always had such tremendous ideas and who by "he" had meant the man next to her, who now cries, "Exactly the same, that is, it's completely different, because the dining room," and who then stops himself whether because he once again can't say what he means or because the others turn to the bride, probably because it's the bride who interrupts him, who while he is saying "the dining room" says, "Our dining room," who as he stops himself goes on to say, "is as big as your dining room. Our bedroom is as big as your bedroom. Our third room, the room between the dining room and the bedroom, the one that's going to be our children's room, is twice as big as your children's room."

"When I was a child," says the man who by himself has said only, "Where would we end up if we thought of everything," and except for that has only said·what everyone else has said and who now breaks off the sentence "When I was a child" and cries out with everyone else, "The bigger the better!"

"Sometimes," says the man of whom the woman sitting

next to him maintained that he always had such tremendous ideas, "a tiny little closet is roomier than a convention hall. I know that's not true, but nevertheless you have to believe me." He turns to the bride.

The bride has bent her ten fingers.

"There's room in it for the first one," cries the bride, stretching out the thumb of her right hand, "for the second, for the third," cries the bride, stretching out her forefinger and the middle finger of her right hand, "for the fourth, for the fifth," cries the bride, holding her right hand out with five outstretched, outspread fingers in front of the bridegroom's face, "for these five children, big and strong as I, for these five children, your spit and image, for the sixth, for the seventh, for the," cries the bride, she laughs aloud, the bride, holding her right hand with five outstretched fingers in front of the bridegroom's face, holding her left hand with two outstretched and three bent fingers in front of the bridegroom's face, "Just look up, now look," cries the bride, "why are you lowering your face," cries the bride, and stretching out ten fingers, she covers the bridegroom's face with both hands. "Just look, all of you, look," cries the bride, "how embarrassed he is!"

Everyone laughs.

Somebody gets up and leaves the hall.

The bride takes hold of her full glass with both hands, she pours it into herself with her head laid all the way back.

"How is Mr. Leinlein," says the one who said the chicken was fine.

"He's busy," says my grandmother, her voice trembling a little, her eyes blinking a little. "So drink, then, drink," says my grandmother to the bridegroom.

"Don't mind if I do," says the bridegroom, and then he drinks.

"So when will you get up?" says the one who said the gravy and the salad were too highly spiced and then that that was the way it was and that it was better that way than some other way.

And the bridegroom answered that he was going to get up at six in the morning.

"When I was a growing boy," says the one who said, "Where would we end up if we thought of everything," and then, "When I was a child," and breaking off this sentence, had cried out with everyone else, "The bigger the better!" and who now breaks off the sentence, "When I was a growing boy," and cries with everyone else, "Why so early?"

And the bridegroom answers that the place where he works is a long way away.

A second somebody gets up and leaves the hall.

The band stops for a break.

"He is going to walk," says my grandmother.

"But why is he going to walk if it's a long way away?" says the woman sitting next to the woman sitting next to the man who said he'd been a witness at every wedding, that he was a witness at only very few weddings, that a tiny little closet is roomier than a convention hall, that it wasn't true and that nevertheless people had to believe him.

"For heaven's sake, open the windows!" cries the bride. "He ought to know why he's going to walk!"

"Someone here knows why he's going to walk," cries a spectator outside. It is the one who cried that they were at the third course and who afterward reported a great many things about the musicians and the bandleader and who finally cried that it was a mean trick and who by "it" meant the shutting of the windows.

"When I was a young man," says the one who said, "When I was a child," and, "When I was a growing boy," who broke off these two sentences and who now breaks off the third sentence, "When I was a young man," and cries out with everyone else, "You've got to find out what you want to know," and says this while several people outside who want to know what's going on, who can't see it themselves, cry, "And why is he going to walk?"

"How should I know why he's going to walk," cries the spectator outside who cried that someone there knew why he was going to walk. "He's bound to have his reasons!"

A third somebody gets up and leaves the hall.

"It's going to be hard work!" cries the bride, and she pushes her head past the bridegroom's back so that her white rump lies headless for a moment next to the bridegroom's black trunk, and with both hands she clutches at the white jacket of a waiter, the bride, and she holds her empty glass in front of the waiter's face, the bride, and then she cries, "But it'll bring in something!"

"Mainly," everyone cries, "you've got to live within your income!"

"He's going to go to bed early," says my grandmother. And while the spectator who called out, "A word that sounds like God," now calls out, "A woman is saying a word that sounds like bed," my grandmother goes on to say, "If he's going to get up so early, if he's going to work so hard."

"When I was a married man, when I became a father," says the one who said, "When I was a child, a growing boy, a young man," and who now breaks off this fourth sentence, like the three others before it, and calls out together with everyone else, "Mainly, you've got to keep busy," and says this while outside several spectators cry, "Someone is talking about himself. Two people are getting up and leaving the hall!"

A fourth somebody gets up. A fifth gets up. They leave

the hall walking one behind the other, while the first, the second, the third of the ones going out step into the hall one after the other and sit down one after the other.

"So when will you go to bed?" says the one who said, "So when will you get up?" and now adds, "If you're going to get up so early because the way to the place you work that you're going to take, and you'll surely know why, is so long, and the work during the day is going to be such a strain?"

And the bridegroom answers that he is going to go to bed at eight o'clock in the evening.

"He's not only going to walk the whole way there," says my grandmother, "he's going to walk the whole way back, too."

"But why is he going to walk the whole way back, too," says the woman sitting next to the woman sitting next to the man who said he'd been a witness at every wedding, that he was a witness at only very few weddings, that a tiny little closet was roomier than a convention hall, that that wasn't true and that people had to believe him nevertheless, "if the way there is so long already, so exhausting, and the work during the day is such a strain. One day he's bound to collapse."

"A woman there is saying he's bound to collapse one day," cries the spectator outside who had said before that someone there knew why he was going to walk.

"Why," cry several people who want to know what's going on, can't see it themselves, "is he going to collapse?"

"Because the way to work, which he is going to go on foot twice, once there and once back, how should I know why, is so long!" cries the spectator who had called out, "There he goes, along there behind the table" and who by "he" meant the minister.

A sixth and a seventh and an eighth somebody stand up, they leave the hall walking one behind the other.

"When I was a widower," says the one who said, "When I was a child, a growing boy, a young man, a married man, when I became a father," and who now, breaking off this fifth sentence like all the sentences before, now calls out together with everyone else, "When he gets his vacation, he can rest up."

The fourth and the fifth of the ones going out step through the hall walking one behind the other. They sit down next to each other one after the other. A ninth somebody gets up and leaves the hall.

"What's the widower going to do when he gets his vacation?" cry several people outside who want to know what's going on, don't see it, don't understand it, and if they understand it, understand it incorrectly.

"If you want to know what's going to happen," cries the spectator outside who had called out after the windows had been opened again that someone there knew why he was going to walk, "then don't shout so much, or you'll find out just as little about it as you will about what was up with that criminal up there!"

"So when will you get home?" says the one who said, "So when will you get up, go to bed?"

And the bridegroom answers that, if he were to hurry, he would be home at seven-thirty in the evening.

"But then he will hardly have time to have supper," says the woman sitting next to the woman sitting next to the man who said he'd been a witness at every wedding and only at very few weddings, that a tiny little closet was roomier than a convention hall, that it wasn't true and that people had to believe him nevertheless, and who now says, "You go on living, no, on the contrary, you don't go on living at all," and breaks off, looks helplessly at the woman next to him who said that he always had such tremendous ideas, whether because once again he can't say what he means or because the others are turning to the bride, probably because it's the bride who interrupts him, pushing her torso past the bridegroom's chest in front so that for a moment his head is lying rumpless against her white back, cries, "He'll hardly have time to brush his teeth! Not in the morning and not at night. That's because for a long time he loafed. You couldn't go on that way any longer. Over a long period of time he couldn't look at himself in the mirror. No one's asking him to get very far. But at least he ought to get somewhere."

"When my son became a father," says the one who said, "When I was a child, a growing boy, a young man, a married man, when I became a father, when I was a widower," and who, breaking off this sixth sentence like all the sentences before, now cries out with everyone else, "What was that?"

"So that's how it's going to be," cries the spectator outside who after the windows were opened again said that someone there knew why he was going to walk. "He'll have to get up early, without taking the time to brush his teeth, because it's a long way to work. He'll have to walk there in a hurry. Because if he walks slowly, you understand, he'll either have to get up earlier or else get there too late. He'll be the one to know why he's walking. Mainly, he ought to know what he's doing. The work during the day will be a strain. Mainly he's got to be busy. The work will bring in enough for him to live within his income. He'll hurry back the whole long way from work to his house on foot, even though the way back is long and exhausting and the work during the day is a strain. He'll know why he has to come back on foot too. Mainly he ought to know what he's doing. Mainly he's got to be busy. One day he's bound to collapse. If one day he gets a vacation, he'll rest up. Mainly he's got to be busy. The way it was, you couldn't go on that way any longer. The way he had to look at himself in the mirror, he couldn't look at himself in a mirror that way over a long period of time. He'll be going to sleep early, without taking the time to brush his teeth, because he's got to get up early in the morning and has to hurry in any case, so as to not to come too late. No one's asking him to get very far. But he's surely got to get at least somewhere."

The musicians play. The bandleader swings his arms, conducting. Couples stand up. Couples go to the dance floor. Couples push, shove each other, pulling each other from one wall to the other wall back to the first wall.

A tenth somebody gets up and leaves the hall.

"Isn't that the little Leinlein?" says the one who said, "When I was a child, a growing boy, a young man, a married man, when I became a father, when I was a widower, when my son became a father," and who now cries out together with everyone else, "Who? That one?"

It is advisable to get up.

I get up.

It is advisable to leave this hall.

I leave the hall.

"What number," I ask a waiter outside the entrance to the hall, "comes after ten?"

"Eleven," says the waiter.